David Wellington was born in Pittsburgh, Pennsylvania, where George Romero shot his classic zombie films. He attended Syracuse University and received an MFA in creative writing from Penn State. He lives in New York City.

To find out more about David, visit his website at www.davidwellington.net

Praise for David Wellington's novels:

'These books are great, fast-paced, modern, pulp action machines, yet Dave Wellington somehow manages to preserve the weird mystery, the magic, of the old classic vampire stories'
Mike Mignola, creator of *Hellboy*

'Wellington is moving the literature of the undead into the twenty-first century'
Los Angeles Times

'Vampirism is the dark side of the idea of immortality, as well as a nightmare personification of parasitism, viral infection and the concept of sharing blood. Wellington uses all of these ideas and they make his novel more than just a gory story . . . a well-constructed novel with a good plot'
Sydney Morning Herald

Also in the Laura Caxton Vampire series:

13 Bullets
99 Coffins
Vampire Zero

Other titles by David Wellington:

Cursed
Ravaged

23 Hours

A Vampire Tale

DAVID WELLINGTON

piatkus

PIATKUS

First published in the US in 2009 by Three Rivers Press,
An imprint of the Crown Publishing Group,
a division of Random House, Inc., New York
First published in Great Britain as a paperback original in 2011 by Piatkus

A CIP catalogue record for this book
is available from the British Library.

ISBN 978-0-7499-5441-3

Typeset in Caslon by Palimpsest Book Production Limited,
Falkirk, Stirlingshire
Printed and bound in Great Britain by Clays Ltd, St Ives plc

Papers used by Piatkus are from well-managed forests
and other responsible sources.

MIX
Paper from
responsible sources
FSC
www.fsc.org   FSC® C104740

Piatkus
An imprint of
Little, Brown Book Group
100 Victoria Embankment
London EC4Y 0DY

An Hachette UK Company
www.hachette.co.uk

www.piatkus.co.uk

For Carrie

Bellows

Come, let's away to prison.
We two alone will sing like birds i' the cage.
—William Shakespeare, *King Lear*, V.iii

1.

The Marcy State Correctional Institution, in Tioga County, Pennsylvania, had been designed and built in the 1960s as a state-of-the-art facility for the rehabilitation and therapeutic treatment of adult female prisoners. The walls were painted bright but tasteful colors. The cells were spacious and airy and laid out on an open plan to improve social communication between the inmates. It had a psychiatric ward, a well-stocked library, three full-sized gymnasia, and 768 beds.

Forty years later, with a population of over 1,300, it always hovered one incident away from a full-blown riot. On March 7, that incident came when no one expected it – except those who had planned it out meticulously in advance.

Laura Caxton was at her usual spot in the cafeteria, over by the wall where she didn't have to watch her back every second. She was eating soup. Everyone was eating soup – you didn't order from a menu at Marcy, you sat down and waited for what they brought you, and then you ate it or you went hungry. She could look down the long length of her white

3

Formica table and see women of every color and creed, but they all wore the same orange jumpsuit and they all were eating beef barley soup.

Her first indication that anything was wrong was when she heard a loud plunking noise and then a cry that was half the scream of an inmate scalded by splashing soup and half a chorus of barely suppressed giggles and curses.

Ten seats down, an overweight Latina woman was brushing soup off her face and her chest. A rock-hard dinner roll had been thrown into her soup bowl, hard enough to splatter the table and the inmates on both sides of her.

The inmate who had thrown the roll, a slimmer and younger woman, white, blond, glasses (Caxton made mental notes of everything she saw – it was an old habit, one that served her as well inside as it had in her life before), leaned back on the bench and gave an exaggerated shrug. 'Sorry, bitch,' she said, laughing and turning away.

It had nothing to do with Caxton. She put her head down over her own soup and kept eating. She knew what to do if there was a problem. All the inmates had been drilled on what to do – you got up, went to the wall, and raised your hands above your head. The correctional officers would take it from there. She looked around, trying to find where the COs were. Three of them, wearing their regulation navy blue stab-proof vests and carrying batons, were over on the far side of the cafeteria, chatting among themselves. They weren't paying enough attention, but Caxton knew better than to try to signal them.

The offended woman, the overweight Latina, rose stiffly from the table. No one stopped her, even though it was strictly forbidden to get up during meals. She didn't look angry, particularly. She was breathing a little heavy, maybe. Without a word she grabbed the blond inmate and smashed

4

her face against the table, shattering her glasses and breaking her nose with a sickening crunch. Then she pulled the blond's head back again and slammed it down a second time.

That got the attention of the COs. The three of them split up and started working their way between the tables, moving carefully in case this was a setup. Before they'd covered half the distance someone had stabbed the big Latina with a sharpened toothbrush handle. Caxton saw it still sticking out of her side. She was pulling at it, trying to tear it free. Someone else had pulled the blond away from the table and had her down on the floor, either to protect her from further attack or just to kick her while she was down. Everywhere Caxton looked women were jumping up from the tables, grabbing their trays or reaching for concealed weapons, looking to defend themselves or to settle old scores while they had the chance.

Time to get to the wall, Caxton decided. She put down her plastic spoon and placed her hands on the table so she could slide out of the bench.

Before she was even halfway up, someone grabbed her ankles and yanked her downward, under the table. Caxton landed flat on her back with the breath knocked out of her lungs. The hands on her legs were like iron claws, digging into her skin. She was hauled down the length of the table past a double row of feet, all clad in the disposable slippers the inmates wore. Some of the feet kicked at her, maybe just on principle.

Her head smacked against a leg of the table and then she was pulled free and she was looking up at the ceiling. Hands – many hands – grabbed her and hauled her upright, then shoved her forward before she had a chance to see where she was headed. All she could hear was screaming, roaring, bellowing, the clatter of women being hit with trays, the noise of bodies hitting the floor. She smelled blood, but not from anywhere close by. Her face hit a door that yielded and swung open and she spilled through into the kitchens, where inmates with white aprons over their jumpsuits were clustered around the doors she'd just come through, all of them having tried to see at once through the tiny plastic windows.

'Get out of here, all of you,' someone said, kicking the doors open. One door slammed into Caxton's side, making her wince. 'Move this piece of shit out of view.'

Hands reached down and grabbed Caxton, hauled her deeper into the kitchen. She was rolled over on her side and then someone kicked her in the stomach. She hadn't caught her breath yet and couldn't ask any of the questions that occurred to her, couldn't yell for help.

A tall, thin Asian woman knelt down next to Caxton and grabbed her lower lip. She yanked on it as if she might tear it off, and Caxton was forced to raise her head. The Asian woman had black tears tattooed underneath her eyes, four on one side, five on the other. Her hair stuck out from either side of her head in a long pigtail. 'You're Caxton, right? I'd hate to think we went to all this trouble and got the wrong cunt.'

Caxton didn't answer. She didn't see what good would come of doing so.

'That's her,' someone else said. Someone standing behind the Asian woman. Caxton couldn't see who the new voice belonged to – she didn't dare break eye contact with her captor. 'She's a cop. Are you sure the pigs won't—'

'Ex-cop now,' the Asian woman said. She didn't smile. 'The COs hate her more than we do, because she used to play for their team and then she fucked up.'

6

She turned back to Caxton. 'I'm Guilty Jen. They call me that because there was another Jen on our dorm who used to tell the screws every night how innocent she was. If I'd tried that they would have laughed at me. I mean, just look at me. Guilty as fuck and it's written all over my face.' She tapped the place below her left eye where there were only four tears. 'Every time I finish a stint, I get a new one. Come next October, I get out and it'll be number ten. See what I mean?'

Caxton tried to bring her knees up to protect her abdomen, but hands from behind grabbed her legs and pulled them back. Other hands grabbed her arms and her shoulders. Guilty Jen had a lot of friends.

'I don't know you, ex-cop,' she said. She reached into the pocket of her coveralls and took out a cigarette lighter and a long iron nail. 'I've got no history with you, and no beef. But as many times as I been inside, this is my first time at Marcy, and in here, now, I'm nobody. I need to make a name for myself all over again. Sucks, but that's how we play. So I asked around and found out who's tough in here, who people are afraid of. I got a pretty short list. Most of the names I could eliminate because they had serious protection. They were ganged up. But you – everybody hates you. Dyke ex-cop. No friends in here. I fuck you up and I'm looking at zero consequences, other than a couple days in a special housing dorm for violence.' She flicked on the lighter and held the point of the nail in the blue part of the flame.

'There are quicker ways to kill me,' Caxton managed to say. 'I figure you only have about thirty seconds before the COs realize we're in here.'

'Oh, I'm not going to go that far,' Guilty Jen said. 'I'm just going to mark you. Put a J on you so you're mine.

7

You just lie there, stay quiet, this doesn't have to go bad for you. Just tell me one thing?'

'What's that?' Caxton asked, as Guilty Jen took the nail out of the flame. Its tip was scorched black by the flame.

'Left cheek, or right?'

2.

Caxton stared at the point of the hot nail. It was beginning to turn red. She knew if she didn't struggle, if she let this woman brand her, she would be marked in more ways than showed on the skin. She would be giving the prison population a signal that she was weak, and vulnerable, and could be preyed upon.

There were a lot of women in SCI-Marcy who would be thrilled to get that sign from an ex-cop inmate. This would be only the first assault of many.

She waited until Guilty Jen flicked off the lighter and scooted forward on her knees, ready to bend down and place the nail against her face. She waited for a second longer, until she could feel the heat of it near her skin.

Then she twisted her wrists simultaneously, slipping them free of the hands that held her, and brought her hands around to smack Guilty Jen's hand sideways. The nail went into the calf muscle of one of the women standing over Caxton. That woman howled and jumped in the air.

The hands on Caxton's ankles slackened their grip, just a

little. Caxton had been expecting that – it's hard to pay attention when one of your friends is screaming in pain – and she capitalized on it by bringing her knees up to her chest as fast as she could and then kicking out, knocking Guilty Jen backward and away.

In a second Caxton was up, feet spread on the floor, torso bent low with her arms up to protect her head. Someone tried to grab her back and she rolled into it, head-butting them in the stomach hard enough to make them let go.

She still had no idea how many assailants she was facing or how long she had to hold them off before the COs bothered to check the kitchen. She could try to make a break for it, run out of the kitchen and back into the cafeteria, but she figured Guilty Jen had to be organized enough to have someone watching the door.

Her other option was to fight her way out. She danced backward, trying to get a wall behind her, and let her eyes flick around the room, assessing. She counted six orange jumpsuits. Jen's girls were a mixed set, black, Latina, white, and Asian. That was weird: prison gangs normally formed up on racial lines. It looked like Jen had found something else to unite them.

Caxton could think about that later, if she got the chance. Right now she had a fight on her hands. Six women she would have to fight, including Jen, including the one with the burnt leg. They were already regrouping, getting ready to mob her. If they all came at her at once she would be done for. They could just pile on top of her and hold her down and beat her into submission.

She needed to thin the herd, right away. She looked for the opponent closest to her. To her left was a brown-haired white girl. Tattooed on her earlobes was a pair of tiny swastikas. She must have been a member of the Aryan Brotherhood once.

Caxton felt no moral compunctions about grabbing a huge tureen full of boiling soup and sloshing it all over her.

The Nazi girl went down in agony, out for the count. A black woman wearing a do-rag came at Caxton from the right, puffing with anger. Caxton laid her out with a haymaker punch that probably fractured her jaw.

A third inmate tried to be sneaky and attack while her back was turned. Caxton threw her head back, hard, and felt her skull connect with the unseen woman's nose. She felt the bones there break. Hot blood went spurting down the back of her collar. That must have hurt, Caxton figured, but it wasn't necessarily enough to put her assailant down. Caxton spun in place and brought both fists toward each other, the knuckles digging hard into the woman's kidneys.

She dropped to the floor, grabbing at Caxton's hips and legs, but her hands just didn't have the strength to grapple properly. Caxton looked down at her victim and thought about stomping on her head or her stomach. For a second she almost did, but she managed to pull back.

It was going to be hard to end this fight without killing anyone. Caxton had gone through plenty of unarmed-fighting courses at the State Police Academy in Hershey, but she'd never really bothered learning how to incapacitate enemies. On the perps she'd been taking down outside, those kinds of moves were never enough. You had to fight to kill or be killed yourself.

Caxton had spent years learning how to fight and kill vampires. Vampires were bigger than she was, much stronger, and much tougher. Any wounds she gave them healed over almost instantly. She had to remind herself constantly that Guilty Jen's set didn't have supernatural resistance to injuries.

Killing the downed woman would be a big mistake here.

11

It would get Caxton in all kinds of trouble and mean losing what few privileges she had, as well as draw the kind of attention she most wanted to avoid. So when she turned to face Guilty Jen and her remaining two gangbangers, she hesitated for just a second, to give them a chance to run away.

They didn't.

'Impressive,' Guilty Jen said. 'But stupid. This counts as disrespect, you know that? And I can't allow that, or I look like a bitch. So now I *do* have to kill you.'

'There are other ways to resolve—' Caxton began, but Jen's two underlings were on her before she could finish her thought. One of them, a Latina wearing lipstick and mascara, came at her low and fast, hands stretched out to grab.

It was a feint, Caxton knew. The other one, a Korean woman, had a shank made from a metal spoon, flattened out and sharpened all around its edge. The leg of her coveralls was smoldering – it must have been she who caught the heated nail. The injury was slowing her down a little, but not enough.

Caxton took a step toward the Latina and raised one arm as if to strike – then launched herself at the Korean and came down hard on her burnt leg. She felt the knee there give way, and the woman collapsed under Caxton's weight. She grabbed the shank out of the woman's flailing hand and threw it underhand at the Latina, who was still coming toward her.

It went right into her eye.

For a moment everyone was screaming and rolling around on the floor. Then the two people who weren't – Caxton and Guilty Jen – made eye contact, and everything else just fell away. Caxton's entire focus shifted to the gang leader. It was a showdown, an old-fashioned gunslinger standoff, but without the guns.

Caxton didn't need them. If she was tough enough and fast enough to fight vampires, one human woman shouldn't pose

12

a problem. She'd just proven she could handle a couple at a time.

Guilty Jen, however, was a little more than just the average gangbanger. She spread her feet, getting a good stance. Then she did something Caxton would never have expected. She leaned forward slightly. She bowed.

What that meant wasn't lost on Caxton. She just had time for a brief spike of fear to go running through her veins before a roundhouse kick came at her face so fast she couldn't avoid it.

Jen had martial arts training. That made her dangerous, even to someone like Caxton. Caxton threw up one arm in time to fend off the kick, but it connected with her wrist and made every nerve in her hand fire at once. Her fingers rattled around in her skin and she wondered if her arm was broken.

Caxton dropped to one knee and leaned over hard to the side as Jen followed up her kick with a sweeping arm attack that was aimed right at Caxton's neck. The arm went instead over Caxton's head, but Jen recovered and pulled back almost instantly, long before Caxton could bring her own hands down on the gangster's knee. Jen's leg flashed backward, out of Caxton's reach, and Caxton knew she'd made a bad mistake. She had avoided the worst of Jen's attacks, but only by putting herself in a vulnerable posture. The next attack was going to be a killing blow, and—

Jen cried out at the same time as something exploded behind her. She staggered forward, her stomach colliding with Caxton's face, and they both went down in a heap. Caxton struggled to get free so she could see what was going on.

'You fucking shot me!' Jen howled. 'That's unnecessary force!'

A team of COs stormed into the kitchen. The one at the front had a guard sergeant's stripes. He also had a smoking shotgun in his hands. 'Just a beanbag round, gal,' he growled. 'You'll have a nasty bruise for a week, but nothing permanent. Alright,' he said to the guards behind him. 'Forced extraction on all of them. Don't take any chances.'

Someone hit Caxton with a thick blanket – shoving it down over her face and body, pinning her to the ground. She knew better than to fight back. There was nothing to grab, no one to punch, just heavy fabric that stank of sweat and blood pushed down over her mouth and eyes. Plastic handcuffs wrapped around her wrists, and her arms were pulled painfully back behind her. Then her ankles were cuffed together, too, and she was hog-tied. She was lifted off the floor and carried out of the kitchen by a pair of COs wearing so much armor they looked like baseball umpires.

She never got a chance to look back at Guilty Jen, to see what they were doing to her, but she knew one thing without a doubt. They would meet again.

3.

Almost two hundred miles away, in Allentown, Clara Hsu was about to be sick. She was surrounded by bodies, corpses drained of their blood and then discarded like old ragged dolls. The women around her ranged in age from thirty-five to fifty, but with some it was hard to tell – their arms and throats had been torn at, savaged by vicious teeth, by a vampire who needed their blood and didn't care how much pain she had to cause to get it.

Clara felt her gorge rising and knew she had to do something, quickly. The smell and the colors – oh, God, the colors – were too much to take in, too much to bear. Luckily, she had a way of dealing with it. Taking a digital camera from the case around her neck, she started snapping pictures, creating a permanent record of the crime scene.

Clara had been just a police photographer once. Even a year ago that had been her whole job. She had worked for a rural county sheriff's office, documenting methamphetamine busts and car accidents. Then she'd done something stupid. She'd fallen in love with Laura Caxton. Caxton's life had been about vampires and nothing else. To stay a part of Caxton's life Clara had agreed to go back to school for forensic criminology, where she'd learned all about latent fingerprints and hair follicle matching and the legal ins and outs of DNA testing. It had gotten her a place on the SSU, the special subjects unit – the Vampire Squad – and exposed her to parts of the human anatomy she had never guessed existed. Or wanted to.

She'd learned the trick of using her camera's viewfinder to shield herself from the gore back in the old days, and luckily it still worked. You focused in on a flap of skin hanging loose over a ravaged jugular vein and you thought about composition, and lighting, and getting the color values right, and suddenly it was just a picture. Something created, something not quite real.

It was the only way she could handle this mess.

'They were having a Tupperware party,' Special Deputy Glauer said, squatting down next to her. Even if he'd sat on the floor he would have been a head taller than Clara. Big and muscular and with the kind of stiff mustache Clara always thought of as police issue. He'd been just a local patrol cop in Gettysburg when he met Laura Caxton, a good, solid peace officer from a town that went most years without seeing a single homicide. Now he and Clara were partners, in charge of tracking down and killing the last known vampire in Pennsylvania.

They were both in way over their heads.

'The hostess – she's over there, most of her,' Glauer went on, pointing at a body he'd partially covered with a sheet, '– is one of the top advertising executives in town.'

Clara squinted through her camera. 'That seems wrong.' She'd noticed, of course, when she came in that this wasn't their typical crime scene. Usually the bodies turned up under bridges, in abandoned buildings. This apartment was in an

16

old warehouse, but one that had been converted to expensive loft space. It was in one of the trendiest neighborhoods in Allentown. 'It doesn't fit the profile.'

Glauer nodded. Together they'd been following the trail of Justinia Malvern, the last living vampire, through one murder scene after another. Vampires needed blood to fuel their unholy existence. The older the vampire got, the more blood it needed every night, or it weakened. Eventually it would lose the strength to crawl out of its own coffin at night and had to lie there rotting away in a body that couldn't die. Justinia Malvern was the oldest vampire on record, well into her fourth century. Most of that time she'd spent trapped in her own coffin, too weak even to rise to feed. That had changed in recent years. She had been feeding a lot recently. Bodies had been turning up all over Pennsylvania. Always before, though, they'd belonged to homeless women or illegal immigrants, migrant workers or housekeepers, the kinds of people who didn't get reported as missing when they failed to turn up for work one day. Malvern was smart. On bad days Clara was sure Malvern was smarter than she was. She'd known that the police would be after her, that she had to keep a low profile if she wanted to keep hunting.

And now – this. 'If she's taking this kind of risk,' Clara said, 'it must mean one of two things. Either she's desperate, she needed blood and she didn't have time to find a safe supply. Or—'

'Or,' Glauer said, nodding, 'she's not worried about us anymore. We've been following her around, cleaning up her messes. Not giving her any reason to worry. Not since Caxton was arrested. Yeah.' He stood up slowly, the joints in his knees popping. 'We don't scare her enough to make her hide anymore.'

They both froze in place at the same time. They'd both

been trained by Laura Caxton, the world's last living vampire hunter, and they knew better than to jump, even when a shadow loomed over them from behind.

'Interesting theory,' their boss said. Deputy Marshal Fetlock of the U.S. Marshals Service was a thin man with jet black hair that had turned dramatically white at his temples. Clara sometimes thought it looked dashing, and sometimes thought it made him look like a skunk. 'Write it up and send it to my email.'

Clara gritted her teeth. 'Yes, sir,' she said.

The deputy marshal had come in through the main door of the loft and walked right through the one splash of blood in the entire place. Malvern had been careful not to spill a drop from most of the victims, but when she forced her way in she had attacked whoever came to the door first and there had been a short struggle. Clara was 100 percent certain that the blood's type would only match one of the corpses in the room – Malvern had no blood of her own to spill, even if an unarmed human opponent could somehow injure her – and therefore the blood evidence was probably useless. There was no such thing as a forensic specialist, however, who could watch someone walking all over a clue and not wince.

'A change in her modus operandi,' Fetlock said, putting his hands on his hips. He looked very pleased with himself. 'That could be good. It could be the break we've been waiting for.'

Laura Caxton had fought vampires successfully by doing things most people considered suicidal. She had gone into their lairs at night. She had sprung their traps just to see what would happen. Somehow she had survived and the vampires hadn't, because she was a warrior, a throwback to the time when vampire hunters had tracked their prey with swords and crossbows. Fetlock, on the other hand, was a very modern bureaucrat. He believed in doing every last thing by

18

the book – which included disciplining anyone who broke protocol.

It also meant he made sure none of his people ever got in harm's way. Clara was one of his people, so she could appreciate that. Up to a point. It hadn't been lost on her, however, that in the time Fetlock had been tracking Malvern, a lot of innocent people had died. A lot more than Caxton would have felt comfortable with.

'I prefer your first theory about what we're seeing here. It's desperation. Malvern is running scared. She knows we're close,' Fetlock said. He bent down next to one of the victims and closed her eyelids with two fingers. Clara winced again. Now he was touching bodies that hadn't even been documented properly. 'All we need is one good clue. One mistake on her part. One lucky break.'

'All we need,' Glauer said, folding his arms across his chest, 'is Caxton back on the team.'

Fetlock didn't even look at the big cop. 'Not going to happen. She's in prison. End of story.'

Clara tried not to say anything. She knew it was futile. Fetlock had been the one who'd arrested Laura in the first place. Worse than that. Laura had freely confessed to her crime and said nothing in her defense at her trial – she had pleaded guilty and let her lawyer go through the necessary motions. When it came time for the sentencing, the judge had asked if anyone had an opinion on what the sentence should be. Fetlock had actually stood up and asked for the maximum sentence allowed by law. After all, he claimed, Caxton had been a cop and should have known better than anyone the consequences of her actions. She had a duty not just to uphold the law, he had argued, but to epitomize it. Clara had started hating him that day, and yet . . . she had felt a certain grudging respect, as well. Because she knew if he was the one being

19

sentenced, he'd still have asked for a maximum penalty. Fetlock was a by-the-book bureaucrat, but at least he had utter faith in his own convictions.

If Clara had spoken up then, and made an impassioned plea to have Laura brought back onto the team, she knew Fetlock's first counterargument would be that Clara had been Laura's girlfriend. That meant she couldn't be objective about this. So there was no point in opening her mouth. And yet—

—Glauer was right. She knew it. She knew for a fact that the only person in the world who could catch Malvern at this point was Laura Caxton.

'She could consult, in a purely civilian capacity,' Glauer went on, saying it so Clara didn't have to. 'She could give us insights on this case that might crack it wide open, and—'

Fetlock frowned. 'There's no good way to set up that kind of relationship, not with her all the way up in SCI-Marcy.'

Clara couldn't take it anymore. 'You could request the court to have her transferred to SCI-Cambridge Springs,' she said. 'That's a minimum-security facility. The prisoners there are allowed real phone privileges. We could set up some kind of arrangement where she could get in on conference calls with us, tell us what we're doing wrong.'

'She's a criminal,' Fetlock growled. He made it sound like this conversation was about to end. 'Do I have to remind you what she did? She kidnapped and tortured a federal prisoner.'

Clara sighed. 'That guy was a sociopath – he'd killed his entire family just to impress a vampire. He knew where the vampire's lair was and it was the only way Laura could get the information.'

'And that makes it okay?' Fetlock demanded. He stepped closer to Clara, picking his way through the carnage on the floor. 'We're law enforcement, Special Deputy. We swear to uphold the law. To put our faith in the law.'

Clara bit her lip. Laura had sworn that, sure. She'd also sworn to protect the innocent. How many lives had she saved that night? Lives the vampire would have taken, if she didn't get to him first? If she'd been forced to kill the bastard for the information, Clara knew she wouldn't have hesitated. Despite Fetlock's attempt to have the book thrown at Laura, the judge had taken all circumstances into account before sentencing her and had thrown out most of the charges against her. Laura had still been required to plead guilty to a charge of kidnapping, and accept a sentence of five years' imprisonment – the mandatory minimum sentence for that crime in Pennsylvania. Even with early release for good behavior it would be years before she was free.

How many people would Malvern kill before that day came?

'I know this is hard for you, Special Deputy,' Fetlock said, his voice dropping into an almost gentle pitch, 'considering the relationship you had with her. But you have to accept the facts. She's in jail because she broke the law.'

'It's not right,' Clara said, knowing she'd already lost. 'She deserves better. For all the people she saved – for all the good she did, she deserves better than to rot in a cell for so long. I mean, hell, without her there wouldn't be a special subjects unit.'

Fetlock gave her a warm smile. 'And because of her, it was almost disbanded. We walk a very thin line, Hsu, and we can't afford to forget that. We have special powers to execute vampires on sight – the legality, the constitutionality of those powers has never been questioned, but if it ever was they would evaporate in a heartbeat. Then our job wouldn't just be hard, it would be impossible. The three of us have to be above suspicion, at all times. Even just associating with a known felon is putting the future of the unit at risk.'

He had a point, of course. The SSU had been created as

21

an ad hoc working group within the Marshals Service, but no high official had ever written up a charter for it or done anything to give it legal standing. So far no one had come forward to complain about what they were doing – the vast majority of people preferred not to publicly acknowledge that vampires were a real threat. But if they ever really screwed up, say by shooting a living human being by mistake, the press, government watchdog groups, and Internal Affairs would descend like vultures and the SSU would be no more.

'Alright, alright,' she said, holding up her hands in surrender. She walked away from Fetlock, not even wanting to look at him. He turned instead to Glauer, who gave him a good-natured shrug.

Suddenly she didn't want to be around either of them. She went over to the far corner of the room and pretended to study some scuff marks on the wall. Far enough away that Fetlock must have believed she couldn't hear what he said next.

The Fed leaned in close to speak to Glauer. Man to man – they would be elbowing each other in the ribs soon enough. 'So she's in prison,' Fetlock whispered, and she could tell from his tone of voice that he was about to try to make a joke. He did that, every once in a while, and every time it made Clara cringe. 'It's not that bad, is it? I mean, come on. She's gay. For her, this has to be like going away to summer camp.'

Glauer earned a little credit in Clara's book then, because he didn't laugh.

4.

They carried Caxton through the prison halls at a fast jog. She was wrapped up in a thick blanket that pressed against her nose and mouth and made it difficult to breathe. She couldn't see where she was, much less where they were going. Finally they brought her into a small echoing room and dumped her on the floor. COs in full riot gear stood around her with stun guns, ready for her to jump up and attack them on sight. When she didn't, they stepped out of the room and a pair of female COs in stab-proof vests replaced them.

'What's going on?' Caxton asked. She looked around and found herself in a room lined with dingy white tiles. There was a large steel bathtub on one side of the room and what looked like medical equipment hanging on the opposite wall.

'Strip,' one of the COs said. A big woman wearing eye protection. She leaned against a plastic table and stared out the window. The other CO, who had a harelip, kept her eyes glued on Caxton. She didn't even blink.

Caxton knew this routine. She'd been a cop in her previous life. There were times when you were handling a prisoner when you couldn't predict what they were going to do, so you made sure they didn't have any options. She understood that she wouldn't be allowed to ask any questions and that if she didn't do exactly what the guard told her, the men with the stun guns would come back in and do it for her. Looking down at the floor, she unfastened the Velcro strip that held her jumpsuit closed in the front.

'Everything. Off,' the big CO said, while studying her own fingernails.

Caxton kicked off her slippers, then peeled off her underwear and her bra. It was very cold in the little room and she started to wrap her arms around herself, but the CO with the harelip took a step forward and grabbed her arms and pulled them down at her sides.

'Don't touch anything. Keep your hands where we say,' the big CO told Caxton. 'Now, we're going to search you. Do not move. Do not swallow. Do not flinch.'

Harelip pulled on plastic gloves and then ran her fingers through Caxton's hair. She took a flashlight from her pocket and pointed it into her mouth and her ears. She lifted up Caxton's arms and checked her armpits, then told Caxton to lift up her breasts so she could check underneath.

'Turn around,' the big CO said when that was done. 'Lean over the table. Now spread your buttocks. Wider.'

Caxton gritted her teeth. Harelip squatted down to get a good look.

'Stand up. Turn around again. Spread your vagina.'

Caxton squeezed her eyes shut in shame. But she did it. She knew they had the legal right to handcuff her and do it to her if she refused. When she opened her eyes again she saw Harelip staring up at her from between her legs.

'You like this, lesbo? You having a good time?' Harelip whispered.

Caxton said nothing.

'Clear,' the big CO said. 'Alright, prisoner. You can put your underwear back on.' She picked up Caxton's jumpsuit and balled it up under her arm. 'This gets searched separately.' She left the room. Harelip went over to the door and stood next to it, her boots slightly spread, her hands clasped behind her.

Caxton pulled her bra and panties back on. Then she just stood there, waiting for whatever came next. There was no place to sit down except on the edge of the bathtub, and it looked very cold. She made a point of staring at the floor, thinking the last thing she wanted to do was antagonize Harelip by looking at her.

Eventually there was a knock on the door and another woman came in. She was older than most of the COs Caxton had seen, maybe fifty-five or even sixty. She was wearing a conservative jacket and mid-length skirt, with a stab-proof vest over the top. She was carrying a metal folding chair and a BlackBerry, which she worked with one thumb even as she set up her chair and took a seat.

For a while longer nothing happened. The newcomer didn't speak, and Caxton didn't think she ought to try to start up a conversation. The older woman used her thumbs to type something on her BlackBerry, which held her whole attention.

Finally, without looking up, she said, 'I think we have a problem here.'

Caxton scratched her nose. Harelip leaned forward, her eyes very hard.

'I don't like it when you girls don't get along,' the older woman said. 'It makes it difficult for all of us. I need to find a way to restore the peace, you see. So we're moving you to Special Housing. Effective immediately.'

25

Caxton looked up. That was very bad news. 'What? But I—'

'We have a zero-tolerance policy for stabbing in this institution.' The older woman was still playing with her hand-held device. She smiled at something on her screen.

'I only acted in self-defense,' Caxton said. 'It wasn't even my shank.'

'Hmm? I have three inmates in the infirmary right now. One has second-degree burns on her face and chest. One has a broken nose that's going to have to be rebroken if she wants it to set right. The third might lose an eye.' She glanced up at Caxton. 'You have a bruise on your wrist.' She looked back down at her email. 'You tell me who should be put in confinement, hmm? There are two kinds of women in this place. There are the ones who just want to get along, work off their time, and go home. Then there are the ones who will stab somebody because they got bored. It's my job to separate these two groups. Today you volunteered for group number two, and I don't care who started it. Beyond that, you're a high-risk prisoner, so you ought to be in protective custody anyway. It's all been decided. You'll be in administrative segregation for the rest of your sentence. Do you have a problem with that?'

Caxton bit her lip and thought about how to respond.

Prisoners who complained about the conditions in Marcy always regretted it. If you complained, that meant you weren't cooperating with the staff. That meant you weren't demonstrating 'good behavior,' and that meant you spent even longer inside, longer until you could go before the parole board, until you could walk free again. Inmates at Marcy did not, on the whole, complain.

On the other hand – AdSeg was the worst part of the prison. It was where the truly violent women were housed, along with

26

those so crazy they couldn't be allowed to roam free and those who were at such a risk of getting killed by their fellow inmates that they had to be watched around the clock. AdSeg was more than maximum security. It meant no privileges, no privacy, and not even the slightest illusion of freedom.

If Caxton had to spend the next five years in an AdSeg cell she would probably go crazy. She had to say something, anything, to avoid that fate.

'I want to talk to a manager or supervisor about this,' she said. 'I want to appeal your decision.'

The older woman stopped pressing buttons with her thumbs. Then, slowly, she put her BlackBerry on the table next to her. Smiling, she reached out one hand. 'Augie Bellows,' she said. 'I'm your warden.'

Crap, Caxton thought. She'd made a bad mistake. She had to try, though, anyway. 'You should know I'm a model prisoner when I'm not being attacked. I have a background in law enforcement and I—'

'I know exactly who you are,' the warden said. She smiled brightly. 'And you should know not to expect any special treatment because you used to be a cop. Many of us here on the staff feel that cops gone bad are the worst kind of prisoner, honestly. You were entrusted to know the difference between right and wrong, and you did a bad thing anyway. How could we possibly take anything you say seriously, ever again?'

'If you look at my record, you'll see I've cooperated fully at all times. I've never started trouble and I've done everything that was asked of me,' Caxton said.

Bellows shrugged as if to say it didn't matter. That it couldn't possibly matter. 'We'll move your things for you. No need to pack. Of course, there are severe restrictions on personal items in AdSeg, so most of your personal belongings will be confiscated. You won't need any makeup or hair care products in

27

special housing, anyway. Now, if things go as I hope they will, you and I will never have to meet again until it's time to send you home. If I were you, I would do everything in my power to make sure we don't.'

'Are you doing this to me because I was a cop – or because I'm gay?' Caxton demanded.

The warden gave her a prolonged, searching look. 'It's because you're in my way. That's all. You're a minor obstacle in the road of my life.'

Then she rose and picked up her folding chair, then went to the door and knocked on it. The door opened and she went out without another word. And that was that. Caxton was doomed to spend the rest of her time in the prison in the worst hell they could create. There was nothing she could do about it. She felt invisible doors slamming shut all around her.

'Wait there,' Harelip said. 'Do not move. Someone will be along to escort you shortly.'

Caxton did what she was told.

Except.

Warden Bellows had left her BlackBerry sitting on the table.

Caxton had been a cop. Cops were nosy. They couldn't help it – it was how they solved crimes, and how, sometimes, they stayed alive. She felt a compelling need to look at the handheld device. She could almost, but not quite, make out the screen from where she stood. She took a step sideways.

Harelip leaned forward again like a dog on a chain.

Caxton held up her hands in surrender. And took another step sideways. When no one burst into the room to restrain or beat her, she stopped in place and looked down. On the screen of the BlackBerry she could see a fragment of a chat transcript. Warden Bellows must have been chatting with someone the whole time she was sentencing Caxton to her new fate. Caxton had no reason to care about the warden's personal correspondence, really, but there was one thread that jumped out at her.

ABell: It feels like forever. I can't wait to get started.
DamaNoctis: It shalln't be long. Patience, I say to ye. 'Tis worth the wait.
ABell: I hope so. I'm risking a

That was all she had a chance to read before Harelip stomped across the room and grabbed the thing off the table. 'Get the hell back, bitch, or I will fuck you up,' she screamed in Caxton's face, knocking Caxton backward until she fell to the floor.

A few minutes later a detail of COs came to walk her to her new cell. They at least gave her a brand-new jumpsuit so she wouldn't have to show up in her underwear.

5.

The special housing unit at SCI-Marcy was constructed in a circle around a central guard post two levels high. The cells all faced the glass post and were all identical – narrow rectangles, eight feet wide by sixteen deep, each with a toilet at the back and a solid steel door at the front. The doors were three inches thick and padded on the inside. Each had a small square window set in it at head height and underneath that a narrow sliding panel, a 'bean slot,' where the guards could hand in food at mealtimes. There was no separate cafeteria for the women in the SHU. They ate in their cells. They did most things in their cells: they stayed inside of them for twenty-three hours out of every day.

Three types of prisoner were kept in the SHU. There were AdSeg cases, like Caxton – the most violent or the craziest inmates in the prison, who were deemed a danger to others. Secondly were the protective custody prisoners, who were a danger to themselves. Either they'd pissed off some particularly vengeful gang, or turned evidence against other prisoners, or had committed some crime so heinous that the general population hated them enough to want them dead. There were only two child molesters in SCI-Marcy, but they were both in protective custody. Two-thirds of the women in the prison were mothers, separated by the law and circumstance from the children they loved. Being so far from their kids made some of them crazy. Some of them liked to prove they were still good mothers by attacking baby-rapers on sight.

The three women in the SHU who were not in AdSeg or protective custody were model prisoners who kept mostly to themselves, passing the time as best they could. These three women alone were given the privilege of a 'Cadillac' cell, a private room with some small luxuries allowed. They had barred windows that looked out over the exercise yard and were even allowed to keep radios as long as the volume stayed low. No one in the SHU complained about their getting special treatment, however, because those three cells made up Pennsylvania's only all-female death row.

When Caxton came into the SHU for the first time she was nearly blinded. The walls were scuffed and dinged, but they had been painted a brilliant white, and they caught all the light coming down from above from a ring of powerful klieg lights in the ceiling. The light was merciless and all-revealing. She was brought in through the only door leading into the SHU, where a row of COs in riot gear waited for her just in case she tried to make a run for it or, even stupider, tried to fight her way out.

She could understand why some inmates would try. For a lucky few who had just pulled temporary AdSeg by stabbing someone or bringing drugs into the prison, a stay in the SHU could last only a few days or weeks. For the women on protective custody and death row, the SHU would be their home for years to come.

Just like Caxton.

31

The CO sitting in the guard post lifted one hand and the COs in riot gear took a step back, letting Caxton come forward. Her legs were shackled together and her hands were bound behind her with plastic handcuffs. One guard grabbed her wrists and guided her to the left. There was a red line painted on the floor, equally distant from the cell doors and the guard post, and she was made to walk along it with one foot on either side. She was marched up to a cell door marked with a seven. Two transparent plastic brackets were mounted on the door. One was empty, while the other contained a photograph of a woman with bad acne and the name STIMSON, GERTRUDE R. Below this was a list of known allergies (peanuts) and special restrictions (zero stimulants) and the legend PC, which Caxton assumed meant that the woman inside was in protective custody.

Caxton looked up and saw the woman from the picture staring out at her through the window in the door. Her complexion was much clearer in person.

'Wall up,' one of the guards shouted. Caxton didn't know what that meant, but apparently it wasn't directed at her. The woman in the cell – Gertrude Stimson – moved away from the window at once.

'Prisoner Caxton,' the CO said, bending down to unshackle her legs. If she felt like kicking him for his trouble she only had to look to the side and see the stun gun another guard was pointing at her neck. 'Welcome to the SHU. You will be confined to your cell at all times unless we come for you. When we do, we'll say "wall up." That means you move to the back of the cell with your back against the wall. If you don't wall up, we will perform a forcible extraction. You don't want that. Meal-times are at six-thirty, noon, and four-thirty. Your exercise period will be from one in the afternoon until two. You'll be taken to the showers once per week, at six P.M.

32

every Thursday. You just missed your slot, it looks like. We'll bring around a deodorant stick for you a little later on. If I remove your hand restraints now, will you behave?'

'Yes,' Caxton said, in the meekest voice she could manage.

He unfastened the plastic handcuffs. Caxton flexed her fingers to try to get the circulation going again. 'Here's a clean blanket and a clean washcloth.' They were both made of the same scratchy nylon that looked like it couldn't be torn or burned. 'Prisoner on the floor,' he shouted, and COs all around the circular housing unit repeated the call. 'Door opening!'

An alarm sounded, a high-pitched clanging that went on for ten seconds, and then an electronic lock in the door thunked open. The CO pulled a lever that released a second mechanical lock and then hauled the door back.

Inside, Gertrude Stimson was standing up against the wall, her hands above her head. She didn't move at all except to blink as Caxton stepped inside the cell.

Before they could close the door on her Caxton turned around to say, 'I'd like to make a phone call. An email would be fine as well. Is there a sign-up roster, or—'

'No outgoing calls. No computer time. If you want to write a letter, let us know and you can dictate it to us through the bean slot. Now wall the fuck up so I can close this door.'

Caxton hurried to the back of the cell and pressed her back against the wall.

The CO poked his head in to peer into the corners of the cell, as if someone else might be hiding inside. 'Enjoy your stay.'

The door alarm rang again for ten seconds and then it was shut with a double thunk of closing locks.

For a long time Caxton just stood there with her back against the cold wall. She didn't move. Didn't say anything.

Eventually she realized she was waiting to be told what to do next.

It was getting to her already. They were turning her into an inmate, even inside her own head.

Stepping away from the wall, she rubbed at her wrists and looked around. There wasn't much to see. The cell wasn't wide enough for two beds side by side, so much of the space was taken up by a tall bunk bed made of scratched aluminum. It had been designed in such a way that it had no sharp corners nor any pieces that could be broken off, even by a determined prisoner with a lot of time on her hands.

The only other furniture in the cell was a combination sink and toilet made of the same rounded aluminum construction. There was no seat on the toilet, and its opening was narrower and long rather than round.

'It looks funny, I know, and it ain't comfortable. It's made that way so you can't shove my head in there,' Gertrude Stimson said. 'You know, if you had a mind to.'

Caxton turned and stared at the other woman. Her new roommate – her celly. In the general-population dorm where she'd been before, Caxton had seven cellies in a cell about three times as large as this one. They had been morose women, relatively quiet unless one of them was moaning about how badly she wanted a cigarette or another was shaking and moaning with withdrawal symptoms. They had mostly been black, with two Latinas, and they had all spoken Spanish most of the time, a language Caxton barely understood.

Gertrude Stimson was pasty white, with stringy red hair that she kept tied back in a stubby ponytail. Her fingernails, Caxton noted, were chewed down to round red stubs.

'You can call me Gert, or Gerty, it's one and the same,' she said.

'Caxton.' Caxton didn't offer her hand.

'Oh, I know you, for sure. You're famous. They made a movie about you, and those vampires you killed. And then at the town of Gettysburg—'

'I don't like to talk about that,' Caxton growled.

'I never thought I'd have a famous lady in here, is all,' Stimson said, with a little laugh.

Caxton tried to ignore her and went to the bunk bed. The bottom bunk was clearly Stimson's. Photographs of babies had been taped up along the wall, but not snapshots – these were just pictures of babies torn from magazines. The bed was unmade, with the blanket shoved down at the bottom in a heap. The top bunk was empty, with nothing on it but a mattress that crinkled when she pushed on it and a pillow made of the same rip-stop nylon as her blanket and washcloth. A plastic bag containing her personal effects lay at the foot of the mattress.

'I want you to know, I'm a little famous myself,' Gert chattered. 'But you shouldn't believe everything you hear.'

Caxton did think the name was slightly familiar, though she couldn't place where she'd heard it before. No doubt she would get to hear about Gert's moment of fame in excruciating detail soon enough, so she didn't bother to ask.

She made the bed carefully, knowing she had plenty of time to keep things neat. Then she opened the bag. The warden had said her things would be moved for her, but there was very little in the bag – her brush, her comb, and most of her books were all missing. She'd been left a couple of dog-eared paperbacks and one photograph. It was a picture of Clara that Caxton had taken one day at a sheriff's office picnic. It had been in a frame before, but the frame had been seized and the picture removed. One corner had been torn in the process.

'Who's that? Friend of yours? Or – girlfriend?' Stimson

asked, her voice rising slyly at the end. 'I heard you was a lesbo, too. So is she? Your girlfriend?'

'None of your business,' Caxton said. She climbed up on the bunk and laid herself out flat. Breakfast was at six-thirty, she thought. That was a long time away. She wondered what time lights-out might be. Stimson would know, but she might also take that as a desire on Caxton's part to start a conversation.

Not that she needed much prompting.

'You been here long? How much longer you got?'

'If it's alright, I'd like some quiet time,' Caxton said. 'I have a lot on my mind.'

'Sure thing,' Stimson said. She disappeared under the bunk and Caxton relaxed a little. She closed her eyes and tried to clear her mind. She could do this. She could stay strong, and do the time quietly and without losing her mind. She could.

From beneath her she heard a high-pitched squeaking sound. Then a muffled grunt of pain. The squeaking sound came again a second later. And again. Eventually she realized that Stimson was chewing her nails.

It was going to be a very long five years.

6.

Lights-out never came.

The light in the ceiling never went out. Caxton wasn't allowed to have a watch in her cell, and there was no clock, either, but as she lay on her bunk listening to Stimson snoring below her, she eventually realized that midnight must have come and gone, and nothing had changed.

She stared at the light for a long time, waiting to feel sleepy. The light came from a single bulb set in a shatterproof fixture designed in such a way that Caxton could neither open it nor get any kind of grip on it. A single cockroach had found its way inside the fixture and died there. It had only five legs. One of them must have rotted away.

Next to the fixture was a small black rectangle that Caxton knew must hide a camera. The light was left on so that the camera could watch her while she slept. She stared at the rectangle for a long time, too, because it was difficult to know she was being watched and not try to watch back.

Then she rolled over and pressed her face into the scratchy

37

pillow for a long time, trying to keep her eyes closed. They kept drifting open of their own accord.

She tried pulling the pillow over her head to block out the light. That just made it difficult to breathe. She tried giving up, next, and sat up so she could read one of her paperbacks by the unblinking light. She was too tired to focus on the words, though, and eventually she gave up on that, too.

Time passed. The night must have passed, somehow, though she couldn't see anything but the walls of the cell and so she had no way of measuring how long she'd been awake until, out of nowhere, a buzzer sounded in the ceiling and Stimson stopped snoring with an abrupt wet sound and rolled out of her bunk.

'Wall up.' The sound came from the same place as the buzzer – a small speaker set into the ceiling, next to the light fixture and the camera's black eye. Caxton jumped down from the top bunk and went to stand next to Stimson against the wall.

Together they waited for quite a while. Then the bean slot in the door slid back and a tray came through. Stimson stepped forward to grab it, then jumped back against the wall. A second tray came in and Caxton did the same thing. Then the bean slot slid back into place. It was designed so that the prisoners couldn't open it from the inside.

Both trays were identical. They were wrapped in plastic. When Caxton pulled the plastic back on hers she found it contained three slices of toast, already slathered with butter, and two slices of melon that weren't quite ripe. A shallow paper cup held apple juice. 'No coffee?' Caxton said, a little upset.

'That's my fault,' Stimson said, scraping at a moldy spot on one of her melon slices. 'Sorry. I have a little teensy problem with, um, speed. I can't have anything that's an upper. Not even caffeine.'

'You're a meth freak,' Caxton said, because she wasn't feeling very charitable. 'But I'm not.'

38

Stimson shrugged. Her mouth was full of toast. 'I guess,' she said, showering crumbs everywhere, 'they're worried I might steal yours. So you don't get none, either.' She washed down her mouthful with the juice. 'Sorry.'

Caxton was hungry enough to eat everything on her tray quickly. That turned out to be a good thing – ten minutes after the trays had arrived, the order to wall up came again and the bean slot slid back so they could pass the trays out, whether they were finished or not.

The slot closed once more. And that was it. Breakfast. Afterward nothing happened. Nothing was going to happen, Caxton realized, until lunchtime. She imagined that meals were going to become the high points of her day.

Clearly conversation with Stimson wasn't going to provide much in the way of entertainment. All Stimson wanted to talk about was what she was going to do when she was released. 'Babies,' she said, and her eyes blazed with excitement. 'I'm going to have some more babies. Babies are what life's all about. You know how they smell? Babies smell good. I love playing with babies. I love the noises they make. Even when they cry.'

Caxton had never wanted children. It had just never occurred to her to think that might be a good use of her life. She tried to steer the conversation into another arena. She considered asking what Stimson had done to get sent to Marcy, but she had an idea that it was impolite to ask. Instead, she tried, 'How long are you in for?'

'A good jolt. Twenty years,' Stimson said.

Caxton frowned. 'Won't you be too old to have babies then?'

Stimson wasn't about to be brought down. 'I'll be forty-two, that's not too old. And if it is, I can adopt. I know it's hard to adopt when you've got a record, but when they see how much I want a baby, and what a good mother I can be, they'll have to give me one. They'll have to give me a baby.'

Caxton nodded politely and climbed back onto her bunk. Stimson kept talking, even after Caxton stopped listening. It seemed she was happy enough chattering away to herself.

Lunchtime came, eventually. A cold chicken sandwich and a cup of apple juice. They had ten minutes to eat it. Then nothing happened, again, for a while. Then the command to wall up came again and Caxton realized it was exercise time. The one chance she would have all day to get out of the cell.

A smile actually crept onto her face. She ran her fingers through her hair and tried to smooth the wrinkles out of her jumpsuit. She knew she was overreacting, but it was something, something different. Something to look forward to.

She waited for what felt like far too long and then finally, magically, the cell door was opened. A CO stood in the doorway and gestured for the two of them to step forward. Another CO was waiting with two pairs of shackles. Caxton's feet were bound together. Then the CO did the same for Stimson. The whole time a third CO was always hovering over them with a stun gun.

They were made to shuffle forward until they were standing on the red line that ran around the circumference of the special housing unit. In his glass watch post, a CO eyed them carefully. He reached for a microphone and his voice was amplified until it squalled off the glaring white walls. 'It's raining outside, so exercise is indoors today.'

Caxton heard an angry moan go up from somewhere on the far side of the guard post. She glanced around the side of the post and saw four inmates over there, all of them shackled as she was. If every cell was full to capacity, there would be forty-eight women in the SHU, Caxton figured. Apparently only six were allowed to take exercise at any given time, with three COs supervising. Nothing in the SHU was ever allowed to get out of control. Nothing was ever left to chance. As a law enforcement officer, or rather, an ex–law enforcement officer, she had to admire the efficiency of the system. As an inmate she felt like she was being ground down, all her humanity scraped out of her one indignity at a time.

The COs got all six women in a line, then made them stand six feet apart from each other. Then the exercise began in earnest. They were told to walk around the SHU in a circle, keeping one foot on either side of the red line at all times. They were required to maintain the distance between them, to keep their hands in plain sight, and there was to be no talking. 'Okay, walk,' one CO ordered.

Caxton walked. She watched the inmate ahead of her, a woman with frizzy brown hair, and did exactly as she was told. And liked it, despite herself. It felt good to use the muscles in her legs. It felt good to breathe air that she and Stimson hadn't already breathed and exhaled a thousand times. It even felt good to be silent for a while, and not have to listen to Stimson talk or chew her nails.

She passed the time watching the cell doors go past on her left. She counted them and knew how many laps she'd made around the SHU, which kept some tiny part of her brain occupied. She wanted to see how many laps she made in an hour. Then she noticed that the woman ahead of her had a dark spot on the back of her jumpsuit. It grew steadily as she walked, never slowing down for a moment, and ran down the inside of her pantleg. Caxton watched in fascinated horror as a drop of yellow liquid fell from the orange cuff and splattered on the floor. Then another. Soon a narrow trickle was dribbling out behind the woman, and Caxton had to step carefully to avoid getting her slippers wet.

One of the COs came rushing in and pushed Caxton back. He grabbed the woman from behind and pulled her into a

41

painful-looking armlock, then frog-marched her over to the guard post.

'Keep walking,' another CO ordered, and Caxton realized she'd stopped and that Stimson was right behind her, less than six feet away. Caxton got back to the line and started walking in circles again.

Eventually exercise time was over, and she was taken back to her cell and had her shackles removed. She went in and walled up next to Stimson and waited for the door to be officially closed again before she spoke.

'She peed herself!' Caxton exclaimed. 'Did you see that? She peed – on herself. I think she did it on purpose. Why on earth would anyone do that? Was she sick, or just crazy?'

Stimson's face broke into a wry and knowing smile. 'When you been in here awhile, you'll understand. She pissed herself,' Stimson said, as if it were perfectly rational, 'so that one of the COs would have to clean her up.'

7.

The guards had been busy while Caxton and Stimson were out. They had put a picture of her on the door, right next to Stimson's. Underneath, where the guards were advised not to give Stimson any stimulants of any kind, they had written in, 'Caxton prone to violence. Use anti-stab and anti-bite precautions.'

It was official, then. She was a resident of the SHU for the duration.

She quickly learned what that was going to mean. How it was going to change her whole philosophy of life.

For instance: when you had nothing, you learned to appreciate the little things. When you had no freedom and no civil rights you learned to treasure any shred of dignity or hope you were permitted.

Caxton finally got her first shower a week after she arrived in the SHU. She even got a shower stall all to herself. Of course, two female COs watched her the whole time and she had to wash around the shackles on her legs, but the hot water made her feel almost human for the first time since she'd

43

been moved to her new cell. It was over all too soon. As she was dressing she was told she was in for another treat: a one-hour therapy session. She was allowed one every six weeks and her number had come up. 'You're allowed to refuse therapy,' a CO told her, but Caxton couldn't imagine why she would. Any human contact that wasn't with Stimson sounded like heaven.

She quickly discovered that the therapy she was being offered wasn't what she had expected, though. She was led to a small room near the SHU. It had padded walls and it smelled of antiseptic. There was no one in the room except for Caxton and two COs, but there was a telephone mounted on the wall. She was told she could pick it up and speak directly with one of the prison's staff psychotherapists. When Caxton picked up the handset she saw there were no buttons on the phone. It was strictly for this purpose and there was no way to get it to call outside the prison.

'Um, hello?' she said, placing the handset to her ear.

'Yeah, hi. How are you feeling?' a bored male voice asked from the other end of the connection.

Caxton licked her lips. 'I, um, I've been better.'

The psychotherapist said nothing.

Caxton let her head fall forward a little. 'It's tough, you know? It's just tough adjusting to this routine. It's kind of. Um. It's nice talking to a friendly voice. Everybody else I talk to around here is either yelling at me or they're crazy.'

Caxton blushed. She couldn't believe she was opening up like this with a complete stranger, one she couldn't even see. But the chance to unload her problems, even in such a clinical way, was affecting her in a way she couldn't have foreseen.

'I miss my girlfriend,' she said. God. It felt good to say that out loud. She'd been afraid to say it even to Stimson. 'I

44

get pretty scared in here. I can't sleep, and the food doesn't taste like anything, it tastes like cardboard. I think – I think maybe I'm having a harder time of it than I even let myself believe. I think I might be going—'

'Are you depressed?' the therapist asked.

Caxton thought about it. 'Um, I—'

'Depression doesn't just mean you're sad. Everybody's sad in here. What about voices? Are you hearing voices? Voices that tell you to do things you don't want to do?'

Caxton's body tensed up again. 'No,' she said.

'Let me know if you start hearing voices or having hallucinations. I can give you Thorazine for that. If you think you're depressed I can send over some Prozac. You just have to be careful with this stuff. If you start feeling suicidal you need to alert a guard right away. Do you want the Prozac? We'll start with a low dose and adjust as necessary.'

'No. Thank you,' Caxton said, and hung up the phone. Her therapy session was over.

On days when it didn't rain, the SHU inmates were allowed outside for their exercise period. Sort of. They were let out of their cells in groups of six, and as before their feet were shackled and they were never allowed to be less than six feet away from each other. They were then taken out of the SHU through a short corridor to a door that led to sunlight, and open air, and a patch of blue sky.

It was the most beautiful thing Caxton had ever seen. It was also carved up into sections by a mesh of wires so close together that Caxton couldn't have put her hand between them, even if she'd had the chance. The SHU exercise yard was a cage twenty feet wide by fifty feet long. Wire mesh formed a ceiling and four walls. The concrete floor of the cage had a red rectangle painted on it, and the inmates were never

45

allowed outside of that rectangle, which kept them always six feet from the mesh.

They were allowed to do as they pleased inside the rectangle, as long as they didn't approach one another or talk. A row of yoga mats had even been set up along one side of the cage, and a couple inmates made use of them to do sit-ups or stretching exercises. The rest just milled around, careful not to get too close to each other. One of them, a big woman with no left ear, only a lump of twisted scar tissue, made a nasty game of it. She would start walking toward one of her fellow inmates until they would be forced to step backward. The COs weren't timid about shouting for them to keep their space, and anyone who broke through the invisible limit was dragged off, forfeiting their exercise period for the next day. They made no attempt to stop the big woman from herding the others back and forth across the yard, however.

Back in the cell Caxton asked Stimson why the big woman would do such a thing. She was only causing trouble for the others. 'She's a convict,' Stimson said, as if that explained everything.

'So am I. So are you. We don't pull that kind of bullshit.'

Stimson shook her head excitedly. This was another chance to initiate her celly into the ways of life inside. 'No, see, I'm an inmate. There's a difference. Inmates try to get along. We want to be model prisoners so we can get days on our good-behavior jackets. Convicts are different. They know they're going to be in and out of prison all their lives, so they got no reason to try to be good. If they can be bad, though, like, real tough, they can get a rep for it, and that's a good thing, how they see it.'

Caxton thought of Guilty Jen, who had been obsessed with

46

respect and reputation to the point she was willing to kill to get it. 'I think I'd rather be an inmate.'

'Yeah?' Stimson asked. 'I had you pegged different. A hard case.'

Caxton climbed up onto her bunk and lay back on her mattress. She had to think about what that meant.

As usual, Stimson wouldn't just let her be. 'I'm pretty useful to you, huh?' she asked, pulling herself up onto the side of Caxton's bunk and leaning her chin on the mattress. 'I mean, I can tell you stuff you didn't know. I can help you out.'

'I guess,' Caxton said.

'We're connecting, right? We're bonding. That's good. 'Cause if I'm useful to you, maybe you can be useful to me. You can protect me. If I get in trouble, you can vouch for me. That's how it works, right? We're getting together?'

'Whatever,' Caxton told her.

'I am going to be so useful to you,' Stimson said. 'You wait and see. I'm gonna be your road bitch. That's what you call your best friend inside. See? Useful. I'm gonna be your best friend in the world. And then, and then, and then you can be my mama. If – if – if, you know. If you wanted to.'

Caxton couldn't look into those trusting eyes anymore. They reminded her too much of the eyes of the dogs she used to rescue. She turned her head away. It was impossible to spend twenty-three hours a day in the cell with Stimson and not talk to the woman. To not interact with her. But the last thing she wanted to do was lead Stimson on. They weren't friends. Caxton couldn't imagine ever being friends with someone like this baby-obsessed speed freak. The second she got out of SCI-Marcy she would never think about Stimson again. It wasn't fair to pretend otherwise. 'I won't be in here that long,' she said, trying not to put too

47

much edge in her voice. 'Maybe your next celly can be your mama.'

'I didn't mean nothing by it,' Stimson said, dropping back down to the floor. 'Shit. I didn't mean I was going to suck your pussy or nothing.'

'Okay,' Caxton said. 'Good to know.'

8.

Malvern struck again and the body count was even higher this time. She'd hit a roadhouse outside of Allentown, just after midnight. One patron had managed to escape to call the local police, but by the time they arrived Malvern had slaughtered two cocktail waitresses, a bartender, a bouncer, and six good old boys who'd just wanted to have a few beers after work. By dawn Clara and Glauer were there, checking for clues. Fetlock was busy in Harrisburg, catching up with his paperwork, so for once the two of them had the scene to themselves.

'She must have had help,' Glauer said, pacing back and forth from the rear exit and the front door. 'Look at the arrangement of the bodies. She got the bouncer here, and one of the waitresses – but the rest of them tried to flee out the back. They got – this far,' he said, stopping next to a bad stain on the carpet by the restrooms. The bodies had already been removed by the local coroner – which Clara appreciated, because it meant she didn't have to see them, even if it also meant some evidence might have been destroyed. 'The exit was blocked, so they couldn't get out.'

'We know she has to have some kind of accomplice,' Clara agreed. 'Someone has to drive her from victim to victim. She's too weak to walk from scene to scene.' A vampire at full strength could outrun a speeding car, but Malvern hadn't been that strong in centuries. 'It could be a human sympathizer. Or a half-dead.' Vampires had the ability to raise their victims from the dead – for a short while. The resulting servants were called half-deads. They rotted away almost fast enough to watch, but as long as they could still stand under their own power they were forced to do the vampire's bidding.

'There's another possibility,' Glauer said, meeting Clara's gaze. He held her eye for a second and then said, 'The accomplice could be another vampire.'

Vampires could make more of their kind. In fact, Malvern was an expert at it. Every vampire Laura Caxton had ever destroyed had been one of Malvern's creations.

Clara shook her head. 'That's not in our profile for her. It saps her strength to create new vampires, and she's running on fumes as it is. It would put her back in her coffin for good if she tried that now.' Deputy Marshal Fetlock had built his whole strategy around the idea that Malvern was indulging herself in one long orgy of blood and that she had no grand scheme in mind, no master plan. That she would start making mistakes any night now.

'You know what Caxton would have said about that profile,' Glauer muttered.

'She would have said that he was underestimating Malvern. And that underestimating a vampire is the surest way to get killed by one.' She stepped behind the bar and ran a hand behind the bins of lime and lemon wedges. Her fingers touched something metallic and she drew it out. A sawed-off shotgun. She knew she'd find something there – every bar had a gun, in case things got so far out of hand that the bouncer

50

couldn't handle it. She cracked open the shotgun and found a pair of shells inside. She sniffed the barrel and decided it hadn't been fired in a long while.

'Something – something occurred to me, after that last scene,' she said. 'After the Tupperware party. Malvern has changed her MO.'

'Sure. She's stopped hiding her kills so carefully.'

Clara nodded. 'Yeah. Fetlock thought it was because she was getting scared, and that made her sloppy. You and I had a different idea, if you recall – that it was just the opposite, that she's stopped thinking of us, of law enforcement, as a threat.'

'Yes,' Glauer said. 'I remember.' He stopped pacing and looked at her. 'You think you have a better explanation?'

'Maybe. I think she might be building up to something.'

Glauer sighed. 'I don't like the sound of that.'

'We know she's a smart one. Every time Laura had Malvern in her sights, Malvern managed to get away almost on a technicality, or at the last minute. And even when she was stuck in her coffin, too weak to move, she always found a way to cause trouble. I can't imagine she doesn't have a plan right now.'

'But what could it possibly be?' Glauer asked. 'She needs blood, lots of blood. More blood every night. That's a zero-sum game. It means we'll never stop looking for her. And no matter how inept we may be, eventually we're going to find her. No matter how clever or how careful she is, she can't keep doing this forever, but she can't stop, either. What kind of plan would get her out of this mess?'

'I don't know. I'm not as smart as she is,' Clara admitted. 'I just have a feeling, that's all. She hasn't finished surprising us yet. Shit. Is that really the time?'

Glauer looked up at the clock over the bar. 'Almost. Places

51

like this set the clock ahead about fifteen minutes, because they know when last call comes, it'll still take the patrons that long to finish their drinks and get out. They call it bar time.'

Clara smiled at the big cop. She probably knew a lot more about closing down bars than he did. 'Listen, I know Fetlock doesn't want to bring Laura into this investigation. But I'm going to run her through it anyway and see what she says. I'm going up to Tioga County today to visit her.'

'Really? He's not going to like that,' Glauer said. 'For one thing, he's definitely going to want you on call, and if he can't reach you—'

'It's only a four-hour drive,' Clara told him. It was almost noon and she really needed to get on the road. 'You . . . heard, right? About where she is now?'

'That they segregated her?' He shrugged. 'Yeah.' Every cop knew a few corrections officers – they ran in the same social circles. And any time an ex-cop ended up inside it made for excellent gossip. Probably every state trooper and sheriff's deputy in Pennsylvania had heard about Caxton's descent to the hole. 'Probably the safest place for her is in an SHU. She can't have a lot of friends in the general population.'

'Yeah, well, it's not all good. Prisoners in the SHU only get one hour of non-contact visitation a month. If I don't get up there by five o'clock today it'll be the end of April before I can get another appointment. It's four hours up there, an hour visit, and four hours back. I'll be back here by ten at the latest. So if Fetlock comes calling, stall him for me, will you? Just pretend you can't reach me, that I'm out of cell phone range or something. Please. It's really important that I talk to her now.'

Glauer smiled at her. 'You know I will. It's got to mean a lot to her, to have someone come see her as regularly as you do.'

'Yeah,' Clara said. 'It must.'

52

'You're a good person,' he told her. 'A lot of people wouldn't have wanted to wait for her to get out. Maybe they would hold out for a while, you know, but eventually they wouldn't be able to handle it. They would have to break things off.'

'Um. Yeah,' Clara said.

His eyes went wide. 'Oh,' he said. 'You're going to—'

'I'm going to be late,' Clara said, 'if I don't get going right now.'

Glauer turned his face away from her. 'Tell her I said hi.'

9.

They checked Clara's ID at a guard post, then waved her through. She drove up a long gravel drive toward the prison complex, a group of low brick buildings connected by brick walkways. There were fences everywhere, and rolls of barbed wire, and signs telling her not to get out of her car, not to use cameras or cell phones on the grounds, and whatever she did, to never, ever pick up hitchhikers. She pulled into a small parking lot directly underneath a looming brick wall between two watchtowers. Men with assault rifles looked down at her from the towers, waiting for her to try something.

Her stomach hurt. It was nerves, just nerves – nobody could really relax in a setting like this, and Clara had a lot to be nervous about anyway. She was going to tell Laura that it was over. She'd wrestled with the idea for a long time. She'd gone over and over in her head all the reasons why it had to be done. Why it was better to do it now than to wait. Why she had to say it in person. Her reasoning was sound. She didn't need to feel guilty.

Their relationship had started at a bad time in Laura's life. Her previous girlfriend, Deanna, had been succumbing to a vampire's curse. She had ended up taking her own life. Laura had clung then to Clara like a drowning woman holding on to a floating tree branch, and for a while it had been so good – she'd been so attentive, so affectionate. Clara had never had a relationship like that before.

But then the vampires hadn't gone away. They kept coming back, and suddenly every time she reached out for Laura, Laura wasn't there. She'd thought it was a temporary thing, maybe. That Laura would learn to balance her job and her love life. Instead the love life had been sacrificed for Laura's obsessive quest to wipe out vampires once and for all. And even that had been okay – for a while. Because when your lover isn't there, but it's only because she's out saving the world, well. You feel guilty if you start making demands. If you start drawing attention to your own needs. So Clara had done her best to support Laura, to always be there for her whenever she finally did come home.

Now she wasn't coming home for years. It was too much to take. Clara was hardly of one mind about breaking up with Laura. But she knew she had to do it if she ever wanted to have any kind of life of her own. It was the smart thing to do. The mature, grown-up thing. To just make a clean break of it, so they could both get on with their lives.

And yet, she still felt like a sixteen-year-old about to take her first driver's license test. Her stomach hurt, and she had a weird headache that wouldn't go away. She hadn't eaten anything all day because she hadn't been hungry, and now, perversely enough, she felt ravenous. She could get something to eat when it was done.

Just do it, she told herself. Do it quickly, like pulling off a—

A big black dog shoved its wet nose against her window.

Clara screamed a little. The dog wasn't barking or snapping at her, but it had a suspicious look in its eye.

'Please step out of the car, ma'am,' a corrections officer in a blue stab-proof vest said. Clara nodded and opened her door. The dog lunged inside the car, sniffing at her skirt and her shoes. Clara held her hands up where they could be seen. She stepped out of the car and let the dog smell her, let it do its job.

'You here for a visitation?' the CO asked. 'ID, please.'

Clara nodded and reached for her purse. The dog sat back on its haunches and stared at her, daring her to try something.

This wasn't her first time visiting Laura. Clara knew the drill. The silver star on her lapel should have been enough, but she handed over her driver's license and her U.S. Marshals Service ID card anyway. The CO shoved them in his pocket. 'I'll make a copy of these and they'll be returned when you leave,' he told her. 'This way.'

He grabbed up the dog's leash and walked her toward a low, narrow gate in the wall. Inside she was led to a waiting room where a number of other visitors, mostly women, were sitting on plastic chairs watching a videotape about what they were allowed to bring inside the prison and what was expressly forbidden. COs with dogs circled the room, searching for contraband.

'Ms. Hsu? You're with me,' another CO said. This one didn't have a dog. 'I'll take you to the SHU visiting area now.'

Clara nodded gratefully. Behind her someone shouted, 'Hey!'

It was a visitor, a middle-aged woman with dry hair wearing a tie-dyed sweatshirt.

'How come she gets to go first? I been waiting an hour,' she insisted.

'Watch the tape. We'll come for you when it's time,' a CO said.

'Shit,' the woman said, sitting back down. 'And you can't even smoke in here!'

Clara was taken through a series of gates, each of them designed to be opened electronically by a CO behind a bullet-proof window. Finally she was brought into a little antechamber where her fingerprints were taken and a female CO brushed a long cotton swab across her shoulders and down the side of her skirt.

'Is this really necessary?' Clara asked. She hadn't gone through this the last time.

The COs didn't answer her. The female one pushed her swab into the waiting maw of an Ionscan machine that could detect even minute traces of explosives or narcotics. Everybody waited for forty-five seconds until the screen lit up red. 'Gunpowder residue,' the female CO said.

The male CO, Clara's guide, pulled a stun gun off his belt and held it down by his thigh. 'Empty your pockets, now. Everything goes in the bucket.' He kicked a plastic bin at her so it skidded across the floor. 'Watch, belt, shoes, too. Wallets, keys, cell phone. You have a camera on you?'

Clara frowned. She took her camera out of her purse and placed it carefully in the bin. Then, with exaggerated slow-ness, she opened her jacket and showed them her empty shoulder holster. 'It's okay,' she insisted. 'I'm a federal agent. You're picking up gunpowder residue because I normally carry a sidearm. I didn't bring it in with me. I really don't see why you need my belt.'

'No exceptions. In the bin, now!' the male CO demanded.

Clara did as she was told.

With one hand on her skirt to keep it from falling down, and wincing with every step – the prison floors were ice cold on her stockinged feet – she was finally allowed into a visitation room. A row of carrels ran down the middle of the room, each booth facing an identical one but separated from it by a plate of inch-thick Lexan. There was a telephone handset in the booth and one just like it on the other side.

'You will not be allowed physical contact with the prisoner,' the male CO told her. 'Everything you say will be monitored, recorded, and analyzed. The recording may be used as evidence in a court of law. You may not use obscene language or any kind of code words, do you understand? And under no circumstances will you be allowed to remove your clothing during the visit. You will have one hour with the prisoner. If you do not wish to use the full hour, you may hang up your telephone handset at any time and the prisoner will be returned to her cell. Do you understand?'

'Yes, yes,' Clara said. She sat down in a hard wooden chair and stared forward, through the Lexan. *This is it,* she told herself. *This is where you get your life back.*

Then they brought Laura in.

She looked terrible. Her face was pale and lined. Her hair was lifeless and fell forward across her forehead. Laura had never spent a lot of time on hair care – she'd always said that was one of the chief benefits of being gay – but she'd always used a little mousse, always kept her spiky hair brushed and neat. Now it was all floppy and dull. She looked like k.d. lang on a bad day.

Laura rushed forward and grabbed her handset before she'd even sat down properly. 'Clara,' she said. 'Clara. I – I'm so glad you came.'

'Of course I did,' Clara told her. She should just clear her throat, she knew, and say it. Just say it in as few words as possible. *It's over, Laura.*

Too cold.

I've been giving this a lot of thought, and—
No. Too wishy-washy. Laura would try to argue with her.
I'll still come and visit, but when you get out—
You know, you would do the same in my shoes—
It's just so hard, being alone, and we were never that great together anyway—

'I need to talk to you about something,' Clara said. She could hear the blood rushing in her ears. 'Something important.'

'Of course,' Laura said.

'It's about.' Clara stopped. Her tongue wouldn't work. She couldn't say the next word.

'It's okay, pumpkin,' Laura said. Her eyes were full of tears. 'You can say anything to me. You can always say anything to me. If there's something . . . something you need to discuss, something we have to talk through, you should just go ahead and get started. So we can work it out together.'

She knows. She knows why you came. So just say it.

'It's,' Clara said, trying again. 'It's about – it's about Malvern.'

You little chickenshit, she thought to herself. *You coward.*

But Laura's face went hard and professional instantly. She wasn't Laura anymore, she was Caxton, the vampire killer. 'Okay,' she said. 'Go ahead.'

'She's stepped up her attacks,' Clara said. Relief flooded through her. This was ground she felt a lot more comfortable on. 'She's started hitting high-profile targets. Groups of victims, all together. This last time she even let a witness get away. He couldn't tell us anything useful, but still – that isn't like her.'

'No,' Caxton said.

Clara shrugged. 'Deputy Marshal Fetlock says she must be getting desperate. She knows she can't keep hunting forever, that we'll eventually find her. So she must be changing her pattern, because she's in some kind of death spiral. Ready to be caught. Glauer disagrees. He thinks it's because she doesn't think we're a threat to her anymore, with you in here.'

'What do you think?'

Clara frowned. 'I think she's working some kind of angle.'

Caxton nodded. 'Good thinking. If we know one thing about Malvern, it's that she's always got a plan. She's always two steps ahead of you. Do not underestimate her. Don't let Fetlock underestimate her, either.'

'I'll do my best,' Clara said, with a little laugh. 'It's good to see you,' she said.

'Yeah. It's good to talk about this stuff. I need to be back on the case,' Caxton said, and Clara could see the wheels turning behind her eyes.

When the hour was up, and the CO came to stand behind Caxton and put a hand on her shoulder, they'd managed not to talk about anything but vampires the whole time.

'I'll see you in a month,' Clara said, with a sigh. 'That's the next visiting appointment I can get.'

Caxton nodded as if that was satisfactory. Then she let them take her away.

For a second Clara just slumped in her chair, unable to believe what had happened. Or what had failed to happen.

Eventually she got up and looked around for the CO who had brought her into the room. She needed to get her things back and get out of there. She needed to get back to Allentown before Fetlock knew she was gone. A CO came to get her – she didn't think it was the same one, but it was hard to tell. They kind of all looked alike. This one had a bad scratch down the side of his cheek, though, which she didn't remember from before. It was bright red and looked infected.

'Are you alright?' Clara asked.

He reached up and scratched vigorously at the wound. Clara

thought about telling him he would just make it worse, but she doubted he wanted to hear that from her. 'Come with me,' he said. 'I'll take you where you need to go.'

The CO didn't lead her back to the anteroom, though. Instead he directed her down a long hallway that led deeper into the prison.

'What's going on?' Clara asked. 'I'm done here.'

The CO looked straight ahead. 'The warden wants to see you for a second.'

Clara checked the name tag on his uniform. 'What's going on, Franklin? I'm not in any trouble here, am I?'

He straightened up a little. Making himself taller. 'I'm sure you'll want to cooperate with us.' There was something weird about his voice. It was a little too high-pitched for a man that size.

Regardless – he was starting to scare her. He had his stun gun in his hand. Held low, against his thigh. She glanced at it, then at his face, which was completely expressionless.

'I'm sure I do,' she said.

10.

Caxton was barely aware of her surroundings as she was taken back to her cell. There was too much going on in her head. It had been alright when she and Clara had been talking about Malvern – Caxton could always switch everything else off when vampires were involved – but now that she was left alone with her own thoughts, it all came crashing in.

Clara was going to break up with her.

Caxton had watched her girlfriend trying to get up the nerve to say it. She'd been able to read Clara like an open book – they'd been together long enough to know each other's gestures, each other's private body language. Clara hadn't been able to get the words out, but Caxton knew that there would come a time when she could. Either next month, at her next visit, or maybe even just in a letter, it would come. *I've been thinking about this a lot*, she would say, *and the time has come*.

Caxton couldn't even get angry about it. She understood perfectly. She had never been a very good girlfriend. Always, as long as she'd known Clara, her life had been about other things. Well, one other thing – vampires. There had never been enough time for romance, for intimacy, for just sitting around talking about nothing, for casual glances, for lingering touches. There had never been a week when her job hadn't got in the way, and there had been far too many nights when she'd been out chasing bloodsuckers and Clara had been forced to sit home alone, worrying, waiting for her to come back, waiting to get a phone call saying she'd been killed.

Now, with Caxton in prison, the relationship must seem utterly doomed.

The honorable thing, Caxton knew, would be to make it easy on Clara. To just accept defeat and give her back her freedom. And yet that would destroy Caxton utterly. Without Clara, what would she have in the whole world? She was never going to be a cop again, even after she served her time and got her release. Fetlock would never let her hunt vampires. So without her work, and without the woman she loved, what remained?

She had rescued dogs in the past. That had given her some sense of satisfaction. But the idea that dogs could replace both Clara and her calling was laughable.

The cell door closed behind Caxton with a buzz and a double thunk of locks slamming shut. She looked up and realized she had walked inside and walled up without even thinking about it. She glanced sideways and saw Stimson standing next to her, but her celly might as well have been in a different city. She wasn't looking at Caxton. She wasn't acknowledging her in any way.

The urge to talk to anyone, even Stimson, the need to unburden herself of her troubles, was compelling, even maddening. And yet she'd blown that chance, too, hadn't she? Because she could never reach out to another human being without screwing it up somehow. Stimson had offered her kindness, and companionship, even friendship of a warped kind. And she'd pushed it away.

Caxton climbed up on her bunk and lay back. She closed her eyes and tried not to sob. It took some work.

Dinner came and went. She ate, but without paying much attention to what was going in her mouth. When she was done she got back up on the bunk and stared at the light fixture again. Just as she had the day before. Just as she would, she imagined, for the nearly eighteen hundred days yet to come.

When she heard the screaming start it barely registered.

In the dorms used by the general population of the prison you heard screams at night, sometimes, and you quickly learned to block them out. Women in prison had nightmares. A lot of them were mentally ill, but not in dangerous ways, so they were just crammed in with the rest of the inmates and convicts. The screams didn't mean anything, and there was nothing you could do about them, anyway.

The SHU was much quieter at night, because the COs responded quickly to any excessive noise by forcibly extracting the offenders from their cells and dragging them away to cool-down rooms – what the prison called its padded cells. Still, even after the third or fourth scream, Caxton didn't move, didn't even roll over to wonder what was going on.

Stimson responded much more quickly. She climbed out of her bunk and went to the small window in the cell door. She shielded her eyes with her hands as if she were studying what was going on out there.

A scream came next that sounded much closer. It was different from the screams Caxton expected, as well. It was longer, more drawn-out. It was a scream of real pain, of someone being violently hurt. Of someone being killed.

'Stimson,' Caxton whispered. 'What's going on?'

Caxton's celly didn't reply.

'Stimson!' Caxton hissed. 'Come on. Tell me.' She sighed. 'Gert,' she tried.

The other woman turned and glanced up at her with hard eyes. 'What, are we friends now?'

Caxton tried to think of how to reply, but she was forestalled by yet another scream. This one was cut off quickly. Abruptly. Caxton knew all too well what that meant. Someone had just been killed.

The speaker in the ceiling crackled to life. 'Get back from your doors, right now!' it commanded. 'There's nothing to see.'

That was enough to make Caxton want to look out the window, too. She jumped down from the bunk and shoved her way in next to Stimson, their bodies touching as she tried to get a look.

There wasn't much to see, after all. The SHU looked as it always had, blinding white paint, central guard post, single reinforced door at the far end. One thing was missing, though. Normally, even in the middle of the night, one guard sat inside the glass-walled guard post, while two COs walked circuits around the unit, keeping their eyes open, listening for trouble. Now the patrollers were gone and only one CO was visible inside the post.

'Where'd the others go?' Caxton asked.

'They hightailed it a couple of minutes ago,' Stimson told her. 'Grabbed up their shotguns and booked out the door. That's all I saw.'

Caxton looked at the CO in the guard post, and recognized her at once. It was Harelip, the female CO who had performed her body cavity search. The one who had knocked her down to the floor when she tried to read the warden's BlackBerry.

'Alright, bitches, wall up for me now or there's going to be some ass-whooping,' Harelip said over the intercom. Her voice echoed off the walls of Caxton's cell.

Stimson ran back to the wall, but Caxton stayed where she was.

The screaming was far away again, when it came next. But there was a lot more of it.

'Laura!' Stimson called. 'Get back! They'll beat us both if you don't.'

'Hold on,' Caxton said. 'Someone's coming.' And there was. A shadowy figure was coming down the hallway toward the big reinforced door of the SHU. As it stepped out into the light she saw it was a male CO in a stab-proof vest. His baseball cap had been pulled down low over his eyes, leaving his face mostly obscured. She could just make out his chin. It was red, but not with blood. The skin there had been scratched and torn at until it came away in long strips. She could see muscle tissue underneath, pinkish-gray and rubbery and bloodless.

'Oh, no,' Caxton moaned. 'Not here. Not now.'

'Which one is Laura?' the half-dead CO asked. A moment later every door in the SHU unlocked itself with a heavy thunk.

11.

Caxton shoved against the cell door with her shoulder, but it wouldn't move. The electronic lock had been released, but the mechanical lock was still in place. Someone was going to have to pull the lever on the outside of the door before she could get out.

There were two people on the floor of the SHU, two candidates who might let her out, but neither of them seemed like much of a bet.

'Murphy?' Harelip said, speaking into her microphone. She hadn't turned off the intercom system, so her voice came down from the ceiling of Caxton's cell. The female CO sounded worried but not panicked. Probably because she didn't yet realize that the male CO stalking around the SHU wasn't Murphy anymore. 'What's going on?'

'Where is she? I'll find her on my own if I have to,' the thing said, approaching a cell door and peering in through the window. Its voice was all wrong. Male COs cultivated a gruff, deep voice that commanded respect. The voice this thing used was high-pitched and sounded like it came from just the far side of sanity.

'I called down to central, but there's no reply. I've got chatter all over the open bands. People are freaking out! Is it a riot? It sounds like somebody broke in,' Harelip said. She was getting more scared, which Caxton thought was probably a good thing. Eventually she might notice the big difference between Murphy the CO and the thing that had invaded her SHU.

It didn't have a face.

Oh, it had eyes, and a mouth, and maybe part of a nose left. But its face would be hanging down in ragged strips of skin, peeled away from its cheeks and forehead by its own fingernails. Murphy was dead. He had been dead, anyway, until a vampire called him back and gave him a second chance.

The vampire hadn't done him any favors. The second chance only lasted about a week – reanimated bodies rotted away with incredible speed, and after a day or two they were already falling to pieces. They were also required to obey any vampire who commanded them, without fail, without question.

Perhaps the worst of it was that they came back without a soul. They knew constant pain, and they knew that what they had become was wrong. One look in a mirror and they understood they were not meant to exist. They tore off their own faces. They hurt themselves, and they took a joy in hurting others (especially with knives – they loved knives). They were vicious, and crazy, and had no moral compunctions whatsoever.

Caxton, following a long tradition among American vampire hunters, called them half-deads. When you went looking for vampires, you found half-deads, usually lots of them. And when you found half-deads they were already trying to kill you.

'Murphy! The call came through for EIP stations,' Harelip went on. Caxton knew the acronym stood for 'escape in progress,' the prison guard's equivalent of a red alert or all hands on deck. 'My two boys ran to comply.'

'Yes, I know,' the thing that had been Murphy said. 'I caught them coming the other way. They're not coming back.' It tittered as if it had just made a little joke. It grabbed the lever on the front of a cell door and yanked it back. It took two tries. Half-deads weren't well coordinated, or particularly strong. Eventually it got the door open, however. Then it pulled a long hunting knife out of its belt.

Knives. Always with the knives. Half-deads loved knives, hatchets, cleavers, anything sharp. This was a hunting knife, six inches long and painted green – so the white-tailed deer wouldn't see it glint when you pulled it out in the woods – and had a nasty serrated edge and a wicked curved point. The half-dead brandished it with obvious pleasure and stepped inside the cell.

'Stimson,' Caxton said. 'I mean, Gert, please. Do you know the name of the CO in the guard post?'

Gert frowned. 'Worth, maybe? Or it could be Wendt.'

Caxton shook her head. 'Hey,' she shouted, pounding on the cell door. 'Hey, CO! Hey, Screw! You've got to stop him!'

Harelip glanced in Caxton's direction. 'Wall up, fucker,' she said, and the speaker in the ceiling popped and whistled.

There was a scream from inside the open cell. A prisoner in an orange jumpsuit came staggering out, blood slicking down one side of her leg.

'Murphy!' Harelip shouted. 'Murphy, what are you doing?'

Another scream. Then the half-dead came back out of the cell. There was blood on its knife and all over its stab-proof vest. 'That wasn't Laura. Laura? Where are you, Laura?' it sang. 'I'm going to find you if I have to cut my way through every last one of these cells. Miss Malvern wants to see you.'

Harelip finally got what was happening, or at least some of it. She stood up inside the guard post and grabbed a shotgun. Then she hit a button on her control board. A beeping alarm went off and the door of the guard post started to slide open.

Then the alarm stopped, and it started to slide shut again.

Harelip looked as if she hadn't been expecting that.

The half-dead went to the next cell in line and pulled back on its lever, using both hands this time. The door slid open on its rails. Both of the women inside came rushing out at once, but the half-dead tripped one of them up and knocked her to the floor. It grabbed her hair and pulled her face back. She was a black woman with long cornrows. 'You're not Laura, either,' it said, and then it slit her throat.

In the guard post Harelip hammered at the shatterproof door of what had become just another prison cell. Clearly that door could be opened and closed by remote control – just like the door locks on the SHU cells. Someone in a central command center was intent on keeping Harelip locked up tight. She beat at the door with the butt of her shotgun, but it was inch-thick Lexan and it would probably stand up to the blast of a hand grenade.

The half-dead went to the door of the next cell.

Two inmates in orange jumpsuits had managed to avoid its rampage. One prisoner was screaming as she ran toward the exit of the SHU. Another, the one who'd been carved up inside her cell but managed to get away, was leaning up hard against the wall, only a few cells down from where Caxton watched in terror. She was breathing heavily and her eyes were closed. She must have lost a lot of blood.

'Hey,' Caxton shouted, and beat on the inside of her cell

door. 'Hey, you. Convict! Let me out of here. I know what to do! I can save everybody.'

The wounded woman's eyes flickered open. She looked right at Caxton. Then she slumped to the floor in a puddle of her own blood.

Everyone was shouting by then. The women in the cells were shouting to know what was going on, shouting for help, bellowing in panic and fear. Caxton could still hear the screams that came from the third cell that the half-dead had opened. The screams were cut off quickly. After a moment the half-dead emerged again, covered now in blood and gore. One of its victims had torn the baseball cap off his head and Caxton could see its ravaged face clearly now. Its eyelids were completely gone, as were its lips. It looked both surprised and very happy, simultaneously.

It was really enjoying itself, and it was just getting started, that expression said. It was five doors down from Caxton's cell.

'Gert,' Caxton said, 'when that thing comes in here, you just dive under the bunks, okay? Get as far in as you can. If this goes badly, I'll just tell it who I am, and hopefully, it'll just kill me, or drag me off, or whatever it is it's going to do. If you're quiet and you don't move, I think it'll ignore you. Okay?'

Gert nodded. Her eyes were as wide as the half-dead's.

'Okay,' Caxton said, steeling herself. Half-deads weren't very strong. It was possible she could overpower it when it came into the cell. Of course, there was the knife to think about.

There was nothing in the cell Caxton could use as a weapon. Nothing she could use to defend herself. It was a maximum-security prison cell, and very smart people had spent a lot of time and money making sure she was harmless when she was locked inside.

She would have to crouch by the door, and wait for it to come in, and then—

Her thought was interrupted by a thunking noise from inside the door. With a gentle creak, it slid open just a crack. Lying on the floor just outside, Caxton saw the wounded prisoner, the one Caxton had thought was dead. She must have crawled over and used the last of her strength to pull back the lever.

12.

Inside the guard post Harelip was trying to pry the door open with a wooden baton. It was an act of desperation – she had completely lost control of the SHU.

In a cell just a few doors down, the half-dead was cutting up more inmates, looking for Caxton. It was up to her to stop him from killing anyone else.

There were other problems to think about – the prison was clearly under attack by vampires, for instance – but they were going to have to wait. Caxton eased open the door of her cell and stepped outside.

It felt weird, being outside of the cell without shackles on. Even as bad and scary as things had gotten, it still felt weird. Caxton tried to ignore the part of her brain that kept telling her she was in serious trouble, that the COs wouldn't like this. The only CO who wasn't dead in the SHU was locked inside her own guard post. Caxton considered trying to free Harelip. It would be nice to have some backup, for one thing, and there were weapons in there. But she doubted she could break into the post any better than Harelip could break out of it.

She stooped down to touch the throat of the woman who had opened her cell door. There was a pulse in her neck, but it was faint. The half-dead had really done a number on her, cutting her open from the armpit down to the hip and probably opening arteries and veins all the way down. The woman needed a lot more than first aid, and Caxton wasn't sure she could be saved even by a team of paramedics. As much as she owed the woman, whose name she didn't even know, there were other people she could help more. People she could save.

From inside a cell a few doors down Caxton heard a woman screaming and begging for her life. A trickle of blood rolled out through the open door and glistened on the concrete floor of the SHU. Caxton kicked off her slippers – they made a slip-slap noise when she walked – and padded barefoot over to the open door. It would be suicide to barge in and try to save the women inside. Half-deads weren't very smart, or strong, or fast. But with its hunting knife and Caxton's limited training in unarmed self-defense, this half-dead wouldn't have to be any of those things to hurt her, and badly, if she rushed it. So she leaned up against the wall next to the door, flattening herself against it as tightly as possible, and cleared her throat noisily.

The whimpering moans inside the cell didn't stop, but she heard the scrape of a boot heel against the floor. The half-dead had heard her and was turning around to see what the noise meant.

It could choose to be stupid, or to be smart. If it was stupid it would come running out with its knife held up high. It would trip over her outstretched ankle and fall face forward onto the floor, losing its grip on the knife in the process. Then she could grab the knife and kill it before it could even start getting back up.

If it was smart, it would stay exactly where it was, and wait for her to come to it.

Caxton could hear her heart beating in her ears. She counted thirty heartbeats before she decided it had done the smart thing. Then she cursed to herself.

It heard that as well. 'Is that you, Laura? Are you playing a little game with me? Why don't you come in and say hi? I'm not supposed to kill you, you must know that. Miss Malvern just wants to talk.'

Caxton bit her lower lip. The half-dead might be lying, but she knew that was just wishful thinking. Malvern was behind the attack on the prison, of course. Justinia Malvern, the last living vampire in Pennsylvania. She and Caxton had a long history. Malvern had been making plans to pillage and destroy the good people of the Commonwealth for nearly a century and a half. In that time she'd created a legion of new vampires, whole armies of them, to aid her. For the last few of those years Caxton had been the one who foiled all her plans and slaughtered all her vampiric descendants. She'd never quite managed to track down Malvern herself, and now it sounded like she was going to pay for that failure.

Maybe Malvern wanted to torture her to death. Caxton knew the vampire wouldn't let her die quickly, not if she could help it. Not if she could watch. There were other possibilities, too. Malvern had always wanted to turn Caxton into a vampire. It would be a great coup, and it would turn her greatest enemy into a valuable ally. More than once Malvern had made the offer, and every time Caxton had turned her down. Maybe the whole prison was suffering just so Caxton could have another chance to say no. Or maybe Malvern had something else in mind entirely, some brilliant but twisted scheme that involved Caxton in some diabolical way she couldn't imagine.

Regardless, the last thing she wanted was to see Malvern

just then. Not until she had some serious firepower to back her up.

'I don't have a lot to say to her at the moment,' Caxton told the half-dead. 'But if you come out of there right now, I'll talk to you.'

The half-dead cackled.

'I'll take it that's a no,' Caxton said.

It might have planned on replying, but before it could speak again she was inside the cell. She kept low but moved fast, rushing forward to try to knock it down, her eyes darting from side to side, looking for where the knife might be.

Instead she just saw the cell's two inmates. They weren't begging for mercy anymore, because both of them were dead, locked in a final embrace and covered in each other's blood.

The half-dead was crouching up on the top bunk, waiting for her.

This one was proving way too smart. It leapt down on top of her, one arm back, holding the knife high, pointed downward toward her. Its orders might be to bring her in alive, but clearly it was willing to wound her if that's what it took.

One of its boots clipped Caxton's ear as she tried to roll out of the way. Her head rang and her ear instantly felt hot. She brought her knees up to protect her body and felt them dig into the half-dead's groin, a blow that would have left a living man gasping in agony. The half-dead didn't gasp. It didn't even need to breathe, and what it had between its legs wasn't that sensitive anymore.

Still, the impact left the half-dead off its balance and rolling off of her to one side. Caxton grabbed at the toilet/sink unit and started dragging herself upright, fighting the fuzziness that was spreading through her head. The half-dead jumped on her back and its knife came around to swing at her face.

Caxton couldn't stop the blow – she was moving too slowly.

76

But she was still stronger than the half-dead. She bucked wildly, like a horse, and it flew backward and off of her, the knife sliding through the shoulder of her jumpsuit but not even connecting with her skin. She spun around to find it standing in the doorway, the knife low, holding it out toward her, ready to lunge.

She kicked it in the wrist as hard as she could.

Had she been wearing shoes, or been just a hair faster, that would have disarmed the half-dead and left her with the advantage. Instead the half-dead managed to yank its arm back just as her kick connected. Her toes curled back painfully as they collided with the half-dead's arm. All she accomplished with the kick was to make her opponent step backward, out of the cell. That left her trapped inside the small cell. The half-dead could simply slam the door shut behind her and engage its latch, locking her inside. Then it could call for reinforcements and just wait until they arrived. That's what she would have done, and this one had proven to be no fool so far.

She screamed in rage as it smiled at her and reached for the edge of the door.

It didn't get a chance to push the door closed, however. Harelip appeared behind it and leveled her shotgun at the back of its head. Somehow she must have gotten out of the guard post.

'Freeze, asshole,' the female CO said.

The half-dead started to turn around. It didn't drop the knife.

Caxton dropped to the floor and covered her head as Harelip pulled the trigger. The shotgun roared and fire burst from its muzzle. It didn't contain any buckshot, Caxton knew, or any weight of slug – the shotguns the COs used fired beanbag rounds, soft nylon bags full of ceramic balls that expanded in

77

flight to spread the energy of the impact. For a normal human being, getting hit by a beanbag round was incredibly painful, even incapacitating, but it rarely resulted in permanent damage.

Normal human skulls, however, had a lot more structural integrity than a half-dead's. The head of the thing that had once been named Murphy exploded like an overripe pumpkin hit by a sledgehammer, spattering the interior of the cell – and Caxton – with pulpy brains and shards of bone and plenty of unidentifiable goo. The beanbag itself, which looked like a sweat sock full of marbles, bounced off her back and landed with a squelch on the floor.

'Shit,' Harelip said.

Caxton started breathing again.

'That wasn't Murphy,' the CO told her. She was crouched next to the body.

'You're right. It might be Murphy's body, but—'

'Murphy had a tattoo on the back of his hand. This asshole doesn't.'

Caxton glanced at the hand and saw this was correct.

'So what the hell is this thing doing, wearing Murphy's uniform?'

13.

An hour earlier Clara Hsu had just been taken prisoner.

They walked for quite a while through narrow corridors, passing through a number of doors that had to be opened electronically, and a few gates where COs in glassed-in booths buzzed them through. The prison was a big place, and Clara doubted she could find her way back alone if she had to, much less figure out a way through all those locked gates. Eventually they emerged from an underground tunnel into a building that felt more like office space than jail cells. The ceiling was made of acoustic tile that supported fluorescent light tubes, and the walls were normal plaster instead of cinder block or brick. Clara decided this had to be the administrative center of the prison, a place prisoners would rarely ever see. It made her feel a little more comfortable, anyway, to be away from the echoing cell blocks and the brutal architecture of restraint and control. Not that she thought that she was free, or that she would be unsupervised for even a second.

At the end of a long corridor lined with normal hollow-core doors they came to a reception lobby and then an oak door labeled WARDEN in chipped gold lettering. The CO with the stun gun indicated that Clara should open the door herself. She stared at the scratch on his cheek. The skin was starting to peel away at the edges. She was very afraid she knew what that meant.

She knocked gently on the door – her arms had gone weak – and then turned the knob. Inside the office her eyes were dazzled by orange and pink light. There was a massive picture window at the far end of the room, and the sun was just setting beyond it, a bar of red light on the horizon. The window looked out over a courtyard ringed with watchtowers and a twenty-five-foot-high curtain wall.

'Miss Hsu,' someone said.

Clara shielded her eyes to try to see who was talking to her. 'It's Special Deputy Hsu, please,' she said. There were at least three people in the room, not counting the CO who had come in behind her and had his stun gun leveled at her back. She blinked rapidly as her eyes adjusted to the gloom. There was a desk there, and a long rectangular coffee table running through the middle of the room, and two people in orange sitting on a sofa along one wall—

'I suppose there's no need to pretend this is a routine interview,' said a woman standing next to the window. She was wearing a stab-proof vest over a conservative business suit. She had something in her hand that Clara thought at first must be another stun gun, but a moment later she saw it was a BlackBerry handheld.

Outside the window the sun winked out, done with the day. In a few seconds it would be night. The timing wasn't lost on Clara. 'Maybe so, but I should point out that detaining a federal agent without an arrest warrant is a pretty serious crime,' Clara said. 'If you let me go now, we can both save a lot of really annoying paperwork.'

'I would advise you not to move, or flinch,' the woman said. She had to be the warden of the prison, Clara decided, though she hadn't bothered to introduce herself.

The coffee table stirred, and Clara nearly did jump back. She hadn't been expecting that. She stared at the piece of furniture and saw that her sun-dazzled eyes had mistaken it for something it was not. It was a wooden box, six feet long, with a long, tapered, hexagonal shape.

'Oh, Christ,' Clara sighed, as its lid started to slide back.

Someone whimpered to her left. Clara looked over and saw the two people sitting on the sofa there. Now that the sun's glare was less dazzling, she could see that they were both prisoners dressed in identical orange jumpsuits. Their hands were tied behind their backs and they were gagged. One of them, a blond girl who looked like she couldn't be more than nineteen, stared at Clara with imploring eyes.

Laura Caxton wouldn't just wait and watch this happen, Clara thought, because she was pretty sure what was going to come next. Laura would fight.

But she wasn't Laura. She had never been as brave as her girlfriend, could never be as tough as the famous vampire hunter. She was a glorified police photographer, and there was a big man – or something worse – at her back, ready to beat her into submission if she made the slightest move. So she stood there, still as a statue, and watched.

The lid of the coffin slid a little further, then overbalanced and fell to the floor with a crash. Clara felt as if a puff of cold air blew out of the coffin, but she knew it wasn't that. Vampires were unnatural creatures. Their very existence felt wrong – it made the hair on the back of your arms stand up. It made your skin prickle.

Taking her time, moving stiffly, Justinia Malvern sat up and looked around the room.

81

She'd been born in 1695 in England, and had lived through every year of American history there was. Vampires lived forever if no one managed to kill them, but they didn't age gracefully. Malvern's skin was pale, paper-thin leather stretched tight over protruding bones. In some places it had worn away where it had rubbed night after night against the stained silk lining of her coffin. A patch on her forehead had eroded down to dull yellow bone. She wore nothing but a thin, almost transparent mauve nightdress that was nearly as tattered as her skin, but modesty hardly applied to something that had spent more time in a coffin than it had standing upright.

Her head was completely hairless. She didn't even have eyelashes. She had long triangular ears, one of which looked like it had been chewed on by animals. She had one eye that was yellow and cloudy with cataracts. The other eye socket was empty except for a wisp of cobweb, a dark hole in her head surrounded by rotten skin.

Her mouth was full of broken fangs. Not just two sharp canines – Clara had been raised on that image of vampires, of suave counts with a pair of protruding but tiny fangs. Vampires in reality had teeth like sharks, their mouths packed full of row on row of wicked translucent blades. There were gaps in Malvern's smile, a lot of them, but she still had plenty of teeth to chew with.

Her bony arms were folded across her chest. She opened them slowly, carefully, and placed a skeletal hand on either side of the coffin. With obvious pain but just as obvious determination, she levered herself up until she was standing on her own two feet. She swayed slightly, but she didn't fall.

Clara gasped a little. She didn't mean to. She'd read Laura's notes, though. The first time Laura Caxton had seen Malvern, she'd been confined to a wheelchair, barely able to lift her arms to hold a beaker full of donated blood. Later on, when

82

Malvern had assisted Caxton with her investigations at Gettysburg, the vampire had been too feeble to even raise her head. She'd been trapped in her own coffin, barely able to lick at blood dripped across her mouth. Clearly the blood she'd drunk at the Tupperware party, and at the roadhouse, had gone some way toward reviving her.

She had never spoken more than a few words, as long as Clara had been alive.

'I trust,' she said now, in a voice that was creaky and thick, but clear enough to be understood, 'that my dinner is prepared.'

It was all Clara could do to be still as the warden went to the sofa and grabbed the blond prisoner. She was dragged up to her feet and pushed forward. The warden tripped the girl until she was kneeling next to the coffin, her head bowed. Her hair fell forward, exposing the nape of her neck from the hairline down to the loose collar of her jumpsuit.

Malvern struck like a snake. She might be slow and stiff, but where there was blood involved, there was always a way. Her broken fangs sank effortlessly through the flesh at the back of the prisoner's neck, grating on the thick bones of her spinal column. The prisoner screamed and shook, tried to break free, tried to buck the vampire off her back, but Malvern's fangs had a death grip on her, like a wolf's jaws squeezing shut around the throat of a caribou. Malvern wrapped one spindly arm around the prisoner's waist and pulled her close. That arm should have snapped like a twig, but instead it seemed to possess the strength of an iron bar. It stopped the prisoner's convulsions and stilled her screaming as Malvern crushed her lungs and squeezed all the air out of her.

In a minute it was done. Malvern dropped the corpse to the floor, having no more use for it. Then she climbed out of the coffin and walked over to the warden. ''Tis a treat, to

83

meet ye at last, my dear,' she said, and leaned in to kiss the warden on the cheek. The warden closed her eyes and sighed as if she were being greeted by a lover after a long separation. 'And for you, Miss Hsu, my feelings are none but the warmest.' She came gliding over toward Clara as if she would kiss her as well. Her face loomed toward Clara out of the gloom of the office like a scarred moon. There was a narrow stripe of blood on her chin.

Clara did flinch then. The CO behind her grabbed her into a choke hold, then pinned her hands behind her back with his free hand, immobilizing her.

'Ah, I understand. Ye'll not find this face a pretty sight, not yet. Well, we'll change that anon. For now,' Malvern said, standing up a little straighter, 'there is my second course to consider.'

The second prisoner on the sofa started to scream, even through her gag.

14.

Thank God,' Caxton said, stepping forward, out of the cell. 'I thought he was going to kill me. You saved my life.'

Harelip prodded the half-dead's headless body with the end of her shotgun. She knelt down next to the corpse and touched its back. 'That wasn't supposed to happen,' she said. She sounded like she was a long way away. 'I thought it was Murphy I was shooting. I wouldn't have used lethal force on Murphy, no matter what. I've worked with him for seven years.'

'That thing was a vampire's servant,' Caxton said, trying to explain. 'When a vampire kills someone, they can—'

'Murphy was no fucking vampire!' Harelip shouted.

'That's not what I was trying to say,' Caxton tried, in as soothing a voice as she could.

Harelip turned and looked at the dead bodies on the floor of the SHU, and at the bodies in the cell behind Caxton. Her eyes stopped focusing for a second. Caxton had seen this before: most people, even hardened law-enforcement types, lost their reason for a moment the first time they saw the kind of violence that vampires or even just half-deads could create. Maybe Harelip had seen murder victims before. Maybe she'd seen people stabbed with shanks more times than she could count. But the kind of chaos the half-dead had created was still new for her, and it would take her a while to process it. Caxton just didn't have the time to let her work through it on her own.

'There will be more of them. They'll send ten of those things next time. Or the vampire will come herself. You can't stop a vampire with a beanbag round. We need to get the door closed. We need to lock down this unit. Right now.'

'You giving me orders now?' Harelip demanded.

'No. No, of course not. This is your show.'

Harelip spun around and focused on Caxton. 'You lie down on the floor, hands behind your head. We're going to do this by the book.'

'Listen,' Caxton said. 'Your name is Worth, right?'

'My name is fuck you, bitch,' Harelip said, breaking open her shotgun and taking a fresh beanbag round from a pouch at her belt. 'I said get down on the floor, on your goddamned belly.'

Caxton raised both hands to where the female CO could see them and dropped to one knee. 'There are vampires in the prison. All that screaming – I know that sound. You must know who I am. I'm Laura Caxton. I'm the vampire hunter. I know all about vampires. I know how to keep us all alive, but you have to listen to me.'

'And I damned well know you know who I am. I am your boss!' Harelip screamed, jabbing her shotgun at Caxton like a spear. 'I don't know shit about vampires, maybe, but I know exactly what to do when I got a prisoner out of her cell and acting violent. You're going back in your cell, and you ain't coming out until this emergency is over. We've got a protocol for this.'

Caxton knew that if Harelip put her back in her cell, she would be a sitting duck for the next vampire – or half-dead – to come into the SHU. She was absolutely certain that someone would come looking for her again. She had to do something, anything, to keep that from happening. 'Your protocol must include calling for backup, right? You're not supposed to do this on your own.'

'I already tried calling central. Nobody's responding. It sounds like there's riots breaking out all over the facility.' Harelip shook her head. 'You going to do what you're told, or are we going to have a problem?'

Caxton knelt down in front of the CO, her hands still up and visible. 'We just need to think about this, okay? What's the next step of your protocol? It's got to be to lock down the unit. To close that door.'

She looked over at the heavy reinforced door that was the only way in or out of the SHU. Harelip followed her gaze.

'Shit,' the female CO said. She was breathing heavily. 'Down. Now.'

Caxton nodded and dropped to her belly, weaving the fingers of her hands together behind her head. She could just crane her head far enough up to watch Harelip run back inside her guard post and slam the palm of her hand against a big red button on her control panel. A buzzer sounded and the reinforced door started to slide along its tracks.

Beyond the door something moved. Caxton heard rubber boots squeaking on a cement floor, running right toward her. There had to be more half-deads out there, she realized. They'd been waiting, maybe waiting for Harelip to get Caxton into her cell. Now that the door was closing they were in a real hurry to get inside.

The door kept sliding closed. But it was taking its time.

'Faster,' Caxton breathed. 'Faster!'

It did no good. The door was designed to close slowly so that anyone standing in the doorway would have plenty of time to get out of the way.

Outside, the footsteps were coming closer. It was dark out there, but Caxton thought she could see something moving, moving toward her.

'Come on,' she said. 'Come on!'

The door was still open by a foot when the first half-dead thudded against it from the far side. They hammered and beat on it, making a rattling, clattering noise. Then one of them had the bright idea to try to slip through the door as it closed. A hand speckled with blood came through the gap, followed by a shoulder wearing the brown patch of a Pennsylvania corrections officer.

The door kept closing. Caxton watched as the half-dead's arm came farther inside the SHU – and then as the door crushed it. The half-dead squealed in terror and tried to pull its arm back, but the door was still closing.

It clanged shut when it reached the end of its rails. There was no blood, but the half-dead's severed forearm, still inside the SHU, dropped with a wet sound on the cement floor.

Then it started dragging itself across the floor. Using its fingers as legs, it pulled along the severed stump behind it. It was crawling toward Caxton where she lay on her belly, intent, she was sure, on no good.

'Holy fuck,' Harelip shouted, and came running out of her guard post. 'What the hell is that thing?'

'I tried to tell you,' Caxton said, losing some of her patience. She jumped up and ran over to stamp on the crawling hand until she broke the finger bones and stopped it from moving. 'This is not just a riot. This is not just an escape attempt. The prison is under attack by unnatural, evil creatures.'

Harelip stared hard at her. Her nostrils were flaring.

'It doesn't matter,' she said. 'There are no exceptions. During emergencies prisoners must remain in their cells. The warden will send special teams to remove us when it's safe, and get us to a secure place.'

'Special teams. You mean teams of COs?' Caxton asked.

'Yes, stupid,' Harelip said, scowling.

'You mean – like Murphy? Maybe like the one who gave us this?' she demanded, stamping again on the hand, which was still trying to wriggle around her bare foot. 'He was wearing a CO's uniform, too.'

Harelip might have responded with a curse, or by hitting Caxton with her baton. She didn't get a chance, however. The buzzer sounded again, and the reinforced door started to slide back open on its rails.

15.

'What's happening?' Caxton asked, as the main door of the SHU inched open. She could hear the half-deads on the other side beating on it and laughing. At any moment it would be wide enough for them to squeeze through. She had no doubt there were a lot of them, and they would all be armed.

Harelip ran back inside the guard post and slammed the red button with her palm again. The door didn't stop in its tracks. She hit it again, still with no result. Caxton could see her cursing inside the guard post. She came running back out with her baton drawn.

'They'll have knives,' Caxton said, staring at the CO's truncheon. 'They'll outnumber us. We have to get the door closed again – what's going on?'

Harelip scowled. 'Every door in the facility can be opened or closed remotely. In case of a riot a unit or dorm can be locked down from central command. Somebody – one of those things – must have gotten to the control board and sent down the emergency evacuation signal. That opens all the doors in this wing.'

'You can't override the signal from here?' Caxton asked.

'If prisoners took control of the SHU, central would still be able to lock down the unit, or pop it open if they needed to. So no, I can't override it from here.'

Caxton stared at the slowly opening door as she thought about it. 'Before – when the half-dead came in here – they unlocked all the cell doors remotely.'

Harelip nodded. 'That's right. And locked me inside the post. That's why I couldn't save the prisoners he killed.'

'But – but you got out, somehow,' Caxton said.

Harelip nodded again. 'I yanked the wire that links that door control to central, then I hit my control again and, lucky me, it worked.' She stared at Caxton as if she was just piecing it together. 'I could pull the wire for the main door control, too. Cut off the link to central, and then close the door from here.'

'It's worth trying,' Caxton said, her heart racing.

'It'll take a minute. Those cables are all run through a piece of PVC pipe under the control board. I'll have to break it open to get to them. By the time I'm done the door will be open.'

'I can fight off the half-deads while you're doing that. If you give me a weapon,' Caxton said.

Harelip glared at her. 'You're kidding.'

'No! Look, we have to do something, or they're going to send every one of those things they have down here. Haven't you figured it out yet? They're coming for me. We're wasting time – just give me a gun!'

'Wait,' Harelip said, as if the door wasn't rumbling open while they spoke. Already a half-dead had shoved one foot and part of its hip through the door. It was getting caught on its stab-proof vest, but at any second it would come lurching through, into the SHU where Caxton waited all but defenseless. 'You're saying that if I give you to them, they'll leave the rest of us alone?'

Caxton's heart skipped a beat.

'You're a prison guard,' she said, finally.

'Yeah,' Harelip replied.

'That means you're supposed to guard people. Not let them come to harm.'

'Uh-huh,' Harelip said.

Caxton shook her head. There was no time for this. 'You fight them off – I'll yank the cable,' she said, and ran toward the guard post.

At least this time Harelip didn't argue. She moved to the door and slammed her baton against the head of the half-dead coming through the door. An arm holding a knife scythed down toward her, and she jumped back.

Inside the post Caxton dove under the control board and saw the PVC pipe Harelip had mentioned. It ran from the underside of the board down to the floor. It rattled slightly when she pulled at it, but didn't come free. She could try to kick it free, but without any shoes on she'd probably just break her foot. She needed something to pry it loose with.

She spared a tenth of a second to glance over at the door. It was open nearly a foot wide now, more than enough for a half-dead to slip through. Harelip swung her baton and danced around knives, desperately trying to hold them back. Caxton needed to get the door closed immediately.

The chair that sat inside the guard post was made of wood. She picked it up and bashed it against the Lexan wall of the post and it shattered. Grabbing one chair leg, she ducked under the control board again and got the leg behind the pipe. With enough leverage, and the right angle—

The pipe snapped in half. A dozen thick cables in white plastic insulation were revealed inside. They were all the same, as far as she could tell. There was no way to know which one to yank. If she pulled the wrong one, she might cut power to the guard post, and then she would never get the door closed.

There was no other option. By the door Harelip was striking faster and faster, but she already had a bad cut on one ear and the side of her stab-proof vest was sliced open. It could protect her from a direct thrust, but slicing blows would eventually take it to pieces and then she'd have no protection at all. Caxton grabbed a cable at random and pulled. It came loose easily enough, but she couldn't tell what effect it might have had. With one palm she slammed the red emergency lockdown button on the console.

Nothing happened.

'Okay,' Caxton breathed, and pulled another cable, then hit the button again.

Nothing.

'Come on!' she squealed, and pulled three of them at once. Then she slammed the button.

The buzzer sounded, and the door stopped opening. Then, slowly, far too slowly, it started to close again.

Caxton ran over to the door and nearly got brained by Harelip's whirling baton. A half-dead was reaching in, trying to grab Harelip by the strap of her vest. Caxton grabbed the dead bastard's arm and pulled it hard in the wrong direction. It snapped. The half-dead screamed.

Another one tried to get its foot inside the door, a big foot in a thick, steel-toed boot. Caxton grabbed the leg behind the ankle and pulled, hard, knocking the half-dead off its balance.

Harelip brought the end of her baton down hard on a half-dead's head. The skull split open like a rotten melon. And then—

—the half-deads pulled back, away from the door. They had seen what happened when it closed before, and one of them had lost an arm. They were smart enough not to let any of their number get crushed this time.

When the door was finally, fully closed, Caxton leaned up hard against it and just tried to breathe for a while. She closed her eyes and didn't think about anything. In a second she was going to have to deal with all of this. She was going to have to think about why vampires were attacking the prison, and what she was going to do about it. But for a second, at least, she could just lean there and be safe.

That was when she felt Harelip's stun gun touch the small of her back.

16.

Franklin took off his sunglasses. The skin around his eyes was mostly gone, torn away by his own nails. If she'd had any doubts before, she was certain now – he was a half-dead. Malvern must have ordered him not to scratch his own face off, so that he could fit in better with the living people in the prison. He'd done the best he could, but he couldn't resist gouging himself a little.

He gagged Clara and bound her hands behind her back with a strip of plastic that dug into her wrists. Then he left her alone. No one beat her, or stabbed her, or shoved her down a flight of stairs.

No one drank her blood.

Malvern made short work of the second prisoner, and the blood worked its magic on her.

Already the skin was starting to grow back over the hole in her forehead. Her hands didn't look so much like bundles of twigs anymore – they were still mostly made of swollen knuckles and broken nails, but the balls of her thumbs

95

looked positively fleshy. Her complexion was lightening, transforming from the brownish-yellow look of old, untanned leather toward more of the classic unhealthy pallor of an active vampire.

Her missing eye would never grow back, of course. Any wounds a vampire suffered before its first death were never healed, no matter how much blood they consumed. But the one working eye she possessed was growing clearer, and a dull red ember seemed to burn far back in its depths.

How many victims would it take before she was back to full strength? Until she was as powerful as the bloodthirsty killing machines Laura had been fighting for so long? Even then, of course, it wouldn't last. For a vampire as old as Malvern, it would take a constant influx of new blood to maintain this level of vigor. Probably after the interrupted Tupperware party, or after the bar she'd attacked, there had been this same transformation, and then she had just rotted away again almost instantly afterward. But here, now – there was the promise of more blood to come. These few victims, Clara understood, were just the first of many. Malvern would be able to support her habit for a very, very long time now that she controlled the place. There would be no shortage of bodies for her to drain, not in this prison.

Clara stared at the warden. The older woman stared back calmly, without a trace of guilt on her features.

'If you want me to feel bad for these two, you can save your energy,' the warden said, reading Clara's expression. 'This one,' she said, kicking the corpse of the young blond, 'was in for IDSI.'

Clara winced. IDSI was 'indecent deviant sexual intercourse.' It was what the courts were calling the crime that had once been known as sodomy, and it could cover a wide range of offenses, none of them pretty.

'She raped her little sister with a hairbrush, if you want to know. The other one has been in and out of my prison since she was eighteen. Every time we let her out she would go right to her crack dealer and whore herself for a piece of rock. Before she knew it she would be right back in here. A total waste of human potential, and the kind of recidivist who has no desire to be rehabilitated. I'm not going to lose any sleep over either of them.'

Malvern rose slowly from where she'd been kneeling over the second victim. 'Enough moralizing, girl. What shall ye tell me of the men ye cannot trust?'

The warden looked at Malvern with an expression of pure reverence. 'Your half-deads have been here all day, killing the COs I knew I couldn't trust and replacing them. The rest might take things the wrong way, so they're being herded even now into cells. We'll lock them up and give them the same choice we give the prisoners.'

'Very good. And of the authorities outside these walls?'

The warden held up her BlackBerry. 'I've been in touch with the local police department and the regional bureau of the state police. I've told them we had a small riot but that it was contained and we didn't need any help. That'll make sure nobody comes within ten miles of the prison until I give them the word that everything's clear. We should have at least twenty-four hours before anyone starts asking questions, and even then they won't know what's really going on. During an emergency all the phone lines out of the prison are shut down except for my private line. We're in total lockdown, and therefore in total control of the facility.'

'Very good,' Malvern said.

Clara tried to pay attention to what they were saying. She knew it was important – she had to understand the situation she'd stumbled into. But her eyes kept refusing to look at the vampire or the warden. They kept straying to look again at the bloodless corpses lying on the carpet between them.

Malvern followed her gaze. 'Are ye thinking, Clara, that ye're next?' she asked.

Clara could say nothing with the gag in her mouth. She knew her eyes had to be very wide. She'd been forced to watch as Malvern gorged herself, again and again. Now she could feel sweat rolling down her forehead and toward her eyes. Fear sweat.

'Ah, but ye're different from this pile of corpses,' Malvern told her. There was the ghost of a chuckle in her voice. 'Or at least – ye have somewhat that makes ye different. Special. Do ye know what it is?'

She waited patiently, as if expecting Clara to answer.

Clara turned her head slowly from side to side.

Malvern leaned close, close enough to kiss. Her skin was so cold and – and wrong – that Clara felt her own gooseflesh pulling back away from the contact. Malvern whispered in her ear. 'Ye're loved.'

Clara whined in fear. She knew exactly what Malvern meant. Her throat tried to form a word, even if her mouth couldn't finish it. *Laura.*

Malvern nodded as if she had heard Clara perfectly. 'She'll come for ye, across any measure of space or peril. Right now she's hiding behind a locked door where I just can't reach. Yet when she knows ye're in danger, how long do ye suppose it shall take her to come a-running?'

Malvern smiled. It is not a pretty thing when any vampire smiles. The teeth seem to spread outward, to grow even larger, to grow even in number. Malvern's grin could draw blood all on its own.

She spun away, and almost danced across the room. It

couldn't last, but for the moment her skin looked almost pink. Almost flushed with blood. 'Someone remove that rag from her mouth. I'd speak with her now.'

A half-dead reached up behind Clara's head and untied her gag.

'She's too smart for that,' Clara said, all at once. 'She won't fall for your trap. Anyway, I broke up with her today. Most likely she hates me right now and wants me to die.'

Malvern glanced briefly at the warden, who shook her head in negation.

'I was listening to their conversation the whole time. They spent most of it talking about you, Miss Malvern. They never talked about breaking up at all.'

Malvern smiled again, but it wasn't such a maniacal grin this time. It was more of a shrewd, knowing leer. 'You're very brave. But I must insist – I've planned this ever so well. Timed it to a nicety. I found the one hour, in all the month, when you two were in one place. Have faith, girl. I'm cleverer than you by half.'

Clara bit her tongue before she could say anything more. She didn't want to accidentally tell Malvern something she might find useful. Instead, she thought, she needed to steer the conversation around to where she was learning things she didn't know before. 'That's the whole point of this? Of taking over the prison? Just to get Laura?'

Malvern shrugged happily. 'How I wish life could be that simple. No, child. This dungeon vile can offer me so much more. Look, already, how I bloom like a flower in a hothouse.' She held up her arms, which were clearly plumping out.

'But it can't last. You killed all those guards, and took their blood, but what about tomorrow night? You're going to get hungry again. And just by being here you'll draw attention to yourself. The police will be all over this prison by morning. They'll surround it, set up kill zones around every exit. You may have gotten one good meal, but it'll be your last.'

Malvern's head drooped forward as if she were considering everything Clara had said. Then she lifted it again and stared out the window at the stars she could see over the curtain wall. 'When I was a child of mortality, like yourself, I had taken a profession up, namely, I ran a gaming house. A pleasant enough suite of rooms in Manchester where gentlemen could come together and play pitch and faro – card games. I always forget no one plays faro anymore. They played whist, as well, following the rules that Hoyle wrote. Do men still play whist when they feel lucky?'

'Really, really, old men,' Clara said.

Malvern chuckled. ''Twas all the rage, whist, in the year of our Lord seventeen-and-twelve. It is a game played without speaking, where only the eyes may make strategy. It was considered thus a poor game for women, as we were believed unable to go so long without gossiping.' Malvern shot a sly glance at Clara. 'But oh, how the discriminating gentlemen favored it – for hours they would sit and be still and the only true thing in the universe seemed the fall of the lead, and the dance that followed, as each played looking to take book, and then the odd tricks—'

'Excuse me,' Clara interrupted, 'but I beg your fucking pardon. What has this got to do with anything?'

Malvern had been standing next to the window. A heartbeat later she was leaning over Clara's shoulder, resting her bony chin on Clara's clavicle. Clara had never seen a human move that fast. She'd never seen a vampire move that fast. 'My point is only this, dear. The odds may shift and flow. The wagers may be steep or thin. Yet a result may never be called

100

until the last card is turned o'er. Do not discount me yet, nor until you see my heart torn out and burnt by your lover's hand. Like all good ladies who play at a game, I may just have a high trump down my sleeve.'

17.

The stun gun pressed hard against Caxton's back. It was a flat plastic weapon, almost all grip, with just a pair of metal stubs sticking out from the business end. When they both connected with conductive material, like human flesh, they formed a circuit and an electric current passed between them.

The current wasn't particularly strong. It had a high voltage, upward of fifty thousand volts, but extremely low amperage – it wasn't designed to electrocute the victim, simply to send a pulsed charge through their nervous system that mimicked the body's own neural signals, essentially sending a message to every muscle in the victim's body telling it to activate at full strength and not release.

The amount of power that required was easily delivered by a standard nine-volt battery. To the victim, however, it felt like being hit by a truck.

Electricity surged through Caxton's body. Her muscles spasmed, some contracting, some expanding, all of them fighting each other. Her eyeballs quivered in their sockets and she felt a pure white bolt of pain run up her spine to explode inside her head.

Darkness grabbed her up in its velvety arms and held her like a child.

But just for a second.

When she came to, she felt like she'd been flash-fried. She was lying on the floor. Staring up at the glare of the klieg lights in the ceiling. She blinked her eyes. It was about all she could manage. Eventually she was able to lick her lips.

A boot prodded her in the rib cage. She tried to roll over and get away from it, but that just took too much energy.

Harelip squatted down next to her. 'Don't try to get up,' she said.

'Okay,' Caxton squeaked.

The CO rubbed at her face. 'Listen. I guess I owe you for your help. I guess we saved the unit, together. And I'm not going to forget that. But there are rules, and they're good rules, and they're there for a reason.'

'Ah,' Caxton said.

'It ain't easy, being a CO. I know you cons think we're all sadistic assholes. That's only, see, it's just because you can't see our side of it, you know? You used to be a cop. You know what it's like when you're looking at somebody who would kill you if they could. Who would take any chance to fuck with you, just because of who you are.'

Caxton had to admit that was true. Every vampire she'd ever dealt with had felt that way, as well as a few human criminals she'd encountered.

'Imagine you were surrounded by that kind of aggro every single day of your life. Imagine if the second you came on the floor of a unit, a hundred eyeballs was watching your every move, looking for you to make one little mistake. To forget one little thing, so they could take advantage. It's possible

103

– just possible – in that kind of a situation, to keep your head above the shit. But you got to be a serious hard case to make it work.'

Caxton lifted her left hand a fraction of an inch. Her muscles felt sore and rubbery and they didn't want to obey her commands, but they were starting to listen on a provisional basis.

'Don't,' Harelip said, and pressed her hand back against the cement floor with the tip of her baton. 'Just chill.'

'You got it,' Caxton said.

'We get plenty of training before they set us loose in here. They make us take all kinds of courses. One of the things they teach is what's called CTS. Contain the Situation. That means no matter what happens, when you're a CO, you're in charge. No matter how bad things get you have to be on top of it. And if you gotta be a little mean, you do it. If you gotta call people names that aren't so nice, or even if you gotta stun somebody when their back is turned, you have no damned choice but to do just that. There are no exceptions to CTS. There is no way I can let you walk around outside your cell, ever. So I'm going to have to put you back in. I'm going to have to lock you in. I will protect you, I promise. I will get you out of this situation. I'll evacuate you and all the other prisoners once the warden sends an all-clear signal. Okay?'

Caxton swiveled her head from side to side. 'No. Please. Just give me a chance to explain. They're not going to stop trying to get through that door. They'll bring down cutting equipment and they'll get through. On your own you might stop the first wave, but they'll send more of those things. And if that doesn't work, Malvern will come herself. She's weak, for a vampire, but that doesn't mean much. She'll have fed – a lot – and regained enough strength that you won't stand a chance against her. I know how to kill her, but it's not something I can teach you in the time we have. We—'

She stopped speaking, because suddenly the floor was moving underneath her. Or – no. That wasn't it. She was moving along the floor. She was being dragged by her heels across the rough cement. Her head bounced painfully and she tried to hold it up. She could just see Harelip pulling her along. Then the female CO bent down and picked Caxton up and slung her over one shoulder. Harelip grunted with the effort, but she managed to get Caxton inside her cell. She dumped Caxton on Gert's bunk – Caxton saw the pictures of Gert's babies directly across from her face.

She struggled to get back full control of her body, but it was still fighting her. She managed to flop off of the bunk and get up on one knee – just in time to see the cell door close in front of her, and hear the metallic thunk as the mechanical lock was engaged.

No, she screamed, inside her head. *No!*

She grabbed at the padding on the door and pulled and tugged at it, but it was designed to resist tearing and she could barely get a handhold. She slammed herself against the door, over and over again, knowing full well she would never manage to get through it.

Eventually she calmed down. There had to be something she could do. There had to be a way to communicate with Hare lip. She stared out through the window in the door, but there was nothing to see out there except for the bodies of the dead prisoners and the crushed arm of the half-dead. Harelip was nowhere in sight.

She could hear something, though.

It sounded like someone was having trouble swallowing. Like they were gagging on a piece of gristly food. Caxton couldn't quite figure it out. She pressed her face up against the glass, trying to get a better view, but she couldn't see anything. Eventually she gave up and started pacing back and forth in the cell. The sound went away. It had never been very loud – maybe it wasn't even something happening in the SHU, she decided. Maybe it was just water flowing through pipes in the walls.

She was still pacing, clutching herself for comfort, when the door opened again.

Caxton whirled around in shock. She hadn't had a chance to prepare herself. What if someone was coming to kill her?

The figure that appeared in the doorway was covered in blood. It was clutching the serrated hunting knife, and it was wearing a blue stab-proof vest. But the vest had been strapped on over the orange jumpsuit of a prisoner.

The face was wracked by a grimace of pure madness. It took Caxton a long time to realize that she recognized it. First she had to consider a fact that hadn't yet gripped her: Gert wasn't in the cell. She hadn't been inside when Harelip dragged Caxton in.

Gert had been busy, apparently. She must have sneaked out of the cell while Caxton and Harelip were wrestling with the SHU's main door. She must have found her way to the cell where Caxton had fought the half-dead, and found the knife there.

Now – she had found a use for it.

'Where's the CO?' Caxton demanded, even though she knew perfectly well.

'I told you I could be useful,' Gert said, and stepped inside.

18.

'Oh God, no,' Caxton said, and put a hand over her mouth.

Gert had – had killed Harelip. She stepped outside of the cell and saw the CO's body shoved up against one wall. A pool of blood glistened around her, staining her blue uniform and slicking across her throat and lower face.

'You shouldn't have done this,' she moaned. 'This was the last thing you should have done!'

Gert came up behind Caxton and grabbed her shoulders. She started to knead them until Caxton jumped away from her.

'She was jamming you up,' Gert said. 'Even after you saved her ass. Don't tell me you ain't grateful. I could have let you rot in that cell, girl! I could have kept my head down, played nice. Instead I gave you a chance to survive, right?'

It was true, in its way. Like most crazy people, Gert operated on a logical basis. It was just a basis built on a very shaky foundation.

Caxton breathed through her mouth and tried to think. Harelip could have been a valuable ally. Caxton's plan up until that point had been to find a group of COs somewhere else in the prison and explain to them what was going on, then get them to help her fight her way out. If she'd been able to convince even one of their number, it would have gone a long way toward enlisting their aid. Now she was going to have to approach them as an escaping prisoner, a situation in which they would be likely to shoot first and ask questions later. Furthermore, Harelip had done well against the half-deads. She had kept her cool and thought things through. She would have made a good partner for the fighting to come.

Now Caxton was all alone. She was trapped inside the walls of a maximum-security prison where no one, neither CO nor fellow prisoner, would be likely to offer her any help.

At least, no one except Gert.

'Who are you?' Caxton snapped. 'I mean – what did you do to get put in a place like this? You're no gangbanger.'

Gert sucked on her lower lip. 'I killed some . . . people.'

Caxton shook her head.

'It wasn't my fault! When you're high, you don't always know what you're doing. You can't be held accountable, you know?'

Caxton had never used drugs in her life. She had met lots of people who had, and rarely had she found one of them trustworthy. Never had she found one whom she would want watching her back.

She was going to have to go it alone. Which meant she needed to start planning.

Whether she was locked in the cell or free to move around the SHU, she was still trapped in a prison that was overrun by a vampire and full of half-deads. Malvern wanted her alive, but she really didn't want to find out why. She was going to have to protect herself.

Calling for backup was her first instinct. She'd been trained, as a cop, to never be out of touch if she could help it. She headed inside the guard post and studied the control board. There was a telephone handset mounted on one side to allow the CO manning the post to communicate with the rest of the prison. There was no keypad – instead individual telephones around the prison could be selected from a series of buttons that dialed directly. She picked it up and then started punching buttons at random, calling the infirmary, the commissary, the staff lounge, the main gate. Anywhere but central command, which she knew had been compromised.

She was not surprised when she didn't even get a dial tone. Malvern might be hundreds of years old, but she was conversant with modern communications. Cutting the phone lines had probably been one of her first moves.

Well, if Caxton couldn't call for help, she would have to help herself. That meant finding some weapons.

She only had to look around herself to find a miniature armory. A row of stun guns sat in chargers on one side of the control board. They would be useless against half-deads, who experienced pain in a far different way than human beings did, but she grabbed one anyway, in case she had to deal with any more COs who thought it was more important to contain the situation than it was to save lives. Underneath the board was a twelve-gauge shotgun, held in a pair of metal clips. She noticed for the first time that the stock was marked with a band of yellow paint, which meant it was to be loaded only with nonstandard ammunition. She pulled it free and broke it open, checking to make sure there was no round loaded already. In a bin beneath the board she found plenty of beanbag rounds but ignored those in favor of a box of rubber bullets. The name was doubly misleading: they were neither rubber nor, strictly, bullets. Instead they were shotgun slugs about four inches long made of polyvinyl chloride. They were designed not to penetrate the skin but to hurt someone enough to make them want to vacate an area. Against half-deads they would be even more effective than the beanbag round Harelip had used.

There were other weapons to be had, but they were all what used to be called less-lethal weaponry (the most recent term was 'compliance weapons') – useful for controlling prisoners you didn't want to actually kill. There was a can of pepper spray, a hollow aluminum baton, and a squishy bag of some compound Caxton couldn't readily identify. She took all of it except the bag, though two concerns limited her arming herself.

For one thing, none of it – nothing in the SHU – would be of any use against a vampire, even one as decrepit and weak as Malvern. The hunting knife could carve out her heart, assuming she would stand still long enough, but Caxton knew better than to fight a vampire without proper firearms. It was just asking for a quick and painful death.

The other big concern was that she had no way to carry it all. There was no belt on her jumpsuit, nor were there any belt loops. The jumpsuit had been designed to be bright enough to see in the dark and easy to wash. Fashion hadn't been much of a concern, and it was baggy and shapeless. It didn't even have any pockets.

At least there was something she could do about that, though it was a grisly task to contemplate. Caxton went over to Harelip's body and removed her belt. It fit over Caxton's shoulder like a very thin bandolier, and she was able to clip the stun gun to it and slide the shotgun and the baton underneath it if she pulled it tight. The pepper spray she slipped inside her bra. That left just the knife.

'Gert, you have to give that to me,' she said, and held out her hand.

Caxton's celly looked her up and down. 'You got the utility belt. I'm keeping the knife.'

Caxton sighed. 'I need it more than you do. In fact, you're not going to need it at all.'

'What do you mean?' Gert asked.

Caxton stood up straight. 'You're going back in the cell now.'

Gert laughed. 'You shitting me? I saw what happened to those fools in the cells when that thing came through. I ain't getting locked up again!'

Caxton was about to reply when a loud bang startled her. She whirled around and saw a woman staring at her through the glass window in her cell door. 'I'm with her,' the woman shouted, her voice just audible through the door. 'Let me out! I don't want to die in here!'

Over across the SHU there came a rapid hammering on another door. 'What about me, bitch?' another prisoner demanded.

Soon half the cell doors were rattling in their jambs. Caxton whirled around, looking at the cells, wondering what she was supposed to do about the women inside. Then she ran back to the guard post and turned on the intercom that would broadcast to the speakers inside the cells.

'Listen,' she said, speaking into a microphone on the control board. 'We are in a very bad situation here, but I'm in charge now and I have things under control, at least for the moment. I need all of you to stay calm.'

The cells erupted with shouts and obscenities and manic pounding on doors and windows.

Caxton gritted her teeth and looked around at the cell doors. Almost every window had a face plastered against it. An angry, demanding face.

'There are more of those things outside the SHU,' Caxton

111

announced. 'They've come for me. Just for me – I plan on leaving here soon, and when I do, I think they'll leave you alone. For now, though, you have to trust me! The safest place for you is inside your cells.'

She stared at Gert as she finished.

Gert stared back with a look of utter scorn on her face. 'If you was one of us,' she asked, raising her voice over the chorus of shouts and catcalls, 'would you buy any of that shit?'

They don't have a choice, Caxton thought. They were murderers and gangbangers and women who were a danger to themselves. Three of them were on death row. She couldn't trust them. She might have all the weapons, but they could easily mob her and overpower her and take away even that advantage.

It was just like Harelip had said. You had to contain the situation. You couldn't leave your back unguarded for a second. And yet Gert had a point. Who was Caxton to deny these women a chance to defend themselves? Maybe they could even help her. If they would just pipe down, that would help a lot. It would let her think—

A booming, echoing thud came from the main door of the SHU, and suddenly there was silence. The shouting stopped, though the women stayed glued to the windows, every eye looking toward the door.

The thump came again. Then a high, cackling voice said, 'Keep it down in there, ladies! We're trying to sleep!'

The prisoners started in again with the noise instantly, but this time it was different. Before it had been howls of outrage and anger. Now they were screaming in fear.

19.

'Take off your jacket,' the warden said, pointing a pistol at Clara's stomach.

Clara didn't protest. She removed her jacket and folded it over the back of a wooden chair. The warden gestured and Franklin came forward to fit a nylon cuff around Clara's biceps. A strap held it in place around her arm. He pulled the strap tight enough to hurt, but Clara refused to give him the satisfaction of crying out. The cinch on the strap locked with a special key that he tossed over to the warden. She caught it with her free hand. Clara studied the cuff and saw that it had a small black box attached to it. Metal prongs from the box poked through her shirt sleeve and felt cold on her skin.

'This is the latest thing in compliance measures,' the warden told her. 'We're still trying it out. There were, admittedly, some side effects we didn't like.' She stepped closer and brought her gun around in a wide sweep that missed smashing it into Clara's nose by a fraction of an inch. Reflexively Clara threw her arm up to ward off the blow.

The pouch at her back gave off a deafening shriek. Clara howled in pain.

'There's a motion sensor built into the cuff. If you try to make any sudden movements – say, if you try to run away, or if you attack someone, or just try to take the thing off – it'll give you that warning tone. That lasts for one second. If you don't immediately stop moving, it'll hit you with a pulse of enough electricity to disable every muscle in your body.'

Clara frowned. 'What are the side effects?'

The warden shrugged. 'For one, when it goes off, you shit your pants. We're not going to let that happen, though, are we? You're going to be nice and quiet and obey the cuff. You can walk, slowly, but I wouldn't try scratching your nose too vigorously. With this thing we can keep you close and not have to worry about watching you every single second.' The warden smiled. 'It's better than being hog-tied and gagged and thrown in a locked room, right?'

Clara wanted to spit in the woman's face. 'Why are you doing this?' she demanded.

The warden surprised her by giving her a straight answer. 'I have colon cancer.'

Clara sputtered in surprise. 'I'm – I'm so sorry.'

The warden ignored her sympathy. 'I let it go too long before I got checked out, and now the doctors say it's inoperable. There are all kinds of treatments they can try, but none of them are an actual cure. I've got this evil little blob inside of me that gets bigger every day and eventually, it's going to kill me. Maybe ten years from now. Maybe tomorrow.' She shrugged. 'I don't want to die. That's not so hard to understand, is it? So when Malvern started contacting various staff members here at the prison, looking for someone she could manipulate, I shot up to number one on her list. Luckily for me.'

'Luckily?' Clara said, surprised.

'If I hadn't been so receptive to her advances, she would have attempted to seduce someone else. Any of the administrative staff or even some of the more senior COs would have served her purpose. If it hadn't been me that she chose, I would have been killed first when she took over the prison. This cancer inside of me, which I have been afraid of for so long, turned out to be my ticket to eternal life.'

'She offered to make you a vampire? And you *want* that? It's not a medical treatment option. It's a *curse*. You'll live forever, alright – just like her.'

Together they looked at Malvern, who was deep in conversation with a half-dead standing just outside the door of the warden's office. Her shoulders stuck out like knife blades and her skin looked like cheap paper.

'In a few hours she'll look a whole lot better,' the warden said. 'Besides. It took her three hundred years to look like that. For the first century, she tells me, she was beautiful. Powerful beyond anything a human body can hope for. I'll have my time like that as well, for however long it lasts. Even if I only get another fifty years of health and strength, it'll be worth it. I'll be stronger than I am now. I'll have sharper senses. I don't see a lot of downsides.'

Clara scowled. 'You just have to give up your humanity.'

The warden laughed. 'You cops. You always amaze me when you think you're making a difference. The streets are full of drugs and guns, and the people on drugs have the most guns – when everything goes bad, which it always does, the results end up here with me. I get to babysit the human messes you couldn't prevent. I've seen women come through this office who choked their grandmothers to death for enough money to buy just one more rock. I've met pretty little girls whose teeth are rotted out of their heads because they can't

115

stop smoking meth. Teenagers who killed their own babies because they wouldn't stop crying. You want humanity? You can keep it.'

Clara was shocked. 'How did you ever end up in this job? If you feel that way, then why would you even want it? I would think if you devoted your life to caring for prisoners, you would at least try to believe in them.'

Bellows rolled her eyes. 'I was young once, like you. I thought big, grand thoughts like that. Then I saw the reality. It's been years since I thought of myself as a caretaker. And that's not even the job anymore. We used to talk about rehabilitating prisoners. That was the term we used, the justification for why we lock them up in such brutal conditions. Now – the term we use is warehousing. This prison, all the prisons like this all over the world, they aren't places of healing. They're places where you store people, like you would store toxic waste.'

'That's horrible. I can't accept that,' Clara said.

The warden shrugged. 'Accept it or don't, I'm just stating fact. I don't care – society doesn't care – if Malvern eats every single piece of human wreckage in Marcy. The women in here don't care about each other, even. They fight constantly. They kill each other over the most pathetic of slights. They certainly don't care about me. I can't walk around this place without wearing a stab-proof vest. So why should I care about them? What I do care about is myself. My continued existence. I wasted my life, I see that now. I just want a second chance to get it right, and if I have to drink blood to get it – if I have to rot away slowly, fine. It's better than the alternative, which is death. Life is always worth more than death.'

'And you think Malvern's doing this out of the goodness of her heart? Did it ever occur to you that she's just using

116

you?' Clara fumed. 'Did you think it's a coincidence that she approached you only after Laura Caxton was sentenced to this prison? This particular prison? She doesn't care about your second chance. She cares about getting to Caxton, and that's it.'

Bellows laughed bitterly. 'Of course! I'm not an idiot, and you should make a point of remembering that. Of course she's using me. And in return, I'm using her right back. That's how it works. That's how it always works.' She glanced up. Malvern was beckoning to her. 'Come on. If you walk too fast, you'll know it.'

Clara shuffled forward, glaring over her shoulder at the warden as she followed Malvern out of the office. Franklin, the CO who had brought Clara in, brought up the rear. He seemed to be the warden's personal bodyguard or maybe her chief of staff.

A receiving line of half-deads stood outside, lined up against the walls of the corridor. Most of them were wearing the uniforms of COs, COs who had to be dead by now. It looked like the half-deads were running the prison now, on Malvern's behalf.

Clara thought about the crime scenes she'd investigated with Glauer, the audacious murders Malvern had committed in the days just before she took over the prison. She realized why things had gotten so explosive now. They'd thought it must be because Malvern needed so much blood. Clearly she'd also wanted as many victims as possible – she needed her own private army of half-deads to run the prison. Each and every one of these creatures had been a living human being once with a family, with friends. Now they were just slaves.

Clara found it hard to sympathize, though, when they sniggered and leered at her as she walked past.

The four of them, Malvern, Clara, Franklin, and the warden, made their way through the maze of locked doors deep into the prison. There was no waiting at control gates this time or any checking of IDs. The doors were mostly unlocked, and those that weren't opened before Malvern even reached them. Clara glanced up at the ceiling and saw there were cameras watching every hallway, every small room they passed through. There must be half-deads in a central command center somewhere, watching.

She was starting to worry that everything was not going to be okay. That even Laura couldn't save her from this situation. The idea had never occurred to her before that moment, but once it arrived she couldn't get it out of her head.

She could die there, in that prison. Worse, she could be used as bait to lure Laura into a trap. And then both of them would be killed. Or worse. She was pretty sure that Malvern intended to make Laura a vampire. Malvern had done that to other vampire killers, in the past. She seemed to find it deliciously ironic.

As for herself, Clara doubted she'd be given the same option.

The four of them passed through one last door, a massive sheet of reinforced iron. Malvern smiled and stepped aside. 'Best if they don't see me as of yet,' she said. 'You go first, child.' She gestured for Clara to step forward, through the door. Clara shuffled forward and was instantly engulfed in noise. They had reached one of the dormitories – what a previous generation might have called a cell block – and the women housed inside were going crazy. The noise was intense and oceanic. Though it had to be made up of individual shouts and questions and profanities, the stone walls and steel bars of the prison reverberated with the noise and made it just one clamorous roar.

Clara looked up and saw three levels of cells, rising up to

118

the ceiling far above her head. As she watched, a flaming roll of toilet paper came sailing out of one of the upper-level cells, unwrapping as it flew. She was very careful not to flinch. Elsewhere in the top two rows women were squirting bottles of water through their bars or throwing down bits of broken wood or crumpled paper. On the bottom level prisoners were beating on the bars of their cells with cups or cafeteria trays or just hitting and kicking at them with their bare feet and hands. Everywhere she looked she saw hard faces staring back at her, hard eyes watching her every move. Women flipped her the finger or waggled their tongues at her or showed her their naked buttocks. Others tried spitting at her, though few of them got any range.

The warden stepped into the dorm and raised her hands high. When that didn't change the volume of the shouting, she reached behind her and Franklin handed her a mega-phone. She switched it on and shouted over the din, 'You want to know what's going on? Then shut the fuck up right now! Or you can all just sit here with no dinner. I've got four more dorms to talk to. You lot can be last in that line, if you want.'

The shouts and calls never really died out, but they defin-itely lessened in volume. It took a while. Clara looked around at the cells on either side of her. The women inside were pressed up against the bars, most of them watching the warden now. There seemed to be eight of them in every cell – cells that might comfortably have held four. There was only one toilet in every cell, and no room for the women to move around much. The stink of unwashed bodies and shit wafted back and forth across the way and Clara wondered if it was always like this. If people were actually forced to live in these condi-tions, for years at a time. She remembered Fetlock's nasty little joke, when he suggested that going to prison was like

119

being sent away to summer camp for Laura. Well, everyone did sleep in bunk beds, Clara saw. Otherwise . . .

The warden finally decided that the noise had dropped to an acceptable level. 'There's been some changes, ladies, and they're going to affect all of us. This facility is no longer under the control of the Bureau of Prisons. That means, whatever rights and privileges you thought you were entitled to before, you've got jack shit now. You want to eat tonight, you're going to have to play ball with me. Lucky for you I don't expect good behavior, or a reforming attitude. All I want is your blood.'

The shouting started up again, but the warden just waited for it to pass. Then she gestured back at Franklin and he, in turn, gestured at someone out in the hall. Four half-deads came running into the dorm, each of them pushing a rolling cart loaded down with medical supplies: rubber tubing, packs of sterilized needles, IV stands, and bags to hold collected blood.

'Dinner is ready to be served. You'll be eating in your cells from now on. I hope that's alright,' the warden said, in a tone that made it clear she didn't care what they thought. 'To get dinner, you have to give me a couple ounces of blood, that's all. Not enough that you'll ever notice it's gone. If you want to donate, you just stick your left arm through the bars and make a fist. These guys with no faces will be taking it from you. You can choose to cooperate with them, you can smile and say nice things to them, as ugly as they may be, and make it easy for them to take the blood. Or you can fight them. You can refuse to give them your arm. That's just fine. In that case, she goes into your cell and rips your throat out.'

'She who, cuntlips?' someone shouted from the second level.

Malvern stepped into the dorm then. She turned her ravaged face up to look at the three tiers of cells. Then she smiled, showing all of her broken, vicious teeth.

A hush, a real hush, something very close to silence, ran through the dorm.

The warden let the vampire's appearance sink in for a while. Then she raised the megaphone again. 'Now. Let me tell you about option three.'

20.

The half-deads didn't waste much time. They didn't bother beating on the door or shouting threats through it at the women inside. Instead they decided to cut their way through.

The door of the SHU was a plate of steel a quarter-inch thick. It was designed to resist any attempt the inmates made to tear it down or pull it off its rails, but the prison's architect had assumed they would never have access to an oxyacetylene torch. There was a loud hissing and a couple of high-pitched screams from behind the door, and then a spot near the middle of the door started to glow cherry red.

'Get back,' Caxton said, and she and Gert moved away from the door just as sparks erupted from its surface and molten slag began running down its face. A jet of yellow sparks emerged from the hole the half-deads had made and began traveling down the height of the door. It looked like they intended to cut the door in half. The jet didn't move very quickly – it was going to take a while, so Caxton had time to get ready. She spent that time mostly sitting, watching the door, trying to make plans in her head.

Gert didn't make it easy.

'So what are we going to do?' she kept asking. As if she wanted to know whether they should go to the mall or just get their nails done. 'What's the big plan, vampire killer?' It seemed she had total confidence in Caxton's ability to outwit their enemies. 'When they come through, where do you want me?' Gert asked. There was a nasty gleam in her eyes.

Caxton tried to ignore her. She could have forced Gert back into the cell at any time. Gert had that knife, but Caxton had a shotgun loaded with a plastic bullet. It would be easy enough to shoot Gert and then get the knife away from her in her resulting pain and confusion. Once Caxton had the knife, Gert wouldn't be able to fight back in any kind of meaningful way. Caxton could force her into the cell, lock it, and have one less thing to worry about.

She kept telling herself she didn't know why she was hesitating. Why she didn't do it right that second. In truth she knew exactly why she hadn't shot Gert – and why she wasn't going to. If she did she would be alone. Alone in a housing unit full of women who hated her, looking at a door behind which was a bunch of monsters waiting to kill her, and beyond them a vampire who would try to destroy her soul.

There are times when nobody wants to be alone. Even if your only choice for company is a multiple murderer.

'I mean, you do have a plan, right? We're not just waiting here to get our asses kicked.'

'It would help,' Caxton admitted, 'if I knew how many of them there were. Or how they were armed.' Half-deads never used guns. Their rotting bodies lacked the coordination to aim properly. Beyond that it was anyone's guess. They would try to take her alive, she knew, but they wouldn't be afraid to hurt her. Gert they would kill just to get her out of the way.

Caxton had one round in her shotgun. She was certain she

could take down one half-dead with it. After that she would need to reload. She doubted they would give her the time to do that.

The jet of sparks reached the bottom of the door and fire licked along the cement. It stopped for a moment, then it reappeared at the top of the cut and started working upward. Caxton estimated she had about two minutes left to think of something.

The door was nearly cut in half when inspiration struck. She realized what was in that squishy bag she'd found in the guard post. She ran back and got it, then dropped it about six feet from the door. Then she checked her shotgun again. Made sure it was loaded. Made sure it was ready to fire.

'Caxton?' Gert asked. The sparks were coming from very close to the top of the door. 'Um, is that all you have?'

'Wait for it,' Caxton said. 'When they burst in, don't run at them. Make them come to you. If you can take them on one at a time, that'll help. And whatever you do, don't hold back. They aren't human, so don't worry about hurting them. They're already dead. Just hit them as hard and as fast as you can.'

'Okey-dokey,' Gert said. She turned to face the door.

The jet reached the top of the door. Bright silver slag had run down the painted metal like dripping candle wax, all the way from the top to the bottom. The jet of sparks sputtered and then went out.

One half of the door slipped out of its tracks and fell inward. It hit the floor with a deafening clang. Revealed beyond it was nothing but darkness.

Gert started moving forward, knife out in front of her.

'No!' Caxton shouted. 'Wait.'

The half-deads came at them all at once. A crowd of them, most dressed like COs, a few in orange jumpsuits. Their faces

124

were torn to shreds and their eyes were alight as they swung knives and shanks and shock batons through the air. They jumped over the fallen section of the door and came roaring toward Caxton like a wave of pain.

She lifted her shotgun. Waited for the perfect moment. Then fired her plastic bullet right into the bag at their feet.

Its contents erupted upward like a silent fireworks display, ropy streamers of wet orange goo shooting upward with incredible speed. It splattered across the oncoming half-deads, splashing across their legs and chests and faces and then hardening instantaneously, snarling around them in a mass of slimy tendrils that dried in the air as Caxton watched.

The half-deads weren't even aware of the sticky foam exploding around them at first. They kept coming, legs lifting for the next stride, arms swinging to menace the waiting prisoners – and then froze in place. The hardening foam held them fast, barely able to move, their limbs trapped, their ravaged faces covered in the ropy mess. What little range of motion they had was spent trying to pull the sticky tendrils off their bodies, with little or no success.

Caxton had been surprised to see the foam pack in the guard post. She knew that the air-activated aqueous foam had been designed originally for use in prisons, as a way to immobilize rioting inmates and keep them from attacking the guards. She also knew that after a few live tests it had been all but banned from prison use, because it had a bad habit of covering its victims' noses and mouths in solid gunk, making it impossible for them to breathe. The potential lawsuits had convinced the Bureau of Prisons to look elsewhere in its constant search for the next great compliance weapon.

Half-deads didn't need to breathe. Even if they did, Caxton couldn't care less. They couldn't hurt her anymore, or take her captive, and that was what mattered.

'Oh my God,' Gert said, snorting with laughter. 'Did you see the look on that guy's face when—'

Caxton grabbed her celly's arm. 'Move,' she said. 'There might be more on the way, and I only had one of those.'

Together the two women ran around the side of the stuck mass of half-deads. The creatures cried out in misery and a few, whose arms hadn't been completely pinned by the foam, tried to reach for them or stab at them, but they couldn't follow as Caxton and Gert made their escape from the SHU.

Now Caxton just had to figure out what she was going to do next.

21.

Just after midnight they brought the first batch of blood to Malvern in plastic bags, the kind hospitals used to store whole blood for transfusions. The prison had a full medical ward, and the necessary supplies were all in stores. A half-dead in a CO uniform pushed a wheeled cart into the warden's office and unloaded the blood onto what had become Malvern's desk. Six bags of it, each of them swollen to capacity. Clara knew this would be the first batch of many.

Malvern grabbed one up at random and pressed it to her mouth. She was able to shred the bag and suck the blood out without spilling a drop on her tattered nightdress. When it was gone she sighed, a strangely human sound. She closed her one eye. There were holes in the eyelid through which Clara could see that Malvern's eye had rolled back into her head. As she watched, the holes shrank, the skin there healing visibly.

It wouldn't be long, she knew, until Malvern was whole and healthy again, at full strength and more than a match even for Laura. Of course, that strength wouldn't last – Malvern would start rotting away again almost immediately. But there was more blood where this came from, so much more.

And meanwhile the outside world had no idea she was here. No idea that the prison had been turned into one enormous blood drive. No idea that every prisoner in the facility was at enormous risk.

Clara had watched the first few donations. Hungry women had shoved their arms through the bars of their cells, more than willing to make a small sacrifice if it meant they didn't have to go to sleep on an empty stomach. There had been far more volunteers than there were half-deads to take the blood. Nobody had refused – they knew what would happen if they did. The half-deads had moved down the dorm one cell after the other, moving quickly, stabbing needles into arms almost at random. The work clearly delighted them. They had not bothered to replace their needles between donations, or even to clean them off. Clara had protested – she knew little about phlebotomy, but she knew you could get any number of things from a dirty needle. How many of the prisoners had been IV drug users on the outside? How many of them had hepatitis? Or HIV, for that matter? Or who knew what else?

Her pleas had fallen, of course, on deaf ears. Neither the warden nor Malvern seemed to think that the spread of blood-borne illness was a significant problem. Which told Clara something. It told her they didn't expect the prisoners to live long enough to get sick.

There had been few volunteers for option three. Maybe Malvern and the warden expected that to change. Or maybe they just knew that the prison was a short-term solution to Malvern's long-term need for blood. Maybe they understood they couldn't get away with this forever, and that meant they must have a contingency plan for what happened when SWAT teams stormed the prison, as they eventually must.

128

Clara wondered if she, herself, would live long enough to find out what the contingency plan was.

While she was considering that particular dark thought, a half-dead came into the office and rushed over to Malvern. He whispered in her ear and she smiled.

The warden looked up from her BlackBerry and raised one eyebrow.

'There's been an escape,' Malvern said, her eye twinkling. She reached for another blood bag.

'Care to share with me?' the warden asked. 'It is still, technically, my prison. It sounds like the kind of thing I ought to be aware of.'

'It is a small thing, I assure ye. I sent a company of my slaves to your Special Housing Unit, there to recover the famous killer, Laura Caxton. They failed at this, and she has escaped.'

'What?' the warden asked, jumping up.

Clara's heart lifted in her chest. Only to fall back again when she heard what Malvern said next.

'It was no more than I expected of her. She has at her advantage resources and craft others cannot match. No lock nor prison gate could hold her long. No half-dead is fair sport for her. I knew she would escape. I planned for her to escape, all this time. 'Tis why we needed her,' she said, and jabbed one bony finger in Clara's direction. 'Be not afraid.'

The warden looked largely unconvinced. 'I've heard of Caxton. I've read about what she's capable of. You're sure this is under control?'

Malvern reached for another bag of blood. Her shoulders looked remarkably less bony than they had before. They were almost round. 'Lady Fortuna makes sport of any who would claim such,' Malvern said.

'Sometimes,' the warden said, 'I wish you would just answer "yes" or "no."'

Malvern smiled. And drank down more blood.

A little later the candidates for option three were brought in, one at a time. Clara was gagged so she couldn't warn them what they were getting themselves into. There were four of them, and they were allowed to sit down on the sofa and given a drink of water. They were tough-looking women, all of them. Two were black, one was a Latina, and one was white, but they all had the same cold eyes that kept moving around the room, taking everything in. They didn't smile, or thank the half-deads who brought their drinks. They didn't talk among themselves.

'Forbin,' the warden said, and one of the black women looked up. The warden consulted her BlackBerry and said, 'You're in for murder, is that right?'

'You know it is,' Forbin said. She glanced over at Malvern and licked her lips. 'I killed my husband because he was beating me.'

The warden frowned. 'It says here that your defense attorney couldn't present any evidence to back up that claim. The prosecution said you had an argument with him over some money. You wanted to buy some drugs and he wouldn't give you the money, so you stabbed him. Seventy-one times.' The warden shrugged. 'I don't honestly care. You're in for twenty-five to life and so far you've been a less-than-model prisoner. You've stabbed two other inmates since you were inside.'

'Always in self-defense,' Forbin protested.

'Let's see. You have some family back in the world. An uncle. We're looking for people without a lot of ties or relationships.'

'He used to rape me, when I was a kid. Then I got too old for him.' Clara's eyes went wide. Forbin couldn't be much more than twenty-five. 'I ain't expecting much from him now.

130

There's nothing out there for me. I'll be old like you if I ever get out. I can't get a job with a felony on my jacket, and as soon as I hit the streets I'm gonna start thinking about getting high again. You got something better to offer, I'll take it.'

Malvern leaned forward across the desk. 'You can't imagine the dark secrets I offer, child. Will ye swear fealty to me tonight?'

'You want my bond? You want respect, yeah? I can give you that.'

'Then come closer. Do not speak. What passes between us is called the Silent Rite, and words would only sully it.' Malvern rose from her seat and bid Forbin to kneel before her. She took Forbin's face in her thin hands and stared deeply into her eyes. For a moment there was no sound at all in the warden's office. It felt like the air had congealed and gone bad.

Malvern was passing on her curse. This was option three. If the prisoners chose it, they didn't have to donate blood. Instead they could take their own lives – and tomorrow night, they could rise again, as vampires. As part of Malvern's new brood.

When the rite was finished Forbin was weeping. Malvern opened a drawer of the desk and took out a small glass bottle with a rubber dropper. It was full of straw-colored liquid Clara couldn't identify, but she was pretty sure she knew what it was.

Behind Forbin the office door opened quietly and a pair of half-deads came in carrying a simple pine box. A coffin. Forbin didn't even look at it. She just opened her mouth and stuck out her tongue.

The curse itself wasn't enough to make someone a vampire. They also had to die by their own hand. The curse helped with that – it got inside your soul, made you want to die, to

131

be reborn. You could fight it off if your will was strong enough, or if you had enough to live for. Forbin didn't even try.

The liquid in the bottle must have been some kind of very strong, very fast-acting poison. Malvern leaned forward and handed the dropper to Forbin. The prisoner put the drops on her tongue, put the dropper back on the desk, then sat back on her heels and closed her eyes.

After a minute or two, she started to twitch. Her arm jumped at her side. Her head rocked on her neck. The twitching got worse and graduated to full-blown convulsions – but only for a few seconds. Then Forbin's face turned purple with congested blood and she fell backward. The two half-deads caught her easily and laid her out in the coffin. Then they pushed the lid onto the coffin and carried it away again, with Forbin inside.

It could be that easy.

The other three women sitting on the couch watched it all without a word. Their eyes took it all in, measuring, evaluating. They were clearly working out in their heads whether it was worth it or not to follow the same path.

The warden cleared her throat. 'Hauser,' she said, and the white woman stood up and came to kneel before Malvern. She had a tattoo running down the side of her neck that read 100% PURE. Clara had worked in law enforcement long enough to know what that meant. Hauser was a member of the Aryan Brotherhood, most likely the girlfriend or sister of one of the white supremacist gang.

'I'm not afraid,' she said, looking straight at Malvern. 'Let's get on with it.'

The warden looked at her handheld. 'Two different counts of vehicular homicide – that's pretty suspicious. You ran down an eight-year-old black boy with your van, and got a light sentence because you claimed you merely lost control of the vehicle. Then when you did it again, less than a year later, the judge decided that you either desperately needed to tune up your brakes, or that maybe there was something more to the case than met the eye.'

'I'm not sorry, if that's what you're asking.'

Malvern grinned wickedly.

'Currently serving life without the possibility of parole, because your offense was judged a hate crime.'

'That's right. I confessed everything already. I don't feel the need to do it again,' Hauser said. She turned and stared at the warden. 'You want me for this detail or what? I was planning on offing myself anyway, looking for a chance. This sounds even better than hanging myself in my cell while seven colored bitches look on and cheer. Let's get it fucking on.'

Malvern reached down and grabbed the woman's cheek-bones. 'You'll do as I say, in all things?'

'Absolutely.'

'Then hush, child, and receive the gift,' Malvern said.

Clara could only stand and watch in horror as the grotesque vignette was repeated again – poison, convulsions, Hauser taken away in a coffin. The other two volunteers went down without any more hesitation than Forbin or Hauser.

In a prison as big as SCI-Marcy, how many women would be suicidal? How many were looking at futures without hope, without prospects? These four had volunteered even after seeing Malvern, after seeing what an old and decrepit vampire looked like. They were willing, like the warden, to take the curse even if it meant rotting away forever. It was still better than what they had now. Tomorrow night, Clara knew, there would be more volunteers for option three. When the prisoners saw what brand-new, freshly made vampires looked like – there might be a lot more.

When it was done the warden reached across the desk to

pick up the bottle of poison. Malvern snatched it out of her grasp.

'You're still useful as a mortal,' Malvern explained. 'As a human face, should any curious fellows come to the door asking what has happened here.'

The warden nodded, though she didn't look happy. 'Soon,' she said. 'You promised me it could happen soon.'

'When faced with eternity in a more perfect form, is not a little time of waiting acceptable? Yes, Augusta. It will come soon enough.'

22.

Laura Caxton was completely lost.

It didn't surprise her. She'd never seen a map of the prison – prisoners weren't typically allowed that kind of information. Every time she'd moved around the facility the COs had been there to guide her. She knew in a general way that she was on the western side of the prison. She knew that the main gate was on the eastern side.

There had to be other gates, though. Other ways out.

Her big plan, so far, was to escape. To get out of the prison and find someone in authority and tell them what was going on. If they wanted her to go back and hunt down Malvern, with proper weapons and backup, then fine. If they wanted to return her to custody and take care of the problem themselves, she wouldn't put up a fight.

The trick, of course, would be breaking out of a maximum-security prison. With no good tools, no guards she could bribe. And in the dark. Malvern had shut off most of the prison's lights. Maybe she just wanted to conserve electricity – or maybe she knew that Caxton was loose, and wanted to make things difficult for her. Here and there an emergency lighting unit was still blazing away, but Caxton knew those would only last an hour or so before their batteries died. And then she would be trapped in complete darkness, without so much as a window to let in starlight.

'I knew I could count on you, Caxton. I just knew when I saw you, we were going to be buds. I'm your road bitch now, right? The one you get together with even when we're out of here,' Gert said. 'I mean, I guess I have to be, because we're going to break out together, right? You're going to need me out there. And I'm going to be so useful to you. This is my big chance. If I can get out now, I'll still be young enough to have more babies of my own. I knew I could count on you.'

Caxton nodded but didn't say anything. She wasn't sure who was listening. She knew exactly who was watching. There were video cameras everywhere in the prison, watching every corner, every hallway, every reinforced door. She had no doubt they had night-vision capability. She knew she had to move quickly, that if she lingered too long in one place it would be easy for Malvern to get a squad of half-deads together and send them her way.

So far she'd been lucky. Beyond the door of the SHU had been a long, featureless corridor that led to a hub area, a place where three hallways crossed each other. It was the perfect place to put a guard detail, and in fact the prison's designers had built a defensive post in the middle of the hub, a guard post with narrow windows and gun ports and thick cinder-block walls. It had been empty when Caxton arrived. Maybe, she thought, Malvern just didn't have enough half-deads to cover the entire prison.

She'd learned a long time ago that hoping for anything like that, anything that would make her life easier, was a trap. You had to expect the absolute worst, and capitalize on what little bits of luck you found, but never depend on them.

Of the three hallways she could explore, two had been sealed off with barred gates. The gates could be opened remotely or with an actual key. Harelip hadn't possessed such a key, she knew – she'd searched the dead CO's body – and the remote controls were, she was certain, heavily guarded. She'd tried the third hallway. There was a big fire door at the end of that one, but it opened easily when she pushed on it.

'This feels bad,' Caxton said, out loud, when she looked at the empty corridor that lay beyond. It was lined with doors, normal doors with doorknobs and everything. No one was guarding that hallway. There weren't any guard posts watching the place where the hall turned a corner. 'There is one door that's open, and it's completely unguarded. It feels like a trap.'

'Don't be such a pussy,' Gert said, pushing past Caxton to head down the darkened hallway. 'I thought you were the big tough vampire killer, who never waited for backup, who went into vampire lairs with guns blazing—'

'That's when I had decent guns,' Caxton explained. 'You know, assault rifles with cross-point bullets. One stupid move right now and both of us are dead. And you might have just made a stupid move.'

Gert looked down at her feet as if expecting to find the floor littered with bear traps. 'Nope, don't look like it.' She marched over to the nearest door and, before Caxton could stop her, turned the knob and stepped through.

'Wait, just—' Caxton called.

'This one's clear,' Gert said. 'Just a bunch of boxes and shit.'

Caxton stepped over to the door and brought up her shotgun. She stepped inside and swung the weapon from side to side, daring any half-dead to come jumping out of its hiding place. When that didn't happen she went over to the pile of boxes and tore one open. It was full of cans of peaches in heavy syrup.

'This must be a storage area,' Caxton said. She went to the next door down the hall and repeated her drill of sweeping the room with her shotgun before approaching the boxes inside. She broke open several of them and studied the contents. Powdered milk. Sliced beets. Sweet peas. The next room down was full of plastic-wrapped pallets of the plastic trays the cafeteria used.

'We must be close to the kitchens – you store food near where you're going to prepare it,' Caxton announced.

Gert used her hunting knife to cut open a can of pineapple. She slurped a couple slices into her mouth and chewed noisily. 'This is good stuff. How do they take good stuff like this and turn it into that shit they serve us at mealtimes?' Gert asked.

'Maybe – maybe this is a positive thing,' Caxton went on, ignoring her celly. 'If this is a storage area, then there has to be a way for people to bring boxes in and out. They must off-load delivery trucks close to here – there might be a loading dock right here. Maybe that's a way out.'

Gert shrugged. 'Kinda. The trucks come in through the main gate, then drive around the side of E Dorm. They gotta go through two gates on the way, and there's a place where the hogs can blow out their tires if there's a problem.'

Caxton stared at her cell mate.

'What?' Gert asked. 'I been here a couple years. You think me and my old celly never talked about how we would break out? People see things, yeah, and they talk about them. Everybody wants to know how this place works. And how to get out.'

Caxton laughed. She hadn't considered that at all. 'Okay,' she said. 'So how would you do it?'

Gert shrugged. 'Well, first you have to fuck a guard. Some of 'em will do that, you know. They'll come in the cell saying they're gonna do a shank search, and then you just take your clothes off if you want to do it. You do that often enough, they start bringing you little things.'

Caxton's eyebrows went up. 'Like what? Chocolate? Lipsticks?'

Gert rolled her eyes. She threw her can of pineapples into a corner, then headed for the next door down the hall and threw it open. 'No, dummy,' she called, stepping inside. 'Like rock. Crystal. You know, drugs. That's how a lot of girls in here get high. But if they really like you, you can ask them for things. It can't be anything too obvious. But there's one kind of toothbrush you can snap off the head and it makes a real nasty shank. Or a good hairbrush, the kind that's metal inside, you can do a lot with a piece of metal if you've got time to work it. Make lock picks, say. So either you take a screw hostage, which shouldn't be too hard if his pants are around his ankles and his dick is hanging out – or you pick a couple locks outside the infirmary, and that gets you as far as the wall. Then you just have to get over the wall. We never did figure that part out.'

Caxton frowned and followed Gert into a room full of chairs. Hundreds of them had been stacked up inside, and in the dark the stacks made weird, spiky shadows. 'I can see a couple of problems with us implementing that plan. For one thing, half-deads aren't interested in sex.'

'Yeah, well – hey. You know, it's seriously dark back here,' Gert said. 'Like, deep end of a coal mine dark.'

'Not quite that dark,' Caxton said. She'd been in a few coal mines in her time.

Gert tripped on something and caught herself against a stack of chairs. They rattled and squeaked loud enough to wake the dead. Caxton tensed herself, just by reflex, and grabbed the stun gun off her belt.

When she felt a knife pass through the air inches from her face, she knew there was a reason she had grown so paranoid. She could just see the blade glittering in the low light. She estimated where the blow had come from and jabbed at it with the stun gun, then squeezed the trigger.

There was a loud snapping sound of arcing electricity, and a high-pitched scream. Then the half-dead hit her hard with a fist to the stomach and knocked her down going past. She saw it silhouetted briefly against the doorway, and then it was gone.

'Shit,' Caxton said. 'I was hoping the stun gun would work on them like it does on living people, but no dice. Now we're screwed.'

Gert clucked her tongue. 'No we're not. It ran *away*, girl.'

Caxton sighed in frustration. 'You don't know about these things. They're weak, and cowardly, and they can't shoot the side of a barn. But the problem is, they never work alone. That one wasn't running away. It was running for help.'

23.

Caxton sped out of the storeroom and slid to a stop in the hall. If she could catch the half-dead before it reached others of its kind she could save herself a lot of trouble. She wasted a half-second peering through the gloom back the way she'd come before she heard running footfalls and realized that the half-dead was running farther down the corridor, past the storerooms and into the deep shadows at the far end. Cursing, she chased after the retreating sound – knowing that what she was doing was stupid. She couldn't see a thing. She could trip over something on the floor and break an ankle. She could miss a turn in the corridor and run smack into a wall and break her nose or worse.

She didn't have much choice. She'd been very lucky back in the SHU. The package of sticky foam had provided her with a few extra hours of life, but there'd only been one of them, and she didn't have any more tricks to play.

Gasping for breath, she tore down the hallway anyway, spurred on by the same reckless instincts that had kept her alive for the last few years, kept her alive when so many vampires couldn't say the same. She held her hands out in front of her, which would give her a split second's warning if she was about to run into anything. Not enough time to stop herself, but maybe enough to prevent giving herself a concussion. She almost cried out in triumph as her fingertips brushed cloth and she realized that she was about to catch the half-dead. It collided hard with something in front of it, something softer than a brick wall anyway, and she threw herself onto it, grabbing for anything she could get a handle on, an article of clothing, a stray limb, hair.

The half-dead had run into a door. It turned the knob just as she hit it from behind, and together they went sprawling through, into light so bright it dazzled Caxton's eyes and momentarily blinded her.

The half-dead went down, its face hitting a cement floor with an ugly crunch. Caxton's fall was softened by its body, but still she felt the impact like a punch in the gut. She sucked air into her lungs and looked up, blinking away the glare in her eyes.

She was in the kitchen, the same kitchen where she'd met Guilty Jen and her set. Back then it had been staffed by human prisoners cooking up meals for the other inmates for a few pennies an hour.

Now it was full of half-deads.

They were standing at counters chopping up vegetables or stirring huge pots on industrial stoves or carrying trays of food. One of them, who stood in the middle of the room with its hands on its hips, was wearing a white chef's toque.

Every single one of them was staring at her. They were as surprised to see her as she was to see them, and they had frozen in place, unsure of what to do next.

That wouldn't last.

Caxton had no idea what Malvern had ordered her slaves

142

to do if they found her lying facedown on the floor, all but defenseless. She could guess, however, that it involved a lot of knives and a very brief but furious attempt to hurt her as much as possible without actually killing her.

She didn't have to think very hard about what she needed to do. She grabbed the shotgun from under her shoulder and fired her plastic bullet into the neck of the one in the chef's hat. The first rule of fighting dirty was that your first target was whoever appeared to be in charge.

Fighting dirty was her only option. She watched as the chef's head flopped backward on a nearly severed neck and then rolled to the side, behind a stainless-steel table covered in chopped carrots. She could hear the half-deads screaming in their obscene falsetto voices, asking each other what to do, shouting that they needed to call for backup, or just howling for her blood.

Caxton broke open the shotgun and started loading another slug. Before she could even get it out of her makeshift bandolier, carrot peelings showered down on her head and she looked up to see a half-dead diving over the table to get at her. It had a steel mortar in its hand, the kind used to crush herbs in a pestle, and it was holding it like a club, ready to dash in her brains.

She yanked the pepper spray out of her bra and squirted the thing in its bloodshot eyes. It screamed and rolled to the side, tearing and gouging at its own eyeballs. Half-deads might not feel pain the same way living humans did, but nobody enjoyed getting a full load of capsaicin right in the mucous membranes.

She finished loading the shotgun just as a pair of half-deads came around the side of the table toward her. They were both armed with kitchen knives, wicked and sharp and glowing in the brilliant light of the kitchen. She had time to notice that one of the knives was still flecked with bits of chopped parsley. She fired a plastic bullet into the chest of one half-dead, then flipped the shotgun around and caved in the other one's face with the weapon's stock.

The two of them went down. Whether they were fully dead or just wounded enough not to bother her didn't matter. The point was that they had to stay down. She was much more concerned, anyway, with the six half-deads right behind them, who were all coming straight for her.

She grabbed her baton. It wasn't much of a weapon, just a hollow length of aluminum weighted at one end and with a rubberized grip at the other. Back when she'd been a cop, though, she had trained in how to use it.

The course she'd taken had focused on how to avoid breaking bones with the baton, and how to make sure you never, ever killed anyone with it. Like everyone else in the class, she had made a note of all the things she wasn't supposed to do in case she needed to do them one day.

A half-dead armed with nothing but a steel ladle reached her first. It tried to duck under her arm, probably intending on grabbing her around the waist and knocking her over. She brought the baton around, grip end first, and jammed it in the soft spot just behind where its jaw attached to its skull. The half-dead screamed and dropped to the floor, where she stomped on it with both bare feet.

She really needed to find some heavy boots. Preferably with steel-reinforced toes.

The next half-dead had a cleaver that it brought whistling around to nearly cut open her throat. Maybe it hadn't gotten the message that she was supposed to be brought in alive. Caxton grabbed its arm at the elbow and pulled it into its own swing, overbalancing it and sending it sprawling.

A third one came at her from the side while she was

144

recovering from that move. It hit her hard in the side with a tenderizing mallet. If it had connected with her kidney, that might have been enough to drop her, but it only grazed the bottom of her rib cage. The pain was still intense and it almost kept her from focusing clearly enough to bring the baton down on the back of her assailant's neck. It curled away from the blow, which wasn't quite hard enough to paralyze it.

'Caxton, over here!' Gert shouted at that particular moment.

Caxton had all but forgotten her celly's existence until then – hadn't, in fact, given her a thought since she'd started running down the dark hallway. She looked around wildly and saw Gert standing next to an open door on one side of the kitchen. It wasn't the door Caxton had intended to use when exiting the area. She had planned, or half-planned, to escape into the cafeteria, a wide-open space that would be easy to brawl in. The door Gert had chosen had two things to recommend it, however. It wasn't locked, and there were no half-deads near it.

A kitchen knife flashed in the air and it was all Caxton could do to swivel away from where it was coming down. Instead of puncturing her chest, it flashed in front of her and sank deep into the back of another half-dead.

Caxton took the opportunity to get away from her enemies, rolling under a prep table and then launching herself out the other side, knocking over a pile of dirty pots and pans as she hurried through the door where Gert was waiting, dancing in anticipation. Beyond the door was a darkened area full of wooden crates, stacked high in towers reaching toward a ceiling lost in the gloom. Caxton saw a forklift ahead of her, its bright yellow paint just visible in the darkness. Beyond that were – trucks. Big eighteen-wheelers, white and ghostly and huge.

'This is the loading dock you were looking for,' Gert said. 'Remember?'

145

Behind Caxton the door started rattling in its jamb. Gert must have had the presence of mind to close and lock it after Caxton came rushing through.

'Who's got your fucking back, huh?' Gert asked.

Caxton didn't bother to answer. The door wouldn't hold long. Half-deads were weak individually, but in groups they could bust down any barrier you put in their way. She needed a way to slow them down.

'Help me over here,' Caxton said, and hurried toward one of the tall stacks of crates. Together they kicked and pushed at the crate at the bottom of the stack. The ones above their heads started to totter.

'You're supposed to say thank you now,' Gert insisted.

Caxton gave the bottom box a last kick. One side of it collapsed, spilling thousands of white plastic sporks in individualized wrappers all over her feet. The boxes above it fell with a great dusty crash, collapsing and shattering against the door, burying it in shattered wood and dented cans of baked beans and fingerling potatoes. That might hold the half-deads a minute or two longer.

Caxton sighed and looked around herself, trying to anticipate the next threat. When she saw Gert's crazy eyes glowing in the dark, she remembered herself and managed to say, 'Thank you.'

24.

Caxton had bought a little time. She needed more. She jumped on the forklift and started moving crates up against the door, a painfully slow process but the best way to make a strong barricade. The half-deads in the kitchen kept pushing and beating at the door, but they were making little headway. With half a ton of canned goods behind the door, there wasn't much they could do. After a little while they stopped trying.

Caxton frowned. 'They gave up,' she said.

Gert laughed. 'That's a good thing! What's with you, huh? Every good thing that happens to us, you look like someone put cayenne pepper in your tampon.'

'That's because I'm a realist,' Caxton said. 'Half-deads don't just stop trying to kill you. It's possible they're just going around another way. Check these doors,' she said, pointing at a pair of large rolling doors leading into the kitchen. They were big enough to drive the forklift through. Gert checked them both, bending low to look at their locks, then shook her head.

'Both locked up tight.'

Caxton rubbed her cheek absentmindedly. It was possible

the half-deads were going the long way around, and were going to come at them through the wide-open loading bay doors. Maybe there was something she could do about that.

The loading dock had its own guard post. The door was locked, but Caxton was still riding out the adrenaline rush she'd gotten from fighting the half-deads in the kitchen. She slammed into the door with her shoulder, careful to hit it just above the lock. It held, but she heard something small and metallic fly out of the door and bounce away. She got a running start and kicked the door just below the lock, careful to keep her foot flat against the wood. The lock disintegrated and the door swung open, vibrating wildly on its hinges.

Inside was a rolling chair sitting in front of a control panel. A pair of monitor televisions hung from the ceiling, angled downward so whoever was sitting in the chair could easily keep an eye on them. She studied the control panel, expecting to find a big red button, and was not disappointed. When designing the prison's control systems the architects had at least known that there might come a time when someone needed to secure the loading dock without wasting time looking for the right controls. She slapped the red button with her hand and an alarm sounded as a chain-link gate rolled sideways across the open mouth of the loading bay. Weird shadows flickered across Gert's face as the gate carved up the light. Caxton bent under the control board and found the cable that would let central command override the door controls. She pulled it, half expecting the door to roll open again because she'd pulled the wrong wire.

It didn't.

'Now we're safe, right?' Gert asked.

'There's not a lot of difference between being safe and being trapped, at the moment. But we have time to think. That's the main thing I was after.'

She found a few useful things. There was a stab-proof vest hanging on a hook, the standard vest every guard in the prison was supposed to wear whenever in the presence of an inmate. It was made of ultra–tightly woven para-aramid fabric that would stop an ice pick, but not a bullet, and definitely not a vampire's teeth. She slid it over her jumpsuit and strapped it on tight. There were no boots in the guard post, but there was another box of plastic bullets, sitting under a row of metal clips. 'There should be a couple of shotguns right here,' Caxton said, touching the clips.

'Maybe when the half-deads took over the prison, the guards in here took the shotguns and tried to defend themselves.'

'Possibly – except there were two shotguns. There's only one chair in here.' She shrugged. 'Maybe the guard took both of them, who knows? And then he locked the door behind him when he went off to fight off the half-deads. Leaving a perfectly defensible position to go alone, on foot, into the middle of a dangerous situation.' Caxton shook her head. 'No, I think one of Malvern's people took those shotguns. I think this place was prepared for us.'

'What? Like, they knew we were coming?'

Caxton tilted her head from side to side. 'The doors we need are always open, or easily kicked in. We keep running across groups of half-deads, but they aren't armed properly. Malvern must know exactly where we are,' Caxton said, pointing upward at a camera mounted in the ceiling, 'but she hasn't sent a whole pack of them with good knives after us. It's like she's letting us move around the prison – part of the prison, anyway. The part she wants us in.' She narrowed her eyes. 'I'm starting to think we're being led through a maze like a couple of rats. That Malvern wanted us to end up right here.'

'Sometimes,' Gert said, very slowly, 'when I was high? I

would start thinking that God was trying to tell me something. Just – just listen for a sec, okay? I would have like a really crappy day. The kids wouldn't stop crying. The bitch at the grocery store wouldn't let me buy cigarettes with my WIC coupons. There would be all kinds of bills in the mail for shit I didn't even remember buying, and then when I would run in my room and slam the door, it would turn out that my mom had cleaned my room while I was out and got rid of my stash. She would never say anything, never even give me a nasty look. But she would find my crystal and flush it down the toilet, like it was just some trash I left lying around. Days like that, sometimes I felt like a voice was talking just to me. A voice telling me to do something bad. Like cut myself, or maybe burn some old letters and pictures, you know, stuff I'd been keeping for years.'

'Okay,' Caxton said.

'I need you to think real hard,' Gert said. 'I want to know if this suspicion of yours is anything at all like that voice I used to hear.'

Caxton held her peace.

'Because,' Gert went on, 'I found in general, doing the things that voice told me to do wasn't always such a shit hot idea.'

Caxton took her celly's point. There was no use worrying about the deeper game unless she could win on the surface. There was a diagram above the control panel that showed the whole of the prison's yard, all the structures and features of the grounds between the wall and the building itself. It showed in special detail the layered defenses between the loading dock and the main gate. Gert had done a pretty good job describing the gates and tire shredders a truck had to pass through to get back to the kitchens, but she'd missed a few things. The trucks had to make three tight corners before they

150

could reach the main gate, and each corner was watched by a machine-gun position. Then there was the main gate itself. Caxton had seen it on her way into the prison, a big slab of metal thick enough to resist a direct attack by a tank. If that gate was closed, there was no truck in the world that could just smash through it.

Still. The gate, the exit, was right there – no more than two hundred yards away. There were three trucks sitting in the loading bay, abandoned in place when the prison was taken over by half-deads. It was the best chance she was going to get to break out, to reach safety and help and sanity—

She was still considering her escape plan when the security monitors over her head switched themselves on. In the dark guard post the white light they blasted over her was difficult to look at, and at first she had no idea what the image on the monitor was supposed to be. It was in color, though there wasn't much color to see, just a tinge of red in one corner of each screen on an otherwise unbroken field of white.

Then the view moved backward and showed that the red was the dully glowing pupil of a vampire's eye. The view pulled back farther to display all of Malvern's face, horribly ravaged by time. But just as horrible was the fact that it didn't look as bad as it should. The skin was intact and snowy white. If it was heavily lined, if there were dark pouches under the vampire's eye and eye sockets, if the ears weren't quite able to hold themselves up under their own weight, it was still a face of something vibrantly and dangerously alive.

Caxton had only once in her life seen Malvern look that good, and it had been in one of the vampire's own memories, transmitted to her via a psychic link they no longer possessed. In the real world Malvern's flesh had never looked so healthy, so vital, so whole.

The camera kept moving backward. Soon Caxton could see

all of Malvern's upper body, and what looked like the arm and hip of someone standing next to her. Malvern was quite gently holding the other person by the elbow. Caxton knew that it would take only the slightest muscular pressure on Malvern's part to turn that soft touch into a bone-snapping vise grip.

There was no sound to go with the picture, and nothing moved within the frame. Every once in a while Malvern blinked. Then she said something that Caxton couldn't make out – it was hard to read a vampire's lips since all those teeth got in the way – and the camera jerked sideways, the entire picture swaying. When it stopped moving, two figures were visible on the screens. Malvern and Clara.

Someone off camera handed Clara a piece of paper. Written on it in large block letters was

23 HOURS.

25.

They walked Clara, very slowly, to the central command center of the prison, a round room located on the top level of the facility's main building. Broad windows let in a little light, but far more came from dozens of flickering security monitors, most of them displaying empty hallways and locked doors. Every few seconds the view on each screen would change, or pan back and forth to show another section of the prison. On one screen Clara saw a view of B Dorm. It looked like the prisoners had mostly turned in for the night, though a few were still pacing their cells, obviously concerned about what the next day would bring.

Around the central command center a skeleton crew of half-deads were bent over control panels and computer terminals, monitoring the prison's security systems. The largest number of them were gathered around a monitor at the far end of the room, where they pointed at the screen and giggled among themselves.

On the screen, Laura was standing next to a woman Clara didn't recognize. They were both staring at something intensely, something just above their heads.

Clara's heart sank when she saw her lover there. She had known Laura was at large in the prison, but she'd been able to imagine her crawling through ventilation ducts or hiding in some out-of-the-way spot – she could imagine Laura somewhere safe. From the grainy low-resolution image on the screen, however, she could tell that Laura had been putting herself in danger. As always. Her face was stained with blood or something darker and her clothes were spotted with gore.

Clara turned away from the screen. She couldn't look at Laura anymore, or her heart would start breaking all over again.

In the center of the room a video camera had been mounted on a tripod. Malvern led Clara in front of the camera while the warden stepped over to operate its controls. For a while they just stood there, while the camera's lens zoomed in and out. The warden cursed and adjusted a lever on the side of the camera.

'Dawn approaches,' Malvern said. 'Make haste.'

'This isn't my specialty,' the warden explained, and pressed a button near the front of the camera. Then she cursed and tried another. A red light lit up on the front of the camera, which meant it was recording.

Clara looked out the windows and saw that a smudge of dark blue was fighting with the black night sky. The sun would rise any minute, and when it did she knew that Malvern would have to be back in her coffin. Vampires weren't burned by the light of the sun, but at the moment of dawn each day they died once again, inevitably, no matter how strong or old or clever they might be. Their bodies liquefied inside their coffins, their tissues breaking down so they could repair any damage taken during the night.

'Give her the placard,' Malvern insisted.

The warden leaned around the camera to hand Clara a piece

154

of paper that read **23 HOURS**. Clara held it in front of her. Malvern was holding her arm, and Clara knew if she didn't do as she was bid it would take no effort at all for the vampire to snap her bones like matchsticks.

'Very well, now end it,' Malvern directed.

'Yeah, yeah,' the warden said, and flipped a switch. The red light blinked off. 'You know, you don't have to be so cryptic. Twenty-three hours, fine, that's an hour before dawn tomorrow, but what happens then? You didn't explain at all. And what use is making a threat if you don't even tell her what you want? There are loudspeakers in every room of the prison. We can broadcast your terms over and over, make sure Caxton gets the message.'

'Don't question me, woman,' Malvern said, her usual convivial tone audibly cooling down. 'Laura will know what I expect of her. Some games are best played in silence. Such as—'

'Fine, I've got it,' the warden said. 'Whist must be a hell of a game, I'm sure. Listen, there's still time before dawn, if you wanted to pass the curse on to me. That way I could be by your side tomorrow night, when Caxton comes gunning for you.'

'Play this message on the screen Laura is watching,' Malvern ordered, ignoring the warden's plea. The half-deads around the security monitors jumped to attention and started tapping commands onto computer keyboards. 'Play it again and again until we're sure she's seen it. You lot,' she said, 'ready my coffin. The time has come. While I slumber, see ye mind her as you would me.' She gathered herself up and prepared to leave.

'Wait,' the warden said.

Malvern turned, a cold, imperious look in her eye.

'Please,' the warden said. 'You made me a promise. I've carried out your plan well, haven't I? I've done everything you asked.'

155

'And ye shall be rewarded. In due time. When Caxton is mine, ye shall—'

'Fuck Caxton!' the warden shrieked. 'She's never going to do what you want. She'll never be what you want her to be. Focusing on her is a ridiculous mistake!'

What happened next was impossible for the human eye to follow.

Clara felt as if someone had hit her elbow with a baseball bat. Malvern had run across the room without letting go of Clara's arm first. The pain was intense. Even worse, as her arm flew up in response, the alarm on her electroshock restraint went off. It blared out a warning tone so loud it made her vision go dim. She froze in place, knowing that if she remained motionless for a second the stun package wouldn't fire and she wouldn't be sent into convulsions.

The camera on its tripod went flying across the room, clanging against a chair and knocking a half-dead to the floor. And then Malvern was standing right next to the warden, holding her by the throat.

'Ye come to me as a supplicant, begging the greatest gift any of your kind may receive,' Malvern said, very softly. 'Ye call me your mistress, and beg to offer me your fealty. And then ye question my decisions.'

The warden tried to say something, but all that emerged from her throat was a choking gasp.

'Are ye really so impatient,' Malvern asked, 'to come to my favor? To take on my form? Let us see.'

The vampire needed only one hand to hold the warden in place. She brought up her other hand and laid the ball of her thumb against the warden's eye. 'I am not your friend,' Malvern said, 'nor your partner yet. I am your liege.' Then she shoved her thumb into the warden's eye socket.

The human woman managed to scream as blood and

vitreous fluid ran down her cheek. Malvern kept pressing until the warden's face turned purple and her remaining eye rolled up in her head. Then she dropped the warden to the floor.

Clara could only watch, and slowly bring her arm down, careful not to activate the alarm on her restraint. She didn't want to do anything to draw attention to herself.

'There will be no rebellion in my lair,' Malvern said. 'Cleanse her wound, and pack it with linen.' A half-dead rushed to the door of the command center, where a first-aid kit was clipped to the wall. It brought bandages and antiseptic to treat the warden's ruined face.

'You . . . why?' the warden moaned, clutching her cheek. Her fingers moved up to probe where her eye had been. When she found nothing there she screamed again. 'You didn't have to do that! Now I'll spend eternity looking like a freak!'

Malvern glared down at her. 'Looking as I do, ye mean. I think it well. But perhaps ye'd like more hurts to remember me by? I could pluck out your tongue, ye who think it best to blare my intentions to every corner of this place. I could tear the ears from your head, or pull your nose into a new shape. Would ye like that?'

The warden shook her head violently. She fought away the hands of the half-dead who was trying to staunch her bleeding and grabbed the bandages away from it. 'No, of course not. No. That is to say . . . I. I'm sorry. I forgot myself. For a second.' She paused to shriek as she dabbed at her eye with the antiseptic cream. 'I won't make that mistake again.'

'Not if ye wish to survive 'til morning comes.' Malvern glanced up at the windows. 'Now. I really must away. Ye'll keep our hostage at her ease, I trust.'

'Of course,' the warden said, slowly rising to her feet.

157

Guilty Jen

We who live in prison, and in whose lives there is no event but sorrow, have to measure time by throbs of pain, and the record of bitter moments.

—Oscar Wilde, *De Profundis*

26.

'It means,' Caxton said, trying to explain to Gert what the vampire wanted, 'that in twenty-three hours she's going to kill my girlfriend. Unless I go and surrender myself to her. Agree to become a vampire and serve her forever.'

'That's your girlfriend?' Gert asked. She looked up at the security monitor where the same piece of video was looping endlessly. 'Huh. She's cute.'

The video monitors flicked off and Caxton dropped heavily into the guard post's sole chair. She put her face in her hands and closed her eyes. Let her shoulders fall. This . . . was bad. Up to that point her main concern had been for her own safety. Her big plan was just to escape, and let someone else deal with the hell that had descended on the prison. Caxton had been prepared well enough for that job. It was easy to keep herself alive – it just took desperation.

Now things had changed. She had a new duty to fulfil. One that would take brains.

She looked up, and over at the door they'd used to get into the loading dock. It wasn't jumping in its frame anymore.

The half-deads were making no attempt to get at them. It looked like Caxton was going to be given some time to think over Malvern's ultimatum. 'Okay,' she said, and Gert looked over at her. Gert's eyes were wide and expectant. Like a kid waiting for her mommy to tell her what to do. 'It's dawn. That's why she gave me twenty-three hours. Twenty-three hours from now will be one hour before dawn tomorrow – just enough time to pass on her curse to me before she has to go back in her coffin.'

Gert glanced over at the sky, visible through the gated outer bays of the loading dock. The sky was turning a weak yellow color and a few purple clouds were sailing by overhead. Gert nodded, as if to confirm what Caxton had said. 'Okay, that's not much time. But for right now – it's daylight! So we're safe now, right? Vampires can't do shit during the day. I saw it on the Discovery Channel once.'

Caxton squinted at her celly. 'I didn't take you as the type to watch the Discovery Channel much.'

'What, 'cause you think my family couldn't afford cable?'

'No,' Caxton said, holding up one weary hand in apology, 'I just—'

'And not just basic. We got six channels of HBO, 'cause Mom liked the Sarah Jessica Parker show.'

Caxton rubbed her face. 'Okay. I'm sorry. I didn't mean to imply anything.'

'Discovery has that show about the crab fishermen, I like that one.'

Caxton went on, hoping that Gert had finally run down. 'It is true, as you say, that vampires are harmless during daylight hours,' she said. 'But half-deads aren't affected by the sun at all. So we're still in trouble. I need to think about what we're going to do next. I have to have a little while to myself to think about that. Why don't you find someplace comfortable to curl up and catch some sleep?'

'Sure,' Gert said. As easy as that. Her mommy was going to take care of everything – she didn't need to worry. She picked a corner of the guard post and curled up there in a ball and was snoring a few minutes later.

This left Caxton alone with her thoughts. Which was problematic in itself, because she couldn't seem to focus on out-thinking Malvern. Her brain was too busy punishing itself.

She shouldn't be here, Caxton thought. Clara shouldn't have been at the prison. Caxton should have broken things off with her long ago, back when it still would have been easy. When a phone call would have been enough. Instead she'd forced Clara to come to visit her. To explain things in person, face-to-face. And then she hadn't even been able to do that. If Caxton had been a better girlfriend, if she'd recognized that Clara needed to move on—

It did not strike her as any kind of terrible coincidence that Malvern had taken over the prison at the exact moment that Clara was finishing up her monthly visit. Caxton knew enough about how Malvern's brain worked. For years now Caxton had outsmarted every vampire she met – except for one. Malvern always planned ahead. Caxton tended to improvise. As a result Malvern had won every single time, or at least, she'd gotten away. Survived. And that was what drove Malvern, her primary goal in all things – to live just one more night.

Malvern was more than capable of killing Clara when the deadline came. Any vampire would be. They didn't see human beings as rational creatures with thoughts and feelings. They saw humans as livestock. Malvern wouldn't bat an eyelash she didn't have. In fact, Caxton knew, there was no guarantee that Malvern would even keep Clara alive for another minute, now that she'd served her purpose. She hadn't claimed in her message that Clara would be around for another twenty-three hours. She hadn't said anything of the sort.

But thinking like that was going to get Caxton exactly nowhere. She had to believe that Clara would be alive for almost a full day longer. That Caxton would have a chance to rescue her.

And kill Malvern, as soon as she was sure Clara was safe.

That was essential. She'd been fighting Malvern for years, and while she'd always saved the day, and kept people from being killed – most people, anyway – Malvern had always gotten away at the last second. She couldn't let that happen again. Malvern was clearly planning something big this time. She must be drinking gallons of blood to look so healthy and strong. Caxton could guess where it was coming from. She must be draining the prison population, using them as a captive food source. The administrators of the prison must be dead or collaborating to allow that to happen. Someone in the administration – the warden, she remembered – had been IMing with someone who used the same convoluted, archaic English that Malvern was famous for. She hadn't quite put it together at the time, but it was obvious now. So this had been an inside job.

But turning the prison into her own private blood bank seemed to lack Malvern's usual elegance. Malvern always thought several moves ahead, and she must know that her time at the prison was limited. Eventually someone on the outside was going to wonder why none of the COs had come off duty and gone home to their wives or husbands. Or maybe some prison bus would show up at the front gate, loaded with new inmates, and there would be nobody to let it in. One way or another the authorities would come in force, and then Malvern would be forced to fight her way out of the prison. No matter how tough vampires were, they could still be taken down by enough cops with assault rifles. She couldn't be looking forward to that confrontation.

164

Malvern was on borrowed time. And yet she seemed in no rush. She was giving Caxton almost a full day to think over her offer. A nearly full day, half of which she would spend inside her coffin, unable to direct her minions, unable to fight for herself.

Of course, she hadn't made it too easy for Caxton. The prison was still full of half-deads, and presumably at least one living human, who would keep Caxton from getting into too much trouble. Especially since they could watch her every move, keep track of everywhere she went, through the hundreds of video cameras that monitored every corner of the prison.

Caxton jumped up and grabbed at the camera mounted to the ceiling of the guard post. It held firm, even when she put all her weight on it. Grunting in frustration, finally she grabbed the pepper spray canister out of her bra and gave the lens a good coating. It would at least ruin the camera's focus, even if it made the close air in the guard post stink of spicy food, and that made Caxton's stomach rumble.

Those cameras. She couldn't spray every single one of them. But maybe there was *something* she could do about them.

27.

After Malvern left the command center the half-deads went back to their tasks, some watching monitors, some trying to make the warden more comfortable. Her breathing was heavy and her face went very pale. She sat down heavily in a chair and put her head between her knees. For a very long time she just sat like that, not moving or speaking, while the half-deads tried to adjust her clothing or mop her forehead with wet towels. Clara stood by, watching it all, unable to do a thing to help anyone.

Then the warden sat up very suddenly and stared around the room with a wild eye. 'I'm fucking fine! Don't you dare touch me,' she shouted, one hand lashing out to smack the face of the approaching half-dead. The creature squeaked in pain and spat teeth onto the ground. It had only been trying to change the bandage on her eye. 'It's not going to have time to get infected,' the warden insisted, 'and that antibacterial shit stings like hell.'

She started to get up out of the chair, but clearly losing an eye had taken its toll on her. She nearly collapsed and had to

had been watching. Clara glanced at the screen and saw that it showed one of the prison's shower rooms, currently empty. She was too frightened for Laura to worry much about what the half-dead had seen there.

'You. Get as many others together as you can and go down to the loading dock behind the cafeteria,' the warden ordered. 'Kill Caxton.'

'No! You can't do this!' Clara howled, but no one was listening.

The half-dead's ruined face scrunched up in thought. 'But, um, Miss Malvern wanted—' it managed to stammer out.

The warden grabbed the half-dead by its shoulders. 'Miss Malvern is currently a puddle of goo in a coffin. Whereas I am very much awake and ready to pull your arms out of their sockets. Do this quietly, do it quickly, and don't give her a chance to fight back. Do we understand?'

'Yes, ma'am,' the half-dead murmured, and then headed off down the hallway at a run.

28.

'Gert,' Caxton said, softly.

Her celly woke up instantly, her eyelids snapping open and her hand reaching for the knife she'd kept tucked under her arm while she slept. 'Everything cool?' she asked.

Caxton nodded. 'For the moment. I've been busy, and—'

'What time is it?'

Caxton shrugged. 'I don't have a watch. If I had to guess I'd say it's around nine.' It had felt like about three hours since Malvern had made her dawn ultimatum. Twenty more to go.

'You think there's any coffee?' Gert asked. 'Maybe in one of these crates?'

'We wouldn't have any way to brew it,' Caxton suggested.

'Oh, I'll find a way. You know how long it's been since I had caffeine? Way too fucking long, that's how long. If I have to snort lines of freeze-dried instant, I will do it. You got me operating on three hours' sleep, I'll mainline the shit. What the fuck are those?'

She was looking at Caxton's big project. The things that

had taken her three hours to construct. The things she wasn't sure would work, even so.

As she'd said, she'd been busy. She'd had to improvise and put them together from items she could find in the loading dock. She'd started with tin cans. She had as many of those as she could possibly want. In her search for supplies she'd found a small toolkit in one of the trucks. It had included a flathead screwdriver she'd used as a can opener. Very carefully she had emptied out five big cans that had contained creamed corn. She'd scraped them out and then let them dry. Then she had broken open a couple dozen crates and pried all the nails out of their boards. She had driven nails through the walls of the cans, all around, as many as she could without buckling the cans entirely. She'd made that mistake more than once.

The final step had left her gagging and sick, but it was necessary. There had been a garden hose on the dock, presumably used to wash the trucks. With a pair of bolt-cutters she had clipped off a four foot section of hose, which she had used to siphon gasoline out of the tanks of the three trucks. There had been a lot of spillage – the loading dock still reeked of gas – but she had managed to fill all five cans to the brim and seal them back up.

Sealing the cans took some work. There'd been a big economy-size pack of chewing gum in the glove compartment of one of the trucks. She chewed and chewed until her jaw was sore and used the wet gum to hold the lids on the cans and make seals around the nails to make the cans more or less watertight.

'Homemade fragmentation grenades,' Caxton explained. 'You light one of these on fire and it'll blow up, throwing burning gas all over the place. Even better, when they go off the nails will shoot out in every direction as shrapnel. They should make a pretty good mess.'

'Well, shit,' Gert said, laughing. 'I never took you for a pyro. You're gonna blow down the main gate, huh? And then we just waltz right out of here. Or no – we can drive out, in one of the trucks. Jeez, Caxton, you're pretty smart, huh?'

'I hope so. I hope I can make them work without killing both of us in the process.' She chose not to share what she really had in mind for her big unwieldy grenades. Gert might not understand what she truly hoped to achieve.

Caxton started loading the cans inside the cab of one of the big trucks. She was careful not to slosh them around too much – not because they might explode (it would take more than rough handling for that), but because she didn't want to disturb the chewing-gum seals. They were the weak spot in her design. She thought there was a good chance that when the cans were set on fire, the burning gasoline would erupt upward and pop the lids right off the cans, rather than exploding outward and launching the nails. She would just have to hope for the best.

'Have you ever driven a truck?' Caxton asked Gert.

'Sure, no problem. Half my family had trucks,' her celly told her.

'That's good. That's a very good thing.' Caxton nodded and rubbed her hands on her jumpsuit. 'Here's what I want to do. You get in this one and get it ready to go. I'll run up to the guard post and hit the control for the outer gate, then come and join you. We're going to have to move fast. Once they figure out what we're doing the half-deads will be all over us, regardless of what Malvern might want from me. You ready?'

Gert pulled herself up into the truck's driver's seat and cranked the engine until it was rumbling along well. Caxton threw her shotgun and her stun gun in through the passenger's-side window, then jogged back to the guard post. She glanced up and saw that Malvern's ultimatum was still running over and over on the monitor. She slapped the red button on the control panel and checked through the post's window to make sure the gate was opening smoothly. When she saw it was, she reached for the post's door.

Before her hand even found the knob the door burst inward. A half-dead barreled through it, its knife high and swinging downward to cut into her heart. Caxton shouted for Gert and half-jumped, half-fell backwards, colliding with the guard post's chair. She stumbled and fell hard on her hip, one arm tucked uselessly beneath her.

It was a lousy defensive position. It was a great way to get killed, falling over herself like that.

The half-dead took a step closer to her, the knife held straight out in front of its body. Its torn face split in a wicked grin so wide that the muscles around its mouth bunched and split.

Caxton grabbed for the can of pepper spray in her bra. It felt suspiciously light in her hand and she realized she'd used it too many times. She couldn't be guaranteed there'd be even one good spray left inside.

She rolled to her left as the knife came down at her, and sprayed anyway. The can sputtered out a thin mist of capsicum and then died on her. The half-dead didn't even look annoyed.

Crap, she thought – she had put her best weapons in the truck, thinking she was safe from attack inside the loading bay. This half-dead must have been waiting just outside the outer gate, waiting for its big chance. She should have been smart enough to check outside the gate before she'd hit the red button. She should have done a lot of things smarter, she thought, as she rolled away from another blow.

She still had her baton. She yanked it free of the belt she was using as a bandolier and brought it up fast, just fast enough to parry the half-dead's next strike. The blade dug a bright furrow through the black paint on the baton. Caxton grabbed it in both hands and pushed, struggling to get back up to her feet as the half-dead tried to keep her down on the ground by pushing down with its knife.

Caxton was stronger than any half-dead – their muscles and bones were rotten and got weaker with every second their unnatural existence continued. She got one foot under her and shoved the half-dead back, sending it sprawling backward out the door of the guard post. She followed through and came down hard on it, smashing the pommel of her baton into its forehead with a grotesque crunch.

Breathing hard, adrenaline making her skin feel prickly and tight, she jumped back up to her feet and started running toward the truck.

Five more half-deads were climbing up onto its cab.

29.

'Gert,' Caxton yelled, 'get it moving! Put it in gear!'

The truck didn't move.

Caxton ran forward and grabbed at the half-dead nearest to her. It was wearing a stab-proof vest, so she grabbed the straps and hauled it bodily off of the truck. Spinning it around, she slammed her baton across the back of its head and reached for another. One of them was crawling up onto the truck's hood, using the top of the tire as a foothold. Caxton grabbed it around the neck and twisted, hard. She heard a series of pops from inside its collar as its cervical vertebrae snapped, one after the other. She knocked it to the ground and then grabbed the top of the passenger's-side window. She brought her bare feet up and slid inside the truck, landing with a bounce in the passenger's seat.

Gert was staring at her as if she'd just won the gold medal for gymnastics.

'Don't look at me! Look at them. And get this thing moving – we can shake them off,' Caxton said. A half-dead was climbing up on top of the cab while another was reaching toward Gert's window.

Gert nodded, grabbed the truck's gearshift, and pushed it forward.

The truck's engine roared for a second, then sputtered and stalled. The smell of burning gears filled the cab.

'I thought you said you could drive this thing,' Caxton insisted.

'I said I could drive a truck. Like a pickup truck. I never even sat in one of these before,' Gert told her.

Gert's window exploded inward, showering them both with tiny cubes of safety glass. The half-dead there had a hammer that he swung into the cab. Gert managed to pull back far enough that it hit the steering wheel instead of her jawbone.

Caxton cursed, then lunged across Gert's lap to grab at the hammer and the hand that gripped it. She pulled hard and the half-dead came screaming into the cab with them. Caxton punched its face and twisted the hammer out of its hand, then smashed its head forward against the dashboard. It stopped struggling then, so she pushed it out the window and moved on to the next task.

'Switch places,' Caxton said, and Gert slid toward her across the seats. Caxton grabbed her shotgun and climbed over Gert to get into the driver's seat.

Something hit the top of the cab hard enough to make a dent in the ceiling. Caxton pointed her shotgun at the dent and started to depress the trigger – then realized the mistake in that and stopped herself. The plastic bullet in the shotgun was designed not to penetrate human flesh. It certainly wouldn't pass through sheet metal. If she fired at the ceiling the bullet would bounce off, at dangerously high speed, and probably hit her or Gert.

The half-dead up there hit the roof again, and the dent got wider.

At the same time another half-dead climbed up over the

truck's grille and grabbed the hood ornament. In its other hand it held a can-shaped grenade with no pin.

'They have grenades?' Gert asked, her voice high enough to count as hysterical.

'CS grenades. They don't kill you; they're just full of tear gas,' Caxton said. She couldn't imagine the prison having any other kind of grenade in its arsenal. Not that it mattered. 'If it gets that thing in here it might as well be high-explosive. It'll pump out a hundred cubic feet of gas in a second, and we'll suffocate even with the windows open.'

'So shoot it,' Gert suggested.

'Just a—'

The half-dead on the roof of the cab struck a third time and the metal roof tore open. The sharp point of a pickax came through the ceiling between the two women. Gert screamed, but Caxton just readied her shotgun. The pick drew back the way it had come and Caxton looked out through the hole it had made. She could see the half-dead on the cab's roof. It was looking back down at her.

She shoved the barrel of her shotgun through the hole and fired. There was a scream and then a rattling series of thumps as the half-dead fell off of the cab.

'What about this motherfucker?' Gert asked, pointing through the windshield.

Caxton hit the truck's ignition, then threw it into reverse.

She'd been in the highway patrol once. She knew the importance of double-clutching. The truck lurched backward, out of the loading bay, and the half-dead on the hood went flying backward. Its grenade went off instantly in a spray of yellow smoke that rolled across the windshield. Caxton caught a whiff of the tear gas before they were clear of the yellow plume, and her eyes clamped tightly shut as her throat spasmed with a nasty dry cough.

'Grab the wheel,' she said. She knew better than to rub at her eyes – that would only smear the tear gas deeper into her mucous membranes. It hurt to talk, but she had no choice. 'Watch the mirrors. What's behind us?'

'The wall!'

Caxton forced her eyes to open up. They immediately clamped shut again. They stung like they were on fire, even when they were closed, but when she tried to open them the pain was ten times worse. 'Turn the wheel left. Toward me,' she said, as calmly as she could. 'How far is the wall?'

'I don't know. Too close,' Gert said, sounding panicked.

'We'll be okay. There might be more of them coming, so we need to move, alright?' She kept her foot on the gas a second longer, then braked to keep the truck from jackknifing, then threw the stick into forward gear. 'What are we pointed at?' she asked.

'Nothing,' Gert told her. 'But you're facing the wrong way! The main gate is behind us.'

'That's okay,' Caxton said. 'We're not going to the main gate.'

'We're not?'

'It's too heavily defended. We wouldn't make it halfway there. Trust me. I know what I'm doing.' And I'm not about to share, she thought, so don't ask any questions. She hadn't figured out yet how to explain to Gert that their mission had changed. That they weren't going to try to escape from the prison anymore. She doubted Gert would want to hear that. 'What do you see ahead of us? Open grass?'

'There's no grass. Just – just a basketball court.'

'That's fine,' Caxton said.

'But it's surrounded by a fence. With barbed wire and everything,' Gert told her.

'That's what I needed to know.' Caxton upshifted and

178

poured on the gas. 'Now, just as we're about to hit the fence – get down,' she said.

She felt Gert duck below the dashboard almost at once. Caxton leaned over to her right, covering Gert's body with her own. The truck hit the fence hard, traveling at almost twenty miles an hour.

The truck went through the fence like a knife through paper, tearing through posts and chain link and barbed wire without even losing much speed. The truck had enough mass to shear off the posts at ground level without any trouble. The fence didn't just part in the middle to let them through, however. It wrapped around the front of the truck and stretched – for a few milliseconds. Then it snapped in a dozen places at once and hundreds of pounds of metal wire and three-inch pipe came scrabbling and sparking up the hood to collide with the windshield. It shattered instantly and covered both of them in glass, while one piece of metal post shot through the cab and impaled the seat cushion where Caxton had been sitting up a second earlier.

Gert started to sit up.

'Not yet,' Caxton shouted, as the truck shot across the basketball court – and then through another fence on the far side. A coil of barbed wire dragged across Caxton's back, tearing through her stab-proof vest but missing her skin.

After that it was smooth driving all the way to the powerhouse.

30.

Caxton blinked away the last of the tear gas and blew her nose hard into her sleeve. She could see the low brick shape of the powerhouse ahead of her through the shattered windshield. There was a signpost fifteen yards away and she downshifted and braked carefully to miss hitting it, but she'd never driven a big rig before and she could just make out half of what it said before the truck plowed right into the sign and bent it over backward.

It had read WARNING: THIS AREA PROTECTED BY and then something else, something she hadn't caught before it was too late. Protected by what? Guard dogs? Land mines?

Cursing, she put the truck in reverse and gave it a little gas. What resulted was one of the ugliest noises she'd ever heard – metal grinding on metal, and wheels spinning without getting anywhere. 'Oh, Jesus,' she said. 'Can't anything ever be easy around here?' The sign must have gotten stuck in the truck's front axle. She tried gunning the engine, tried driving forward, tried hauling the wheel all the way over to one side, then back the other way, but nothing worked.

180

She switched off the engine and rested her head on the steering wheel.

The truck settled around her, its vibrations and its rumbles shutting down one by one. Eventually all she could hear was the engine pinging as it cooled down.

'I guess we walk from here,' she said.

Gert looked over at her with wide eyes. She was hugging herself and shivering.

'You alright?' Caxton asked.

'Uh-huh,' Gert said, and licked her lips. 'Just a little scared, I guess.'

'That was kind of a wild ride,' Caxton admitted. 'And I suppose you didn't see those half-deads until they were all over us?'

'Yeah, except, um, no,' Gert said. 'That stuff doesn't scare me. I've seen shit like that in the movies. It's you I'm scared of right now.'

'Me? I thought I was your road bitch.'

'Me too. Except, we had a great chance to escape back there and you didn't take it. That's not how a road bitch is supposed to act.'

'I told you, Gert, it was too well defended, and the main gate—'

Gert shook her head. 'Nope.'

Caxton frowned. 'Nope what?'

'Nope, I ain't buying that bullshit. You think I'm stupid? After all we've been through, you still think I'm some kind of down-home trailer-trash fool? I know what's going on. I know what you're doing.'

'Oh,' Caxton said. She'd hoped to put off this confrontation for a while.

'You're going to try to rescue your girlfriend. Which, you know, hoo-fucking-ray for you, big hero butch dyke, but it's

181

not what I signed on for. She's cute and all, but she's not my type. Mostly because she's got tits and no dick.'

Caxton closed her eyes. She didn't have time for this. According to the clock on the dashboard it was nearly ten – which meant she had only nineteen hours left. For what she had planned that wasn't a lot of time. 'You want to split up, then? You go your way, I'll go mine?' Caxton asked. 'The only thing between you and the outside world is the wall over there.' Which was twenty-five feet high, topped by barbed wire, and in full sight of the machine-gun nests on two different guard towers, of course. If Gert wanted to try it, Caxton wouldn't stop her.

Or – maybe she would, she reconsidered. Gert was a killer. She was in the prison for a very real reason. Caxton might not be a cop anymore, but it was her duty as a citizen if nothing else to keep Gert from escaping.

It was her duty as a celly to keep the girl alive.

Gert stared out her window, rubbing her arms as if to keep warm.

'I think, though, it's still in your best interest to stick with me,' Caxton said. 'I think that's your best chance of getting through this without dying.'

'Yeah. Even a NASCAR-watching, sweatpants-wearing coupon queen's white-trash daughter like me can figure that one out. Let's just fucking go,' Gert said, and popped open her door. A flood of broken safety glass and pieces of chain-link fence sloughed out and spilled across the ground.

Gert put one foot down, careful not to slip in the mess, and started to climb down from the cab. Then Caxton heard a noise like a six-pack of soda cans being opened one after another, pff-pff-pff-pff-pff-pff. An instant later Gert started screaming. Caxton grabbed for her celly's hands and pulled her roughly back into the cab.

'Oh my God, oh my God,' Gert howled, 'it stings – it stings so much – I think I got shot, oh motherfucker!'

Caxton pulled Gert closer and grabbed the leg of her jumpsuit. Something had indeed hit her very hard and left a white powdery residue that flaked away when Caxton scratched at it. She lifted her finger to her nose and nearly screamed herself.

Her eyes had barely recovered from the tear gas. Tears burst out from under her eyelids at the same time as she started sneezing and coughing uncontrollably. There was a distinct smell to the powder as well, one she knew all too well.

It was PAVA, sometimes also called Capsaicin II. It was made of superrefined capsaicin, the chemical in chili peppers that made them burn your mouth and made you want to die, except this chemical was two thousand times hotter than the same weight of jalapeño peppers. It was the same chemical used in pepper spray, but much more concentrated. A direct hit from that stuff on the face or chest would be enough to incapacitate anyone for hours.

Caxton squinted through the windshield and saw what was defending the powerhouse. There was a camera mounted on the front of the building, just above its door, a camera in a complicated housing that allowed it to swivel and point in any direction. Mounted just beneath the camera was a long, thin pipe painted black. It looked exactly like a rifle barrel, because that was exactly what it was.

Caxton had heard about such devices before. They'd been developed for use in understaffed prisons to deny access to sensitive areas. There was no one on the other side of that camera. The rifle was under the control of a robotic system that simply watched its surroundings twenty-four hours a day, looking for signs of intrusion on its programmed territory – and then attacked anything that moved.

It looked like the truck's cab was just inside that territory.

To get to the powerhouse, Caxton was going to have to find a way around that gun.

'Gert, Gert, calm down,' Caxton said, when she realized her celly was hyperventilating. 'Just calm down. You aren't really hurt.'

'It hurts like fucking hell!' Gert assured her.

'It didn't puncture the skin. That thing's firing pepperballs. They look like gum balls but they're just pepper spray in a casing that's designed to break open on impact. It's like it's shooting water balloons at you.'

'Yeah, water balloons full of fucking pain!'

Caxton shrugged. 'That's what it feels like to get hit with a paintball. It stings, yeah, but you'll be okay. And I need you to be okay right now.'

'What? Why? What do you want me to do now, flash my tits at the next half-dead that runs by to distract it? Maybe cut off my head so you can throw it at somebody.'

'Um, no,' Caxton said, explaining as carefully as she could. 'I need you to run out there, as fast as you can, waving your arms. To get that thing's attention and make it shoot at you. For about thirty seconds.'

31.

'You're out of your mind.'

Caxton shook her head. 'Listen, it's just a robot. It has lousy depth perception and it can never really lead a target, especially if you run in a zigzag pattern. If you keep moving fast enough, it won't be able to hit you at all.'

'Oh, boy,' Gert said. 'And I'm going to do this . . . why? To entertain you?'

Caxton picked up one of her homemade grenades. 'It can only track one target at a time – most likely the fastest-moving target it sees. I'll come out a second after you do, and make my way inside there with these. Once I'm inside you can run around the side of the building and you'll be safe. Okay?'

Gert said nothing.

'I need you for this,' Caxton said. 'I know I haven't been straight with you. I know you don't care about Clara, and whether she lives or dies. But I really need you. I need you to be useful to me, right now. I need to count on you. Because we're cellies. And cellies watch each other's backs.'

Gert stared at her for a long time, her nostrils flaring.

185

Her lips compressed as if she was trying to keep herself from saying something. Then, without a word, she pushed her door open and jumped out.

Immediately the robot started shooting at her, pff-pff-pff. Gert screamed and spun and ran with her arms up in the air. Caxton wasn't sure if she'd been hit or if she was just following instructions.

It didn't much matter, as long as Gert kept moving. Caxton pushed her door open and jumped down to the ground, the five cans sloshing in her arms as she bent over and duckwalked toward the powerhouse. The robot's gun started to swing toward her, but she just stopped in her tracks and it went back to shooting at Gert.

Moving as fast as she dared, Caxton made her way to the door of the powerhouse. It was locked, of course, but she hit it a couple of times with her shoulder and it gave way. She stepped into a dimly lit room full of machinery that gave off a crackling hum.

The prison was attached to the local power grid, but it consumed so much electricity every day that it needed its own substation, as well as backup generators in case of a power outage. The powerhouse supplied the entire facility. If she could take it down she would shut off every piece of electrical equipment inside. There would be backups on the backup systems, she knew, and eventually the half-deads would restore some kind of power, but it would give her some time to enact the next stage of her plan, time she desperately needed.

The big turbine generators and the step-down power conditioners were all locked away in cages with thick bars, and anyway she didn't think her grenades would do them much harm. Instead she found a main power coupling, where all that electricity was shunted through one thick bundle of cables that ran down into the floor. The cables would spread out underground and form a network of wires throughout the facility as tangled and complex as the roots of an ancient oak tree, but inside the powerhouse every line was gathered up in one single bundle of insulated cabling. She placed her grenades carefully around the bundle, where they could do the most damage.

The hard part about the plan was setting them off. She didn't have the equipment or the expertise to build any kind of timed detonator. Instead she had to rely on a very crude, very simple source of ignition: a Molotov cocktail.

She had found an old soda bottle in the trash can on the loading dock. She had filled it with six ounces of gasoline, then shoved an oil-stained rag into the neck of the bottle to seal it.

A Molotov cocktail on its own would do very little damage to anything in the powerhouse. The concept behind the weapon was simple: you lit the rag and threw the bottle at your target. The bottle was supposed to smash on impact, and the gasoline inside would be dispersed as a fine mist which would then catch fire from the still-burning rag. This would create a cloud of burning fuel that would last for only a few seconds before it died out. Effective, perhaps, against riot-control cops or anyone who could be psychologically damaged by the threat of being set on fire. However, a little flame inside the powerhouse would do nothing more dramatic than – maybe – melt some of the insulation on the cables.

It would, however, raise the temperature of her makeshift grenades by several hundred degrees for a split second. Which would be enough to make the gasoline inside them expand and hopefully ignite, bursting open the cans and sending the nails flying in every direction at very high speeds. That might just be enough to destroy the cable bundle and cut power to the prison.

It was an awful lot of mights and maybes and hopefullys she was looking at, but Caxton needed to take out the powerhouse if she had any hope of getting Clara out of the prison alive. She was just going to have to trust her luck.

She moved to the doorway of the powerhouse. The robot above her head was still spitting out pepperballs at high speed. There was nothing she could do about that – it was designed in such a way that it couldn't be disabled without special tools. She sent Gert all the positive thoughts she could muster; it was all she could afford. She adjusted her stance so that as much of her body as possible was outside of the door, then gripped the Molotov cocktail in one hand and her stun gun in the other.

Please let this work, she thought. *Please.* It wasn't a prayer, really, so much as a voice of desperation. She was asking herself not to make any mistakes.

She pressed the stun gun to the dangling end of the rag and triggered its test mode. A bright arc of electricity jumped across the shiny terminals at the business end of the gun. She wished, and not for the first time, that the prison didn't have a strict no-smoking policy. A butane lighter or even just a pack of matches would have made this much easier.

The rag refused to light the first time she hit it with the stun gun, and the second time. The third time a tiny ember of orange appeared on the end of the rag. It curled and bent and refused to grow, refused to start consuming the oily rag. Caxton shoved the stun gun into her jumpsuit and blew on the ember, fanned it with her free hand, willed it to enlarge, to expand.

A thin flame leapt up and then the rag caught all at once. Fire dripped from it and evaporated before it could touch the ground. Caxton threw the bottle at her grenades, at the exact same time as she threw herself sideways, out of the powerhouse doorway.

There was a noise like a barbecue grill starting up, then a second where all she heard was metal expanding under heat with tiny noises like pins dropping. Then a wall of noise and pressure hit the side of her head and rolled her over on her side. Black smoke boiled out of the powerhouse door and the orange light of flames lit up its windows.

Above her the robotic gun drooped suddenly, its camera lowering to point at the ground. Caxton got up slowly, unsure if she'd managed to cut the power. When the gun didn't follow her movements, she allowed herself a small yelp of triumph.

Then she looked over at Gert, who was lying on the ground five yards away. She wasn't moving. White powder covered most of her orange jumpsuit and all of her face. It had turned into a thick paste where it had mixed with tears and snot around her nose and her eyes.

32.

'Why can't I see anything?' the warden demanded, smacking the side of a security monitor. 'Is this the right view?'

The half-dead wearing the uniform of a CO named Franklin was standing next to her. It winced as she turned to glare at it with her good eye. 'That's the view from the loading dock, yes,' it told her. It reached up and scratched tentatively at what remained of the skin around its left ear. When Clara had first seen it, the half-dead had looked completely human except for a red scratch down one cheek. Now it had gouged all the skin away from its face until nothing remained but gray and pink muscle tissue, with here and there a pocket of yellow subcutaneous fat. It was one of the most disgusting things she'd ever seen.

'Well, make it focus or something,' the warden commanded. The view on the screen was no more than a blurred smear of brown and reddish yellow. Nothing at all could be made out of that view.

The half-dead winced again. 'The cameras focus automatically. They can't be adjusted from here. It's possible that . . .'

'That what? Don't keep me waiting, just spit it out.'

The half-dead nodded. 'It's possible she smeared something on the lens. Like Vaseline. Or lipstick. Just about anything viscous would do.'

'Pepper spray,' the warden said. 'I'll bet it was pepper spray. There's enough of it in this place to paint the curtain wall.' She smacked the monitor again. 'I need to know what's going on in that loading bay. I sent a detail down there to kill Caxton and I would very much like to know if they succeeded or not. I imagine you would like to know that as well, hmm? Because it looks like she's killing every half-dead she runs across, and if I don't find out what I need to know, I'm going to send you personally down there to check and see what condition she's in.'

Clara laughed. 'You're wasting your time.'

The warden turned and glared at her. 'You have something to share?'

Clara started to shrug, then thought better of it. The band around her arm might interpret that as a sudden move and hit her with a near-lethal electric shock. 'You can't threaten them with death. They've been there once already, and believe me, they aren't afraid to die again. It would be a mercy. You're in pain, aren't you?' she said, addressing Franklin.

The half-dead sneered at her. 'None of your business, cunt.'

'They like to talk tough. But look at its face. You think that doesn't hurt? But it can't stop itself from scratching. Its whole existence is a scab, a temporary scab over a fatal wound. They only last for about a week before they fall apart, did you know that? All that's left then is a pile of goo with maybe some eyes and fingers sticking out. And twitching. Still twitching.'

The half-dead's eyes were bright and huge as it stared at her. At its sides its hands were clutching at nothing and then relaxing, over and over again.

The warden coughed into her hand. 'She's taunting you,' she said. 'Ignore it. I don't know if she thinks that making you attack her will get her anywhere, or maybe she's just bored. Either way, ignore everything she says.'

'Yes, ma'am,' Franklin said, and seemed to relax a little.

It had been worth a shot.

Clara had come to an inescapable conclusion. Her value to the warden was very small to begin with, and it was about to evaporate. Malvern had ordered her capture for use as an insurance policy. A way to control Laura. If the half-deads did manage to kill Laura – *Please God, no*, she thought, but if they did – then Clara would be completely useless to the warden. In fact, she would be a liability. She'd seen far too much. Knew too many secrets. The warden would have a very good reason to kill her.

If the half-deads failed to kill Laura, which Clara thought was more likely, she might gain a few extra hours of life. More time to sit around watching the warden's plans unfold, more time to fret and worry and wonder just how she was going to die.

She had to do something. The risk was very high that by angering Franklin or the warden she would get herself hurt. But there were no other options. With the band on her arm she was unable to run away and unable to attack them herself. If Franklin attacked her, though, she might be able to get its weapon away from it. Then she could kill it and threaten the warden into removing the band on her arm, and then she could – she could—

The main problem with any of these theoretical plans was that she wasn't Laura. She wasn't fast, or tough. She didn't instinctively know how to fight, or when to duck, or how to escape from a bad situation. She had been a police photographer. She was learning how to do crime lab science. Nothing in her law enforcement career had prepared her for violence. She didn't even know how to shoot straight.

A half-dead ran into the room then, its mouth hanging open in shock. 'They're out of the loading bay,' it said, cowering as the warden came over to look down into its ravaged face.

'I beg your pardon?' the warden asked.

'I – just – I saw them on another camera. There's a truck. It's driving around the yard. It has to be Caxton and her partner. But they're being stupid. They're driving the wrong way. Away from the main gate.'

The warden whirled around to stare at Clara. Clara shrugged, very, very slowly.

'Do you think Caxton is that stupid?' the warden demanded.

'No?' Clara offered.

'Neither do I. She must be up to something. Or maybe she just knows I have a team at the gate, ready to kill anyone who gets close. You,' she said to the half-dead who'd brought the news, 'get back to your post. You,' she said to Franklin, 'let me see this truck.'

Franklin tapped away at a keyboard and the view on the security monitor changed. Clara moved in close to watch – nobody stopped her. On the screen was the view from a camera mounted on one of the prison's watchtowers. It showed a white tractor trailer careening across a concrete apron, with half-deads clinging to its hood. One by one they fell off and were either crushed by the truck's wheels or simply left behind, unmoving and battered.

You go, girl, Clara thought.

The truck stormed right through a basketball court, dragging two lengths of fencing along for the ride. Then it slowed to a stop outside a small brick building.

The warden, Franklin, and Clara watched silently what came next. A prisoner in an orange jumpsuit and a blue vest

– it wasn't Laura – ran toward the building and was quickly subdued by an automatic gun, her body pelted by dozens of red balls that exploded into white powder when they hit.

The camera couldn't really show what Laura was doing at the same time. The truck blocked most of the view.

'What is that building?' Franklin asked.

'It's the powerhouse. She's going to knock out our power. But how can she? She would need some kind of—'

The screen went black without warning. The lights in the room flickered off, leaving them with just the murky gray light coming in through the room's high windows. The prison was suddenly very, very quiet.

And then the shouting began. The nearest dorm was down a long corridor and through several closed doors, but still Clara could hear the faint echo of women screaming and bellowing to know what was going on. By the sound of it, more than a few of them were laughing.

The warden turned to Franklin. 'How did she do that?' she asked. She turned to face Clara again. 'How?'

'Search me,' Clara said.

'Fuck! Fuck fuck fuck! This is going to make things much harder.' Bellows grabbed Franklin by the shoulder and squeezed. 'There are flashlights down the hall in the equipment locker. Go get some. And then find somebody who knows about electrical engineering. I'll take anyone who knows how to fix a toaster. There are thirteen hundred women in the dorms; at least one of them must know how to change a goddamned light-bulb.'

Franklin ran out of the room. Perhaps annoyed by the shouts echoing down the hall, the warden closed the door behind him. 'We had to go and kill the custodial staff. Malvern said they couldn't be trusted. She was right, of course, but we could have kept at least one person who knew how this place worked. What are you—'

She didn't get to finish her thought. Her words were interrupted by an incredibly loud high-pitched alarm. It was coming from Clara's armband.

She was moving fast, and she knew exactly what was going to happen next. She had one second to stop moving, but she didn't. Instead she rushed at the warden and grabbed her up in a very close bear hug.

Clara had time to see the warden's lips curl up in a nasty sneer before every nerve in her body fired at once, jolted to life by a fifty-thousand-volt shock. The pain was beyond anything she'd felt in her life. She felt her teeth burning, felt her eyeballs dancing in her head and then—

33.

Spring came early to central Pennsylvania that year. At the university extension the students in forensic criminology were having trouble focusing during their morning physics class. Physics was probably the dullest of the subjects covered by the school – chemistry and genetics were a lot more exciting, because they had more practical applications for the work the students would eventually be doing. Too many of the students had been caught staring out the window. The trees around the quad were in bloom and more than one class was being conducted out on the grass, so the professor had relented and taken them all outside as well. They sat in a circle under a massive oak tree and held their notebooks at the ready. There had been a stiff breeze, but Clara just hugged her knees to her chest and watched as the professor took what looked like a normal metallic flashlight out of his bag and placed it in the middle of the circle.

'This one is worthy of James Bond,' he said, and got a few laughs. He was about fifty years old and handsome. The majority of the students in his class were female and he certainly didn't lack for attention, though of course Clara didn't swing that way. He handed the flashlight to Clara with a smile. 'Turn it on,' he said.

She flipped its switch and a beam of light, barely visible under the shade of the tree, lit up the side of the classroom building. She waved it around for a second to show all the students it was on.

'Notice anything about it? Anything different from a normal flashlight?'

Clara studied it carefully. 'This part is kind of strange,' she said, not sure what you called the front end of a flashlight. There was a thick ring of metal around the lens, which was divided into two pieces separated by a strip of rubber.

The professor nodded. 'Very good. Now, touch it against my arm, here.' He rolled up his sleeve.

Clara raised one eyebrow, not sure where this was going, but she did as she was told, leaning over to tap it against his bare skin.

'Goddamn it!' the professor swore, jerking his arm away from the flashlight.

Some of the students laughed. Some gasped. Clara jerked the flashlight away from him and then dropped it on the grass.

'My apologies for startling you, Miss Hsu,' the professor said, smiling again. He looked a little pale. He picked the flashlight up from where it had fallen. 'What we have here is a stun gun built into a police-grade flashlight. Pretty cool, huh? We're going to talk today about electroshock weapons. It's important you know about them because they're being used more and more in police work and you need to understand how they work and what effect they have on the bad guys. We're also going to take turns shocking each other so you all know what it feels like.'

There were a few unhappy murmurs. Then the professor

insisted that the student next to Clara take the flashlight and shock his neighbor. That student jumped up to his feet and staggered backward a few steps before laughing and sitting back down. Then he got to shock the girl next to him in the circle. It looked like Clara would be the last in line and that the professor would be the one to shock her. She pulled her knees in tighter in anticipation.

'This is actually a very weak shock, as they go,' the professor said, raising his voice to compete with the giggles and stifled screams. 'A real stun gun doesn't just sting. It causes involuntary contraction of every muscle in your body. You fall down. You bend over at the waist. You get muscle spasms in your arms that make you drop any weapon you're holding. You can see why the police like this. If someone is resisting arrest or threatening a civilian, one good solid shock can just . . . remove the problem.'

One of the students raised her hand and the professor nodded at her. 'I've heard there are problems with them, though. That there have been some deaths,' she said.

The professor nodded agreement. 'Yes, there have. The manufacturers of these weapons claim they're perfectly nonlethal as long as they're used according to strict instructions. But police officers in the field can never guarantee perfect conditions when they're using a new weapon they've had only a few hours' training in. The main thing you need to know about this is that every human body is different. A football linebacker in perfect physical shape is going to have a very different reaction to a stun weapon than an elderly woman suffering from a heart condition. The electric shock is low in amperes but extremely high in voltage: some electroshock weapons can deliver over a hundred thousand volts over a multisecond pulse. Most people will experience some muscle paralysis, a great deal of pain, and a desperate need to lie down. But the duration of those effects varies widely from individual to individual. The general rule of thumb is that a young, healthy, well-rested person will be incapacitated for a few seconds, while an older, sick or physically unfit, tired person can be out of action for several minutes. Now, Miss Hsu. Would you mind taking off your jacket?'

Clara looked up. She hadn't noticed that the flashlight had come all the way around the circle. She took off her windbreaker, then pushed up the sleeve of her sweater. 'Does it hurt a lot?' she asked. The professor leaned toward her.

She opened her eyes. Her mouth was full of hair, and it wasn't her own.

Coughing it out, she forced herself to sit up, though it hurt like hell. Every muscle down her side was sore as if she'd been working out for hours but only exercising her left arm and left leg.

There was a smell of scorched fabric in the air, and her tongue was stuck to the roof of her mouth. Carefully she pulled it free with one finger.

No, she wasn't at school. She was having trouble focusing her thoughts, but she knew – she knew she was at the prison. The prison where they had Laura locked up. And there had been . . . vampires . . . and—

'Shit,' she breathed. She looked down and saw she was still lying half on top of the prison's warden. The warden's face was twitching wildly and one arm was beating against the floor as if she was keeping time.

Clara didn't have much time. She yawned hugely – she couldn't help herself. She needed to get up, needed to get something before – she needed to get the warden's phone. And a key. The key to – the key to the band around her arm. The electroshock band around her arm.

Confusion. Disorientation. Not knowing where you were

or how you got there. That was one of the side effects of electroshock. So was crapping your pants. Clara gave the air an exploratory sniff and smelled urine but not feces.

'Oh, no,' she said, and reached one hand down between her legs. It came back dry. She'd managed to control her bodily functions, but it looked as if the warden hadn't been so lucky.

She had to move quickly.

It was coming back. Her focus was coming back. She had waited until she and the warden were alone in the room, then she had grabbed the warden, knowing the electroshock band on her arm would go off. Also knowing that whoever she was touching when that happened would get shocked as well. She'd been pretty sure that the warden, who was older than she and badly wounded, would get worse effects than she would. That she would recover more quickly than the warden, giving her some time to escape.

She also knew the warden was a tough bitch and that it would be a close thing.

She couldn't just run away, though. The band was still on her arm and she was pretty sure it had enough juice for more than one shock. If she ran now she would just get zapped again. She bent down over the warden – slowly – and went through her pockets. She found the special key that locked the band onto her biceps and removed it easily. She dropped it on the floor and then hurriedly went back to the warden's pockets and took out the woman's BlackBerry – and her pistol, a SIG Sauer P228.

Clara stared at the pistol for a while. She even pointed it at the warden's face. Surely if anyone deserved to be shot while they were down it was this woman. She had betrayed her trust and put over a thousand women at risk. She had fed some of her prisoners to Malvern. She had ordered half-deads to kill Laura.

Clara couldn't do it. She put the pistol in her pocket.

It wasn't that she didn't think the warden deserved to die, though. It was because Laura wouldn't have done it. Laura had no compunctions about killing monsters, but she'd never kill a human being, no matter how much they deserved it. Clara couldn't imagine doing such a thing, either.

So instead, she wrapped the electroshock band around the warden's arm and locked it tight. There was a heating vent in one wall of the room. She slipped the key through the vents and listened to it clunk and ding its way down into the bowels of the prison's ventilation system.

Then she went to the room's door, checked to see no one was looking, and slipped out into the hall, a free woman.

34.

The hallway was almost pitch dark. There were no windows anywhere along its length, and the only light came from an open door down at the far end. A fan of murky light spread outward from the doorway, striped or occluded now and then as a half-dead passed in front of it. Clara could hear them talking down there in their grotesque high-pitched voices. They sounded confused and frightened.

Clara was glad she wasn't the only one. She headed in the other direction, feeling her way along the wall. She wanted to run. Her body wanted to move, to get out of there as fast as it possibly could. She couldn't afford to make any noise, though. If she were discovered now the warden would probably have her killed just for revenge.

Her fingertips brushed the molding around a door. She stopped and leaned close to the door and listened, held her breath and waited to hear anything from the other side. When she was sure that no one was behind the door, she searched for its knob and then turned it slowly. The door's hinges didn't creak as it opened. That was a small blessing, and she was thankful for it.

The room behind the door was almost as dark as the hallway. There was a single narrow window high in one wall that illuminated some uninteresting furniture – a desk, a few chairs. A computer sat on top of the desk, as well as a multiline telephone, but she knew they wouldn't work, so she didn't bother with them. Laura had cut all power to the prison, it seemed. Clara wondered how the prisoners in the dorms would be reacting. They must be going crazy wondering what was going on.

She couldn't help them. Or rather, she could. She was going to help everybody, but not directly. Clara climbed under the desk and took the warden's BlackBerry out of her pocket. It was a high-end model with a full keyboard and a built-in camera. The screen lit up when she touched the space bar and it displayed a list of email subjects. Clara didn't have time for those. They would be important evidence later, when the warden was brought to trial, but for now all she needed was a cell phone. It took her a while to figure out how to just dial a phone number, but eventually she got Glauer's cell number typed in and hit send.

The phone on the other end rang once, twice, three times. Clara bit her lip and nearly switched off the phone when she heard footsteps passing outside the room. This was too important, though. Even if she got caught in midcall, she needed to get the word out to Glauer and Fetlock. On the fifth ring the call went to voice mail.

'This is Glauer. You've reached my official phone. If this is personal, call me back on my other number. If you don't know that number, it can't be too personal.'

Clara cursed silently and waited for the beep. She had practiced what she was going to say and didn't have to think about it. 'Glauer, it's Hsu,' she whispered. 'I'm at SCI-Marcy. Malvern is here and she's taken over, with the assistance of

203

the warden, um, Augusta Bellows. The whole facility is under their control and they're recruiting prisoners to become new vampires. Caxton is here, alive, and at large inside the prison walls, but she's alone and unarmed. I'm currently at large but very much alone and definitely outgunned. Get Fetlock. Get the state police. Get anybody and get up here.'

She hit *end* and pressed her forehead against the plastic screen. How long would it be before he thought to check his messages? It was a workday and she'd called his work phone. Why hadn't he answered it? It must be sitting in his car or, worse, maybe he'd forgotten it when he went in to work that morning.

She heard someone out in the hall and froze in panic. Just footsteps, and they kept going past. She wondered how long it would take Franklin or one of the other half-deads to find the warden. When she recovered from her shock, would she scream for help? Clara couldn't have much more than five minutes.

She couldn't stay where she was. They would search every door on this hallway for her, and this room would be the first place they looked. She needed to get to a different part of the prison without being detected. She supposed there must be heating ducts in the ceiling. People in the movies crawled through heating ducts all the time.

Then she realized that if people did it in the movies all the time, the person who had designed the prison might have seen it done and therefore known not to make the heating ducts big enough even for a petite woman like Clara to get into. She remembered the heating vent she'd thrown the key into: it had been no more than eleven inches across. So that idea was out. She looked up at the window above her, but it was reinforced with chicken wire and had bars on the outside.

She was going to have to chance the hallway. There was no other way.

Clara went to the door and went through the same routine she'd used when she entered the room. She held her breath and listened, and only when she was sure there was no one outside did she open the door and step outside. She closed the door silently behind her and pressed her back up against a wall.

She couldn't go down the hall toward the open doorway. She was certain there would be half-deads down there. So she had only one direction she could head. It saved her from having to make a difficult choice. She pressed on, deeper into the darkness, until she couldn't even see shadows, just uninterrupted blackness.

She very nearly walked right into a wall at the end of the corridor. Her outstretched hand knocked into it and she had to force herself not to keep walking, to stop in midstep so she didn't collide with the wall face first. When she'd stopped completely she let out a long sighing breath.

'Dupree,' someone said. 'Is that you?' The voice was high and hysterical.

Slowly Clara reached toward her pocket where she'd put the warden's pistol. It would be suicide to try to shoot now, of course – there was no way she could hit anything in the darkness, and the noise of the shot would draw all kinds of unwanted attention.

'Dupree?' the voice asked again. From closer by.

She could try to slip past the half-dead. Clearly it couldn't see her – it had only heard the sound of her hand hitting the wall, or maybe her exhalation. If she knew where it was she could just step around it and—

'Gah!' she said, a noise of pure revulsion. A hand had come out of the darkness and touched her left breast.

There was no thought process for what she did then. Clara's hands moved of their own volition, obeying a reflex as old as time. One hand grabbed at the half-dead's clothes and pulled it close to her. The other hand went over its mouth. Then she brought up her knee, right into its crotch.

It struggled and tried to bite her hand. Its own hands grabbed at her lapels, at her hair. In pure animal fear Clara grabbed its head in both hands and twisted, trying to break the thing's neck. She felt bones grinding against each other inside the rotten envelope of its flesh and felt its hands grab ever more desperately at her, but she had the element of surprise and she kept twisting, clamped her hands tighter around the half-dead's head and twisted and twisted—

And then the head came off in her hands. It felt like she was holding a squishy bowling ball. She heard the half-dead's body slump against the wall, but she couldn't see anything.

The head kept trying to bite her fingers where they covered its mouth. Clara threw the head away from herself and heard it smack the floor and go rolling down the hall.

Time to run, she thought. She'd been as quiet as she could, but surely someone had heard her outburst or the half-dead calling for Dupree. Clara pushed forward again and found another doorway. She pulled it open and ran through. The hallway beyond was better lit, though not much – an emergency light box was shedding a fading yellow glow from somewhere far down its length. She couldn't see any half-deads moving through the murky light, so she ran forward, her sensible shoes clopping loudly on the floor. Up ahead she saw a sign and as she got closer she could just read it in the gloom:

INFIRMARY
Stab-Protective Vests
Must Be Worn Beyond
This Point!

There was a massive barred gate beyond the sign. She was just going to have to find a way to get it open. She couldn't go back, couldn't—

She heard two things then, and both of them made ice cubes chatter in her blood. One was a cough, from somewhere in the shadows. The other was the BlackBerry, which chose that moment to start ringing in her pocket.

35.

'Get the fuck off of me,' Gert moaned, but her heart wasn't in it. Caxton opened another bottle of dish detergent and squirted it into her celly's eyes.

'This is going to feel pretty good in a couple of seconds,' Caxton explained as she rubbed the detergent into Gert's eyelids and then used a scrunched-up paper towel to scrape at the girl's cheeks and mouth. Gert kept trying to push her away, but Caxton held on tight. The pepperballs had left a thick pasty residue all over Gert's face that was burning her skin. It had to come off, one way or another.

When she'd scrubbed her celly's face enough she let Gert lie back on the cot and sat down herself in a folding chair. She was exhausted. She used to be able to go without sleep for days at a time, but in the SHU her body had gone flabby and her muscles had started to atrophy. Just fifteen hours to go, she thought. At the end of Malvern's deadline, either she or the vampire would be dead. Either way, she could rest then. In the meantime she had plenty of work to do.

'What the fuck,' Gert said, rolling over on the cot. It had

taken Caxton far too long to revive the girl and get the PAVA residue off her face, but it had to be done. 'What happened? What did you just do to me? My mouth tastes like ass.' She smacked her lips. 'Soapy ass.'

'You were hit in the face with a couple pepperballs from that robot gun,' Caxton explained. 'I got you out of there, but you were suffering from respiratory distress. You weren't breathing very well. So I found the prison's infirmary and brought you inside. I had a hell of a time getting the door open. Then I had to clean you up to get the pepper out of your system. The soap you're tasting is dishwashing detergent. You can't just wash capsaicin off with water – that makes it worse. You need to scrub it off with soap. Milk works, too, but I couldn't find any. They keep a ton of detergent on hand here, probably because there's so much pepper spray in the prison that accidents happen all the time. I tried to be gentle.'

'Yeah, thanks,' Gert said. She tried to open her eyes and grunted in pain. She brought her hands up to rub at her eyes, and Caxton grabbed them and pushed them back down to her sides.

'You'll just grind it in. Trust me – it's nasty stuff, but I've worked with it before.'

'Back when you were a cop.'

Caxton nodded. Then she realized Gert couldn't see her, so she said, 'Yeah. I've used pepper spray on people, a couple of times, when I needed to stop them from running away. It's supposed to be more humane than shooting them in the legs.'

'I think next time I'll try my luck with a bullet.' Gert managed to open one eye and stare up at the dark ceiling.

Caxton handed her an ice pack. The infirmary's refrigerator had gone down when the power was cut, of course, but it was well enough insulated that things in the freezer were still frozen when she opened it. 'This'll help, too. It'll take some of the swelling down.'

Gert's face was a mess, puffy and bruised. There was no permanent damage, though. That was the point of pepperballs, of course. They belonged in the middle of what police called the continuum of lethality – a rainbow of options for controlling subjects that went from demanding in a firm voice that they stop all the way up to gunning them down with automatic weapons. Pepperballs were closer to the latter, but you could live through a direct hit and eventually be fine. Well, most of the time. Caxton had read about Victoria Snelgrove, a journalism student who had been caught in the middle of a riot in Boston where the cops had used pepperballs to control the crowd. The cop who shot Snelgrove hadn't even been aiming for her, but he managed to put one through her eye. It had broken through the bone behind her eye socket and caused massive bleeding in her brain. Ambulances couldn't reach the scene fast enough because the panicked crowd wouldn't let them through. The cop who fired that pepperball had received a forty-five-day suspension without pay.

Gert had been lucky. One of the pepperballs had hit the ridge of her eyebrow. An inch lower and it could have killed her.

'You didn't just leave me there,' Gert said, sounding surprised. 'You went out of your way to help me out.'

Caxton shrugged. 'You were helping me when you got hit. It seems fair.'

Gert shook her head. 'No, sure. But you have somebody else to save, somebody you care about a lot more than me. Wasting time on me maybe makes it harder to save your girlfriend, right?'

'I don't see it that way,' Caxton said. It was just a small lie, she told herself. 'What are you getting at, Gert? Anybody would have done the same.'

210

'You ain't been inside long, you think that,' Gert snorted. 'There's girls in here wouldn't piss on you if you were on fire. And there's some people who . . . maybe you shouldn't help.'

Caxton shrugged. 'Who, like Adolph Hitler?'

Gert laughed, but she looked like she had something on her mind. 'Yes, and maybe some people who aren't as bad as that but who did real bad things. Things that can't be forgiven.'

Caxton shook her head. 'I don't know who I am to judge who's worth saving or not. Lie down and rest for a while. We'll move again soon, but you need to take it easy.' She went over to a desk on the far side of the room. She found paper and a pen and started making a map of the prison, sketching out its layout based on what she'd seen of the place from outside and what she knew about prison design, which wasn't much. SCI-Marcy was surrounded by a squarish wall with watchtowers every hundred feet around its perimeter. The prison itself was made up of eight long buildings: the five dorms, the infirmary wing, an administrative wing, and the cafeteria and kitchens, which also incorporated the SHU. Each building radiated outward from where they were connected at one end to a central tower, like rays coming out of a central sun. At the top of the main tower was the central command center. Outbuildings and covered walkways connected the buildings here and there, making the prison look from above like a half-finished spiderweb.

It was designed to be easy to get around, if you were a guard. If you were a prisoner it quickly became a maze of locked doors and heavily armed checkpoints.

She couldn't see any way around it. If she could rescue Clara and save Malvern before nightfall, that was fine. Malvern couldn't put up a fight during the daylight hours. She would be trapped in her coffin, unable to move, unaware of what was going on, and Caxton could just reach in, pluck out the

211

vampire's heart, and destroy it as she saw fit. Malvern would never even wake up. But if, as was becoming more and more likely, she needed to fight Malvern during the hours of darkness, she was going to need guns – real guns, loaded with real bullets.

There were machine guns up in the watchtowers, but there was no way for Caxton to get through all that barbed wire without a pair of wire cutters and a lot of free time. There had to be an armory full of rifles and handguns inside the prison as well. She had no concrete proof of where it might be located – it wasn't the kind of thing the guards were likely to tell a prisoner – but looking at her crude map, she saw that it could only be in one place. A riot could break out in any dorm, at any time. The COs didn't ordinarily carry lethal firearms on their persons, because it would be too easy for a prisoner to take a gun from an unsuspecting CO and kill him with it. The real guns only came out in emergencies – but that meant they needed to be available at any time. If the warden decided that the less-lethal elements of the continuum of lethality had been tried and found wanting, that deadly force was a reasonable response to prisoner violence, then the guards would need to arm themselves in a hurry and from a central location. The armory had to be on the ground floor of the central tower.

Which was where all the half-deads were, of course. It would be the most heavily defended spot in the prison, she was sure.

It was going to be her next stop.

She put down her pen and got up. Now she just had to figure out how to get there. The central tower was just on the other side of the infirmary, she knew. It was no more than a couple hundred yards away. But Caxton had already made a quick check of the prison's medical wing. There was the pharmacy, where she and Gert were holed up, and beyond that a single long room full of beds. Empty beds. There must

212

have been patients in some of those beds when the prison was overrun, but they were gone now, probably shoved in cells in one dorm or another where they could be more easily watched. Beyond the room of beds was a barred gate that she would never be able to get through, not without heavy-duty cutting equipment she didn't have.

She stretched and rubbed at the bridge of her nose, trying to wake herself up. Maybe she could go around to one of the dorms, and make her way through to—

Suddenly she stopped in place.

'What's going on?' Gert asked, grabbing her hunting knife from where Caxton had placed it under the cot.

'Shh,' Caxton hissed. She'd heard something. Someone screaming. It sounded like it came from the far side of the barred gate. It hadn't sounded like a half-dead. It sounded like a human being, in real trouble.

Whoever they were, there was nothing she could do for them, she told herself. But she kept listening all the same.

36.

The BlackBerry rang again. Clara pressed her hands over her pocket to try to muffle the sound, but she knew there was no point.

In the darkness she could feel people moving around her. Human people. Half-deads, like vampires, were unnatural creatures. You could tell when they were nearby because the hair on your arms stood up. Your skin prickled with gooseflesh, your body reacting to the sheer wrongness of the undead. The people gathering around her were human. She could only sense them by the small sounds they made. The noise of slippers dragging along the cement floor. Their breathing.

They said that when your sense of vision was impaired – say, when you were in a perfectly dark room – your other senses grew stronger. It helped a lot if you were terrified that you were about to die, Clara discovered.

The handheld rang a third time. It felt like time was slowing down. Coming to a stop. Clara expected her life to flash before her eyes.

'Aren't you going to answer it?' someone said, in the

shadows. It was not a pleasant voice, even if it had the normal human timbre. Someone else laughed and it was definitely not a nice laugh.

Clara reached into her pocket and took out the BlackBerry. Its screen lit up the darkness for a few feet around her, but not enough to reveal what was lurking in the shadows. Just enough to hurt her eyes. She fumbled with the handheld, looking for the button that would answer the call.

'Put it on speaker so we can all hear it,' the voice from the shadows instructed.

They could see her. She was sure of that. They could see her face in the light of the BlackBerry's screen. She nodded carefully. Then she looked at the glowing keyboard and pressed the appropriate buttons.

'Hsu? Hsu, are you there?' the BlackBerry demanded.

Clara bit her lip. It was Fetlock on the other end. 'Uh. Hi. Deputy Marshal, this isn't a good time—'

'So I gather,' he said. 'Glauer wasn't here to get your message. I sent him to fetch our lunch while we planned what to do about your absence. Lucky for you I monitor all of your calls, both incoming and outgoing. It sounds like you're in real trouble. I've called the local authorities for Tioga county. They're waiting for me to take the lead on any assault on the prison. As soon as Glauer gets back we'll head up there – it shouldn't take more than a couple of hours. Can you hang on that long?'

Clara gritted her teeth. 'I'm not alone right now,' she said, hoping Fetlock would take the hint. 'I can't really talk.'

'I need information, Hsu, if I'm going to put together an appropriate response strategy,' Fetlock insisted. He was not the type to take no for an answer. 'Tell me about Caxton. You said you went up there to visit her, well, that's very commend-able of you, I'm sure. You get a gold star for being a good girlfriend. It turned out to be lousy timing, though. You said Caxton was at large. Has she killed any vampires yet?'

'No,' Clara said. 'She—'

A hand reached out of the darkness and grabbed the BlackBerry away from Clara. 'She's going to have to call you back, pig. Right now she's too busy begging for her life.' Before Fetlock could say anything more the shadowy hand pressed a button to end the call. The BlackBerry's screen went dark.

A moment later it started ringing again. That would be Fetlock calling back, Clara knew. Wanting more information, even when it wasn't exactly convenient. The handheld was switched off and then disappeared from view.

'I'm warning you,' Clara said, drawing her pistol. 'I'm a federal agent. Assaulting me could get you in real trouble, you could—'

'What?' someone asked. She thought it was the one who had laughed before. 'We might go to jail?' A face loomed out of the darkness. It was grinning from ear to ear. At first Clara thought it belonged to a half-dead after all; the skin on the face was raw and irritated. Then she realized it was just burn scarring. The woman wore a pair of earrings in the shape of swastikas – no, Clara saw, those weren't earrings. They were tattoos. Gaping in horror, Clara raised the pistol and pointed it directly at the woman's burnt face. 'I will use lethal force if you don't—'

A bare foot came in from the left, fast and hard enough to break boards. It hit Clara's gun hand and she screamed in pain. The pistol clattered to the floor.

'I didn't break any bones,' the owner of the foot said. She stepped into the light and just smiled at Clara. It was the kind of smile you might see on the face of a shark as it circles a drowning sailor. Clara was disoriented by the pain in her hand, but not enough to miss the fact that this new assailant had her feet slight apart, in a martial arts fighting stance, and one fist balled at her waist, ready to punch at the slightest provocation.

There were tattoos on this one's face, dark blue prison tattoos that looked as if her eye makeup had melted and run down her cheeks. Clara looked closer and saw that they were in the shape of teardrops.

'I'm Guilty Jen,' the woman said, and gave Clara a slight bow.

Clara had taken four free lessons in Tae Kwon Do before deciding she didn't have the discipline to keep going. She'd thought they would at least teach her how to punch somebody, but instead they had just made her stand in various postures and move her feet back and forth, over and over, for hours at a time. She had, though, learned one valuable lesson about unarmed combat. If someone bows to you like that, whatever you do, don't bow back. That just means you want to fight them.

Judging by the precision and the force in the kick that had disarmed her, Clara very, very much did not want to fight this woman.

'Special Deputy Hsu,' Clara said, keeping her posture perfectly straight.

Guilty Jen's smile broadened. She relaxed her fighting stance a little. 'So you're Caxton's famous girlfriend. Well, well, well. How lucky for you that we found you just now.'

37.

'She looked younger. And skinnier,' someone said. Someone still back in the shadows. These people were smart enough not to all reveal themselves at once.

'What are you talking about, Queenie?'

'You know, in that movie. There was a whole scene of them making out. My man must have watched that scene a hundred times.'

Clara managed to blush, even though it felt like all the blood had drained out of her head and into her feet. She'd never been thrilled with the television movie they'd made of Laura's exploits. It was called *Teeth: The Pennsylvania Vampire Killings* and the actress they'd gotten to play Clara had been Japanese and underage. She'd been beautiful, frankly, where Clara always thought of herself as cute. 'They took a lot of liberties in the movie,' she said. 'It wasn't really like that at—'

'But you are Laura Caxton's significant other?' Guilty Jen asked. 'Think carefully before you answer. If you lie to me I'll break a bone in your foot. Not so you can't walk, mind. Just enough to make it hurt like fuck.'

Clara swallowed convulsively. 'I'm her partner,' she admitted.

'Caxton and I have bad history,' Guilty Jen said. 'She messed up my set pretty bad. Before I could fuck her back the hogs came in and ruined everybody's fun. Fucking hogs.'

'Hogs?' Clara asked.

'The guards here, man, you know,' Queenie supplied.

Guilty Jen nodded. 'So now I have a respect deficit with her, which is no good when I'm trying to organize things and do business in this place. If she was here right now I would just break her face and we'd be even, maybe. But she isn't. You are. Now, I can get my respect back by putting my mark on you. I have my girls train you – you know what that is, a train?'

'No,' Clara said.

'That's when they take turns fucking you. The nastiest way they can think of.'

'Oh.'

Guilty Jen's face clouded with thought for a moment. 'You might like that, though. 'Cause you're a lesbo. So maybe I just kill you, that's a pretty clear sign that Caxton can't protect her own. That she's my bitch. This is a very tempting proposition.'

Clara squeezed her eyes shut and tried to think logically. 'But – but – but you wouldn't even be telling me this,' she said, 'if you didn't have something else in mind.'

'Yeah, good point,' Jen said, as if she hadn't considered it before. 'See, things have gotten weird in here lately. Did you notice? All these vampires and shit?'

Women on three sides of Clara laughed at that.

'Bleeding everybody dry, killing some. Making lots of new rules.' Guilty Jen raised her hands as if to say, what can you do? Vampires will be vampires. 'Now, I considered offering

219

my services to that vampire, but I'm guessing she's not looking for lieutenants. What she is going to be looking for, real soon now, is hostages. She's going to have SWAT teams on top of her, and maybe worse, maybe National Guard if that boss of yours thinks you're in trouble. Worse still, she's going to have Caxton hanging on her tail, and maybe Caxton isn't as tough as me, but I understand she's hell on bloodsuckers. So our friend the vampire is going to need somebody to serve as a human shield. That's where you come in. I hand you over to her, she gives me what I want.'

'Which is?' Clara asked.

'Not much. I just want her to hold the door open while me and my set walk away. We're going to appreciate this shitstorm from a distance.'

Clara licked her lips. 'Maybe we can arrange the same result a different way. Maybe I can talk to my boss. Get your sentences commuted, get you out of here before anything happens. I can get you some money, too, and a car. That'll get you a lot farther than anything Malvern can offer.'

Guilty Jen's smile vanished from her face. 'They teach you that in cop school? Hostage Negotiation 101, offer 'em all kinds of shit, get 'em on your side, then when it all turns out to be a lie you shoot 'em in the back while they're running away, thinking they're home free? Yeah, I bet they teach you that trick. What they should teach you is that I am not fucking stupid.'

Guilty Jen's hand lashed out and Clara's head snapped back, fast enough and hard enough that she worried she would get whiplash. It took a second for the pain in her cheek to arrive, a hot blossom of agony that grew and grew.

'Okay,' Guilty Jen said. 'Lesson learned. Let's move. Featherwood, what's it look like out there?'

The burned woman was over near the door. She cracked it

open for a quick peek, then said, 'Looks clear. Those ugly sons of bitches were running around like welfare moms on a first Monday two seconds ago, but now they've cleared out.'

Guilty Jen nodded. She scooped up the pistol off the floor and put it inside her jumpsuit, deep enough that no one could just reach in and grab it away from her. 'We need to get some-place we won't be interrupted. Lucky for us, my crew here've been in and out of Marcy so many times they got the place memorized. There's an interrogation room up on the second floor of the admin wing. There won't be anybody there, and it's nice and quiet.' She gave Clara a knowing glance. 'Soundproofed.'

The women under Jen's charge moved quickly and silently through the dark corridor that led back toward central command. They acted like a trained military unit, effortlessly responding to their leader's hand signals. There was one excep-tion, though, and it wasn't a woman. Jen had a CO under her care as well, a living human prison guard still dressed in his navy blue uniform. He had some bad cuts on his face and his hands were bound behind him in plastic handcuffs. He moved like it hurt him to do so. Jen made him keep pace with the others by repeatedly jabbing him in the kidneys with his own collapsible baton. Occasionally he would shoot a glance Clara's way, as if imploring her for help, but every time she returned his gaze he just looked away as if he were embarrassed to have anyone see him in this condition.

Clara could sympathize.

Jen led them down a side corridor and through a pair of swinging doors. For a minute they were outside, walking under a covered walkway. Barely a hundred yards away was the wall, separated from them by first fenced-in exercise yards, then three layers of razor wire. Clara looked up at a watchtower, hoping there would be someone there, someone she could signal to, but even if there was someone up there it would probably be a half-dead, and she didn't want them to know where she was.

Back into the prison, then, back into darkness. They climbed a flight of stairs without any light at all, Clara banging her shins again and again but not daring to even gasp in pain. At the top of the stairs they passed through a short corridor and into the promised interrogation room. It wasn't much to look at. There was a simple wooden table and two chairs. One chair had nylon restraints dangling from its arms and coiled around its legs. The walls were covered in a flocked wallpaper that would eat up any sound. Light came from a pair of very narrow windows in one wall. The glass inside the windows was reinforced with chicken wire, even though the windows were too thin for even a child's hand to pass through.

There was a stain on the table that could have been a very old coffee spill or dried blood. Guilty Jen hopped up on the table and pulled her legs into an easy lotus position.

'Who are you?' Clara asked, when the door had been closed. 'I mean – how does someone like you end up doing all this?'

Guilty Jen just smiled. 'Featherwood, Queenie, you get lunch going. I'm starved. Maricón, you're on guard duty.'

The woman called Maricón was a Latina wearing pronounced lipstick and mascara – at least on her good eye. The other one was covered in a thick bandage.

'Okay,' Clara said. 'Can you tell me why you call her that? I know that word, it's Mexican slang for a . . . for a male homosexual.'

'I call her Maricón because she wears so much makeup, she looks like a drag queen.' Guilty Jen's eyes narrowed. 'Don't get any ideas, though. She plays for the straight team. So do we all. If you try to cop a feel or kiss one of us—'

Clara held up her hands in surrender. 'Don't worry. I'm not

exactly turned on at the moment. What about Featherwood, how did she get her name?'

'That's what the Aryan Brotherhood call their women. It's a nicer version of what they call each other – Peckerwoods.'

'Charming.'

'Queenie gets her name the same way. In the black gangs they call their women queens. That's a little more like it, right?' Guilty Jen smiled. Her hands rested palm up on her folded knees. It looked like a posture she'd spent a lot of time in.

'Will you tell me how it is that you and your set aren't locked up right now? I didn't think the warden was the type to just leave one of the cells unlocked.'

The male CO looked up as if his name had been called.

'Marty here helped us out. Didn't you, Mart-o? He brings in the drugs, I sell 'em, we split the money. Until now. Now I'm on top. Yesterday, when everything went bad, right? Marty came and saw me. He asked me for protection. Can you believe that? He knew that COs were going missing all over the place. He tried using his radio for help, but he just got the sound of some asshole giggling in his ear. He knew I was his best bet. So he came to our cell – me and my set, we all got jungled up together in one cell, sweet, right? *That* took some cash money to arrange. Marty came to our cell and we invited him in. He locked himself in there with us and sat tight. Some dude with his face hanging off came by looking for him, but we hid him under some bedding and eventually the dude went away. Then, when the coast was clear, we used Marty's keys to get out of the cell. Now he's one of us, one of the set. Of course, we had to beat him in, a little, and one or two of the girls had some fun with him, but he's my property and I'll keep him safe. You just think of me as your mommy, Mart-o. Mommy's gonna keep you all safe and clean, won't let anything happen to you, isn't that right?'

'Yes,' Marty said, enthusiastically.

'Yes, what, bitch?'

The CO glanced at Clara, but only for a split second. 'Yes, Mommy.'

Guilty Jen laughed. 'Marty's down. Marty's my Tiny Gangster, gonna come work for me outside when this is over. He sure as hell can't ever work as a screw again, not after what he's done the last twenty-four hours.'

Queenie and Featherwood had been hard at work preparing a meal while Jen was talking. None of them had eaten since Malvern took over the prison, and they needed their strength if they were going to keep moving. They had produced from somewhere a carefully prepared tin can and a couple of packets of ramen noodles. One of the cans had been wrapped around and around with toilet paper, maybe a whole roll, meticulously pulled tighter and tighter until it looked as dense as wood. When it was lit on fire it burned slowly but with a good orange flame that didn't give off too much smoke. Soon water inside the can was boiling and the women dumped in the noodles, adding bits of hot dog and a couple dozen packets of ketchup. The result was a nasty, gooey mess that bore some distant resemblance to spaghetti and meatballs. The amount of time and energy it must have taken to get the meal together astonished Clara, but then she supposed when you were serving a long prison sentence there wasn't much to do except wrap toilet paper around cans and steal extra ketchup from the cafeteria.

'You want some of this?' Jen asked, after she'd had the first serving.

Clara had to admit she was hungry. She hadn't eaten anything since before her visit with Laura the day before. 'Yes,' she said. 'Please.'

'Too fucking bad,' Jen said, and laughed, spraying bits of wet noodle in Clara's face. 'There ain't enough to go around.'

224

Clara had been wondering who this woman was, who had the discipline and willpower to master a martial art and the natural leadership abilities to form a gang out of women of different races and backgrounds, and yet still had been desperate enough to resort to criminal activity for her livelihood. Now she was beginning to see.

Guilty Jen was a sociopath.

38.

Gert's finger strayed along a row of boxes on a high shelf. She had a playful, quite innocent expression on her face.

It was not lost on Caxton that they were holed up in the prison's pharmaceutical dispensary, nor that Gert had a history of substance abuse. Caxton was a cop and she knew all about people with drug problems. 'Don't,' she told her celly, and got back to work.

Gert shrugged. Whistled a few notes. And then went back to browsing the shelf. 'There's some good stuff in here.'

'I'm sure it's fantastic. You don't need it. Why don't you come over here and help me? It'll make it easier not to get distracted.'

Gert thrummed her lower lip. Then, as if she were just playing with it, she picked a box off the shelf and closed her hand around it.

'Did you think I didn't see that? What have you got?'

Gert pouted. 'Like I said, good stuff. As in, good for you. It's just Excedrin, okay? That's like aspirin, and I have a really bad headache.'

'There's real aspirin over on this side,' Caxton said. 'Excedrin is full of caffeine. Anyway, if you do have a headache it's just because you haven't eaten in a long time. Have some of this.' Caxton had found a brown bag in the bottom of the dispensary freezer, under all the bottles of insulin. At first she'd been wary to open it, but when she had she'd found inside a green salad, a soggy hamburger, and a beautifully ripe, non-rotten apple. One of the doctors or nurses who worked in the dispensary had apparently brought their lunch to work and never had a chance to eat it. Caxton had been ravenous, enough to eat it all herself, but she'd been very careful to only take half and leave the rest for Gert. It remained untouched on a table next to Caxton's elbow, beckoning to her.

'I'm not hungry. Anyway, what's wrong with a little caffeine now and again? Millions of people all over the world drink coffee all day long and nobody gives them shit for it. You're one of them, aren't you? I bet you got a real Starbucks habit, Caxton. I bet you're just jonesin' for a double tall frothy latte mocha grandecino, or whatever.'

Caxton had never been much of a coffee drinker. She would, in fact, have given one of her weapons in exchange for a two-liter bottle of Diet Coke. She wasn't about to admit it.

'So how is it fair, huh? I need a little help sometimes. I got clinical depression and shit, um, chronic fatigue syndrome. I got drains on my energy you could not believe, and out of all the people in the whole world, I am the one, the only one, who can't have a goddamned motherfucking Excedrin?'

Caxton sighed. She remembered the sign posted on their cell door. STIMSON, GERTRUDE. NO STIMULANTS.

'And besides, we're not exactly in the middle of chill time, here. We are in one bona fide emergency situation. You and I could both benefit from getting amped up right now. It improves your reaction speed. Makes you stronger and faster and it helps you think. I could really use something right now to help me think, how about you?'

Caxton sighed again.

Gert had a point. A very good point. Which was always the problem with junkies. They weren't insane. They were quite rational. They just needed something their bodies couldn't supply on their own. Needed it enough that they felt that need, all the time, in the back of their heads. Like a little man back there, a quiet, unassuming little man who just every once in a while would raise one finger in the air and say, 'Excuse me, but if you aren't too busy . . .' Junkies could develop extremely convincing reasons why they needed their fix. They could explain those reasons patiently to anyone who was listening, at great length, and eventually, always, they could wear down the resistance of whoever it was they needed to get past, whoever it might be who had access to the drugs.

Unless that person happened to know that the calm, reasonable person in front of them was, in fact, a drooling drug fiend underneath.

'You did methamphetamine outside, right? How'd you do it? Snort it? Inject it? Pills?' Caxton asked.

Gert's face didn't betray her at all. She didn't look embarrassed or like she'd been caught out when she said, 'You know, however it came. I wasn't particular.'

'And now you have bad teeth. At the age of twenty-two. You've probably got all kinds of health problems – liver, kidneys, pancreas. How long have you been clean?'

'Since I been inside. I had a little party, I guess, the night before my trial date came up.' Gert twisted her head around until she wasn't looking at Caxton. 'Listen, I heard all this stuff before. Every day I'm clean is a day of freedom, right? But that's a fucking joke. You can't be free if you're locked

228

up. So what does it matter? I'll be clean outside, then I'll really be free. I will show you, I will show the world, that I can do it. And then I will find some nice guy, some guy with green eyes, maybe. I always wanted a baby with green eyes and red hair. And I will be the best mother who ever lived. But that's all in the future. That's if we survive through the night. Right now, I'm looking at almost certain death. I'm looking at the inside of a prison, still, even though we kinda broke out. I cannot imagine why I would try to be squeaky clean right now.'

'No,' Caxton said. She pulled a strap through a buckle and pulled it tight with a loud snap.

'It's just headache medicine!'

'No. Come here.'

Gert shuffled closer. She threw the box of Excedrin down on the cot next to Caxton. Caxton grabbed it and shoved it inside her jumpsuit. It was important not to leave it out where Gert could see it. Where she might try to grab it again.

'Here,' Caxton said, and handed a pair of restraints to Gert. 'Look at this. It's pretty simple. Just a nylon strap, about twenty-eight inches long. Holes all down its length. On one end there's a buckle.'

'Yeah, I can see that,' Gert said.

'Good. This is a restraint. They used them to keep the prisoners in their beds while they were here receiving treatment. There are a whole lot of them in this box.' She kicked the cardboard box at her feet. It was big enough to hold a wide-screen television set. 'Watch what I do.' She took two of the restraints and fed the loose end of one through the buckle of the other. She closed the buckle on a hole about six inches along the restraint, then tied the dangling end in a tight knot around the buckle. When she was done she held up the joined restraints and snapped them. 'As good as a climbing rope, right?' She repeated the process with a third restraint. She already had six good lengths going. When she joined them together they would form a rope twenty feet long. 'We need about fifty or sixty feet. Help me.'

Gert sat down hard on the cot and picked up a couple of restraints from the box. Caxton watched her carefully as she put them together.

'Good.'

'You know, caffeine can improve your manual dexterity,' Gert suggested. 'I could do this a lot faster if I—'

'No,' Caxton said, and snapped another pair of joined restraints.

Eventually they had a rope.

Caxton led Gert out into the hospital ward, where the empty beds lay on either side of a narrow aisle. Together they looked up at the ceiling. The hospital wing was the same height as the other buildings that comprised the prison, but unlike the other buildings only had one floor. That meant the ceiling of the ward was twenty-five feet above their heads. A complicated tangle of pipes and lighting fixtures ran along the ceiling, suspended from thick metal brackets every few feet. Almost hidden among the lights were a row of skylights. There were no bars on the skylights – the architects of the prison had probably thought no prisoner would ever be able to get up there, not without a stepladder. Caxton had searched the infirmary from end to end and had completely failed to find a stepladder of any kind.

Her rope was going to have to do instead. She hoped it would hold her weight.

'Find me something heavy but small to use as a weight,' Caxton said, unreeling her makeshift rope length by length. Gert came back with a metal bedpan. 'Fair enough,' Caxton said. There was a hole punched in one side of the bedpan, perhaps so it could be drained or attached to a catheter. Caxton fed the end of her rope through the hole, then tied it tight.

She looked up at the skylight closest to her. There was a thick pipe running alongside it, as well as a cluster of light fixtures. Caxton paid out a little line, got a good swing going, and cast for the pipe.

The bedpan sailed up between the lights and clanged off the side of the pipe. Gert ran madly to avoid getting hit as it came back down.

Caxton hadn't really expected to get the range right the first time. She took a step back, gathered her line, and tried again. The bedpan went over the pipe this time – and got stuck. It was wedged between the pipe and the ceiling.

Gert started to cheer, but Caxton shook her head and pulled hard on the rope. The bedpan came loose and fell down to hit one of the beds. It bounced off and clanged on the floor. 'Third time's the charm,' Caxton promised. She reeled in her line, swung, and cast. This time the bedpan went right through the gap between the pipe and the ceiling and came down the far side, dropping like a stone. Caxton let the line play out between her hands, then grabbed it before it could get away from her.

'Tie that end to one of the beds. That should be heavy enough to act as a counterweight,' Caxton told Gert. When her celly had done as she asked, Caxton grabbed hold of the other end of the rope and started climbing.

The buckles creaked. The nylon straps groaned. It held. It was even better than a real rope, because it had hand- and footholds every few feet along its length. She was feeling pretty good about herself when she reached the pipe and got an arm around it. Getting what leverage she could, she swung and kicked at the skylight. It was made of dirty, sun-damaged transparent plastic and it cracked when she hit it, even with her bare feet. One more swing and she knocked it right out of its frame. The way to the roof was clear.

'Gert, your turn,' she called. 'It's an easy climb. You know how to climb a rope, right?'

There was no answer. Caxton looked down and couldn't see Gert anywhere in the ward.

'Gert!' she shouted. 'Gert! You get out here right now, or I'll leave you behind!'

Gert came running out of the dispensary when she heard that. She looked up at Caxton with the eyes of an innocent fawn, who had definitely not been doing anything bad.

There was nothing Caxton could do about it. She told Gert how to climb the rope, and waited for her celly to join her up by the pipe.

232

39.

Maricón winced a little as the needle dipped in and out of the skin on the back of her hand, but she didn't make any noise. Queenie kept glancing up at her face as if worried she were hurting Maricón. Then she would dip the needle into Maricón's hand again and leave another dot of ink.

The needle, a normal mundane sewing needle, was held in the barrel of a ballpoint pen, and wrapped around and around with a piece of thread that had been soaked in the ink. The ink cartridge from the pen had been cut open to get the blue ink inside, which was mixed with cigarette ash for color and saliva to keep it from drying up as the thread was dragged through it again and again until it was dripping.

The only concession toward hygiene the women made was to hold the needle under a lighter flame until it was black with soot – which darkened the ink, as well. Clara had cringed more than Maricón the first time the needle pierced the Latina's skin.

This was going to be a cover-up tattoo. Maricón had several tattoos already, some of them done professionally but a lot of them done in this same makeshift fashion. Her prison tattoos tended to be simple, usually just a string of letters – coded gang marks that you had to know how to interpret. 'ALKN' meant Almighty Latin King Nation, Maricón had told Clara, while 'PV' stood for Por Vida, for life, meaning Maricón would die before leaving her gang. The one Queenie was covering up read 'BO,' for Brown Only, and that was unacceptable in Guilty Jen's mixed-race set. So Queenie had drawn a new logo over the faded letters. The new tattoo read 'GJ,' for Guilty Jen, with a crude teardrop dangling from the hook of the J.

'You're up next, Featherwood,' Maricón said, squinting a little as the needle scratched on her hand. 'That Nazi bullshit on your ears.'

'Don't remind me,' Featherwood said. She was standing guard by the door, listening for the sound of anyone moving out in the hallway. 'Anyway, maybe it should be Marty who gets the next one.'

The former CO, who was crouching in one corner as if he was afraid he was about to be beaten, didn't even look up. Clara had tried to talk to him briefly before she realized he wanted to be left alone. When she asked him if he was okay, if the set had hurt him too much, Guilty Jen's eyes had lit up. She was just waiting for a new sign of weakness from him, something she could use to twist him deeper into her clutches.

Now she'd found an opening. 'What about it, hog? You down with me, you gotta wear my name on you somewhere. How about on your forehead, would you like that? Or the palm of your right hand. You can get a lot of respect for ink on your palm, you know. It's supposed to be the place it hurts the most.'

Marty glanced up but studiously avoided making eye contact.

'How about on his balls?' Queenie asked, and the women

234

had a good laugh at that. 'You know,' Queenie added, 'if he can find them again.'

Clara thought she should try to defuse the situation. If Marty reacted, the women would hound him mercilessly – but if he didn't react at all, they would probably hurt him just to make him react. 'That's real loyalty,' she said, louder than she'd meant to. 'Getting Maricón to cover that one up.'

Guilty Jen turned very slowly to look at Clara. Then she got down from the table, moving like a cat, and came over to where Clara sat against one wall. She started to crouch down in front of Clara, then swung around to make clawing motions at Marty while stomping one foot on the floor.

The ex-CO jumped. Not much, but enough to get another laugh.

'My bitches are color-blind,' Guilty Jen told Clara. 'That's the first thing you get rid of when you join my set. It don't help nobody, hating on people of color. That right, Featherwood?'

'That's right, Jen,' Featherwood agreed. 'You helped me see that.'

'I'm impressed,' Clara said. 'I know most gangs in prison gather around racial lines, because—'

'What the boys do in their gangs is bullshit, and it means nothing to us. When you got a dick, you lose the ability to think straight.' Guilty Jen crouched down easily next to Clara. 'Sometimes I think you dykes have the right idea. No men around to fuck things up, no men to play stupid games about who can piss farther or make the smellier fart. Women join gangs for protection, that's all. They don't really care, deep down, if your hair is straight or kinky. They know life is more complicated than that. Oh, they can memorize the bullshit lines the men hand them, about racial purity this, and ten thousand years of history that. They can talk it back to you all day. But they join the gangs in the first place because they

235

want somebody to watch their back. So they don't get stabbed over some drama they didn't even start.'

'Is that why Queenie joined up with you?' Clara asked. 'Or Maricón?'

'No,' Guilty Jen said. 'They came to me because they wanted some respect. They wanted to respect themselves. They wanted to share the respect I get. I taught 'em that, that there's more to life than being safe and protected. Anybody can take a beating if they have to. Maybe they don't believe it at first, but they learn. Not just anybody can fight back, get revenge. That's where respect comes from. These girls know I'm tougher than anybody else they're likely to meet. They know if somebody disses them, somebody puts a hand on their stuff or maybe grabs their ass in the showers, they know I'll be there to kick that somebody's teeth out. That's respect.'

Clara looked at the women of the set. Featherwood's face was scalded. Queenie's jaw was puffy and bruised, and when she tried to eat it hurt her too much to chew. Maricón was wearing thick bandages over one eye. 'You must have kicked a lot of teeth out for these three.'

'You shoulda seen Carol, she had her leg snapped,' Maricón said. 'And Shanice, she's gonna get plastic surgery on her nose, they said, 'cause they didn't set it until it was too late. They were both in hospital when this shit came down. Thanks to your girlfriend.'

Clara's mouth formed an *O*. 'I see,' she said. 'It was Caxton who did all this. And yet – the last time I saw her she was just fine.'

Guilty Jen's face remained calm. Her eyes didn't widen, her nostrils didn't flare. But down by her side, she brought the fingernails of one hand together and then flicked them apart violently. This was clearly a sore spot.

236

'She'll get what's coming to her. She's going to die, there's no question about that. In fact,' Guilty Jen said, and she started to smile again, 'I think we might be able to do a little worse than just kill her, now that we have you. Like maybe, we get her to come in, turn herself in, whatever, for the vampire, and then, just as she's about to get her blood sucked, I cut your throat while she watches. That would work for me.'

Clara felt the skin crawl up and down her spinal column. She had no doubt that Guilty Jen was capable of carrying out her threat.

The phone in her pocket rang then and saved her from having to think anymore. She knew better than to grab for it, and instead let Guilty Jen take it from her. The set leader put it on speaker so everyone could hear.

It was the warden on the other end this time.

'Hsu,' the woman said. 'You're going to die. Do you under-stand me? There's no way out of this that doesn't involve me drinking your blood. I know you can hear me. I watched you take my phone. I couldn't stop you, but I saw everything.'

Clara looked up at Guilty Jen, who shook her head.

'Hsu's here, alright,' Jen said, 'but I'm doing the talking. You know me, Augie. This is Guilty Jen.'

'Oh yes? She went to you for protection?'

'Not exactly,' Guilty Jen said. 'More like I agreed not to kill her on the spot because I figured she might be worth something to you. You want her back? It's going to cost you.'

Clara shook her head. If Guilty Jen turned her over to the warden now it would be all over – the warden would kill Clara immediately. If she could hold out for a few more hours, though, until Fetlock and his SWAT teams arrived, then maybe, just maybe, she would stand a chance.

'You name your price, I'll meet it.'

'Simple. My set and I walk free out of here, no strings

attached. You provide civvies for us to change into, and a car, and you never see any of us again.'

'I doubt that, if you mean you won't be coming right back here the next time a deal goes bad or you get bored enough to kill somebody. But I won't be here then, so fine. Bring her down to—'

Clara had been mouthing, *No, no,* and shaking her head enough to make Guilty Jen at least hesitate. 'Hold on,' she said, and pressed *mute*. 'You got something on your mind, Hsu?'

Clara nodded. 'Listen. She's lying to you. She can't guarantee anything that you want. She's not in charge here anymore. It's the vampire who's running the show. If you turn me over now the warden will kill me. That will just infuriate Malvern. She'll hunt all of you down just because you thwarted her plan. They know all about respect, too,' Clara said. It probably wasn't true. Malvern was far too smart to waste time on petty debts – but Jen didn't need to know that.

'It means waiting until nightfall, right? The vampire's in bed right now.'

Clara glanced at the screen of the BlackBerry. 'It's almost three now. That's only a couple of hours. You give me to Malvern instead, and she will be very grateful. She's the one who really wants Caxton, not the warden.'

Guilty Jen thought about it for a second, then took the BlackBerry off mute. 'Okay, Augie, we'll bring her to wherever the vampire is at dusk. I'll hand her over directly to the vampire. You have our stuff waiting.'

'You're making a mistake, Jen,' the warden said.

'I don't make mistakes. I make corpses,' Guilty Jen replied. 'You want me to make one out of Hsu right now? 'Cause I will.' And then she ended the call.

Malvern

My limbs are bow'd, though not with toil, But rusted with a vile repose, For they have been a dungeon's spoil . . .

—Lord Byron, *The Prisoner of Chillon*

40.

The sky overhead was blue, with only a few fat clouds scudding by high above. After the gloom and oppression of the prison's interior Caxton's eyes had trouble adjusting.

Caxton climbed up onto the roof and held on to the edge of the skylight to keep from sliding off. The infirmary had a pitched, shingled roof that was far too sloped to allow her to stand up.

She helped Gert up and clutched the back of her jumpsuit to keep her from falling. She pulled her makeshift rope up through the skylight and wrapped it around her waist inside her jumpsuit. You never knew when you might need a rope again. Then she craned her head around to look at the central command center, which sat atop the prison's central tower like a UFO on a pedestal. Windows ran all the way around its circumference, and its roof was studded with searchlights, machine-gun nests, and communications antennae. She could see a little bit through the windows and it looked like there was no one inside.

'We've caught a real break,' Caxton said. 'Don't look down.'

Gert was looking at the edge of the roof, down below her dangling feet. If she slid it would be a long way to the ground. She probably wouldn't die from falling twenty feet, but she would most likely break a leg or an arm. Caxton couldn't afford to let either of them fall.

'There's nobody up in central command right now. I cut the power so they couldn't watch us on the security cameras,' she explained. Gert hadn't bothered to ask why Caxton had felt it necessary to blow up the powerhouse – she'd just assumed her celly knew what she was doing. 'They have no idea where we are. And it looks like, without power to run the equipment up there, they didn't think it was worth it to have anyone up there just staring out the windows. If they did, we'd already be in trouble.'

'I think we've got plenty of trouble as it is,' Gert said. She sounded like she was breathing heavily. Caxton wondered if she had a fear of heights. If she did, this next part of the plan was going to be tough. The best way to make somebody afraid of heights, though, was to put them up on a roof and ask them if they were scared of falling off, so she kept the thought to herself.

'We need to make our way over there,' Caxton said, tilting her head toward the central tower, 'and then find a way in. It'll be easy if we work together.'

'You're going to teach me how to fly?' Gert asked.

'No. We're going to walk. Two people can do that, but one can't. So you have to do exactly what I say, alright?'

'Sure.' Gert looked into Caxton's face. There was something funny about her eyes. 'You got it. I do what you say, and I don't die. I like that part of the plan. The part where I don't die.' She glanced down the slope of the roof again. 'Can we just do it now, then? Just, like, right now?'

'Sure,' Caxton said. 'Don't forget to breathe.'

Gert nodded and took a few deep breaths. It seemed to calm her a little.

'The roof is too steep to walk on, as you've already noticed,' Caxton said. 'But if we stand on either side of the peak, we can counterbalance each other's weight. You stand on that side, I'll stand over here. We hold hands – hold on really tight – and neither of us will fall. If you let go—'

'I won't let go,' Gert assured her.

'Good. It's also important we walk at the same speed. So.' She held out her hand and Gert grabbed it. Careful not to overbalance, Caxton rose slowly to her feet and watched as Gert did the same. The grip on her hand quickly became painful, but Caxton ignored it as best she could. 'Left foot forward.'

Gert moved her foot carefully, her toes grabbing at the shingles. Caxton moved her own foot.

'Right foot, now. Left.'

'Hold on! Okay,' Gert said, having taken her first full step on the roof. She looked over at Caxton and started laughing. Laughing a little too much. 'I got it. Left, now. Now. Right, now, left.'

'Slow down, Gert,' Caxton said. 'Let me catch up.'

'This is easy!' Gert laughed again. 'Left, uh, and—'

Caxton's right foot went out from under her. The shingles were old and weatherworn. One had crumbled underneath her. She fought to get her balance, hopping on her left foot as Gert dragged her forward.

'Right! Left! Right, left, right! Woohoo! Left!'

'Gert!' Caxton called, sliding along the shingles, her feet barely finding purchase. If she lost her grip with both feet at once they would both fall. 'Gert, stop for a second. Gert!'

But Gert was nearly running along the shingles, swinging her legs high. Her hand crushed Caxton's in a grip that kept getting tighter and more painful.

'Left, right, right! Ha ha, I tricked you on that one,' Gert said, hauling Caxton forward. Caxton started to scream—

And then she stopped. They had reached the edge of the roof. Beyond was a five-foot drop to a flat concrete roof that covered a walkway leading into the central tower. Gert jumped down without a care in the world, letting go of Caxton's hand.

For a long, drawn-out second, Caxton was all hands and feet as she grabbed at the shingles, trying desperately to hold on. The shingles cracked and fell apart as her toes dug into them. Her fingers found exposed nails and clutched to them as handholds, but she was falling, she could feel herself slipping, it was a losing battle trying to—

Gert grabbed her by one arm and one leg and hauled her down onto the flat roof of the walkway.

'Now, that's teamwork,' she said.

Caxton rubbed at her arm where it had been dragged across the edge of the roof. Her hand was numb where Gert had been gripping it and her feet were raw and red. But she was alive and she had made it down from the roof.

'Come on,' she said.

Ahead of them, in the wall of the central tower, was a window looking into an empty room. There were no bars on it, though it was thicker than an ordinary window and not quite as shiny as glass. Caxton rapped it with her knuckles and listened to the sound it made. 'Bulletproof. We'll never break through,' she told Gert.

'What?'

Caxton stared at her celly. Gert's face was bright red, with sweat slicking down her temples and glistening on her chin. Her pupils were enormous, with only a tiny ring of brown showing around them.

'What? No. Goddamn it, no. I did't come all this way to—'

244

Instead of finishing her sentence, Gert slammed her shoulder against the window, again and again.

'Gert! Stop,' Caxton commanded.

The girl stopped immediately. Then she dropped down to sit on the concrete and started chewing on her fingernails.

'You took something,' Caxton said.

'What?'

Caxton grabbed Gert's sweaty chin and pulled it up so they were looking at each other. 'Back in the dispensary. You took something when I wasn't looking. What was it?'

'I don't know whatcher talking about,' Gert slurred.

Caxton groaned in frustration. She didn't know whether to make Gert throw up or just let her burn it off on her own. Without knowing what kind of stimulant Gert had taken, there was no safe answer to that question.

She would have to worry about it later. In the meantime she studied the window. It was fitted perfectly into its frame, which was set deeply into the brick wall of the tower. There was nothing to grab hold of, nothing she could bend or break. It was built in two sections, one of which was designed to slide over the other so it could be opened, and . . . and . . . the latch wasn't locked.

Caxton put both palms against the sliding section of the window and pushed. It opened almost effortlessly, sliding along a well-greased rail.

She climbed inside, and dropped easily to the floor of the room. Gert followed a second later.

41.

Gert leaned up against the wall, next to the room's only door, and stood there, giggling. She had her hunting knife in her hand, holding it tight until her knuckles turned white around its handle. 'This is. This is. This is. It. Right?' she said, her breath whipsawing in and out of her lungs.

'I ought to leave you right here,' Caxton said. 'That was idiotic what you did. It could get both of us killed. I can't believe you took drugs at a time like this.'

'Keeps me. Keeps me. Keeps me.' Gert swallowed noisily. 'Focused. Alert. Awake. You coming?'

'Hold on,' Caxton had time to shout before Gert tore open the door and ran out into the hall. Cursing, she followed her celly, her shotgun held in both hands so she could bring it around quickly when she needed it. She wanted to grab Gert, pull her back into the room, and beat some sense into her – make her understand the plan better before she went rushing into danger. But frankly, she seemed to have the plan down already.

It was simple enough: kill anything that moves.

They found their first half-dead at the end of a short corridor. It poked its head out of a door as if looking to see what was making all that noise. The answer was Gert, who roared as she stabbed and cut her way through the door, leaving the half-dead in pieces. On the other side of the door was a broad room filled with old ratty couches and darkened vending machines. A staff lounge for COs, perhaps, in better times. The only light came through the door behind the two women, but it was enough to show them the three half-deads crouched around a dead television monitor.

'Get clear,' Caxton yelled, as she brought her shotgun around to blow away the one nearest to her. Gert ignored her and jumped onto the half-dead she'd been aiming at, grabbing its ear and yanking its head sideways to stab at its throat. The other two tried to scramble over the back of the couch, but Caxton was waiting for them. She knocked one's face in with the butt of her shotgun, then brought the other one down with a shot to the back of its neck. The plastic bullet passed right through its throat and its head slumped over to the left, dangling by a few scraps of skin. It kept running. Caxton followed close on its heels and knocked it to the floor, then smashed in the back of its skull with one quick blow.

There was a stairwell on the other side of the lounge. Gert was already racing down its steps, into deep gloom. Caxton followed more slowly, knowing that Gert could be rushing into certain death. Half-deads were cowardly and not very bright, but they were perfectly capable of setting cunning traps for the unwary.

At the next landing down someone had left a votive candle burning to give a little bit of light. It showed Caxton a door leading into the second floor of the central tower. Gert slammed into the door with her shoulder hard enough to knock it off its hinges. She didn't need to – it was unlocked, and it slapped open with a loud bang as Gert staggered out into a large open space.

Caxton reloaded her shotgun as she ran after her celly, knowing that if Gert's drugged-up recklessness was going to get them killed, this was the precise moment when it would happen. The room behind the door would be full of half-deads, she thought. Or it would be booby-trapped. A net would fall down over them as they passed through the door, or who knew? Maybe someone had left land mines lying around. Caxton doubted that a modern prison would have many land mines in its inventory, but she wouldn't put it past SCI-Marcy from what she'd seen so far. She expected to find machine-gun nests inside the big room, or lines of half-deads holding wicked carving knives, or even a cohort of live, human COs holding assault rifles, turned to Malvern's cause through some trickery.

The last thing she expected was to find the warden working at a desk, apparently all alone.

'Gert, get back,' Caxton said, as Gert started rushing toward the older woman.

Warden Bellows was sitting behind a massive desk that was bathed in yellow light. A generator sat on the floor behind her, chugging away and pouring black smoke up at the ceiling. The light came from a pair of portable metal stands holding miniature searchlights, both of which were focused directly on the desk. The warden's face was only partly visible, only her mouth and her nose lit up enough to be recognizable. In the darkness beyond the reach of the light one of her eyes twinkled.

Caxton couldn't see much of the rest of the big room, but she had the impression it was full of cages, full of small prison cells made of nothing but bars and locks.

The warden looked up and must have seen Caxton staring into the shadows. 'This used to be the psychiatric ward,'

248

Bellows said. 'Now we use the cages as cooling-down rooms. When prisoners get too violent we bring them here and let them sit in a cage for a while. Never more than twenty-four hours. If they can't calm down after that long, we move them to the SHU.'

'I need guns,' Caxton said. There was no reason not to get to the point. She had her shotgun pointed at the warden's head. The plastic bullet inside wouldn't kill the woman – she was still alive, and therefore had more structural integrity than a half-dead – but it would make her very, very unhappy. 'Real guns. Where's the armory?'

'Downstairs.' The warden picked up a piece of paper from her desk as if this were the kind of question she was asked every day. 'You'll have some trouble getting in, though. When the lights went out I sent most of my half-deads down there to wait for you. There was nothing for them to do up here, and I figured no matter what your next move might be you would have to go through the Hub.'

'The Hub?' Gert asked. 'What are you, what are – you talking—'

The warden stared at Gert as if she were some kind of rare insect. Fascinating and repellent at the same time. 'Uh-oh,' she said. 'Someone's been naughty. The Hub is where every long corridor in the prison comes together. It's designed as a choke point. In case a riot breaks out in one dorm, we can lock down the Hub and it can't spread to any other wing. Believe me, you won't get through it.'

'Even if I use you as a hostage?' Caxton asked.

'That would be a good plan, normally. With Malvern in her coffin I'm in charge, and if I told the half-deads down there to back off, they would have to. You would march right through there, presumably with one arm around my neck, right? Then I could unlock the armory door for you, and you could go in

249

and get all the guns you wanted. There's a problem with that, however.'

'Oh?' Caxton asked.

'Yes. I'm not going to let you take me hostage.'

Caxton steadied her grip on the shotgun and leaned forward into a firing stance.

The warden leaned forward into the light. For the first time Caxton saw that one of her eyes was missing, a ragged hole in her face ringed with crusted blood. It wasn't even covered by a bandage. 'I've had one shit day,' the warden said. She pulled a pistol out of a drawer of her desk and before Caxton could shoot she brought it up to point at her own temple. 'You give me a reason, any reason at all, and I'll blow my own brains out,' she said.

42.

'You're bluffing,' Caxton said.

'Am I? There's one way to find out.' The warden fitted her finger through the trigger guard of her handgun. 'I'm dead anyway. Maybe not today. Maybe not for years yet. But I have inoperable cancer. My one big chance was Malvern. She could make me immortal, she said. She promised. All it would cost me was a few of my prisoners' lives, which was a price I was perfectly willing to pay. But it looks like she lied. It looks like she never intended to make me a vampire. When she wakes up tonight, she'll probably kill me, and then bring me back as a half-dead. That's almost worse than going out in a hospital bed with a drip in my arm. So I have no reason not to pull this trigger.'

'You think I care?' Caxton asked, trying to keep her voice from breaking.

'Oh, yes, I do,' the warden said. She cocked the hammer of her pistol. The muzzle hadn't moved a hairsbreadth from where she had it jammed against her temple. 'I know you, Caxton. I know you well enough, anyway. I've met enough

251

dirty cops in my time – sometimes they ended up here, as prisoners, and sometimes they were just dropping somebody off. You get so you can tell right away. It's like they have a certain smell.'

'A stink of corruption?'

The warden laughed, a short, bitter sound. 'Ha! No. More like the smell of money. So I know you're not dirty, because you smell like failure. You're a good cop. You're one of the good guys. Or at least that's what you tell yourself. It explains why your life is such a wreck, doesn't it? Because good guys always finish last, but it's okay, because their hearts are pure.' The warden sneered. 'You're in here for kidnapping and torturing some schmuck who had information you needed. I could appreciate that approach – but you can't. You actually feel bad about what you did. You confessed, and pleaded guilty, and now you're doing your time like a nice little girl. It's all bullshit, of course. I've had a front-row seat for twenty years now on what human nature really means. I've watched nice little girls come in here and turn into bloody savages in a week. Nobody's clean in this world, but cops like you want so badly to believe it's possible, you'll do anything not to break the illusion. You won't let me shoot myself because it would make you complicit. It would gnaw at you, for the rest of your life, that you let somebody die when you could have saved them.'

'Are you so sure? The man who taught me how to kill vampires – he would have cocked that gun for you. And I memorized everything he had to teach me.'

'I can see it in your eyes, Caxton. You still think you can come out of this without killing a real live human being. You think you can kill Malvern and walk away – go back to some kind of normal life. So no, you won't let me kill myself. And if you take one step closer to this desk, I will shoot.'

252

The warden was right.

Caxton couldn't let her shoot. The warden was right that it would gnaw at her. It would give her nightmares. Even when she did the right thing, when she protected people from harm, she had nightmares of the things she did. If she let this woman kill herself, it would haunt her forever.

She had no choice but to give in.

'So I guess we have a stalemate,' Caxton said. 'A . . . hostage situation.'

'What? What what what?' Gert looked up and stared around the room. 'Who has a hostage? What's going on?'

Caxton sighed. 'I'll explain later.'

'You want me to kill her?' Gert asked, pointing her knife at the warden.

'No. Not right now,' Caxton said.

Gert's head slumped forward. She was crashing – whatever drugs she'd taken were wearing off. In a minute she would probably fall asleep.

The warden smiled. 'Interesting,' she said. 'I put you in a cell with Stimson because I expected her to throttle you in your sleep, but instead, you've made a friend.'

'I couldn't have made it this far without her.'

'Hmm. You honestly believe it, don't you? That everyone deserves a second chance. That there's a little bit of good in everyone. You must. I watched her kill Wendt, the CO in the SHU. You were right there, you know how that happened. Yet even still – you brought her along. You relied on her. Do you even know why she's in prison? You might want to ask her some time. It might make you think twice about your choice of partners.'

'She's done fine so far,' Caxton said, but she sounded half-hearted even to herself. 'If I lower my shotgun, will you lower your sidearm?'

'No,' the warden said. 'I think not. If you lower your weapon, I'll shoot you where you stand.'

'Why?' Caxton demanded. 'How does that help anyone?'

'It could help me a great deal. Malvern's obsessed with you. She wants you alive so she can make you her plaything. Oh, she has big plans for Laura Caxton. But if you're dead when she wakes up in a little while—'

'She'll kill you. For thwarting her.'

'You really think so?' the warden looked upward as if considering it. 'I know she'll be angry, sure. But she's too smart to throw away someone she needs, just because they disobeyed her once. And when she's not fixating on you, she can be a very rational creature.'

Caxton had to admit that was true.

'And then at least I would have a chance of getting what I want – the curse. No, your dying right now would be great for me. I'm thinking about shooting you right now, shotgun in my face or not. I'm wondering if I can kill you before you kill me.'

'I doubt it,' Caxton said.

The warden pursed her lips in thought. 'Yes. So do I. So that's not how we're going to play it, either.'

'Alright,' Caxton said. 'Tell me how it goes.'

'I'm going to walk out of here. You aren't going to follow me. After that, you can do whatever you want. Go downstairs, get yourself killed. That way I still win.'

'There's a chance I won't die down there.'

The warden laughed. 'A slim one, I suppose. But say you do live to see the sun go down tonight. What will you do then?'

Caxton shrugged. 'I'll rescue Clara. Then I'll kill Malvern.'

'You think she'll make it that simple? A woman who has spent the last three hundred years surviving when all the world wanted her dead, and it will just come down to one last showdown with her latest nemesis? She's too smart to let you get close enough to try.'

Caxton had to admit the woman had a point. 'She's made a mistake this time. She's decided she's willing to risk everything for a chance to turn me into a vampire, and now she's got herself stuck in a corner. She can't leave the prison – there must be a hundred cops outside right now, waiting for her to make a move. So she's got nowhere left to run.'

'You may be underestimating her.'

Caxton's blood surged in her head. That, of course, was always the worst mistake you could make with a vampire. Especially a smart one. She'd spent the last few years learning just how foolish it was to underestimate Malvern. But she didn't see what kind of trick the old vampire could pull this time. She had finally run out of clever ideas.

Hadn't she?

'If you live long enough, you're going to find that things aren't exactly what they seem here. Where Miss Malvern is involved, I suppose they never are.' The warden stood up very slowly from her desk. 'Well. I'll be off now.'

'Wait,' Caxton said, as the warden started edging toward the door. 'Where's Clara? Just tell me that much.'

'She escaped,' the warden said. 'The little bitch hurt me, bad, and got away when I was lying on the floor curled up in a ball of pain. Last thing I heard she was shacked up with one of the gangs. I don't know where.'

Caxton nodded in gratitude, and relief, and a funny mixed-up pride in Clara for being so tough. 'And where's Malvern? You said yourself that you're afraid of what'll happen when she wakes up. Tell me where she is and I'll make sure that never happens. If I can find her before nightfall—'

'I wouldn't tell you, even if I knew. I'm still holding out a certain hope that this is going to work out for me.'

'That you'll become a vampire? That's what you really want?'

'Everyone has a dream,' Bellows said. She shrugged. 'I'll tell you what I know, because it isn't going to help you. She went off somewhere at dawn with a couple of half-deads. Presumably to her coffin. I don't know where the coffin is. It's not in my office, which is the last place I saw it. When I asked the half-deads where they put her, they said they were sworn not to tell me. That's when I realized, you see, that she didn't trust me. That she might not fulfill her promise.'

Caxton grunted in frustration. 'Good-bye, warden. I'm sure we'll meet again,' she said, with as much menace as she could put in her voice.

'Yes, I think we will. Though perhaps not the way you're hoping for. Now, if you'll excuse me – there's much for me to do before the sun goes down. I really must be going.'

Bellows headed quickly for the door then. Caxton turned in place, keeping the shotgun trained on the warden. But the older woman didn't even look back as she left the room.

When the door had closed behind Bellows, Caxton went over to the desk and studied the papers there. There were several dozen sheets, all of them printouts of chat transcripts. Caxton remembered when she'd seen the warden's BlackBerry, and thought there was something familiar about the archaic language on the screen. It had been enough to make her think – if only on a subconscious level – that Malvern was involved. Now she could see that it had definitely been Malvern talking to the warden.

The transcripts went back for months, since shortly after Caxton's trial. Malvern must have been following the news very closely, and she had learned what prison Caxton would be sent to, then had begun to seduce the warden, making promises to get her to betray her duty. It looked like it hadn't been very hard. The transcripts revealed how much the warden hated her prisoners, saw in them everything that was wrong with herself and every other human being she'd ever known. Over just a few pages of conversation, Malvern had convinced the warden that sacrificing everything – her career, her life, the lives of all her COs – would be worth the curse Malvern offered as reward.

Caxton was a little surprised to find the papers. It would have been easy for the warden to take them with her, to fold them into her pocket before she left, and yet she hadn't. She'd left them in plain sight.

The transcripts were a confession of sorts. Caxton wondered – had the warden left them behind because she had no desire to hide her guilt? Or was she just so convinced that Caxton was going to die that it didn't matter whether she saw them or not?

Or was it all part of Malvern's latest insidious scheme? Did she want Caxton to see the transcripts? Had she ordered Bellows to leave them behind?

'Where – where are we – what's – next?' Gert asked. Her eyelids were drooping and she was swaying back and forth on her feet.

'I'm going downstairs,' Caxton said.

'Oh? Okay, let me just get my stuff and—'

'But you're not coming with me,' she told her celly.

43.

'Gert. I'm sorry about this,' Caxton said.

'About what?' Gert asked. She was barely able to stand up straight. She was crashing hard.

Caxton grabbed the quick-release tabs of Gert's stab-proof vest and tore it off of her. Then she pulled down on the plastic zipper of Gert's jumpsuit, stripping her to the waist. A white cardboard box fell out from between Gert's breasts and crashed to the floor. Caxton picked up the box, zipped her celly's jumpsuit back up, and then steered her over to the warden's desk and made her sit down.

The box held a bottle of pills. The plastic safety seal on the bottle had been torn open, and when Caxton took the lid off the bottle she saw the foil seal underneath had been pushed in. She shook out a few pills into her hand and saw they were simple round, white tablets. She didn't recognize them – her training had been in illicit street drugs, not prescription medication. 'Methylphenidate 20mg,' she read from the side of the box. 'What are these?'

'Vitamin R,' Gert slurred. The hunting knife fell out of her hand and clanged on the floor.

'You mean – Ritalin? You took Ritalin? Do you have ADD, then, too?'

'Chronic fatigue,' Gert said. 'I said! You know. It's just a little . . . boost. A little boosty to keep me goin'.'

'How many did you take?'

Gert didn't answer. Caxton went over to the other side of the desk and grabbed Gert's chin. The younger woman made a grab for the bottle, but Caxton held it out of reach.

'Just stay with me a second, and I promise you can sleep as long as you want,' Caxton said. 'How many did you take?'

'Five or six.'

Caxton shook her head in dismay. On the box it said that dosage should not exceed two tablets a day. There was a warning on the side of the box that told you what to do in case of an accidental overdose. You were supposed to call your local poison control center immediately.

Caxton ran a hand through her hair in frustration. She was no doctor, and she had no access to medical care. Gert could be in serious danger, but there was absolutely nothing she could do.

There was a possibility that Gert could just sleep it off. That she would be fine after a little nap. *Keep telling yourself that*, Caxton thought. She took Gert's wrist between her index finger and thumb and felt her pulse. It was racing – and yet the girl looked as if she couldn't stay awake a moment longer. That had to be a bad sign, didn't it?

The only thing that Caxton could think to do was make Gert vomit. If some of the pills were still in her stomach it would at least keep the problem from getting worse. Of course, she also knew that in some cases of poisoning, inducing vomiting was the last thing you wanted to do – but she would have to take her chances. She had no other ideas. She tried grabbing Gert around the waist and squeezing her, but Gert just pushed her away, with surprising strength given how exhausted she seemed. Caxton sighed and tried another way. She yanked Gert's mouth open and shoved her index finger down her celly's throat.

Gert's eyes went wide and Caxton worried she would clamp down and bite the intruding finger clean off. Instead she jerked backward and then vomited explosively all over the desk, the floor, and her own jumpsuit. She coughed and gagged and spat up long ropes of drool. Caxton lowered her to the floor, well away from the puddles of sick, and got her on her side. She knew that much – if someone was throwing up and passing out at the same time, you put them on their side so they couldn't choke on their own puke. Then Caxton wiped her finger on her own jumpsuit and sat back on her haunches, wishing she had any idea of what to do next.

Other lives depended on her. She couldn't just sit with Gert until the girl woke up and felt better. By then Clara could be dead – and half the prison's inmates, as well. Twilight was coming at six o'clock, and when the sun set Malvern would wake up and be ready for another night's rampage.

And yet . . . if she just left Gert, if she walked away while the girl was still moaning and wheezing on the floor . . . how was that different from watching the warden shoot herself and doing nothing to stop it?

While she was trying to decide what to do, Gert's chest started to shake. Caxton thought she might be having a seizure, but when she checked she found that instead Gert was just sobbing, letting out huge, noisy gusts of tears.

'It's not fair,' she cried. 'It isn't fair. It was an accident!'

'Shh,' Caxton said, and rubbed her celly's shoulder. 'Shh. Try to lie still.'

'I never meant to do it. Nobody would ever want to do that! How can they lock you up for something you didn't even want to do? Something you can barely remember doing at all?'

Caxton's hand stopped moving on Gert's arm.

She had never asked Gert what it was she had done to get herself in prison, or why she was under protective custody in the SHU. At first, when she'd been locked up with Gert, she'd figured she didn't want to know. That asking would just get Gert talking, when what she'd wanted at that point was for her celly to shut up. Later there hadn't been time.

She still wasn't sure she wanted to know. The warden had seemed to think it was something bad, something that would make Caxton regret partnering with Gert even if the option was going it alone.

'They wouldn't stop crying,' Gert said. She wiped at her nose with one sleeve and it came away slick with snot. 'I couldn't seem to fix them. I would feed them, I would change their fucking diapers, and they never . . . they never stopped. And then my mom said I had to move out, and I was packing up but still, still they were crying . . .'

'Gert, stop,' Caxton said. 'Please don't say any more.'

'Little Charity, she was sick, she had colic, and it made her crazy, and Blaine, her brother – he would hear her crying, and it would wake him up, and nothing would make him go back to sleep. I just needed Charity to be quiet, just for a little while, so I could think. Think about where we were going to go. And she wouldn't. She just . . . wouldn't. I'm a good person. I know I did something horrible, but in my heart, where it counts, I'm still good . . .'

'Enough!' Caxton said. She didn't want to know any of this. She didn't want to think about what came next in this stupid, sordid little story. She didn't want to remember why Gert's name had been familiar the first time she'd heard it. Why Gert had said she was a little famous, and why she'd told Caxton not to believe everything she'd heard.

Half the women in the prison were mothers, mothers of children they got to see for an hour a week at most. Children they couldn't play with, or help with their homework, or feed, or put to bed – children being raised now by other people. Those prisoners would do just about anything to prove they weren't bad mothers. And for a certain kind of person, a person prone already to violence, to not thinking things through carefully, it made sense, that to prove you were a good mother, you had to hurt someone who'd already proved she was the worst kind of mother of all.

A baby killer.

Gert had been locked up for her own safety. Because half the women in the prison wanted to see her dead.

'Enough,' Caxton said again. 'I don't care,' she told Gert. 'I don't care what you did, that doesn't matter – I mean, of course it matters, but – but you helped me, you were there for me when I needed you, maybe not in the ways I wanted you to be there, but – but—'

Gert started to snore then.

Caxton closed her eyes. She saw Clara, in her head, as plain as if she was standing right in front of her. She knew what she needed to do.

Leaving Gert to sleep it off, she headed down the stairs toward the Hub.

She took the hunting knife with her. And Gert's shoes, as well.

262

44.

There was another votive candle waiting on the landing of the stairs leading down to the Hub. Its flickering light illuminated the doorway that led out into the bottom floor of the central tower, a very simple door painted white with a brushed aluminum knob. All Caxton had to do was turn that knob and walk through.

She didn't like walking into a bad situation without knowing what she was about to face. That wasn't how you lived through moments like this. She had no choice, however. Not if she wanted to save Clara. Not if she wanted to finally kill Malvern, and be done with vampires forever. She checked her shotgun one more time, making sure it was ready to fire, making sure she had one of her few remaining plastic bullets loaded in the chamber. Then she reached out and touched the knob.

She hesitated.

The bulk of the warden's half-deads were in there, she knew. So far she'd been very lucky. She'd only faced a few at a time, she'd been able to surprise them, mostly, and she'd had Gert watching her back.

263

Laura Caxton wasn't immortal, and she certainly wasn't invulnerable. She'd been wounded many times in fights with vampires and half-deads. She knew it only took one knife wound to kill a human being, and she knew that if she marched out into the Hub, into a small army of the faceless abominations, she would be asking to die. She had her limits, and she'd finally reached them.

She reached for the knob again.

And then she turned it, opened the door, and stepped through.

The first thing she saw in the Hub was a half-dead staring at her, surprised to see anyone come through that door. It was dressed in a prisoner's orange jumpsuit and it was clutching a long-bladed kitchen knife close to its chest. Its face hung in tatters from its cheeks and chin like a dry, papery beard. She brought her shotgun up fast and put a plastic bullet into its chest, high up near its throat.

It dropped its knife and sank to its knees, clutching at the wound. It shrieked, a horrible, high-pitched keening that hurt her ears.

The second thing she saw in the Hub was the group of six more half-deads standing in the center of the room, huddled around a metal trash can full of burning paper. They all looked up when they heard the scream, and turned to see what was happening.

They all had knives. These weren't kitchen staff armed with ladles and rolling pins. These were soldiers in Malvern's undead army. They were fresh, their bodies still mostly intact, and some of their faces were still partly attached to their skulls. One by one their knives came up, held high as if they were slashers in a horror movie. One by one they peeled off from the trash can and came running at her.

Caxton waded in, knowing that in a knife fight the only

good defense was to get inside your opponent's reach. She dropped the shotgun, empty now and useless, and drew her baton with one hand and Gert's hunting knife with the other.

A heavy, serrated bread knife whistled through the air toward her face. Caxton stepped under it and sank the hunting knife into the first target she found – the arm that was swinging toward her. The half-dead it belonged to screamed and jumped back.

Another half-dead came at her from her right. Caxton flipped the baton in her hand until she was holding it hilt first. The baton was collapsible and hollow, meant for inflicting pain rather than breaking bones. Its rubberized grip was the only solid part of its construction. She caved in a half-dead's torn face and then brought her knee up between its legs, knocking it backward.

A knife touched the back of her neck, sliding through her skin, and she gasped in pain. She was moving too fast for them to stab her effectively, but little wounds like that could add up in a hurry – if she started losing blood, if she started letting herself react to the little cuts, she would slow down and they would have her. She brought her head back fast and hard, pushing the knife there back, then whirled around and sank the hunting knife into the ear of the half-dead behind her.

They didn't die like human beings. They were already dead. You couldn't knock them down with electric shocks or stun them into submission by hitting them hard on the forehead. They didn't need to breathe, so tear gas and pepper spray had minimal effect on them. Having already been drained by the vampire who killed them, there was no blood in their bodies to spill. But they were weak, and cowardly, and they felt pain. If you hurt them enough they fell down, or ran away to lick their wounds, or just collapsed in pieces. The pieces kept moving but could safely be ignored.

It was horrible work, it was butcher's work. Their very existence was wrong, though, an abomination. You were doing them a favor, Caxton told herself, when you cut them to pieces. When you sent them back to dreamless sleep.

Another knife in front of her. Caxton brought the baton around fast and smacked the wrist, knocking the knife free. Then she spun and parried another blow, and cut a half-dead across the eyes, blinding it.

They kept coming. Had she taken out the original six? She'd lost count. She could hear footsteps running toward her. Reinforcements on the way. She needed to at least get her back against a wall, or they were going to mob her. It would all be over if they could effectively surround her. Their blows were slow and unsteady, but she only had two hands and could only counter two attacks at once.

She glanced up and around – but before she could see anything useful, a knife sank right through her stab-proof vest.

The vests were designed specifically for the kind of attacks COs met with in normal prison situations. They were very good at stopping shanks – sharpened toothbrushes, flattened-out spoons, at worst a blunt icepick. They could stop most commercially available knives, too, but by *stop* the designers of the vests had meant 'Allow a blade to penetrate no more than one-quarter inch.' That was enough to keep one from being killed instantly by a knife wound, but it still allowed for a serious injury.

Caxton gulped air and tried not to throw up. The knifepoint caught the small of her back, just left of her spine, cutting through skin and subcutaneous fat and just piercing the layers

266

of muscle underneath. She felt something in her back give and she sagged to the side.

She didn't stop to think. Instead she roared and ran backward, pushing the knife in deeper but knocking over the half-dead behind her and wrenching the weapon from its grip. She kept going, fast enough to throw off any other half-deads who were trying to sneak up behind her, kept going until her back collided painfully with a cinder-block wall behind her. She was sweating hard, and panting, but for the moment she was free of the pack of murderous bastards.

They took a moment to regroup and come at her again. She took the pause this gave her to firm up her grips on her two weapons, and to grit her teeth so she didn't scream from the pain.

Then the half-deads came at her like a brick wall. She didn't have time to count them. She didn't have time to look at what they were wearing, or where their weapons were, or what their faces looked like. Sometimes time slowed down at moments like this, when death was so close.

Sometimes it didn't. Caxton brought her weapons up in front of her chest, ready to push back the first attack. And then a noise like thunder rolling through the room made the half-deads jump and spin.

One ravaged face exploded in a red cloud. An arm flew out of the group and smacked the wall next to where Caxton was crouching. Some of the half-deads just fell down like sacks of broken bricks. A few of them managed to run away.

When they were gone, when the room in front of her was clear, Caxton saw what had happened. She just had time to swear before it happened again.

There was a machine-gun nest built into the Hub, a narrow

guard post at the very center of the room with gun slits carved into its concrete walls. The smoking muzzle of a machine gun was sticking out of one, pointed right at her. Without any preamble it started roaring and spitting bullets at her, hundreds of them per minute.

45.

Guilty Jen peered out through one of the narrow windows of the interrogation room. 'Not long now. Maybe an hour until the sun goes down. Then we get out of here, right, girls?'

Queenie said, 'Fuckin' yeah.' The others seemed to agree with the sentiment.

Clara glanced over at Marty the former CO again, but he wouldn't meet her gaze. She had bought herself a little time, it was true. By convincing Jen to hand her over only to Malvern herself, she had kept herself alive a little longer.

Now it seemed like it wasn't going to make any difference. Fetlock had to be out there somewhere. He'd had half the day to gather SWAT teams and get in place. And yet she'd heard nothing from him on the BlackBerry, nor had she or any of the others noticed if the prison was being noisily surrounded by cops. What was holding him up?

Maybe she'd been a fool to put her faith in her boss. She knew how slow he was to take action. He thought of it as being cautious. She also knew what Laura thought about people who were overly cautious when dealing with vampires.

269

They might, it was true, survive through the night. But other people just died in their place.

Fetlock had been willing to bide his time when Malvern was at large, murdering people every night. He had wanted to let her have time to make a mistake, to give herself away. Instead he'd just given her time to work the kinks out of her master plan, to make sure of every little detail in her bid to take over the prison. Now – how many lives would he waste, waiting for the perfect time to strike? He had to be out there. He knew what was going on. But he wanted to make sure he, too, had every little thing just in place before he made his move.

Clara knew that the second the sun went beneath the horizon, her life was effectively over. She had long since given up hope that Laura would rescue her. Or maybe . . . maybe there was one tiny shred of hope left, but it was undernourished and rapidly fading away.

She looked up at the table as the BlackBerry rang once more. She stared at it, then at Guilty Jen. Maybe it was Fetlock, saying he was on his way—

'Hello?' Jen asked, pressing the button to set the handheld to speaker mode.

'Hello, Jen. Your friendly neighborhood warden again, just checking in.'

Guilty Jen slapped the table so hard the phone jumped. 'I told you, bitch, we're not negotiating with you. I want to talk to the cunt in charge, and I'm more than willing to wait until she wakes up.'

The warden chuckled. 'Oh, I heard you the first time. I just wanted to bring you up to speed with the latest news. I know you and Laura Caxton are old friends, and I thought you'd like to know I just ran into her.'

Clara's heart sped up. She made a point of not staring at

the phone with wide eyes, not wanting to give away her excitement.

'She didn't kill you, I see,' Guilty Jen replied. 'I knew she was weak.'

'She might have, but I'm more slick than you give me credit for. Anyway, I left her heading down to the Hub. You know where the Hub is, don't you, Jen? It can be reached easily from anywhere in the prison. Wherever you're holed up, for instance, can't be more than a few minutes away from there. All the doors between you and the Hub are open, by the way. Not that you have any reason to go down there, of course.'

'That's right,' Jen said. 'You're not going to catch me out like a sucker. I'm not going down there just so you can ambush us and get your hostage back. What do you take me for, an idiot? Anyway, Caxton'll be dead in an hour. When the vampire wakes up, she'll suck her blood.'

'Are you so sure of that, Jen? You've never actually met Miss Malvern, have you? I have. I've spent quite a bit of time with her, actually. Enough to know she appreciates a nice ironic turn of events. She doesn't want to kill Caxton. She wants to turn her out. You know, make her a vampire.'

'Bullshit.'

The warden was silent for a moment. 'You can believe what you want. But I want to remind you of something. The first time you met Caxton, when you jumped her in the kitchens – she didn't kill any of your set in that fight. She didn't want a murder rap on her jacket. Even pulling her punches, though, she managed to make mincemeat out of every one of your girls.'

'If your hogs hadn't come in before I had a chance, I would have—'

'You might have taken her, I know. You're a real hard case, I get it. But when she's a vampire, she'll be ten times as strong and tougher than you can imagine. And she won't have a single compunction left when it comes to killing worthless scum like you and yours. Just a thought I wanted to share.'

Every pair of eyes in the room was staring at the phone. Slowly, as each brain worked through what had just happened, the eyes turned toward Guilty Jen.

Clara knew what the sociopath was thinking. It might as well be written on her face. Laura Caxton had made a fool of her. She had disrespected Jen in a way that could not be forgiven. Under the very strange code of ethics that Jen followed, that meant Laura Caxton had to die. It would be preferable if she could die at Guilty Jen's hands, but if Malvern wanted to shred her to pieces in a very painful way, that would have been enough.

If Malvern had different plans for her, though – if she wanted to make her stronger, more dangerous, and nearly bulletproof—

At the best, Guilty Jen would never get her revenge. At the worst, she would have a merciless bloodsucker dogging her trail for the rest of her life, which wouldn't be a very long time.

'Stop looking at me, Featherwood,' Jen said. She chewed on her lower lip.

'Sorry, Jen,' Featherwood stammered, looking away.

'I don't like being stared at.'

Featherwood shook her head. Clara wasn't sure, but she thought the burned girl looked scared of something. 'I'm not, I swear I'm not looking at—'

Guilty Jen hit the white girl hard enough to knock her halfway across the room. Featherwood's head bounced off the wall and she slid down into a heap, but Guilty Jen was already on top of her, punching her again and again in the stomach.

Queenie and Maricón grabbed at her shoulders and tried

272

to haul her away. For a while Guilty Jen fought them off, still punching her underling over and over, but eventually she let them pull her clear.

Featherwood sat up very slowly. She was bleeding from her mouth and she couldn't seem to catch her breath. She looked down at the floor and wouldn't lift her head, even when Guilty Jen said, 'You got something to say?'

With a clearly painful effort, Featherwood gathered herself together enough to wheeze, 'I'm sorry, Jen. I shouldn't have looked at you like that, I – I'm sorry.'

'It's alright,' Guilty Jen said. 'Don't do it again.'

'That's good, keep your people in line,' the warden said, and Clara jumped at the sound of her voice. She hadn't realized the BlackBerry was still transmitting. 'You'll need them all if you're going to take down Caxton.'

'Shut up, bitch,' Jen said, and grabbed up the PDA. 'Did I not tell you, I'm not dealing with you?'

'Fine. Be that way. I have to go now, Jen. Good luck.' The warden ended the call abruptly.

Guilty Jen growled and shoved the BlackBerry into her pocket. 'I've made my decision,' she said, 'but it's got nothing to do with what that dried-up old twat wants. This is about what I want, and that's what—'

A sudden noise interrupted her. The sound of a gunshot, coming from quite nearby.

'What the hell was that?' Marty asked. Then he turned his face away as Guilty Jen stormed toward him. She didn't bother to hit him – maybe all she'd wanted was to see him flinch.

'It don't matter what that was,' Guilty Jen said. She glanced around the room, staring long and hard at Marty and at Clara. 'Alright,' she said, 'pack up. We're moving out.'

46.

For a while it was all Clara could do to stay on her feet. Queenie was dragging her along by one arm and didn't mind twisting it whenever Clara stumbled or slowed down, even for a second.

Guilty Jen's set moved quickly and silently. She'd trained them well. They had their marching orders – follow Jen – and they didn't need additional supervision. Clara shuddered to think what they would be capable of if they did manage to escape from the prison. She was a cop, of sorts. Enough to know that a cop's worst nightmare is not some raving killer on the loose or a drugged-out maniac with a machine gun. It was a well-organized group of criminals with a leader smart enough to know exactly how to operate on the wrong side of the law and get away with it. A killer on a rampage could do a lot of damage in one night before he was inevitably gunned down, but a smart gang could do immeasurable amounts of harm over a period of years before they were caught.

When she managed to get her feet properly under her and match her stride with Queenie's, she knew what her next duty was. 'You're making a mistake,' she said, calling out to Guilty Jen, knowing she was asking for trouble. She needed to do something, though, needed to make a case for Laura no matter how pointless it seemed. 'You're letting the warden lead you around by the nose. Do you really think she has your best interests at heart? And killing Caxton won't gain you anything right now. It won't get you out of here any—'

The set stopped instantly as Guilty Jen froze in front of a doorway. Slowly she turned and glared at Clara. 'I'm the only thing keeping you alive right now,' she said. 'It would be easier, and safer, to kill you, got it? I'm about ninety-eight percent ready to do it with my bare hands. I'm not at one hundred percent because there just might come a time in the next couple of minutes when you'll be useful to me alive. The thing of it is, it don't matter much if you're alive and able to walk, or just alive. I know exactly how to kick you in the back so that your spinal cord would snap. You believe me?'

Clara nodded. She couldn't have spoken at that moment if her life had depended on it. She was pretty sure her life depended on *not* speaking, which was fortunate.

'I can leave you in a wheelchair for the rest of your life, and it'll only take me about ten seconds to do it. Queenie, Featherwood, and Maricón could carry you from here – you ain't that heavy. Caxton would still want you, even if you were a useless cripple. Now, we'll move a little faster with you on your own feet, so I'm giving you one more chance. But you say another word and we'll take a nice little ten-second pit stop. Okay?'

Clara nodded again.

'Good. Move, now.' Guilty Jen pulled open the door in front of her and they flowed out into the yard. Clara was shocked by how dark it seemed. The sun was still above the horizon, but it was below the level of the prison's walls and long shadows were draping the grounds in gloom.

They headed around the side of a low outbuilding. Judging by the number of pipes sticking out of its walls, it must have been the control center for the prison's water supply. Featherwood dashed up to one corner of the structure and peered around its side for a second, then flashed a hand signal back to the rest of them to say the way ahead was clear.

This couldn't be the fastest way to the central tower. Clara remembered the route Guilty Jen had taken before, and this was a far more roundabout path. She wasn't surprised by that, however. Guilty Jen was smart enough to know that the warden might be laying a trap for them, and so she was taking an alternate route to throw off anyone who might be lying in wait for them.

It wasn't much farther to the Hub. They passed around the side of a softball diamond and then entered a covered walkway that led back to the central tower. Long before they reached it Clara started hearing a noise. A repetitive, metallic, hammering kind of noise, as if someone were dropping rocks off a high place onto a corrugated tin roof. She wasn't the only one who heard it, either.

'Sounds like some artillery in there,' Queenie said. 'Sounds automatic. Big caliber, too.'

Guilty Jen nodded. 'It might be Caxton. Maybe she got into the hogs' toy box.'

'We ain't got any guns,' Maricón pointed out. 'I ain't sure about this—'

One look from Jen shut the woman up.

'We're going in,' Guilty Jen said. 'You know the drill.'

47.

Caxton pulled her knees in closer and made sure the top of her head wasn't exposed. She wanted to take a peek to see what was going on, but she didn't dare. Every time the smallest part of her body was exposed, the machine gun started firing again.

She hadn't been prepared for this. Half-deads never used guns. They lacked the coordination to aim properly, and the recoil from anything heavier than a derringer could rip a half-dead's rotten arm right off. Apparently the half-dead in the machine-gun nest had figured out the answer. A mounted gun didn't transfer its recoil to its operator, and with something that big and fast you didn't need to aim. You could spray down the whole room as if you were using a garden hose. Some of the other half-deads had been killed in the process, but they weren't known for looking after one another's well-being. The thing in the nest wanted only one thing, which was to kill her as quickly as possible.

Caxton had barely survived the first volley of the machine gun, diving behind the only cover available. It wasn't even

277

particularly good cover. There was a small kiosk built into one wall of the Hub, a counter where COs signed in and out every time they moved a prisoner from one wing of the facility to another. Behind the counter was a tiny booth just big enough for a chair. Caxton had dived over the counter when the machine gun started firing and now had a concrete wall between her and certain death, but she was pinned down. The other half-deads, cowards to the last, had fled the Hub when the shooting started. If they came back she would be a sitting duck. She couldn't stay there forever, and she couldn't leave her hiding hole, either. If they came back – but then, they didn't have to, did they? Sundown was very close now. Caxton didn't have a watch to time it, but she'd been fighting vampires long enough to have an uncanny sense of where the sun was in the sky, even when she couldn't see it. When you hunted vampires, knowing when it was day and when it was night was something that kept you alive.

The moment the sun was down Malvern would be coming for her, Caxton knew. She didn't need to send in waves of half-deads. She could just come to the Hub herself, and drag Caxton out of her hiding place with her own two hands.

Caxton needed to get out of this trap before that happened. But how? Her weapons were useless to her. She had dropped her shotgun, thinking she wouldn't have time to reload. It was still sitting on the floor outside the kiosk. It might as well be on the far side of the moon. She had a stun gun, a hunting knife, and a collapsible baton. They were worth nothing against the bad end of the continuum of lethality.

Maybe at least she could get a look at what was going on. The kiosk had originally had a plastic window set above the counter, designed to be pulled down by the CO inside in case of an attack. It had been meant to protect against knives and thrown objects, not machine-gun rounds, and the first time it was shot at it had collapsed in long, jagged shards. Some of them lay on the floor around Caxton. She picked one up. If she held it up, just so, she could see a reflection in it of the room beyond the counter, and by turning it slowly from side to side she could scan the room.

The machine gun opened fire again, chewing through the paint on the wall behind the counter. The half-dead inside the nest must have seen a flash of light from her improvised periscope. Caxton tried not to flinch as she turned the shard slowly to the left. There – she could see the machine gun firing. It was impossible to see into the nest from where she was, though. She couldn't tell how much ammunition the half-dead had left, or whether anyone else was coming, or—

—except, maybe she could. It looked like – it could just be that – something was moving on the far side of the room. Behind the machine-gun nest. It wasn't a half-dead, though. At least, Caxton was pretty sure it wasn't, because it was sticking very carefully to the shadows, staying out of the machine gun's fire zone. Moving slowly, not showing much of itself at all.

Then something else rushed out of the shadows, a flash of orange. The machine gun pivoted quickly to track it, and the orange blur started zigzagging back and forth. The machine gun opened fire, but for a moment it seemed the orange blur was moving too erratically, too randomly.

Then – then there was a scream.

It was a human scream, not the high-pitched piteous wailing of a half-dead. It was human and it went on and on. Caxton turned her shard of plastic to try to see what had happened, but the orange blur was nowhere to be found. Instead she could see the machine-gun nest. Its door had been pried open. The machine gun was pointed up at the ceiling, its barrel smoking but silent.

There was another scream, and it was a half-dead this time. It was cut off very abruptly.

Then a living woman said Caxton's name very softly.

Caxton knew the voice. She knew she'd been rescued. Sort of. She started to stand up, the hunting knife held carefully in one hand she kept out of view beneath the counter. The other hand held the collapsible baton. She brought that one up in plain view. 'Guilty Jen,' she said.

It wasn't the gangbanger she saw first, though. It was one of her set, a black woman with a broken nose. Caxton remembered breaking that nose. The scream she'd just heard, the horrible drawn-out scream of pain, had come from that woman's throat. It was the last noise she was ever going to make. Her orange jumpsuit had been torn open along one side by the machine gun, and her rib cage was a gaping, steaming mess. She was dead, her eyes staring up at the ceiling, her hands curled lifelessly at her sides.

Guilty Jen stepped out of the machine-gun nest. Her hands were empty, but she was smiling, which Caxton knew was a bad sign. 'Hey,' she said, and waved cheerily. 'You want to come out of there?'

'You going to give me a good reason?' Caxton asked. She kept glancing down at the dead woman on the floor. She wasn't squeamish about dead bodies – in her line of work that would be a serious problem – but something about this death bothered her. Not the cause of death, not the severity of the injuries, but the sheer stupidity of it.

Guilty Jen had sacrificed one of her set to distract the attention of the machine gunner. The dead woman had been utterly loyal to her leader. She had run into gunfire just because Guilty Jen had ordered her to. That act of stupid courage had saved Caxton's life. But for what?

'I got a couple reasons,' Guilty Jen said. She didn't move

280

closer. She kept herself half concealed by the door of the machine-gun nest, ready to jump back inside if Caxton was holding a gun underneath the counter. 'One is, I can just come over there and pull you out whenever I want to.'

'You can try,' Caxton said.

Guilty Jen nodded, her pigtails swinging back and forth. 'The other one is, I got your girlfriend. I know you'll come out of there for her.' She shook her head when she saw Caxton peering into the shadows of the Hub. 'Not here. But close by. I got people sitting on her, of course.'

Caxton sighed. 'So . . . what now? I come out, and then we fight. If I lose, you kill me. And probably Clara too. If I win, you'll let her go?'

'Nah.' Guilty Jen's smile broadened. 'If you win, and that doesn't seem real likely, but let's say I trip and crack my head open before I can even touch you – if you win, they got orders to kill her anyway.' The gangbanger shrugged. 'That's just how I roll.'

48.

She could jump over the counter and be through one of the Hub's many doors before Guilty Jen could catch her. She could find Clara somehow and overpower her guards. There'd be time for a quick hug, and then they would take down Malvern together and—

No. It wouldn't work. She would never find Clara in time.

She had the hunting knife, which would work as well on Guilty Jen as it would on a half-dead. She could throw it, because Jen wouldn't be expecting that. It was painted green, so it wouldn't even glint as it sailed through the air. She could make sure it hit Jen somewhere painful but nonfatal, and then she could make the gangbanger tell her where Clara was being kept, and then—

Not a chance. Jen was too fast. She would hear the knife coming, or something.

There didn't seem to be any way of saving Clara. There didn't seem to be a real chance of surviving a fight with Guilty Jen. She'd tried that once already, back when she'd actually had a full belly and a night's sleep. Jen was too fast, and her training in the martial arts just made her too deadly. Caxton was great at killing vampires. That took brains, determination, and high-tech guns. She knew next to nothing about unarmed combat against human opponents.

Across from her, still standing in the doorway of the machine-gun nest, Jen glanced at her wrist. She wasn't wearing a watch, but Caxton understood the gesture. Nodding in resignation, she put one knee up on the counter. 'I guess you know me pretty well,' Caxton said.

'I know your type,' Jen agreed.

Caxton slipped the hunting knife inside her stab-proof vest. Her best plan was to keep it hidden, then bring it out when Jen least expected it. She doubted it would work, but it was the only clever idea she had. 'What type's that?'

'The type that cares about people getting hurt. You'll do just about anything if I threaten your girlfriend. You'd get down on your knees and lick my cunt right now if I said I'd spare her life, wouldn't you?'

Caxton grunted as she grabbed the edge of the counter and hauled herself out of her hiding place. 'Is that an offer?'

'No,' Guilty Jen said.

Caxton dropped to her feet on the far side of the counter. The burning trash can that was the Hub's sole source of light was slightly to her left. She moved so that it was between her and the other woman.

'It's a weakness. It's something your enemies can exploit.' Jen tilted her head to one side. 'So why do you let yourself feel that way?'

Caxton squinted at the gangbanger. Did she really need to ask that question? Maybe she did. Guilty Jen seemed to live in a world with a few very basic rules. Love and its obligations did not seem to be one of them. 'I don't think I can explain it very well. I guess you could say it's what separates me from the monsters. I knew a guy once, my mentor. He didn't care about people. He only cared about killing vampires. He was willing to use innocent people as cannon fodder. As diversions. Even as bait.' He'd used Caxton as vampire bait more than once. She had put up with it because she was learning from him every time he put her in danger. He was dead now. She wasn't. 'I swore I'd never be like that, that I would manage to have some kind of life besides just killing vampires. That meant having people like Clara, who—'

'Bored.' Guilty Jen sighed dramatically. 'You want the first swing?'

Caxton smiled. She knew a trap when she heard one. 'Let's just wing it,' she said. She flicked her baton outward, extending it to its full length.

Jen bowed. And then she attacked.

She had to cover five yards of empty space before she could land a blow on Caxton. Those five yards included the burning trash can. She started to dodge left around it, signaling the move to force Caxton to dodge the other way and keep it between them. Caxton chose instead to roll to her right, closing the distance between them faster than Jen expected. She came out of her roll with her baton swinging upward, grip first. If she could shatter Jen's kneecap straight out of the gate, this could be over very fast.

But Jen's knee wasn't there when her swing followed through. Instead her leg was up in the air, spinning through the deadly arc of a roundhouse kick. Caxton managed to get her head down before it was knocked off her neck, but that left her in a bad position, one knee and one arm down on the floor, her back arched up in the air, unable to see very well where the next blow would come from.

Jen spun around like a top and brought her feet down in a fighting stance like a sumo wrestler. Her hands were bunched into fists at her waist and she cried out in victory as she readied a double punch toward Caxton's kidneys.

A punch like that would kill her. The trauma to her kidneys could lead to massive internal bleeding. Without prompt medical attention, which was definitely not available, there would be no way to stop the bleeding, and she would die in a matter of minutes. Caxton's body knew what to do next, even if her mind was stuck for ideas. Her legs flashed out and backward like the legs of a frog jumping off a hot stone. It wasn't much of a sweep, but it caught Guilty Jen off guard and made her stumble backward to keep her balance.

That gave Caxton just enough time to get back up on her feet and facing Jen.

Guilty Jen grinned and dropped into a low fighting crouch, one fist extended toward Caxton, the other at her hip.

'We're wasting each other's time here,' Caxton said. 'The vampire—'

'Bored.' Without warning Jen lunged forward in an attack.

Caxton shoved her hand under her vest and pulled out the hunting knife. She didn't have time to swing, so it would need to be a lunge, right into the other woman's attack. Hopefully the knife would be a surprise for Jen, one she couldn't prepare for. Caxton braced herself against the blow, bringing her other arm up to protect her face, just as Guilty Jen's body twisted in midair. Jen's back collided painfully with Caxton's chest and her arms lifted up, hard. The knife was tugged out of Caxton's grip and flew through the air to clatter on the floor.

Jen's hands grabbed Caxton's now-empty knife hand in a tight grip. She felt something hot and wet slick against the back of her hand – she must have cut Jen, anyway, must have sliced her palm – and then—

Hot agony raced up Caxton's arm, all the way to her

shoulder. She felt her arm twisting under pressure, felt her bones resisting, felt them start to give way—

She screamed as half the bones in her hand and forearm snapped, all at once. Guilty Jen gave her a last sadistic yank and dropped Caxton, moaning, to the floor.

She tried to force herself to get up, tried to will her body to obey her, but her muscles were twitching wildly and her blood was roaring in her ears. It was all she could do to breathe, all she could do to keep from passing out from the pain.

Leaning over her, Guilty Jen reached down and placed a hand on either side of her throat. And started to squeeze.

It was at that precise moment that the lights in the Hub came back on.

49.

There was a blaring, high-pitched tone and a series of deep clunking sounds as the lights came on one by one. The ventilation system kicked in a second later, sighing out dusty warm air on the back of Caxton's neck.

Guilty Jen looked up, but she was disciplined enough not to let go of Caxton's throat. She twisted her hands together and Caxton started to feel the pressure on her windpipe.

'Jen? Jen, what just happened?' a voice said near Caxton's ear. It sounded like a cell phone set to speakerphone mode. 'Jen? Is Caxton dead?'

Caxton tried to raise her baton, which was still clutched in her good hand. She couldn't find the strength to even begin to swing it, though, before Jen brought one leg around and knocked it out of Caxton's grip with one knee.

'Jen? Can you hear me?'

Guilty Jen rolled her eyes and stared down at Caxton. 'Gimme a second,' she said.

'What? Jen, there's something you should know, the—'

'I said fucking hold on!' Guilty Jen cursed. Then she growled in frustration and released Caxton's throat. Caxton started to get up, but Guilty Jen just kicked her in the face and she went back down, hard.

Jen pulled the zipper down on her jumpsuit and reached into her panties. She brought out an expensive-looking BlackBerry and held it up near her mouth. 'You got lousy timing, Featherwood. What the hell is going on that's so important it can't wait, huh? I got Caxton right where I want her, but I need about thirty seconds to finish things here. Okay? Is that too much to ask?'

'Sorry, Jen, but the sun's down. I thought you'd want to know. It's getting pretty dark outside, so the vampires should be waking up any second. I don't see them on any of the monitors yet, but I figured – hey. Do you want us to kill the girlfriend now?'

Guilty Jen started to open her mouth to respond.

Down on the floor, at that same moment, Caxton was staring at the gangbanger's ankle. Guilty Jen was wearing prison-issue slippers, but her ankles were exposed. Caxton could see bare skin there.

In a moment, Jen was going to tell her set to kill Clara. This was Caxton's absolute last chance. Jen had already disarmed her of her hunting knife and her baton. Her shotgun was lying on the floor somewhere nearby, but there was no time to reach it and it wasn't loaded anyway.

Luckily for Caxton, she had one weapon left. Her stun gun. Striking like a snake, striking for Clara's life, she lashed out with it and zapped Guilty Jen right in the side of her foot.

The gangbanger dropped the BlackBerry as her whole body started to shake. Her eyes wobbled in her head as she staggered back and forth, trying not to fall down. Caxton released

288

the gun's trigger and scrambled up to her feet, pivoting before she was even upright to head for the stairs.

Behind her Guilty Jen grabbed at the back of her stab-proof vest.

Hell no, Caxton thought, but she didn't waste time processing what was happening. She got to the stairs and started stumping up them two at a time, even as Guilty Jen came rushing up behind her.

Caxton must not have given Jen a full charge from the stun gun, she decided. Or maybe Guilty Jen was just that tough. Caxton had heard stories about bikers who could take a full stun gun jolt and not even slow down, but they were always huge guys, big mountains of fat, and they tended to be extremely drunk or high when they did it. Guilty Jen couldn't weigh more than one-twenty, but she looked like the stun gun had just pissed her off.

Caxton sped past the second-floor landing. She didn't bother looking into the cooling-down rooms there for Gert – there was no time. She kicked aside the votive candle that still burned on the landing and started up the last flight of stairs to the central command center.

The woman who had called Guilty Jen had said she could see the security monitors. That could only mean that she – and Clara – were up in the top of the central tower. Caxton was sure of it. And Jen's underlings would never dare to hurt Clara until they knew whether Jen had killed Caxton or not. They would follow her orders to the letter, lest they tick Jen off and suffer the violent consequences. Caxton was sure of it.

She couldn't afford not to be sure. This was Clara's only chance.

The door to the command center was right in front of her. She had only to reach up and turn the knob. The gang members in there would be surprised to see her, she could overpower them before they could really react, and then—

Caxton's legs went out from under her. Guilty Jen had grabbed one of her feet and yanked upward. Caxton went flying and bounced off the steps, sliding downward. Her broken arm collided hard with one wall and she sang out in pain as she slammed into the landing, her teeth grating on the concrete there.

Above her, higher up the stairs, Guilty Jen stood looking down. She was breathing a little faster than normal, and there was a drop of sweat on one of her cheeks. One of her hands was striped with blood where Caxton had cut her. Otherwise she was unscathed. The door to the central command center was right behind her. Caxton would never reach it now. She wasn't going to save Clara. She wasn't going to save herself. In a few seconds she would be dead, and everything she had ever cared about and the one woman she had ever truly loved would be destroyed. This was it. The moment she'd known was coming for years now. The moment when her calling failed her.

'I gotta say,' Guilty Jen told her, 'you can hold your mud. Well. It's been fun.'

The gangbanger took a step down toward Caxton. Another step.

Caxton couldn't have fought back against a kitten just then. Pain, exhaustion, and utter desolation were all dragging her down. Telling her she was finished.

Behind Guilty Jen the door to central command swung open.

Guilty Jen just had time to look surprised as a snow-white hand reached around her face and yanked her backward, out of Caxton's line of sight.

There was a muffled scream. The instantly recognizable

sound of a human neck being snapped, the vertebrae letting go one after the other like popcorn popping. And then a sound that Caxton found far too familiar. The squelching, sucking noise of human blood being drained from a grievous wound.

The vampires were awake, alright.

50.

Maricón and Featherwood were arguing. Clara was paying attention with half an ear, just enough to hear if they started talking about her. Occasionally they did, and always it was to ask each other whether it was time to kill Clara or if they should wait for some kind of sign from Guilty Jen. The second that Laura was dead, they were supposed to cut her throat. Of course, they would have no way of knowing whether or not Laura was dead until Guilty Jen came up the stairs, probably brandishing some grisly trophy from the fight. Laura's severed head, maybe, or just an ear to—

Stop it! Stop it! Clara howled inside her own head. She had managed to make her face blank, and had even stopped shivering. But she couldn't stop the fear from getting inside. She couldn't stop thinking about the future. About the very brief future.

The possibility that Laura might kill Guilty Jen never seemed to occur to the members of the set.

Clara put most of her attention in front of her. If she

concentrated on something else, if she really focused on the fine details, she could keep from crying in panic. It was the same trick, really, that she had used with her camera when she started feeling queasy at Malvern's crime scenes. If you just focused on what your eyes were actually seeing, just the colors and the shapes, you didn't have to think about what anything actually meant.

So she studied the prison's nerve center. Its controls. The prison had been updated frequently since it had been built, almost fifty years ago. The technology of warehousing human beings had advanced by light-years since then. Instead of tearing out all the old equipment and replacing it all at once, however, clearly the prison's keepers had kludged everything together, shoving computer terminals in beside old black-and-white analog closed-circuit television equipment, stringing bundles of Ethernet cable as thick as Clara's arm along the top of control panels in old worn steel cases and covered in black plastic knobs. Everything was patched together with duct tape and ancient wiring furry with dust, and all the controls had been relabeled with pieces of masking tape, written on with Sharpie pen. The communications board was a nightmare of dials and switches and toggles. The master control board that opened and closed the prison's doors was simpler but built to be taken seriously, in black enamel lined with scuffed rivets. Big red panic buttons were everywhere, usually accompanied by labels that read in huge letters, DO NOT TOUCH! EVER!

All of it was dead, of course, and perfectly silent. Without power the prison couldn't breathe, couldn't live the way it was meant to. So when the power did come back on, all at once, for a second Clara could do nothing but gasp as red and white lights flared to life, as sirens, buzzers, Klaxon, and alarms rang all over the boards, as every television screen and computer monitor in the cluttered space flickered back on at the same time.

'—why it matters, she's supposed to die anyway, and then we only have to worry about Marty, and he's nothing. You and me could take turns having a nap, right, and—'

'Hey,' Featherwood said.

'—just a thought, but maybe—'

'Hey!' Featherwood shouted. 'You! The girlfriend. What the fuck did you just do?' the burned woman demanded. She ran over to the control board, where Clara stood dumbfounded, and ran her hands over the dials and knobs, obviously unsure of how to turn it all off.

'I didn't do anything,' Clara said. 'It just happened. Look – there.' She pointed at one of the television monitors. It showed a monochrome view of a claustrophobic room full of machinery. A shaky time stamp in the corner of the screen read 12:00:00 PWRHS, CAM 1. 'That's a view inside the power-house. Where the power comes from,' Clara explained. 'Caxton cut the power, but the warden sent a bunch of half-deads to get it back online, somehow. I guess they found a way.'

On the screen a couple of half-deads were giving each other a high-five. They looked up at the camera and waved cheerily, obviously proud of what they'd accomplished. On the floor a third one lay, its torn face blackened and its fingers burned down to little more than stubs. Clearly they'd had some trouble with the repairs.

Maricón chose that moment to look out the window. 'Just in time,' she said. 'It was gonna get real dark in here soon. Look. The sun's down.'

Featherwood spun around. 'Oh, shit. I didn't realize this

was taking so long. Goddamn it. I know Jen has a real hard-on for whacking this Caxton, but we cannot still be here when the vampires wake up. Here – how does this phone work?' she asked, looking at Clara. She had picked up a phone handset from the communications panel. 'Do I need to dial nine or something?'

Clara shrugged. 'How should I know?'

'You really are useless, aren'cha?' Featherwood grimaced and dialed a number.

'What are you doing, *loca*?' Maricón asked. 'You think she wants to be disturbed just now?'

'I ain't dying here just because she lost track of time.' Featherwood glanced over her shoulder as if worried Guilty Jen might be standing right there. From what Clara had seen of the set and how it operated, that was a pretty sane precaution. 'Here, you,' she said, slapping Clara on the back, 'get me a picture of what's going on down there. Let me see if Caxton's dead or not.'

They all waited while Featherwood stared at the ceiling, presumably listening to the phone on the other end ring.

Then Featherwood said, 'Jen? Jen, what just happened? Jen? Is Caxton dead? Jen? Can you hear me?' She glanced at Maricón and said, 'She picked up, so it must be okay, right? You – I said, get me a view of the first floor.' She smacked Clara in the ear, hard enough to really hurt. Clara studied the controls on the video board, looking for a way to figure out which camera showed what part of the facility.

'What? Jen, there's something you should know, the—'

Maricón growled. 'Ask her if we can off the *cerda* already.'

'Sorry, Jen, but the sun's down. I thought you'd want to

know. It's getting pretty dark outside, so the vampires should be waking up any second. I don't see them on any of the monitors yet, but I figured – hey. Do you want us to kill the girlfriend now?'

Featherwood held the phone away from her ear. 'What the fuck? There was this really loud buzzing noise and now all I get is a dial tone. What happened, stupid?'

She hit Clara with the phone. Clara shied away, but didn't protest. 'I think I have a picture for you now. This one says it's of the Hub.' She flipped a switch and a monitor over their heads flickered. When the image cleared it showed a brightly lit room with many exits. The floor was littered with gun refuse – brass shell casings, an abandoned shotgun, craters in the floor tiles dug up by high-velocity machine-gun rounds. Lying in the middle of it, in a pool of blood, was Queenie. She was clearly very dead.

For a while the three of them just stared at the image.

'Holy fuck,' Maricón said. 'What the hell happened down there?'

Featherwood grunted. 'She said she had Caxton down to rights. I don't know any more than you fucking do, so shut up and let me think!'

'Um, excuse me,' Marty said. It was the first thing Clara had heard him say in hours. The three women spun around to stare at the ex-CO, who had been sitting quietly in a rolling chair in the middle of the room. His hands were still bound, so Featherwood and Maricón had figured he was harmless there. His eyes were wide now and sweat was rolling down his forehead. He was trying to kick his way across the room, but one of the wheels on his chair was stuck so he was just going in pathetic circles.

Clara looked up and saw that one of the window panels of the central command center was missing. Not broken, not torn

296

out of its frame. Just gone. Cold evening air was blowing in, lifting her hair and getting it in her eyes.

Then the shadows in the room moved. Five white shapes stepped out of the gloom. And within the space of twenty seconds everyone but Clara was dead.

51.

Marty was the first to die. Malvern moved forward faster than he could push himself away in the chair and snapped his neck, turning his head almost all the way around. Before she could scream, Maricón was grabbed by one of the others, a female vampire in an orange jumpsuit with the sleeves torn off. The vampire started to lean in to savage Maricón's neck, but Malvern flashed across the room and slapped the vampire away from the Latina gangbanger.

'None of you shall drink here,' she said. 'Ye can't yet handle the madness the blood brings.' Then she choked Maricón until her face turned purple and her tongue stuck out of her mouth.

'Stay the fuck back,' Featherwood said, brandishing a shank. Another of the new vampires – this one naked – ran up to the burned woman and laughed as the shank sank into her chest again and again. As it came out each time, the wounds were already healing.

'You didn't say it would feel this good,' the vampire growled. Then she spun around and slammed her forearm up against

298

Featherwood's throat, crushing her trachea. The burned gang-banger dropped to her knees and stared up at Clara as she struggled for a breath she couldn't take.

Another of the vampires, this one wearing panties and a stab-proof vest, was behind Clara before she could even turn to run. The vampire's hands settled on Clara's shoulders. It felt like she was being pressed down by heavy stones. 'Kneel,' the vampire said.

Clara knelt.

'She lives, for now,' Malvern announced. The vampire holding Clara nodded but didn't let her go.

The five of them came and stood around her, looking down at her. They were beautiful, in a way. They were hairless and their skin was perfect, creamy smooth and perfectly white. Their bodies were tight and lithe, even Malvern's. All the blood she'd drunk the night before agreed with her – she didn't even look wrinkled anymore. The only reason Clara even knew it was Malvern was that one of her eyes was missing, leaving just an empty socket in her head. That, and that she was wearing her old mauve nightdress, which didn't look like an empty sack on her anymore. Now it clung to the filled-in curves of her body.

Otherwise they were all identical. Their ears were long and came to sharp tips. Their eyes glowed a dull red. And their mouths were filled with rows of wicked, translucent teeth.

There was a clattering sound from the stairwell – from the stairs that led down to the Hub. It had to be Guilty Jen, coming up to announce that Laura was dead. Clara's head dropped forward, her body unable to support its weight anymore.

For a moment the five vampires just stood looking at the door. It didn't open. One of the vampires moved to the door, eventually, and stared at it as if she could see right through it. Then she tore it open, reached through, and pulled Guilty Jen into the room so fast the gangbanger barely had time to scream. The vampire holding her grabbed Jen around the waist and around the mouth, effortlessly holding her motionless. But then Guilty Jen did something Clara would have thought impossible. Writhing like a snake, she slid right through the vampire's arms and ducked between her legs, rolling out the other side. Immediately she sprang upward into a combat stance, one hand held out in front of her like a blade.

The vampire turned on her heel, her face lit up with excitement. Even Clara could see the deep cut in Guilty Jen's palm. And the drop of blood rolling down her forearm.

Malvern growled, no words at all, just a pure animal noise. The vampire facing Guilty Jen didn't seem to notice. She was watching the hand, watching the blood. Malvern started to move, but the vampire got there first. Grabbing Jen again, she pulled the gangbanger's hand into her mouth and bit down hard. There was a noise like someone trying to suck up the last bit of frozen strawberry from the bottom of a milk shake, and then Guilty Jen lost all her color.

The gangbanger tried one last roundhouse kick. She got halfway through her arc before collapsing to the floor. She wasn't breathing.

The newly fed vampire dropped to her knees. Her chest shook and her hands grabbed at the floor, her fingernails digging deep channels through the linoleum tile. When she looked up her cheeks were slightly pink, as if she'd applied a layer of blush, and her eyes were on fire.

Malvern hadn't stopped moving. She collided with the blood-drunk vampire, hard enough to knock her over on her back. Then she raised one arm and brought it down like a pile driver, her fingers sinking into the vampire's flesh as if through so much milk. There was a horrible sucking noise

300

and an elastic snap and then Malvern pulled the vampire's heart out right through her shattered rib cage.

The fire went out of the dead vampire's eyes.

'Ye shall not defy me,' Malvern rasped, getting to her feet again. 'Ye may be strong, but I am stronger.'

Every single red glowing eye in the room was fixed on the heart in Malvern's hand. It was dark, almost black in color, and it was still beating, though without any kind of human rhythm. It slowed down as they watched, and eventually stopped.

Clara didn't think about what she did while they were distracted. It wasn't as if she had any kind of plan. Her hands crept across the control board behind her, the one that monitored and administered the prison's communication systems. She turned a knob here, flipped a switch there. And leaned toward a microphone that stuck out from the top of the board on a flexible wand.

They weren't going to kill her. Not right away. She could get away with this, and still they wouldn't kill her. She just hoped they didn't know spinal anatomy the way Guilty Jen did, or some even more horrible way of letting her live but making her wish she was dead.

'Fetlock,' she shouted at the microphone, 'if you're waiting for the right time to attack – this is it!'

Every intercom speaker in the prison picked up the message and relayed it at ear-shattering volume. Clara could hear her words echoing around the prison yard and bouncing upward into the darkening night sky.

The vampires looked around the room as if they expected federal agents to come storming out of closets and crawl spaces, machine guns blazing.

That didn't happen.

Clara begged, silently, for some sign. Some signal, of any

301

kind, that meant Fetlock had heard her. That he was out there, ready to save her. Maybe he could have shot a flare over the prison. Maybe he could have called in on the prison's multiband radio system.

But he didn't.

Malvern took a step toward Clara, and suddenly she was right there, so close that every hair on Clara's body stood up at once. Then Malvern hit her, and—

52.

'Jesus,' Clara said, 'that hurt.'

She was conscious again. She kind of wished she wasn't. Her whole jaw felt like it had been dislocated, knocked backward off its joints and into the fleshy part of her neck. It hurt to talk. It hurt to sit up. It hurt a little every time she breathed, a twinge that went all the way up to the top of her sinuses and deep into her chest. She touched, carefully, the skin of her neck and throat and felt it swollen and tender. It hurt to touch her face, so she stopped doing that.

It hurt to open her eyes, but she had to know where she was. She was still alive, and she presumed she was still a prisoner of the vampires, but beyond that what her eyes told her didn't help explain very much.

She was in some kind of cage, just tall enough for her to stand up in if she ducked her head, and just long enough that she could lie down in it. It was made of crisscrossing bars, spaced about six inches apart. All the bars were wrapped with yellow spongy foam rubber, which was patched here and there with duct tape. The cage had a rubber sheet on its floor that smelled like someone had peed on it, then hosed it off with harsh detergents but not very thoroughly.

Similar cages filled the room around her. Two of them were occupied but the people in them were either asleep, unconscious, or dead. Both of them wore orange jumpsuits.

There was also a desk in the room, with a portable generator sitting next to it. The generator was switched off. Sitting at the desk was a vampire. The one wearing a sleeveless jumpsuit. The vampire was reading a magazine.

Or trying to. She would bring it up close to her eyes as if she had trouble making out the words in the dimly lit room, then sigh angrily and flip rapidly through three or four pages before repeating the operation.

'I can read, sort of,' the vampire growled. 'I can understand the words. I mean, I was never a big reader before, but I knew how. But now they mostly look like weird little squiggly shapes. And even when I try hard, I can read a sentence and then forget how it started before I reach the end. It just don't seem to matter, you know? Like whatever this asshole was trying to say about Brad and Angelina just isn't all that important anymore.'

'You knew I was awake,' Clara said.

'Well, you sat up, for one thing. That's a fucking easy sign right there. Plus I saw your blood go faster. When you sleep your blood slows down. Your heart beats slower. Did you know I can see your heart? It's like I got x-ray eyes. That's pretty cool, I guess.'

It's seriously creepy, Clara thought. 'You're not human anymore,' she told the vampire.

'What the fuck you just say, girl?'

Clara cringed. But she knew that as long as she was engaged in a nice, civil conversation with this bloodsucker, she wasn't being dismembered, eaten, or tortured. That was worth

304

something. 'I didn't mean any offense. It's just – vampires don't care about the same things human beings care about. You're not supposed to. Celebrity gossip has got to be pretty low on the list of things important to vampires.'

'Yeah? What's at the top?'

Blood. Clara tried very hard not to say that out loud. Even if it was true. Blood was the single thing vampires truly cared the most about. Pretty much the only thing. 'I don't know,' she said, instead. 'I guess you'll have to figure that out for yourself.'

'I still feel pretty human. I mean, better. Stronger. But I'm still wondering about my kids, and what they'll think about this change. And about their daddy. Except . . . I keep thinking about the hair on his back. It never used to bother me before, or at least, I put it out of my head. But now I keep seeing it, seeing him on top of me like I'm looking down at him from the ceiling and all I can see is this thick rug of hair. Oh, and his smell. He never would shower before we did it, that always bugged me. Now when I think about it, it kinda makes me sick.'

Vampires had their own body odor. One that didn't wash off. They smelled like the bottom of a hamster cage – a sick hamster's cage. It was a nasty, animal smell, very faint, but it was one of the signs a vampire was nearby. Clara could just smell it now from ten feet away.

'You're – Hauser, right? I was there when you took the curse,' Clara said, for lack of anything better. 'In the warden's office. Where is the warden, by the way?'

'Dead,' Hauser told her. 'That was pretty much the first thing Malvern did, when she woke up tonight and found out how fucked up things got during the day.'

Clara closed her eyes. If she'd had a plan – she hadn't, not really, she knew she was screwed. But the brain kept trying to piece things together, even when all hope was gone. If she had consciously tried to think of a plan, it would have involved playing Malvern and the warden off each other. Widening the rift between the two of them. Apparently Malvern had taken the expedient course toward solving that problem.

'Hey, you. Hey,' Hauser said. She got up from the desk and took a step toward one of the other cages. 'I know you're awake.' The vampire kicked the cage and made it slide a foot and a half across the floor. Inside it someone struggled to grab at the bars and pull themselves upright.

'Laura,' Clara breathed, when she saw who it was.

Laura said nothing. She just sat down on the floor of her cage and lowered her head. One of her arms looked wrong. It was tucked up across her chest in a way that looked painful. Her face was bruised and one lip was puffy and swollen. But she was still alive.

'And you. Who the fuck are you?' the vampire snarled, and grabbed the third occupied cage. She picked it up easily and then dropped it to the floor with a deafening clang. The woman inside rolled over and batted at the bars with one weak hand.

'You can call me . . . Gert. Or Gerty, whichever . . . you like.'

'She was Laura – I mean Caxton's cellmate,' Clara told the vampire. If she could get Hauser to sit down again, to sit calmly, there was less chance of her accidentally killing one of them. Clearly she had orders not to, but vampires sometimes didn't know their own strength. 'She helped Caxton escape from the SHU.'

'This piece of trash got out of the hole? Shee-it,' Hauser said. 'She's about likely to have a heart attack right now. Well, fuck her. She don't have to survive very much longer. Just 'til five o'clock.'

Clara frowned. 'What happens then?'

306

The vampire shrugged. 'Ain't up to me. It's you three that decides. Malvern said twenty-three hours, and that's what she's got. When it's almost up I'm supposed to ask you, do you want to be like me. Tougher than nails and live forever. Or do you want to die? Only there's a catch.'

Of course there was. 'What's the catch?' Clara asked.

'You gotta be unanimous. All three of you become vampires or all three of you die. It seems kind of simple to me, but if even one of you vetoes it, you all get eaten.'

And so we're going to die, Clara thought. There was no way any logical, thinking person would take the other choice, and become—

'I say yes, please,' Gert whispered.

In her cage, Caxton said nothing. She was picking at a piece of tape holding the foam rubber around a steel bar, just scraping away at it with a fingernail. She hadn't even looked over at Clara. Hadn't said a word.

Clara couldn't help but think that was a bad sign.

53.

The tape came away, leaving Caxton's fingers sticky and one fingernail broken. She dug a finger into the foam rubber wrapped around the bar of her cage and felt a sharp edge underneath. It was as she'd suspected – the bars weren't bars at all, but strips of steel as flat as ribbons. You could cut yourself pretty well on the edge.

She looked up and saw the vampire standing over Clara's cage. They were still talking. Well, that was fine. For now. She knew what Clara was trying to achieve. Hauser was a brand-new vampire. There was still plenty of humanity left in her – it took weeks for the bloodlust to take hold. Over time it would erode Hauser's personality until there was nothing left. Each night she woke in a coffin she would feel less connection to the person she had once been. Each night she would think more and more often about blood, and how good it would taste running down her throat, and how little it mattered if she had to hurt people to get it. But for now, on her first night post-death, Hauser could be reasoned with. She could be talked around.

That wasn't what Caxton had in mind, though.

They'd taken all her weapons. They'd taken her stab-proof vest when they came and found her in the stairwell, reeling in pain, barely able to move. They couldn't take away her brain, though. Her knowledge of what made vampires tick.

She grabbed the naked steel bar of her cage and jerked her hand along the sharp edge. The pain was intense but short-lived. It barely made her gasp. She felt her skin give way, though, felt hot wet blood well up across the creases of her palm. She flexed her hand over and over again, pumping blood out of her veins, until it was dripping on the floor of her cage.

The vampire's head lifted and she looked around. As if something was calling her name.

'Did I say something wrong?' Clara asked, trying to sound innocent. 'I was just asking about your parents because—'

'Hold on,' Hauser said. Her nose twitched. Vampire senses were sharper than those of human beings. Where blood was involved they were positively acute. Like a shark, a vampire could smell blood a mile away. 'There's something – I shouldn't—'

Caxton flicked her wrist. Droplets of blood stained the foam rubber bars in front of her. A few of them sailed through the air and splattered the floor outside the cage. She flexed her hand a few more times and then brushed her palm against the bars, spreading even more blood all over them.

There was no apprehension in her, no fear that this wouldn't work. It would definitely work. It would almost certainly get her killed, too. That was okay. She'd stopped believing she could end this neatly. She couldn't see a lot of positive outcomes. But she would die trying, and that had to count for something.

Hauser padded over toward her, nose rummaging through the air. Her red eyes fixed on a spot of blood a few feet outside of Caxton's cage.

'I cut myself,' Caxton said, her tone flat and emotionless.

'That was kind of stupid, bitch. It's not like I'm going to come in there and bandage you up,' Hauser said. But she was still looking at the blood.

'I wonder what it tastes like,' Caxton said. 'You know. If we're going to be vampires. I wonder what it tastes like to you.'

Hauser seemed to recover herself a little. 'Yeah. Well, you can lick it off the floor later. I'm supposed to sit at that desk and just watch you guys. Make sure you talk over Malvern's offer real good.'

'I bet it tastes like – what? Wine? Maybe really good chocolate,' Caxton suggested. She hadn't expected Hauser to put up this much resistance.

The vampire squatted down and put one white fingertip next to the blood spot. And just stared at it. Didn't touch it. Didn't move. When they wanted to, vampires could stand so still you'd think they were marble statues. They didn't breathe. Their muscles never got stiff or tired.

'You don't have to do this,' Clara shouted. 'You can fight it.'

'Clara, please,' Caxton said, trying not to sound too angry. 'Don't. Not right now.'

'She'll kill you on the spot,' Clara whispered. 'Suck you dry!'

'No I won't,' Hauser said. 'The last one did that, Malvern tore her heart out while we watched. I ain't stupid, you know? I may not be a genius, but—'

She stopped talking in midsentence as if something had interrupted her train of thought. Then she trailed her finger

310

through the cooling spot of blood. Lifted it carefully to her face and sniffed at it.

Then she licked her fingertip. And her eyelids drifted shut.

For a while there was no sound in the room. No one moved or spoke. Caxton held her breath. Then, when the vampire didn't open her eyes again, she said, 'Look. I got it all over these bars. I kind of made a mess.'

The eyelids snapped open. The red eyes were burning.

For a vampire the first taste of blood was like a junkie's first fix of heroin. It would never taste as good as that first time. It would never be so clean, and pure, and fulfilling. It took them places, took them to dark new worlds that were theirs to explore. Places human beings couldn't go.

It made them want more.

Endlessly more.

Hauser attacked the cage with a sudden savagery that had Caxton reeling backward. She felt her bad arm hit the side of the cage and she winced in pain, but her brain wouldn't let her feel much. It was too busy overloading her body with adrenaline. Getting her ready to run. But there was no place to run. The cage bars bent inward and snapped as Hauser licked and tore at them, tearing the foam rubber to crumbs, smashing through the lock on the cage's door.

Caxton had been careful to smear as much blood as she could spare on that lock.

The door flew open and Caxton rolled out onto the floor. She grabbed the first thing her hand could find.

The vampire turned and glared at her. Her mouth opened wide and Caxton could see the dozens of nasty fangs in there. A few of them were wet with her blood. There was no intelligence in Hauser's eyes now. There was nothing to reason with.

311

No thinking going on at all. Just pure vampire instinct.

The vampire pounced. Caxton braced herself and twisted her head away at the last possible moment. Hauser's teeth clicked on the floor where her jugular vein had been. The vampire lifted her head up again to howl in frustration—

—and screamed in agony instead.

Caxton had grabbed a broken piece of steel bar, part of her cage before the vampire demolished it. She had held it in front of her like a spike and let momentum do the rest. The bar had been broken off at an angle, giving it a good point. Caxton knew exactly where to place it for maximum effect.

It pierced the vampire's heart like a needle, and came out through the skin of her back.

The vampire's body convulsed, demonically strong muscles pounding the floor, thrashing at the air. A blow hit Caxton in the thigh, instantly numbing the flesh there. Another slapped at her face, but they were getting weaker now. Hauser's jaws flashed open and closed as she tore and rent at death itself, but she couldn't put it off for long. Little by little the red fire in her eyes went out. The tension in her muscles eased. She died a second and final time, pinning Caxton underneath her corpse.

Using the impaling bar as a lever, Caxton pushed the body off of her. Then she searched the vampire, looking for keys. She found one that had a tiny white label on it reading CDR, which she assumed meant Cooling Down Rooms. That was what the warden had called these cages.

She unlocked Clara's cage, and, after a moment's hesitation, Gert's, too. Her celly crawled out of the cage with a look of sheepish self-hatred on her face. 'I was supposed to be useful to you,' she said. 'I was supposed to help. I let you down.'

'Don't worry about it,' Caxton said. 'I—'

312

She didn't bother finishing the thought. Clara was too busy grabbing her in a desperate embrace. Then she pressed her lips hard against Caxton's and kissed her, again and again.

54.

Clara filled Laura in on the situation as quickly as she could. There were two remaining vampires other than Malvern in the prison, and an unknown number of half-deads. The warden was dead, and so were Guilty Jen and her set, which meant there wasn't a single living person at large in the facility other than herself, Laura, and Gert. Fetlock was supposed to be outside with a small army of SWAT troopers, but so far he hadn't made his presence known.

There were nine hours left until the twenty-three-hour deadline.

'We're not going to be here when the deadline comes,' Laura said. 'One way or the other. Malvern's playing a game with us. I don't want to play anymore.'

'She's trying to torture you. That whole business with us having to make a unanimous decision – she's trying to get under your skin,' Clara said, grabbing Laura's arm. She felt the muscle there, under the sleeve of her jumpsuit. Laura had always been so strong.

'Maybe. That almost seems too simple for Malvern – she

likes to be two steps ahead of me, always.' Laura shook her head. 'Anyway. I know what we do next. We all get guns.'

'Fuck yes,' Gert crowed, and slapped hands with Laura. Clara wondered what there was between the two of them. She wasn't jealous, really, just—

There was no time for that sort of thing. The three of them raced down to the Hub, which was deserted except for the corpse of Queenie. With the lights on it was easy to find the armory door. It was a heavy reinforced door with multiple locks, but when Laura pushed on it, it swung open easily on well-oiled hinges.

Too easily. Clara's heart sagged in her chest even before they got inside and found that the armory had been wrecked. There were piles of guns on the floor – pistols, shotguns, submachine guns, heavier stuff, too, by the dozen, and box after box of ammunition – but the barrel of every single weapon had been bent out of shape. One assault rifle was still clamped in a table vise. The half-deads had been busy.

'No,' Laura said. As if she could change reality by denying it. 'No. We worked too hard to get here.' She picked up a riot gun. Its barrel turned ninety degrees from its stock and pointed at the wall. In disgust she threw it hard against the far wall to make an impotent clattering noise when it hit the floor.

'It makes sense, I guess,' Clara said. 'The half-deads couldn't use the guns, and the vampires don't need them. Why leave them lying around? Just in case anybody wandered in here. Say, someone like Guilty Jen.'

Laura shook her head. 'No. No! This wasn't just about hedging bets. Malvern knew I would come here. She's been leading me around like a bull with a ring in its nose. She *let* me get this far. Her pal the warden even gave me directions! She wanted me to see this.'

Clara sighed. 'Does it matter?'

Laura didn't answer. Instead she grabbed Clara's arm and pulled her out of the armory and back to the stairs. Together they headed up to the top level, to the central command center. Gert came trailing after.

Laura kicked open the door and stepped through. There was one half-dead in the room, sitting in a chair watching a bank of monitors. It had its back to them. Before it could turn around Laura ran up behind it and bashed its head forward against the HVAC control board. It didn't fight back.

'You stay here,' Laura said. 'You can watch me on the monitors. You know how to work all this stuff?'

'I can figure it out,' Clara said, 'but—'

'If you see me walking into trouble, use the intercom. I'll be able to hear you just about anywhere. If you find Malvern, let me know where she is.'

'Or,' Clara began.

Laura gave her a cautious look.

'Or,' Clara continued, 'you could stay here with me. We can call Fetlock. Let him storm this place and take care of Malvern. That way we'll both live.' She gave the cautious look right back. 'You know perfectly well that without a gun you don't have a chance against her. You're going down there to kill yourself.'

'No,' Laura protested. 'I'm going down there to kill Malvern or die trying. I thought that was clear.'

'I thought—' Clara said. But she knew she couldn't change Laura's mind. 'It doesn't matter what I thought.' *I thought you were the same woman I fell in love with*, she was thinking. *I thought the last couple of years didn't matter anymore, that this could all be over, that we could try to work things out, to be a couple again. That I wouldn't have to break up with you.*

The look in Laura's eyes said different. When Clara had first met Laura she was already fighting vampires. She hadn't

316

stopped since, not even long enough to be a proper girlfriend. To be in love, even for just one day.

'Go,' Clara said. For the same reason she always had. Because it was selfish and stupid to ask someone to stop saving the world just because you thought they were sexy. 'Go! You need to do this. It's who you are. I've got your back.'

Laura nodded. It was a serious nod. A businesslike nod. It broke Clara's heart, but she would never admit it out loud.

The second she left central command, Clara locked the door and pushed a chair up under the knob. That should hold against any half-deads who came up to get a look at the monitors. She had no doubt a vampire could get through the barricade without lifting more than a finger or two, but it was something. She shoved the half-dead out of its chair and started working the boards. She needed to call Fetlock. She needed to figure out how the video board worked.

'You can help me,' she said to Gert, and turned to look for Laura's cellmate. But the red-haired girl was gone, too. She had taken apart the pathetic barricade and left the room without a word, leaving Clara all alone. She felt absurdly familiar with the situation. Laura was out chasing vampires and Clara was stuck alone watching TV.

55.

'Laura — I've got her. Malvern's in C Dorm, along with a couple of half-deads. They're taking donations.' Clara's voice wasn't as loud as Caxton had expected it to be. 'I've figured out how to use individual intercoms without turning on the entire system at once — so they didn't just hear me say that.'

'That's a plus,' Caxton said. She stopped for a second and looked up at the camera in the stairwell's ceiling. 'Did you just hear me?'

Clara didn't respond. So the intercoms didn't work both ways. She would be able to hear Clara but not talk to her. It was still better than going it alone.

'No sign of the other two vampires,' Clara said. 'I don't think they know we're free yet, but I'm thinking that someone will go and check on us eventually. I don't know how much time you'll have.'

She was halfway down the stairs to the Hub when she heard a clattering behind her and saw Gert coming down the steps.

'Go back,' Caxton said. 'Go back and guard Clara.'

Gert shook her head. 'I came this far with you. I'm not

backing off now. Are you really going to tell me you don't want an extra pair of hands right now, when you only got one that works?'

'Fine. Just don't get yourself killed.' Caxton reached the door to the Hub and glanced up at the nearest camera.

'All clear,' Clara told her. 'Nothing moving in there, anyway.'

Caxton pushed open the door and stepped inside the circular room at the heart of the prison. She scooped her shotgun off the floor – no one had bothered to remove it – and went straight to the armory and found a box of shotgun shells. They were loaded with plastic bullets, of course, and therefore absolutely useless against vampires. But maybe she could do something about that.

'Here,' she told Gert, handing her a box of .22-caliber bullets. 'Pry six of these out of their casings.' There was a pretty good set of machine tools in the armory, useful for adjusting and refitting the now ruined guns. With a pair of pliers she pulled the plastic bullet free of its casing and threw it away. It wasn't easy doing it with one good arm, but she gritted her teeth and got through the pain. As Gert handed her the bullets she loaded them into the shell casing as if they were buckshot. They weren't perfect. They weren't spherical, so they would tumble when the shell's gunpowder went off, making them even less accurate that normal shot. They were too big, as well, and the shell had half the load of powder a normal shotgun shell used – the plastic bullet didn't need to travel as fast as a lethal round. But if she got up close, very close, and fired point blank into Malvern's chest – maybe. Maybe the makeshift shot would punch a hole right through the vampire's chest cavity. Maybe it would be enough to destroy her only vulnerable spot, her heart.

She would be well fed, which meant she would be able to resist an awful lot of damage. Caxton would never get in more than one shot, not even if she took Malvern completely by surprise. But it was better than the alternative, which was to try to shiv the vampire with a sharpened spoon. She knew that would never work.

When she'd finished loading her hand-built shell, she checked the shotgun a couple of times to make sure it hadn't been tampered with. She shoved it into the armpit of her good right arm. Then she nodded to Gert and stepped out of the armory.

Now. Which way?

There were exits leading out of the Hub in every direction, some of them darker than others, some of them behind heavy barred gates, some wide open. 'Third exit on your right,' Clara said. C Dorm was behind a locked gate, but as Caxton approached a buzzer sounded and the gate clanked open on its hinges automatically. 'I can open any door in the prison from here,' Clara said.

Caxton looked up at a camera and mimed turning a key.

'You're asking – oh, you're asking if I can lock them, too? No, unfortunately. The controls up here are just for emergency use, if there's a fire or something. They have to be locked by hand with an actual key.'

'At least we can go wherever we want,' Gert said.

Caxton didn't bother replying. She headed through the open gate and into a long hallway that led straight to the dorm. It was lined on either side with checkpoints and defensive kiosks, but Caxton ignored those.

Except – there was a weird smell in the air. Caxton had learned a long time ago that when weird things happened around vampires it didn't pay to ignore them. She sniffed around and found the smell was coming from one of the kiosks. It was a smell almost like roasted pork, though more sickly sweet. Like someone had been burning the hair off of a pig, perhaps.

'Smells like my daddy's barbecue,' Gert whispered when Caxton asked if she smelled it too. 'He had a half an oil drum full of coals, big enough to roast a horse if he wanted to, he always said. He used to do a whole suckling pig for Fourth of July.'

Caxton hadn't eaten in a long time. She was pretty sure that what she found in the kiosk would not be a pig roast.

Except – in a way, it was. In a very sick, very darkly humorous way.

'I think that's the warden,' Caxton said, when she popped open the door of the kiosk. Inside, lying on the floor, was a charred human corpse. 'The clothes look right.'

Clara's voice came very softly over the intercom. 'That's the warden!' she said.

'Yeah.' They had known already that Malvern had killed the warden. Now they knew how. The vampires must have doused her in gasoline and set her on fire. 'I don't get it. That's not Malvern's style. Sometimes vampires like to torture their victims – they get off on it – but she was never that kind. I think this is a message, except I don't know how to read it, you know?'

Gert's open face suggested she didn't know. 'You been after Malvern a long time, huh?'

'You could say that.' It had only been a couple of years, really. But in that time Malvern had cost Caxton a girlfriend, a mentor, half the police force of Gettysburg, Pennsylvania, and, least of all, her career.

'You really want her dead.'

'Oh, yes.' Caxton wanted nothing more in the entire world. She would let Fetlock take the other two. She didn't know them, had no history with them. But Malvern had to die now. Once it was done, Caxton would be finished with vampires. She could go back to being a model prisoner, do her bit, and then restart her life.

Or she could die in the next thirty seconds.

She was pretty much okay with either scenario, as long as she got one shot in.

There was nothing they could do for the warden, even if they wanted to. They left her body where it lay and moved to the far end of the corridor, where another barred gate was all that stood between them and C Dorm. 'The plan's pretty simple. We rush in there. You distract the half-deads, however you can. I get as close as possible to Malvern and I shoot.'

'And then what?'

'Then we play it by ear. You ready?'

Gert nodded. Caxton looked up at the video camera in the ceiling.

'She's close to the far end of the dorm,' Clara whispered. 'There are three half-deads between you and her. It's just a straight run and she doesn't look like she has any idea that something is up.' The intercom crackled for a second – Clara had left it turned on, though she wasn't saying anything. Finally she came back and said, 'Laura. Good luck.'

'Thanks,' Caxton said, even if Clara couldn't hear her. Then she pointed at the gate and held up three fingers. Two fingers. One.

The gate popped open with an electronic buzz.

They stepped through. Every light in the dorm was on, and Caxton had no trouble seeing the rows of cells, the medical carts in the walkway, the half-deads drawing blood from the arms that prisoners shoved through the bars. Dead ahead, not fifty yards away, Malvern had her back turned. She was wearing her decrepit mauve nightgown, and the skin on her head and bare shoulders was perfect, creamy, unblemished.

Caxton's vision narrowed down to a spot just left of Malvern's spine, just below the wing shape of her shoulder blade. Right where her heart would be. She was running so fast, she didn't even feel her feet moving beneath her.

You didn't aim a shotgun, she told herself. You pointed it. You didn't squeeze the trigger. You yanked it. You could do all that with just one hand.

Caxton had closed half the distance, Gert right by her side, when the intercom blared again. Clara wasn't whispering this time.

'Laura, look out! They were hiding on the upper level the whole time!'

Caxton stumbled to a stop. Malvern turned around to look at her with a wicked grin full of nasty teeth. Caxton turned around and looked up at the galleries above her, to the second tier of cells. From either side, a female vampire dropped down, landing effortlessly like a pair of cats.

As if they had all the time in the world, they started walking toward her, their red eyes locked on her face.

56.

'Have ye made your choice, then?' Malvern asked. 'And were ye three unanimous in the choosing?'

Caxton brought the shotgun up to shoulder level. She swiveled from side to side, pointing the weapon at one of the new vampires, then the other. She thought of how she'd tricked Hauser, but she didn't have the time or the imagination to come up with something like that again. Anyway, she knew Malvern. Malvern would have stuck the stupidest of her brand-new brood with guard duty. These two would be smarter than Hauser.

They were getting closer. They clearly enjoyed the anticipation, the moment before the kill. One of them, the one in a stab-proof vest and panties, was licking her lips. The other, dressed in a jumpsuit with the sleeves torn off, kept wiggling her fingers in the air as if trying out a new set of claws for the first time. Vampire fingernails looked just like their human counterparts (if paler), but they could tear through sheet metal without breaking. They had no trouble at all taking apart a human body.

'Forbin, please secure Miss Caxton,' Malvern said. As scared as she was, Caxton thought that was odd. Always before Malvern had referred to her by her first name. What game was the old bat playing? 'I think we can forgo the niceties now. She's turned me down, and more's the pity. We could have made history together, dear.'

Forbin was the one with the torn sleeves. The other one didn't have to be told to go for Gert. Maybe, Caxton thought, she could give Gert a chance to run away. Not that she could outrun a vampire, but—

Forbin lunged for Caxton, trying to grab her shoulders, but she telegraphed the move and Caxton just ducked under her arms. She spun around on her heel and stuck the muzzle of her shotgun right into the other vampire's stab-proof vest. Without any hesitation she fired her one and only shell.

It was too bad, then, that Forbin was even faster than Caxton had reckoned. Forbin recovered from her failed lunge and brought her elbow backward, into the small of Caxton's back, throwing her across the room – and ruining her aim.

The shotgun went off with a roar and the hand-loaded shot tore through the vampire's body, but well to the left of her heart. The vest caught fire and for a second the vampire's arm swung free at her shoulder, barely connected to her torso. She looked down at it with a grimace and lifted a finger to touch the edge of the gaping wound.

On the floor Caxton rolled over onto her back, her broken arm flopping painfully at her side. 'Gert, get out of here!' she screamed.

Gert didn't need much encouragement. She was already running for the door behind her. The wounded vampire didn't try to stop her. She was too fascinated by the wound in her chest. It was healing rapidly, white smoke filling in the hole, new skin flowing over the exposed muscles and bones. When it was done she lifted her arm and made a fist, perhaps checking to see if the arm still worked.

Only then, after all that, did she begin to chase Gert. She got to the door before Caxton's celly was halfway there. Gert stopped running. Started to back up.

Meanwhile Forbin straddled Caxton's body, one foot on either side of her stomach. She raised one index finger and curled it repeatedly, gesturing for Caxton to get up. Caxton knew it was useless, but she flipped the shotgun in her hand so she was holding the hot barrel and rammed the stock into Forbin's stomach as hard as she could.

It was like hitting a boulder with a rubber mallet. It just bounced off.

Forbin took the shotgun out of Caxton's hand. It would have been incorrect to say she grabbed it away from Caxton, because that would have implied there was some kind of struggle. She lifted one knee and broke the shotgun in half across her thigh, springs and bits of metal flying down to bounce off Caxton's face and chest. Then she threw the two halves of the weapon behind her. And repeated her come-hither gesture.

The second Caxton got up, she knew, Forbin would repeat the move on her spine. Of course, if she didn't get up, Forbin might just stomp her to death.

None of the vampires, however, had counted on Clara.

As the half-naked vampire stalked Gert around the dorm, Malvern came closer to watch the free entertainment. She was the first to look up, as if she'd heard something inaudible to Caxton. That didn't last long. Half a second later the dorm was shaking as an electronic buzzer sounded loud enough to wake the dead. A strobe light near the dorm's main exit started to flash and then a row of red lights went on, one over each cell all along both tiers.

Then, all at the same time, every door in the dorm slid open on well-greased rails. All the exits. All the cell doors. At the other end of the dorm, the far end from the Hub, a green sign lit up reading EMERGENCY FIRE EXIT.

Caxton looked over into the cell nearest her face. There were eight women inside of various ages and races. Most of them had had their arms sticking through the bars with their jumpsuit sleeves pushed back. They had to jerk their arms backward quickly or have them torn off as the door opened. Suddenly they weren't behind bars anymore. Suddenly they were just standing there, not ten feet away, watching the vampires, watching Caxton and Gert, or just staring at empty space where a second ago there had been prison bars.

It took only a few seconds before one of them decided to make a break for it. A white woman with glasses who couldn't be more than twenty raced out of the cell, looking over her shoulder the whole way as she headed for the fire exit. When no one tried to stop her, a middle-aged black woman came running down the stairs from the upper tier. And then suddenly there was a stampede.

Women from every cell were coming out onto the floor of the dorm. With no COs to corral them and with the vampires distracted, it fell to the half-deads to try to stop them. That didn't work very well. Three women from the same cell on the upper tier picked up a half-dead between them and threw it over the railing. Its skull made an audible pop when it hit. Another half-dead tried to flee but was trampled by the rush for the fire exit. Most of the women were bent on escaping, or at least getting away from the vampires, but some of the younger ones, the gang-banger convicts covered in jailhouse tattoos, were sticking around to play with the half-deads.

Then there were so many of them that Caxton couldn't see what any of them were doing individually. She could only see them as a faceless crowd in constant motion. She had to roll to the side and dash into an empty cell to avoid being crushed. Forbin started after her, but even a vampire had trouble fighting against the current of two hundred women all moving in the same direction. She tried grabbing them and throwing them out of her way, but that just increased the desperate pace of the crowd and made it harder to slog through. Of the other vampire, the one she'd shot, there was no sign. Caxton saw that Gert had climbed up on one of the medical carts and was trying to keep her balance as it was rocked by colliding bodies. The noise was intense, a surging, oceanic roar of shouts of excitement and also panic, of hundreds of feet pounding on the steel catwalk of the upper gallery, of cursing and pleas for help when the fire exit was jammed with bodies. Some of the women seemed to think they'd have better luck heading toward the Hub, and soon there were two currents flowing through the dorm. Bodies filled up all the available space outside the cells and suddenly Caxton couldn't even see Forbin anymore.

Her spine went rigid when she realized she couldn't see Malvern, either.

57.

Clara took her hand off the panic button and sat back in her chair. She could barely believe what she'd just done. The board was alive with red lights. The telephone on the communications board wouldn't stop ringing. And on the monitors—

She hadn't known what else to do. Laura was about to be killed. Malvern was going to get away. So she had hit the panic button on the fire emergency board. A big sign at the top of the board said you weren't supposed to do that unless local police units were ready to assist with an orderly evacuation. Otherwise, you could let hundreds of murderers and rapists escape into the surrounding community.

And a lot of the women had taken the opportunity to run away. The main gate was wide open now and inmates were streaming out, some forming small groups, some just running into the woods in random directions. The really dangerous ones, though, had stayed behind.

The women with nothing to lose.

On the monitors she could see it all. A middle-aged woman with a butch haircut was having her head slammed repeatedly against the tiles in one of the shower rooms. The five women holding her down were all half her age. A white gang had taken over the cafeteria and had barricaded the doors. They were armed now with shotguns and stun guns and pepper spray, and it looked like they planned on staying awhile – they had control of the prison's food supply, which meant they could outlast a very long siege.

Out in the yard fights were breaking out everywhere she looked. People were being trampled. People were dying. Because she pushed a button.

In C Dorm, at least, she saw Laura and Gert both still alive. Both okay. Some of the worst violence in the prison happened in C Dorm, but it wasn't directed at the ex-cop or her old cellmate. Instead the prisoners had turned on the vampires. It made sense, of course. When the doors opened, the vampires had been in the middle of draining the inmates dry. Malvern had never meant for any of these women to live more than a couple of days – either they would become part of her new brood of vampires, or they would become food – and they seemed to understand what that meant. They knew what they had to do.

In the Middle Ages, Clara knew, vampires had been like a plague on Europe. Every little fiefdom had its bloodsucker, sometimes whole lineages of them. But the people had learned ways to fight back, even with the most primitive of weapons. They had made up for their lack of firepower with superior numbers. If enough people jumped on top of a vampire, they would eventually weigh so much the vampire couldn't shrug them off. If enough desperate warriors threw themselves at a vampire's ravenous maw, eventually one of them would get close enough for the killing blow.

The women of C Dorm were trying their own version of the tactic. The half-naked vampire was down on the ground, fighting desperately to get up. Prisoners were clinging to her arms and legs and pushing her back down, dozens of them for just the one vampire. They had nothing but shanks and razor blades and homicidal frenzy.

Meanwhile Forbin and Malvern were moving. They'd been smart enough to realize they couldn't contain the situation and had made a break for it very early on, heading out through the open fire exit and across the sheltering shadows of the yard. So far Clara hadn't picked them up again on any of the monitors. She hoped, frankly, that they would keep running. That they would run right out of the prison and never come back. That was one way Laura could survive.

But she knew it wouldn't happen that way. It couldn't.

The phone kept ringing next to her left elbow. 'Shut up!' she howled, but that was pointless. Finally she picked up the handset and lifted it to her ear. 'Hsu here,' she said, thinking that was a stupid way to answer the call. The fire department wouldn't know who she was—

'Clara?'

'Jesus. Oh my God. Is that you, Glauer?'

'Yeah,' he said. 'I'm so glad – you're okay, right? You're alive in there? Oh, boy, am I glad to hear it. Fetlock and I have been sitting out here in the trees for hours now, wondering what the hell was going on inside.'

'You've been there for hours? Didn't you hear me telling you it was time to move in?' Clara demanded.

'We did, but Fetlock—'

'You son of a bitch! People have died in here because you didn't listen to me. You were supposed to storm the place. You were supposed to come in here and save me! I am not a field agent. I am not equipped for what I just went through, do you understand? It is not acceptable to ask me to deal with this shit!'

'You're alive. Is Caxton alive?'

Clara squeezed her temples. 'Yes. For now.'

'Then I guess you did okay. Listen, I wanted to attack as soon as we got here. I promise. But Fetlock held me back. He's got every SWAT team from every town from here to Baltimore assembled out here. Right now we're just scooping up the prisoners as they try to escape.'

Well, at least that was something. Something to assuage her guilty conscience.

But not enough. 'I could already be dead and you wouldn't even know it!'

Glauer sounded like he was in physical pain when he responded. 'I wanted to go in there alone. Just me and a gun to get you and Caxton out. But he wouldn't let me. He gave me his big speech again. About how the SSU can't afford public scrutiny, how we can't make any mistakes. You know that speech.'

'Yeah,' Clara said.

'I listened patiently and then I waited for him to turn around and then I tried making a run for it. I was going to come in anyway. He had me arrested. I guess technically nobody's got me in handcuffs right now. But he's made it clear that if I make a move without his authorization, I'll be going to jail. And we've seen what he does with his agents when they break the law.'

'Christ. You did what you could, I guess—'

Glauer was still talking. It sounded like a confession now. 'I wasn't the only one. The SWAT teams wanted to move in hours ago. So did the local cops. But Fetlock called the governor's office to make sure he had proper approval first. Big mistake. The governor sent down word that nobody was to make a move. That this was a hostage crisis, and that he was going to get the FBI to send trained negotiators down here.

332

If anybody moved before the negotiators arrived, they'd lose their jobs. What I'm trying to tell you, Clara—'

'Is that Fetlock screwed us over good.'

'Yeah,' he admitted. 'Yeah. But listen, that's all changed now – the hostage negotiators got here a couple of minutes ago. They took one look at the situation and gave up. Said they should never have been called in – that things are too far gone for them to help.'

'Fetlock. That stupid dick,' she said. 'He's afraid of his own shadow, and they put him in charge of vampire cases.' She was angry. She was, to be honest, righteously pissed. But even so, she could recognize the logic. Fetlock's orders always made sense, in an abstract fashion. They usually ended up in people getting killed, but they made perfect logical sense.

'I need you to tell me anything that can help us raid this place,' Glauer said.

'Alright. Alright! Fine! Listen. We're down to two vampires in here. The half-deads are all, well, full-deads now. Laura's alive but unarmed, and Malvern is going to kill her on sight.' She went on for a while providing a full situation report, telling him everything she knew about the gang wars and what was happening in the cafeteria. When she finished she took a deep breath. 'How does Fetlock want to proceed?'

'We're moving in en masse, as fast as we can. We'll take the yard first, then secure the facility wing by wing. You stay put. We'll extract you as soon as it's safe.'

'Okay,' Clara said. 'Thanks.'

'Listen. We're going to get her,' Glauer said.

'Who? Malvern?'

'Yeah. And the other one. And do you know what that means? After tonight, there won't be any more vampires. They'll be extinct.'

Clara closed her eyes and started to weep. That couldn't

be right, could it? There would always be more vampires – except. Except the only two vampires left in the world were inside the prison walls. 'After all this time,' she said. 'After so many people died – it'll be over,' she said, trying the words out to see if they sounded real when said aloud.

'Yeah,' Glauer said. 'We did it.'

58.

'Laura, the feds are—'

Caxton couldn't hear the rest of what Clara had to say over the intercom. The women of C Dorm were making so much noise that they drowned her out. She pushed her way through the crowd as best she could without being trampled and finally made her way over to the cart where Gert was crouched, barely keeping her balance.

The crowd was starting to thin out a little. Most of the women had run out the fire exit. Those who remained were mostly in a heap on top of the half-naked vampire. Caxton could only see the occasional flash of milk-white skin underneath the pile.

'Let's move,' Caxton said, and Gert nodded eagerly.

They made their way slowly back toward the gate that led to the Hub. There was a thick crowd around the warden's body back there – it seemed more than a few prisoners had enough of a grudge against Augie Bellows to want to defile her corpse. The very thought sickened Caxton, but she knew there was no way she could stop so many of them. She also had more important things to do.

'Did you see Malvern leave?' she asked Gert. 'Do you know which way she went?'

Gert shook her head. 'I was too busy trying not to get killed.'

Caxton sighed and pointed at the ceiling. 'Clara was trying to tell me something, but I couldn't hear her. Let's get some-place quieter so she can try again.' The two of them headed deeper into the prison, toward the Hub. Rioting prisoners filled the hallway, but they didn't seem organized or dangerous. Some of them actually looked like they were having a good time.

Then Caxton saw the flames, and she knew there was going to be trouble. Up in the Hub someone had found a bunch of filing cabinets and dragged them into the center of the room. Caxton had no idea what the cabinets contained, but she knew any facility like SCI-Marcy had to be stuffed full of paperwork. Prisoners were pulling out files and setting them alight, maybe with the intention of burning down the prison – maybe because they just wanted to see them burn. They'd built up a couple of pretty good bonfires already. Craning her head around to peer through the massed bodies there, she saw others filing in and out of the armory. They must have been disappointed to find the guns all destroyed, but they were arming themselves anyway with batons, with pepper spray, and with stun guns. More women were streaming into the Hub all the time, coming from the other dorms, and despite the smoke from the fires the central room was rapidly filling up. It would be next to impossible to get through there.

'Come on,' she told Gert. 'We'll try another way.'

She turned – and then stopped. Because there was a woman,

a huge woman with a butch haircut, looking right at her. One of her former cellmates from when she'd been housed with the general population.

'Hey, I know you – you're that ex-cop,' the woman said. She didn't sound particularly unfriendly. She and Caxton had never bothered each other much. Caxton nodded, tried to smile pleasantly, and pushed past.

She was not surprised, though, when the crowd noise died around her, or when some of the women in the hallway started moving toward her, very nonchalantly, with no obvious violent intent.

Every woman in the prison had a reason to hate the police. They'd all been arrested, after all, by cops. A sizable fraction of them were willing to do something about that resentment.

'Run,' she shouted to Gert. She started to follow her own advice – and then a pair of thick arms grabbed her from behind. She managed to break free, even with only one good arm, but someone else tripped her and a third convict grabbed her bad arm and twisted it behind her back.

All around her women were moving in, shanks appearing in their hands, or just bare fists drawing back to hit her. She tried to fight her way out, but the pain searing through her arm kept her from making any headway. Already she could smell nothing but unwashed bodies, and the light was growing dim—

Then she heard a hissing sound and a meaty thud and Gert was spinning through the crowd, causing screams. Her pepper spray flicked across half a dozen eyes and her baton crashed down on wrists holding shanks, sending the makeshift knives clattering on the floor. She pushed her way in and got her shoulder under Caxton's good armpit, then levered her up out of the mass of bodies.

'Get the fuck back or you'll be looking at a whole thirty-one flavors of this shit,' Gert growled, her voice low and angry. Even Caxton shrank back from that voice.

'Just having a little fun,' one of the women in the crowd said.

Gert sprayed her right in the eyes. She screamed and ran away. The crowd started drawing back, no one wanting to be Gert's next victim. They must not recognize her, Caxton thought. It was bad enough to be an ex-cop in a prison without supervision – but Gert was the hated baby killer. They'd put her in protective custody from the day she'd arrived.

Except now she wasn't Gertrude Stimson anymore. Now she was Caxton's celly. Her road bitch. And somehow that transformed her from a pimply speed freak into some kind of Viking warrior goddess. Nobody, not a soul, tried to stop her as she moved Caxton quickly through C Dorm and out of the fire exit.

Outside, in the dark, she set Caxton down on a patch of dry grass.

'Thanks,' Caxton said. 'That was pretty good.'

'I got your back, no prob,' Gert said. She watched Caxton's face for a while, then said, 'Listen. One thing I gotta ask.'

Caxton nodded.

'We ain't escaping, are we? I mean, I know you said so before. But I was still holding out some hope. You're not going to get me out of here, though.'

Caxton stared at the girl. She supposed, in a way, she owed Gert the truth. She could lie and say she expected to live through the night. She could lie and say she would get Gert out of the prison, somehow. It would make her celly feel better to hear it. More willing to help Caxton with what came next.

But it just wasn't possible. Gert had killed the CO in the SHU. Worse than that, she had killed her own babies. Maybe prison wasn't the best place for her. It was a degrading place, a soul-killing place where no one even pretended to want to rehabilitate her. But she couldn't just be allowed to walk the streets, either.

'I guess . . . all I can say is, I'll still be your celly if we survive.'

'And we'll get along okay? We'll be useful to each other, right? If I talk too much, you won't try to make me shut up. That kind of thing.'

Caxton smiled. 'It's a deal.'

That seemed to satisfy Gert. 'Cool, I guess. What next?'

Caxton looked up and saw stars overhead in half the sky. The other half was blocked out by the great looming expanse of the prison's wall. Inside the wall groups of prisoners were storming the prison's outbuildings and looting them of anything that wasn't bolted down. She saw a dozen of them outside the back door of the infirmary, where she and Gert had reentered the prison after blowing up the powerhouse. She thought of all the drugs in there. There was going to be one hell of a party in SCI-Marcy tonight, she told herself, and—

She looked up at the wall again. It was twenty-five feet high. Every hundred feet along its length was a watchtower with a searchlight and a machine-gun nest. The towers were all dark at the moment. There was no one up there to man them.

Except maybe a pair of vampires. It was where Caxton would go to get away from the riot. If you could get up on top of the wall, into one of those towers, you could see everything. And once you were up there you could escape anytime you wanted – assuming you were a vampire – by jumping down the far side of the wall.

Caxton looked for the nearest camera and found it in the angle made by C Dorm and the wall of the Hub. She waved at it until a loudspeaker mounted on a pole nearby said, 'I see you, but I don't know where Malvern went. She's not on any of my screens.'

Caxton shook her head and pointed at the nearest watchtower. It was a pain in the ass not being able to talk to Clara. She sighed and then pointed at it more emphatically.

'What, up in the towers?' Clara asked. She was silent for a while, but a crackling buzz from the loudspeaker told Caxton the circuit was still open. 'Oh, wait – yeah! There! They're hiding in some shadows, but it looks like Forbin hasn't mastered it yet. One of her feet is in the light. Listen, let me find a way to get you up there.'

There was a muffled crump from the far side of the yard. Caxton raced around the side of C Dorm and saw tendrils of white mist snaking around the outbuildings. Another crump, closer this time, and a group of prisoners came racing out of a roiling cloud, coughing and rubbing at their eyes.

'Shit!' Caxton said. 'Fetlock!'

Gert grabbed her good arm. 'What is it?'

'The cops,' Caxton explained. 'They're here. They're using tear gas. If we get caught in that we're done.'

'So you just have to explain to them who you are and what you're doing. Maybe they'll even give us guns.'

Caxton shook her head. 'They won't ask questions, they'll just scoop us up and drag us back inside. Come on, Clara! Find something!'

The intercom buzzed back into life. 'There's a way up to the wall,' Clara said, as if she'd heard Caxton. 'It's an underground tunnel. The entrance is at the side of the

340

administrative wing. Go – go left, three hundred yards.' Caxton and Gert hurried to follow Clara's instructions. As they passed each loudspeaker it came on and Clara gave them a new command. 'You can't just go straight there or you'll run smack into a SWAT team,' Clara explained, as she sent them all the way around a row of baseball diamonds. When they finally reached the door they wanted it was standing open.

It led to a flight of stairs going down into the earth. At the bottom was a long tunnel with bundles of wiring and dripping pipes overhead. 'Go left at the next junction, and you'll come to a flight of stairs going up. It'll take you all the way up to one of the towers.' The intercom was buzzing when they reached the tower stairs.

'Listen,' Clara said, and then couldn't seem to find any more words.

Caxton looked at a camera mounted above a door and gave it her most patient look. She was running out of those.

'You don't have to do this. Fetlock has the place buttoned up. She can't get away. I know you think this is your responsibility—'

Caxton nodded emphatically. There was no way to tell Clara what she was really thinking. That Malvern was a sneaky monster, and that no matter how good Fetlock's perimeter security might be, she would have some plan of escape. If Caxton waited for Fetlock to mop up the prison, there was no chance of catching Malvern. And then it would just go on. The nightmares. The long sleepless nights worrying who was going to be killed next. The blood. Always there would be more blood.

Clara was silent for a while. 'Just. Just – I was going to say be careful. But that's not your plan, is it? Okay. Just do it, then. Do what you do best.'

Caxton wasn't sure how to reply. Blow a kiss at the camera? Salute? In the end she just patted her heart and then pointed at the lens. Clara would know what she meant.

Then she headed up the stairs, with Gert close behind her.

59.

Caxton grabbed Gert's forearm and pointed into the darkness. Something was moving there, right next to one of the towers. She pulled her celly back into the shelter of the stairwell door.

'What's the plan?' Gert asked in a whisper.

As if it was as simple as that. Caxton was facing two well-fed, desperate vampires. Between her and Gert she had a can of pepper spray, a collapsible riot-control baton, and three working arms.

She had thought, of course, about what she would do when she found Malvern. She had thought about very little else since she had saved Clara. Most of her plans had involved heavy weaponry.

'We can't take them ourselves,' Caxton said, thinking rapidly. 'But we can keep them from getting away. If we can get them back down into the yard, the cops can take care of them.' It wasn't a plan she liked. It didn't allow her to kill Malvern with her own two hands. But it had the advantage of being plausible, whereas taking on Malvern without guns was not.

'How do we do that?' Gert asked.

Caxton smiled to herself. 'We use bait.'

The trick she'd used on Hauser – using her own blood to drive that vampire crazy – would work on Forbin, but not on Malvern. Caxton had seen Malvern turn away from readily available blood before when the cost was too high. Over her three centuries she'd learned some kind of self-restraint.

She had another idea, though. She explained it carefully to Gert, who started breathing heavily and blinking a lot. It scared Gert. It scared Caxton, too, but fear had stopped meaning much to her.

'Okay. We need to be together on this one. If you don't think you can handle it—'

Gert nodded. 'I can be useful to you. I can be your road bitch. That's all I've wanted this whole time, right? So let me do it.'

Caxton grabbed Gert's biceps and squeezed by way of thanks. Then she stepped out of the doorway and into the starlight. 'Malvern!' she called.

There was no answer. The shadows she'd seen moving before had stopped, still as statues. Maybe she'd been completely wrong and there were no vampires there. Maybe they had already escaped.

No. That wasn't an acceptable thought. She banished it from her mind.

'Malvern, you know how I feel about vampires. You know I would never accept the curse willingly.' She grabbed Gert and pulled her forward, to her side. 'But it's not just about me, is it?'

She could sort of see a red glow in the darkness of the tower wall. Or maybe it was just her brain wanting it so badly that it was filling in details that weren't there.

She had to keep this up. 'Gert shouldn't have to die, just

because I'm stubborn. I want to make a deal with you. Clara gets to live. She's out of your hands now, anyway – the police got to her first. But Gert and I . . . we'll . . . join you.'

A pale shape detached from the shadows and stepped forward. It was Malvern, her red eye positively burning with excitement. She looked so healthy, so whole. Caxton couldn't get used to the transformation. Always before Malvern had been a rotting corpse in a coffin. Now she was a sleek and deadly predator.

Her voice was a rough growl. 'You – uh.' She paused.

Caxton frowned. She'd never heard Malvern mumble before. It didn't matter, she told herself.

'Ye will forgive me, Miss Caxton, should I doubt ye.'

Caxton nodded. 'Sure. I would, too. But I owe this to Gert. She's saved my life a bunch of times, and – I can't repay that debt any other way.'

'It's what I want,' Gert said, right on cue. 'Please.'

The red eye flicked from Caxton's face to Gert. It looked the girl up and down carefully. Then it focused again on Caxton.

'Ye misunderstood my intentions, though,' Malvern said, in a flat tone. 'I never meant to make ye come to my estate.'

Caxton frowned. 'No?'

'No, dear. I only wanted to watch you beg for your life.'

Forbin came out of the shadows then as if she'd been launched from a catapult. Caxton didn't see her feet touch the ground more than once or twice. Her hands were outstretched, her fingers curled like talons. For a killing blow.

'This is bullshit,' Gert had time to scream. And then her shoulder was in Forbin's stomach. Ordinarily she had as much chance of moving a Mack truck with her shoulder as she did stopping Forbin's attack. But Gert didn't need to stop the vampire. She just needed to throw her a degree or two off course.

345

They went over the side of the wall together, arms and legs flailing, teeth flashing in the starlight. There was a brief scream, and a horrible thud.

Gert – Gert had—

Gert had just saved her life, again.

'Gert!' Caxton shouted. 'Oh my God, Gert!'

There would be no more babies for Caxton's celly. She would never finish her jolt and walk out the main gate of the prison. It was a twenty-five-foot drop. Straight down into coils of barbed wire. If Forbin killed Gert on the way down, it would be a blessing. Otherwise – Gert would be snarled in vicious barbed wire, struggling still with a hurt and angry vampire. There was no way that fall would kill Forbin.

'Gert!' she screamed again, wanting to close her eyes. Wanting to sink to her knees and start crying.

Unfortunately, there was no time.

Malvern was still watching her.

'You . . . bitch,' Caxton said.

Malvern smiled, showing all of her teeth.

'Why do you kill everyone I care about?' Caxton asked. 'Why do you have to destroy my life, over and over? Is it because I'm dangerous to you? Because I'm the only one who can kill you?'

Malvern shrugged. 'It's because you're in my way.'

Something clicked inside Caxton's head. A puzzle piece attached to another puzzle piece. Connections started being made. She did not, however, have time to finish her thought process.

Without any further words, Malvern disappeared. She just stepped back into the shadows and vanished.

Caxton knew perfectly well that she wasn't gone, though. Malvern didn't know if Caxton was armed or not. She didn't

346

know how badly Caxton's arm was hurt. She wasn't going to take any chances. This time – she would go for the kill.

Caxton had chased Malvern long enough to know that what happened next would not be a game. Some vampires liked to play with their food. They would tease and scare and startle their victims until their eyes were bugging out of their heads, until they were gibbering in panic, and only then would the vampire move in to feed.

Malvern didn't have a sadistic bone in her body. Not out of any nobility or morality, though. It was because sadism was inefficient. It didn't help her meet her goals. She would circle around Caxton and strike from behind, and she would do it quickly. Caxton had maybe a second or two to get ready.

She ran toward the tower. It was the last direction she would be expected to go – straight toward where she'd last seen Malvern. Right into danger. It was, however, the best move defensively. The tower had walls she could hide behind.

The door to the tower was open. Caxton pushed her way inside and closed it behind her. Locked it, for all the good that would do her. Inside the tower was a small circular room containing a mounted machine gun and a searchlight that could be moved around by hand. There was also a chair, an unfinished thermos of coffee, and a dead CO.

Caxton nearly stepped on him in her haste. She pulled her foot back just in time and crouched over the body. Judging by the smell, he must have been killed back when Malvern's half-deads took over the prison, more than a day before. Killed and then just left to rot. She apologized to him, then grabbed his stun gun and his stab-proof vest. As she clicked open its quick-release buckles, something heavy thunked against the floor. She couldn't see very well in the gloom, so she reached down to see what had made that sound, but—

Malvern hit the door like an enraged sledgehammer. It

shattered in its frame, chunks of wood and broken glass bursting through the tower room like a vicious rain. Caxton sat down hard, the stun gun held up in front of her as if it would do any good at all, and braced herself for an impact. But it didn't come.

The doorway was empty.

'Oh shit oh shit,' Caxton breathed, because she knew what that meant. Malvern had destroyed the door just as a distraction. In point of fact, she would be behind Caxton, sizing up the back of her neck.

Caxton scrabbled upward as cold fingers brushed her spine. She swung around and threw herself behind the searchlight.

Malvern howled in joy. She bent at her knees, getting ready to pounce.

Caxton switched on the searchlight and hauled it around by its handle. A light as intense as a million candles hit Malvern right in the face.

Vampires are creatures of the night. They do not do well in bright light.

Malvern's single eye burst and ran down her cheek as white goo. She screamed in pain and rage and her arms lashed out, smashing again and again at the lens of the searchlight, shattering the bulb inside and warping the metal reflector out of shape. It didn't matter – the light's work was done. Malvern was blind.

'Do ye think this matters? Ye've bought ye – yourself a second's grace, that's all,' Malvern growled.

'All I need,' Caxton said.

Malvern's eyeball was already growing back, white smoke filling in the cavern of her eye socket. She didn't even need the eye to track her prey, Caxton knew. She could smell Caxton, could hear her as she stepped backward.

348

Caxton raised her pistol and fired three times into Malvern's rib cage. Right into her heart.

She had expected the pistol to fail. That its firing pin had been filed down or that there would be no bullets in the magazine. When she'd found it on the belt of the dead CO, she had been unable to believe her luck. A gun. Right where she needed it. Right when she needed it. It was too much to ask for. It had to be a trick.

The bullets tore through Malvern's undead lungs, her sternum, and her heart. She screamed and thrashed and howled, crawled across the floor toward Caxton, her fingers reaching for Caxton's ankles, her monstrous jaws snapping at thin air. But the red light in her fully healed eye was already going out.

The vampire dropped to the floor, suddenly very small. Very compact. Caxton thought she could pick Malvern up with her one good hand. Strange to think a creature that could do so much damage would ever come to look like that. She was dead. Caxton fired the rest of her bullets at point-blank range into the monster's chest, into her heart, just to be sure. 'Finally,' she breathed. It wasn't the most profound thing she could say, she knew, but it was all she had strength for.

Then she closed her eyes and wept.

But not for long.

Another puzzle piece clicked into place. A gun, loaded with real bullets, exactly when it was needed the most. The half-dead who killed the CO hadn't bothered to take it away. Even though every other gun in the prison had been carefully, methodically ruined.

There had been a package of sticky foam in the SHU, when Caxton needed it. Even though sticky foam was experimental and was banned from use in prisons until the kinks could be worked out.

Doors had been left open in the prison, doors that should have been locked. Oh, not the doors she had hoped would be open. But enough that she'd been able to move around relatively freely.

It hadn't been easy, not at all. But then – if it had been easy, she would have seen through the game right away, wouldn't she?

She bent down over Malvern's corpse and studied its face, ran the fabric of the mauve nightdress through her fingers. She wasn't sure what she was looking for. But something felt wrong. Something was wrong.

Then she got it. All at once, the puzzle put itself together in her head.

'Smart,' she said, through gritted teeth. 'Always so smart.'

She saw the whole game now, from beginning to end.

And she knew Malvern had won.

60.

By five o'clock in the morning the fires had all been put out. The vast majority of the prisoners were back in their cells, grumbling but more or less happy once the Feds started handing out food and coffee. A few were unaccounted for. The white supremacists barricaded in the cafeteria were still making demands, but it sounded like they were arguing among themselves in there and there was no place for them to go. A SWAT team of hostage negotiators had assured Fetlock that they could resolve the situation peacefully.

Up on the wall, Clara looked down at a prison that was as close to being back to normal as she could hope for. A lot of people had died, and a lot of people had suffered. But it was over.

Kind of.

Five o'clock. Clara checked her watch again. This was it, the end of the twenty-three-hour deadline. An hour still to go before dawn. By now she was supposed to be dead. She shuddered at the thought.

Fetlock and Glauer came up the stairs huffing and puffing.

351

She had called them and said there was something they needed to see. She wasn't sure how she should present it, though. As the team's forensic analyst, it had been her job to look at all the bodies, including Malvern's. Fetlock didn't seem to know what he expected her to find, but it was part of any investigation that you checked the bodies afterward, and he was a man who did everything by the book.

'She was here,' Clara said, when they looked at her expectantly. 'Laura. I mean, Caxton. This is where she left the prison.' A makeshift rope had been dangled over the outside of the wall, tied at the top to a window of a watchtower. The rope looked like it was made out of nylon restraints buckled together, and it was more than long enough to reach the ground. 'Most of the police units were inside the wall at that point, and the ones outside were busy at the main gate rounding up attempted escapees. Caxton could scale the wall here and run into those woods without being seen. She's had at least a couple hours to get away.'

'I'll find her,' Fetlock said. 'The U.S. Marshals Service is good at that sort of thing, at least.'

Glauer looked sharply at their boss, but he didn't say anything. What could he say? Laura was a fugitive from justice now. If she had returned to her cell and just waited for the cops to arrive, maybe all could have been forgiven. She could have served out the rest of her sentence quietly and then been released. But now she was a problem, and she had to be hunted down and arrested again, prosecuted again. Given a whole new sentence. Fetlock was never going to just let her go. He wasn't that kind of man.

'Why did she run?' Glauer asked, confused. 'I don't get it. She was done! The vampires are all dead. Why would she make more trouble for herself?'

Clara knew that Glauer had personally been responsible for

352

killing Forbin. He had been leading a SWAT team when they found two persons tangled up in a coil of barbed wire, apparently trying to struggle their way out. He'd had the presence of mind to realize that one was dead and the other was a vampire, and he had dispatched the latter without much fuss. Sometimes you got lucky.

Clara cleared her throat. 'This isn't actually what I wanted you to see. The vampire's corpse is in the tower over here.' She led them toward the tower, working out her next words precisely. 'I'd like to have a pretty serious autopsy done on the warden.'

'Why?' Fetlock asked. 'You made a positive identification based on her clothing and build. This looks like a closed case to me. Do you know how badly I want this to be a closed case, Special Deputy Hsu?'

'Yes, sir. No more than Special Deputy Glauer or I do, I'm sure. The warden's body was almost unrecognizable, though. The face and the hands suffered fourth-degree burns, making it impossible to get fingerprints or even dental records to fully identify her. I'd really like to see if we can do a DNA screen.'

'Whatever,' Fetlock told her. 'I don't see the point, but if it makes you happy. You want to tell me why you think that body isn't Augusta Bellows, though?'

'I think Malvern was playing a very deep game here,' Clara said. 'I think she never intended to occupy the prison for very long, and that the vampires she created here were not meant to survive. I think she had something in mind other than just a ready supply of blood and recruits.'

'Well, obviously she came here because of Caxton,' Fetlock said. 'She wanted revenge. And it backfired on her.'

'Perhaps, sir. I just want to make sure. Let me show you

why.' She led them into the tower room. The corpses inside had not been moved. She would perform a more in-depth examination eventually, but for the moment she wanted to wait until she could get a camera up there and fully document the scene. It had to be done before Laura's final message was disturbed.

On the floor there was a large amount of debris from a broken searchlight. Bits of glass and shards of broken mirror littered the floor. Laura had quite carefully arranged the pieces to spell out three words. She hadn't possessed any normal writing utensils or any other way to leave a message, but like a smart prisoner she'd learned to make do with what she had. The message was very short. It simply read:

it's not her

There was an arrow pointing to the vampire's body.

'Oh, come on,' Fetlock said in disgust. 'She only has one eye, the dress is the same. She looks a lot more . . . fresh than we're used to, but that's simply because she was full of blood. That has to be Malvern. It has to be!' .

The last time Clara had seen the warden, she'd been missing an eye. She'd been missing her left eye, just like Malvern. She could have easily killed herself before sundown and then been put in a coffin by waiting half-deads – no one had seen her after she left her desk above the Hub. Clara remembered the call Bellows had made to Guilty Jen, and how immediately after it ended she had heard a gunshot she couldn't explain. That could have been the sound of Bellows taking her own life, the last step necessary before the curse consumed her and turned her into a vampire.

As for Malvern – she probably had left the prison long before the police had secured its perimeter. She could have left the prison as early as sundown the day before, immediately after sending her '23 hours' message. Clara had wondered why the message had been so brief, and she saw now that it didn't have to mean anything, really. It could very well mean that, twenty-three hours after the message was sent, Malvern would be a free vampire. Far, far away from the prison.

She could have left the warden in her place, to act like her and speak like her and wear her old tattered dress. The two of them could have worked it all out in advance. Bellows wanted very badly to become a vampire. In exchange Malvern might have insisted that Bellows pretend to be her. To kill Caxton herself. But Bellows wouldn't have known about the loaded gun, left just where it needed to be – the final double-cross in Malvern's plan.

And she'd almost gotten away with it.

After all, if Laura Caxton, the world's foremost expert on killing vampires, claimed that she had killed Justinia Malvern – who would ever doubt her? Fetlock would close his case. The long hunt for Malvern would be over. Which was exactly what she wanted. She wouldn't have police studying her every move. Laying traps for her. She could lie low, and scheme her schemes, and wait for the right moment to come back. Maybe after all of them were dead.

It was the perfect plan.

And looking at Fetlock's face, Clara wasn't sure it hadn't worked. He looked skeptical. 'You think we should just take Caxton at her word? When all the evidence points in a different direction? As far as I'm concerned, Malvern is dead. Truly dead. Case closed. And if she's dead, then vampires are extinct, and we win.'

His face made it very clear he refused to accept the other possibility. That Malvern had beaten them once again.

Laura had known he would have that reaction. That was why she ran.

Because it wasn't over.

Acknowledgments

I'd like to thank everyone who had a hand in writing this book, but many of them have asked not to be named. They could get in trouble at their jobs, or, far worse, at the places where they temporarily lived. I will thank Byrd Leavell and Carrie Thornton, without whom this book would never have existed, and Julian Pavia, who did such an excellent job editing it. If it fails to please at this point, that's because I didn't listen closely enough to what he had to say. As always I would be remiss if I did not thank Alex Lencicki and my very patient wife, Elisabeth Sher.

13 BULLETS

All the official reports say they are dead – extinct since the late '80s, when a fed named Jameson Arkeley nailed the last vampire in a fight that nearly killed him. But the evidence proves otherwise. When a state trooper named Caxton calls the FBI looking for help in the middle of the night, it is Arkeley who gets the assignment – who else? He's been expecting such a call. Sure, it's been years since any signs of an attack, but Arkeley knows what most people don't: there is one left. In an abandoned asylum she is rotting, plotting and biding her time in a way that only the undead can.

But the worst thing is the feeling that the vampires want more than just Caxton's blood. They want her for a reason, one she can't guess; a reason her sphinxlike partner knows but won't say; a reason she has to find out or die trying. Now there are only 13 bullets between Caxton and Arkeley and the vampires. There are only 13 bullets between us, the living, and them, the damned.

978-0-7499-5426-0

99 COFFINS

Laura Caxton vowed never to face them again. The horror of what the vampires did is too close, the wounds too fresh. But when Jameson Arkeley comes to her with an unfathomable discovery, her resolve crumbles. Arkeley leads Caxton to a recently excavated tomb in Gettysburg. While the town, with its legendary role in the Civil War's worst battle, is no stranger to cemeteries, this one is remarkably, eerily different. In it lie one hundred coffins – ninety-nine of them occupied by vampires, who, luckily, are missing their hearts. But one of the coffins is empty and smashed to pieces.

Who is the missing vampire? And does he have access to the ninety-nine hearts that, if placed back in the bodies of their owners, could reanimate an entire bloodthirsty army. The answers lie in Civil War documents that contain sinister secrets about the newly found coffins – secrets that Laura Caxton is about to uncover as she is thrown into the deadly, gruesome mission of saving an entire town from a mass invasion of the undead . . .

978-0-7499-5431-4

VAMPIRE ZERO

U.S. Marshal Jameson Arkeley taught police investigator and vampire fighter Laura Caxton everything she knows about monsters. When an army of vampires attacked Gettysburg, Arkeley gave up his own life to save others. Except he didn't exactly die . . .

He accepted the curse and is now a vampire himself – one that knows all the tricks better than anyone else. Now Laura is faced with the task of destroying him before he succeeds in his quest to exterminate his own family, one member at a time. But Arkeley knows all her tactics too; after all, he taught her.

Worse still, if Laura fails to stop him then Arkeley will become a beast exponentially more dangerous – a Vampire Zero.

978-0-7499-5436-9

Do you love fiction with a supernatural twist?

Want the chance to hear news about your favourite
authors (and the chance to win free books)?

Keri Arthur
S. G. Browne
P.C. Cast
Christine Feehan
Jacquelyn Frank
Larissa Ione
Sherrilyn Kenyon
Jackie Kessler
Jayne Ann Krentz and Jayne Castle
Martin Millar
Kat Richardson
J.R. Ward
David Wellington

Then visit the Piatkus website and blog
www.piatkus.co.uk | www.piatkusbooks.net

And follow us on Facebook and Twitter
www.facebook.com/piatkusfiction | www.twitter.com/piatkusbooks

piatkus